Gift of Gamman

*"The more the universe seems comprehensible,
the more it seems pointless..."*

Steven Weinberg

Nobel laureate in Physics 1979

...an original and gripping read. ... an epic journey that could only be brought to us by Stan I.S. Law. ...Author Stan I.S. Law has outdone himself with Gift of Gamman. ...The story has incredible characters, scenery and dialogue. The humor and seriousness flow together beautifully. The underlying possibilities fill us with wonder and intrigue. The ending is beautiful and hopeful. I highly recommend it!

Ally McMahon
Amazons

I highly recommend Gift of Gamman by Stan I.S. Law and look forward to reading more of his work!

Mary Leckie, Author, USA

...adventure, mystery, spirituality, suspense... interesting plot, great characters, dynamic happenings, surprises and overall, it is well written, entertaining, exciting and most important - it really draws you into it and takes you to a new world!

Janja Litiju, Slovenia

After reading the Gift of Gamman, I'm entirely convinced that this is our very near future. It's almost as if this journey has already taken place, and by Stan I.S. Law himself, because of the detail-oriented nature of the book, the flow of events, and the way everything culminates into something grander that will move mankind further ahead.

Stan I.S. Law, I am looking forward to your continued ownership and raising the bar of the science fiction genre!

Chameleon
Amazon.com

The novel has an originality to it that I haven't ever come across before, blending together fiction with non-fiction elements to weave a fantastically imaginative tale that never ceases to keep the reader sucked into the plot.

The author has a clear talent for storytelling that can't be denied and I am eager to read more from Stan I.S. Law.

L. Collins
TOP 1000 REVIEWER

By the same author

ALEC (Alexander Trilogy, Book I)
ALEXANDER (Alexander Trilogy, Book II)
SACHA—The Way Back (Alexander Trilogy, Book III)
YESHUA—Personal Memoir of the Missing Years of Jesus
PETER AND PAUL (An intuitive sequel to Yeshûa)
ONE JUST MAN (Winston Trilogy Book I)
ELOHIM (Winston Trilogy Book II)
WINSTON'S KINGDOM (Winston Trilogy Book III)
THE AVATAR SYNDROME (Prequel to Headless World)
HEADLESS WORLD—The Vatican Incident
(Sequel to *The Avatar Syndrome*)
MARVIN CLARK–In Search of Freedom
THE GATE—Things My Mother Told Me
NOW—Being and Becoming
GIFT OF GAMMAN
THE PRINCESS
ENIGMA of the Second Coming
WALL—Love, Sex, and Immortality (Aquarius Trilogy Book I)
PLUTO EFFECT [Aquarius Trilogy Book II]
OLYMPUS—Of Gods and Men [Aquarius Trilogy Book III]

Short stories

THE JEWEL & OTHER STORIES
CATS AND DOGS
Sci-Fi Series 1
Sci-Fi Series 2

Non-fiction Books by Stanislaw Kapuscinski

VISUALIZATION—Creating Your Own Universe
KEY TO IMMORTALITY
[Commentary on the Gospel of Thomas]
BEYOND RELIGION: Volumes I, II and III
[Collections of essays on perception of Reality]
DICTIONARY OF BIBLICAL SYMBOLISM
DELUSIONS—Pragmatic Realism

Poetry in Polish
[with illustrations by Bozena Happach]
KILKA SŁÓW I TROCHĘ GLINY
WIĘCEJ SŁÓW I WIĘCEJ GLINY

INHOUSEPRESS, MONTREAL, CANADA
http://inhousepress.ca

GIFT
OF
GAMMAN

A Novel by

Stan I.S Law

INHOUSEPRESS, MONTREAL, CANADA
SECOND EDITION

Published by
INHOUSEPRESS
http://www.inhousepress.ca

Design and layout
Bozena Happach
Email: info@inhousepress.ca

ISBN 978-0-9731184-7-6

For Madeleine
in gratitude for her work on this
and a number of my other books.
Her commitment
surpassed that of Delta

PROLOGUE: 2140

PART ONE: EARTH 2300

PART TWO: ZIIRCON

PART THREE: EARTH 2371

The
Prologue
2140

The Black Hole

Commander Adam Blake became vaguely aware of his surroundings when his body temperature reached 35.8º C. He remained quite still, eyes closed, the respirator filling his lungs with air rich in oxygen. Within the next few minutes, he became acutely aware of a prickly, fairly painful consequence of blood forcing its way, with increased pressure, through the veins and arteries of his awakening body. Gradually, after a lengthy time of considerable discomfort, the thousands of dancing needles gave way to a sensation of profound sensual pleasure. His artificially maintained, previously greatly reduced, cardiovascular pressure was returning to normal. Adam Blake felt alive. Fully alive. After a long, long time. His breathing was becoming deeper, more relaxed. The humming respirator sighed, hesitated, then turned itself off.

Adam remained quite still—strangely afraid to open his eyes.

The cabin, jet black for nearly fifty years, now glowed with soft, conveniently diffused light, designed to lessen the impact on Adam's still half-dormant retinas. It took quite a while for his optical nerves to adjust, focus; for the mist to rise, the cobwebs of accumulated dreams, chimerical phantasms, to clear.

"I am alive", he whispered, attempting to enunciate every syllable. "I am alive," he repeated softly, thinking that is was the most understated expression in the universe. His voice sounded as though it belonged to someone who had just fought his way through the singing sands of the Sahara.

Sahara desert, he thought, so many light-years away.

Commander Blake's body temperature registered 36.6° C. He glanced at the chronometer. The dial recorded 17,842th day since breaking Moon's orbit—about 49 solar years. Next, Adam looked at the gravimeter. An expression of surprise mixed with disbelief twisted his inelastic, long stagnant features. Adam blinked repeatedly, refusing the evidence of his eyes. The gravimeter registered exactly 10 g's.

"TEN GEES!" he exclaimed, or tried to, yet only a harsh rasp escaped his throat.

Ten times the gravitational pull of the earth. The scientists back home had been right. He was still alive. The anomaly followed its own rules, obeyed its own laws. Had they been wrong, he would have had no one to blame. Adam Blake volunteered for this mission.

A few seconds later, automatically, the transparent polymeric cover of his berth slid silently over his head into the ship's bulkhead. Considering that Adam had spent close to fifty years in suspended animation, his arms and neck manifested amazingly little stiffness. He grinned, though rather grotesquely, in appreciation. This lack of stiffness did not apply to his facial muscles, though he had little control over them.

Adam Blake's athletic body said nothing of the string of Ph.D.s in pure science as well as in various disciplines of ancient and modern philosophies he had acquired while waiting for some, undefined mission. He had no way of knowing, when he would be assigned, to what task, on what expedition. Perhaps, as a direct result of such a broad spectrum of knowledge, his mind retained the inquisitive freshness of a young man. At 36, ignoring the nominal aging process during his hibernation, even under these unique circumstances, he took life as it came, met it face on, without any preconceived ideas. Physically and mentally Adam Blake was an extremely resilient individual.

He reached overhead and pulled on a thin plastic tube. By biting on it and sucking, in quick succession, he initiated the flow of a soothing liquid. Mostly glucose. Next, he pressed the 4th button to the left of the main console. Within two seconds, two brown biscuits of reconstituted protein, carefully balanced with the three other dietary groups, popped up from a thin slot. He bit off a tiny piece. Almost instantly it distended itself, into a healthy morsel. Considering his protracted period of fasting, its taste was satisfying. During his hibernation, Adam's body had been supplied with the necessary nutrients intravenously. This was different. This tickled his taste buds.

The slow chewing did wonders to his stiff facial muscles.

"I am alive," he repeated again.

He noted that his voice began to resemble his normal, deep baritone. If anything could be referred to as normal, after fifty years of deep, very deep slumber. Fifteen minutes later Adam felt alert enough to inspect his ship.

The slim, cigar-shaped hull had not been designed for a return trip. The cockpit at the prow left no room for maneuvering. Adam, echoing his ancient predecessor, traveled quite naked. Massage units built into his berth had provided all the physical exercise necessary to maintain his basic bodily functions. A series of strategically placed electrodes, when activated, sent a micro-voltaic current which contracted, held and released practically all the muscles of his body. In spite of the fact, that Adam had little use for most of his muscles. A humanitarian concession? The ship was little more than an interstellar communication computer. Adam's presence was almost incidental.

The original rocket, behind the capsule he occupied, had once measured over three hundred meters. When all the fuel necessary to arrive at the required velocity had been exhausted, the length of the hull had shrunk to a mere fraction of its former glory: barely 19.8 meters, including the cabin. Little more than a Moon-shuttle. Virtually the whole space behind Adam's exiguous quarters housed a nuclear generator, whose sole purpose was to sustain his life as long as possible. Officially.

In a different reality, it served, principally, to provide the power necessary for the ship's laser communication system. Adam had been considered expendable; the data shipped back to earth—were not. They were the purpose of this one way mission.

There were no portholes anywhere. Adam's eyes and ears to the outside universe consisted of a mass of gauges, dials, and six main colour screens, which provided visual and audio contact fore, aft and in the four remaining cardinal directions. An added concession to the pilot's intellectual and emotional needs was a considerable library of fibro-optical memory storage units. Therein, a fair share of mankind's literary and musical heritage remained at Adam's disposal. The eggheads, back home, had not been completely heartless.

In a nutshell, the ship had been designed as a missile that was to accelerate at a constant 1.67 gravities. The various stages of the rockets had been discarded, progressively, when empty. It had been hoped that by the time the impulse power runs out, Adam Blake and his communication system would be trapped, or at the very least, within the influence of the gravitational field of the XM742 anomaly, commonly referred to as the Black Hole.

Years of arguments preceded Adam Blake's mission: arguments about quantum mechanical uncertainty principle, as regarding the apparent emission of particles from rotating and/or non-rotating black holes. The obvious paradox had been settled, albeit hypothetically, by the theory postulating that the radiation had originated not from the black hole itself, but from the 'empty' space, just outside the black hole's event horizon. Nevertheless, what had finally motivated the United Planets Federation to spend billions of dollars on expediting Adam Blake towards and into the elusive non-space, had been the phenomenon of XM742. A series of independent observation satellites reported, that light from a number of stars had been noticeably bent around an invisible fulcrum, in the midst of darkness of space. While the particle emissions from XM742 had been relatively negligible, the photons refusing to follow their predestined path had been the determining factor. This discovery had mobilized armies of theoretical astrophysicists. Twenty-seven years later, ADAM ONE, a spaceship constructed for a one-way mission, had left the lunar orbit.

Adam had little reporting to do himself. The laser-oriented instrumentation transmitted, automatically, all the data that the sensors collected. It would continue to do so, up to that certain—as yet undefined—point, whence the photons would no longer have the power to overcome the monstrous gravitational pull of the Black Hole. Assuming Commander Blake's cranium did not cave in onto the mushy grey matter it had been meant to protect, Adam had been expected to add his own observations, a human touch, an insight, into the unknown characteristics of the anomaly.

Within a very short time, the gravimeter advanced a few decimal points towards the 11g mark. Adam knew that the gravitational field increased exponentially to the distance from his objective. A paradox. Subjectively, Adam Blake remained in zero gravity. Observed from an astrophysical distance, an anomaly, such as XM742, appeared to generate a directional, gravitational pull, as indeed it did, within a vast radius of influence. A black hole's horrendous gravitational attraction might vary from a few parsecs, to tens of thousands of light-years. The hub, the very center of a galactic core, might well hide a prodigious anomaly, exacting its majestic, gravitational influence so great as to hold hundreds of billions of stars in its flamboyant grasp. Once within the space matrix distorted by its influence, its event horizon, the theoreticians theorized that space would have been distorted sufficiently for the gravity to act as a field rather than a directional force.

So much had been predicted, suspected, assumed. At the home base.

To understand his own predicament, Adam drew an analogy with the theory of the expanding universe, which holds that every major star cluster, a galaxy, is moving away from every other such system. Within the space distorted by the anomaly, however, a partial reversal took place. While the laws governing the expanding universe tended to pull solid objects apart, or, at the very least, away from each other, the intense gravitational field of the anomaly provided the reverse motive. Such a resultant, singular field, could be expected to hold every atom in perfect, if delicate or precarious equilibrium in relation to every other atom.

This effect had been suspected at the home base, if only within the peripheral behaviour of the anomaly. If they were right, Adam would confirm their reasoning by merely staying alive... a little longer.

Adam grinned.

"I'm alive!" he repeated again, as if this fact was reason enough to give his life in exchange for new knowledge.

For the first time his voice sounded normal, if elated. He did not regard himself as a hero. Adam competed with many young astronauts for the privilege of taking part in this unique experiment. He had won. The privilege to venture into the unknown. To boldly go where no man....

No sane scientist dared to even speculate what enigmatic laws, gargantuan forces or fields, secrets or paradoxes, governed reality near the centre of a black hole. Let alone one wielding the effect of XM742.

"Space is bent upon itself. Completely!" One genius announced. The consequences of such hypothesis, however, were beyond the scope of human imagination.

Adam smiled boyishly when he realized that on earth, under his present conditions, he would weigh over 800 kilos!

"And you ain't seen nothing yet, kiddo!", he said out loud, lightheartedly.

He forgot that every word he uttered was instantly converted into laser impulses and transmitted at 300,000 kilometers per second, towards base. Fifty years into the future, countless solons would analyze his every word, each syllable, probably mystifying over the depth of his statement. Adam Blake must have been the only human being within a good few light years, who found his predicament funny. He roared with laughter.

On finishing his second biscuit, Adam performed all the routine checks and reported AAA to whoever was, or rather will be, listening. The obvious had eluded him, till now. Back home, a number of his friends, colleagues, must have already died. From old age. The rest of them will be dead by the time any of his transmissions reach earth. How ephemeral is human existence...

For a moment, Adam grew pensive.

He dialed Mozart. One of the screens displayed a complete selection of Mozart's works. Adam punched 'Don Giovanni'. He needed something amusing, irresponsible, and Leporello footed the bill. The hapless servant never failed to make him laugh. The overture filled the cabin. A little later, a tiny, holographic stage shimmered, then solidified, just over a meter away, directly in front of his eyes. Though the human figures were no more than ten centimeters high, each seemed perfect in every detail.

After the first act, Adam glanced at the chrono. The time registered 17,842.79.

"Bloody nonsense!" he shook his head.

He punched CHRO and then the code for the elapsed time since he'd been 'reactivated'. The dial now read 0.1284 ET. He could reset the Elapsed Time chrono whenever he wanted. For whatever reason.

"That's better", he muttered, "just over three hours".

The gravi climbed to 11.89.

At 1.729 ET he pressed for another biscuit. This time a fresh salad taste tickled his palate. He washed the 'salad' down, with a near perfect taste of white Burgundy.

"Cheers," he gurgled lifting an empty hand cupped around empty space. The same tube provided an excellent facsimile of black coffee.

Adam lowered his consol, stretched out and pressed the relax button. His berth began vibrating. A pleasant, almost seductive, undulating motion. Within ten seconds he was asleep. The moment his brain began emitting alpha rhythms, all the dials, screens and coloured buttons went black. Black as the blackness of deep space itself.

Blackness and silence.

And endless space.

During Adam's sleep various sensors continued to monitor his physiological activities. The same instant the data were transmitted back home. Adam's diet had been designed to induce maximum hours of sleep. No one at home base could have guessed how long the 'star' fall would take. Sleep had been regarded as the best means of preserving Adam's sanity. Should anything unforeseen happen during his rest period, Adam would be instantly awakened. If necessary, the drug in the coffee would be counteracted through a permanent intravenous implant grafted under his left knee. Permanent? Adam slept like a newborn baby. After all, he deserved it. This was the first real sleep he enjoyed in almost fifty years!

At 2.73ET, the electro-mechanical massage started. At 2.8 Adam was awakened. The moment he regained control over his senses, he looked at the gravimeter. For the second time since reactivation, he challenged the evidence of his eyes. It never crossed his mind to question the efficacy of the instrumentation. The dial reported 74.89 g's.

"My God!" he thought, "I shouldn't be here. At least not in one piece!" His momentary horror gave way, with equal dispatch, to his usual, irrepressible humor. "Or at least, in a much, much smaller piece..."

Three sleep cycles later, at 17,000 g's, it became apparent, that within this incredible environment, the centrifugal and centripetal forces maintained the individual particles of matter in a superb, quantified, equilibrium. Adam Blake's ship was no longer subject to the established laws an expanding universe. It responded to a field where perfect harmony prevailed, defying the principally directional forces governing the space left behind. As each individual atom, each subatomic particle—whatever concept, idea, could be quantified—became subjected to the fantastic stresses, they each contracted within their own, individual orbit of existence or activity, while the concentric acceleration continued to increase their mass. The result was that as the mass increased, the nuclei shrank further and further apart. Each quantum collapsed in, upon itself, while its mass grew, exponentially, towards infinity.

A Paradox, a Singularity, a Black Hole within—yet without the universe.

Adam spent the next few subjective hours pondering the possible consequences of such conditions. Finally, with considerable trepidation, indeed, stretching his courage to the outer limits, he decided to test his theory.

He extended his hands at arms length. Then, joining his palms he began pressing them together. The next instant, Adam witnessed the seemingly impossible. His stomach fought its own battle to retain its state of balance. And biscuits. You must never be sick in a free fall. Never! Adam's mind, demanding, screaming for a familiar point of reference recoiled in horror. The sensation was that of immersing his hands in wet sand, or a bucket of ready-mix concrete. Only there was no sand or wet concrete. Not within fifty light-years. By an effort of sheer will, he increased the pressure. His palms began to merge into each other and then reappear on the opposite sides.

When he pulled his hands apart, Adam's throat and mouth felt arid. In perverse contrast, fresh beads of perspiration formed on his forehead. He suddenly realized that during the feat he just performed, he experienced absolutely no pain. Nevertheless, he did not dare to wipe his forehead, lest his hand penetrated his own skull. He lay back exhausted. He had been right.

Would this knowledge be communicated back home, to Earth? Ever? Or did the universe extract the ultimate penalty from all who reached out, who dared to penetrate its inner, esoteric secrets.

The ship now travelled within a few decimal points of the speed of light. There was no sensation of motion. Absolutely none. The four digital gravimeters, running sequentially like puny electric meters back home, were all working overtime. Only a blur on the first three dials testified that they were still working. Incongruously, Adam became acutely aware of the advantages of electronics systems. Had the gravis been designed with rotating needles, they would have, long ago, merged into the surrounding casing.

During the time taken by Adam's experiment and the subsequent effort to regain his sanity, the g's had climbed to 22,600. Even as Adam watched, spellbound, the dial climbed faster than he could count.

23,000....24,000....26,000....29,000....

Such figures, numbers, concepts, no longer held any rational meaning!

Time and motion merged into the same category. Adam lay back, inert, silent, rapidly losing awareness of his physical body. At 35,000 g's he no longer retained any perception of pulmonary or cardiovascular activity. Yet, evidently, he occupied the same space in the same cockpit. As he diverted his attention to his body, it seemed to vibrate with a slight shimmer. He 'saw', though hardly with his optical senses, that his 'body' consisted of countless millions of shining, spinning, constantly oscillating points of light. Electrochemical discharges?

"Stars", Adam thought, in abject wonder. "I am a galaxy of stars held together by an act of my will. The substance of my body is moving, acting, functioning, behaving in direct relation to my imagination. Whatever I think or imagine— must follow."

As if to prove the point, Adam imagined himself outside his own ship. Within a split second he was looking at the hull, himself hovering, suspended in a dark gray emptiness.

Strangely calm, Adam thought of his physical body. The hull
of the ship became instantly transparent to his vision. Inside,
reclining in total repose, he regarded his own physical body.
His mind accepted the phenomenon.

"I accept as reality whatever I perceive with my senses."
A thought formed in his mind.

"What senses...?" someone asked.

He shrugged. Whatever I sense isn't real...

"Where am I?"

Adam was acutely aware that the capacity of his
consciousness was expanding in direct proportion to his
ability to absorb it. The next thought placed him back in his
reclining body, though he no longer felt its limitations nor
depended on it for his self-awareness.

His thoughts drifted to his past. Rather than becoming
aware of Adam Blake, the astronaut, his mind showed him a
sequential kaleidoscope of incidents, seemingly spanning
millions upon millions of years. He saw himself as a
rudimentary consciousness embodied in various animal
forms. A flash of light brought him into a two-legged
creature. Hairy, primitive. Proud? His mind registered a
critical difference from his previous states of awareness. The
animal form he now occupied, registered a spark of self-
awareness. The first spark. It possessed an embryonic concept
of 'I am'. Adam's mind examined the various stages of his
own growth. He perceived a slowly emerging, very gradual,
yet distinct pattern. Suddenly he knew. He understood the
evolutionary process. It was as though all that had ever
happened to him manifested the implicit purpose of driving
him relentlessly to this present moment. Nothing, not one
single event in the eons of his existence occurred without
reason. Each cause had its effect. Every effect was preceded
by a cause. The essence, the sum total of the relationship
between his growing awareness and his personal, individual
environment, was an intractable, obstinate tendency towards
a state of balance. Towards order.

Balance, harmony, equilibrium.

Beauty.

His mind reached out to the stars. As his attention left his own, puny pattern, Adam sensed a similar matrix in the universe around him. It was no longer a physical universe. Yet the patterns, the forces at play, all had their effects in energy and matter. Mostly energy... it was as though matter no longer existed. The earth, the solar system and the most distant galaxies were all suspended in a single lattice of intergalactic forces. No part had more importance than any other. Each served its predestined purpose, its predestined position, in the balanced state of the unified field of forces. An atom, a molecule, a speck of dust, a rock, an asteroid or a planet; they all meshed smoothly into the Pattern. Even as the subtle, harmonious vibration held them together and imbued them with life, with the individual existence, so the light was akin to knowledge, an awareness growing, expanding, of the final effect, of the universal interplay of the primeval forces.

Adam sensed the mystery of eternal becoming. His mind watched, absorbed. Through it, through the expanding scope of his mind, he witnessed the birth of countless stars, as the vast clouds of gases had been ignited into convoluting, focal centers through which light entered and distributed energy necessary for the next step on the endless journey of destiny and fulfillment.

Then, even as a tsunami sweeps everything in its path, Adam's mind, fired by an overwhelming realization of purpose, became flooded with a single, all-exclusive, deSire. He needed to be one with this glorious pattern. He needed to unify all forces within his own being into a singular state of total awareness. His awareness hovered at the very edge of space-time continuum.

In an endless ocean of absolute, intense darkness, a single point of light commanded Adam's attention. As the light swelled, increased in magnitude and intensity, Adam continued shedding the remnants of his human awareness. He was becoming one with that which he perceived. Within seconds or eons, beyond time or space or any limitations, the light source grew, augmented, distended, until it burst with such ferocity that billions upon billions of suns could not rival its brilliance.

The blaze filled, penetrated, overwhelmed, the deepest recesses of Adam's consciousness. Burning, destroying, cleansing, liberating. Nothing, nothing existed but pure, white essence of light. The essence of the undifferentiated, unfulfilled infinite potential of all Knowledge. All Power. The single Unifying Force of yet unmanifested universes. It was the Light that was, that is, that forever will be.

Within that single instant of realization, Adam, or the consciousness which had once been Adam, became one with the blaze around him. He was no longer within it, nor part of it — he, himself, he was the Light Itself.

I AM   I AM   I AM   I AM   IAMIAMIAMIAMIAM sung a single atonal vibration, so fine and pure as to enfold infinity with aliquot harmonics. It held, sustained and glorified the essence of his being.

I AM, it reverberated in a limitless glory of pure consciousness.

I AM the birth, the sustenance and the fulfillment
I AM the source of all knowledge
I AM the power of my own being
I AM life itself
I AM

Adam Blake chose to return to earth four decades after he had been sent on his unique mission. His return was as easy, as his departure—difficult. Just as Black Hole satisfied the centripetal laws of the universe, so his own sun, like every other, served as a focus for the centrifugal emission and distribution of Life energy. Adam did not have to come back. He gave his life in order to gain Life. This fact alone liberated him from the need of assuming, once again, a human form.

He chose to return. He wanted to help those who were ready, though not lucky enough, to have been selected for his last, his one-way mission.

At a particular moment, a fragment of eternity, a young, healthy, proficient pilot had been falling to his death from an exploding ramjet. The ejection seat worked, but the parachute failed to open. As the pilot's consciousness vacated the falling body, Adam entered it and brought it gently to the ground. No one witnessed the accident. No one followed up on the seeming departure of the young man. His parents were already dead. He was a single man with no emotional attachments.

The next day, John Galt, for that was the name of the body which Adam had entered, reported the accident to his superiors. He failed to mention just one pertinent detail. He did not mention that his parachute did not open. John Galt simply reported for duty. The error in the ramjets' engine design was readily corrected.

Four years later, John Galt was promoted to Commander and transferred to the Moon Base. He arrived in time to help the colony of scientists decipher the endless string of data, arriving from a relatively primitive spaceship, falling, relentlessly, into a strange phenomenon known as the XM742 anomaly.

John Galt knew it as the brightest Black Hole in the Universe.

***

PART ONE

Earth

2300

Chapter one

JOHN GALT

"Reporting as ordered, Sir!"
Commander Galt's lean, supple body lingered in a state of expectant attention. Face relaxed, neutral, noncommittal; dark eyes staring directly ahead. This was the manner in which lower ranks reported when summoned by an Admiral, some forty odd years ago. That was the last time John had visited earth.

The Admiral looked up.

For a moment, he searched the younger man's face. Then he met his eyes. Dark, brooding, deep set eyes. Staring. Beyond the next horizon? Farther. Beyond material limits? John Galt's eyes rejected the confines imposed by the physical universe. They even denied the reality of the immediate surroundings; detached, locked in a search for some elusive freedom, haunting the boundless void of Outer Space.

"Ah, yes, my boy... or should I say Sir, or... old friend?" The Admiral's heavily lined face broke into an unfamiliar smile.

The First Admiral of the Galactic Navy, Hermes D. Grant, had first met Commander John Galt more than sixty years ago. At that time John had been a mere hundred and twenty four years old—earth-time, and Hermes Grant had just been promoted to the rank of second lieutenant. A young, sprightly lieutenant. So many years ago...

As the Admiral, now a young eighty-four, smiled recognition, John Galt reached deep into his memory. Unsure of himself, John remained silent.

"Relax, John." The Admiral presumably referred to John's stance of perfunctory attention. "This is me, old friend. Hermes. Remember? You beat the daylights out of me in the Kendo final. Had you been standing like this then, I would have laid you out in one second flat!" A sonorous sound rolled deep in the Admiral's throat as he walked over to John and embraced him.

Gentle waves of retrospection washed over John like a warm, pleasant breeze. He relaxed his straining memory cells. The Admiral's face changed, practically beyond recognition. People who carry great responsibilities, especially those not coveted but thrust upon them, have a tendency to show that burden in their heavily worn features. Also, the Admiral's broad shouldered physique had now become even more square, perhaps a little stocky, though he still radiated the power of a dormant volcano. Only the eyes of Hermes Grant had not changed: the same penetrating gaze, direct, unflinching, defying anyone to question his absolute dedication to duty, uncompromising honesty and courage. John may have beaten him in Kendo, some sixty years ago, but the Admiral would never lose to him, nor to anyone else, in a game of chess. In a way, it was a kind of chess game that the Admiral had to play, these last twenty years, trying to maintain the Galactic Navy at the prestigious level it had presently reached. The Admiral was the Navy.

"Thank you, Sir!"

John was unsure how to behave. Hermes D. Grant was the Admiral, the Five Star variety. There was no one above him in the whole of the Galactic Navy, nor anywhere in the Federated Republics. With the exception of the Council. A Commander does not meet the top man in the Navy often. Certainly no Commander who had spent most of his last one hundred and sixty years, earth-time, in Outer Space.

"Hermes, to you John, if you insist—Harry, if you don't mind." The Admiral's initially strained smile now appeared easy, almost relaxed. Hermes Grant did not share his leisure with many people. Did not enjoy many friends. Since his wife died, thirteen years ago, he allocated all his time, all his efforts, his quite astounding energy, to the Galactic Navy. In this stagnant, dying world, what else was there? The Admiral did not have much time to smile. Not with the constant game of chess, otherwise known as politics, claiming most of his time. He hated politics, but he loved the Navy more. It was his sole pride. It had been, and continued to be, the essence, the substance, the one true love of his life.

Suddenly, John Galt's eyes filled with a new light. Old memories came flooding back. John recalled a mass of details. Ordinary every-day details, all held back, denied, during his last trek. His last, yet again unsuccessful, expedition. During his missions, each lasting on average close to forty years, earth-time, John had learned to suppress, to consciously eradicate, all irrelevant memories. He had to. Had he allowed himself to think of Earth, he would have gone insane—light-years away from his home planet. From mankind. A miniscule grain of dust in the vastness of cosmos. Now, a single word, the name "Harry", brought it all back. John embraced the Admiral with reactive, hungry vigor. His eyes filled with tears. Emotions restrained for so long, now, suddenly, caught up with him.

"Harry... Harry..." he whispered, "Oh my God, Harry..." He swallowed hard. "Let me look at you..."

John's normally impassive face couldn't hide a shadow of pain. All the family he had ever had, ever hoped to have, were long gone. Dead. Harry, this old faithful friend, was the last. His comrade, his buddy, was now over eighty. How adamant were the laws that ruled this vast, cold universe. John, who had walked on Earth over one hundred and ninety years ago, now looked no more than in his late thirties. His white hair might have given a hint of his age, but he shaved them clean. His eyebrows, by some trick of nature remained black, bushy. They cast deep shadows over his impenetrable eyes. Eyes more used to staring into the black void of infinite space than to facing and holding the gaze of the First Admiral of the Galactic Navy.

"I've put on a couple of years?" The Admiral shook his head. "You know John, I don't know if this is actually funny, but I must say it. You haven't changed a bit!"

The Admiral laughed. Probably the first spontaneous laughter since he last saw his friend. It was contagious. The two men stood at arms length, tears swirling in their eyes, rumbling with deep, too long-restrained laughter. Finally, like a child's toy wound up but for a time, haltingly, as though with regret, they stopped. Harry Grant put his arm on John's shoulder and led him to the sitting area of his spacious office.

The Admiral seldom went home, these days. His office was his home. This was where he felt the most useful. They sat down. The Admiral dialed for drinks. The same drinks they had shared together before. Time seemed to collapse, roll back. Again John felt an arid constriction squeezing his throat. Just emotions. It passed with the first sip of the Venusian brandy. They shared a moment of silence.

"How up to date are you, John?" The Admiral asked some time later.

They both had to rearrange their thoughts, their emotions, to be able to get back to more mundane matters. John soon learned that very few things were ordinary in Hermes D. Grant's life. The Admiral was a charging dynamo. To get things done, he seemed bent on burning a candle at both ends. He functioned, efficiently, within an ocean of horrendous bureaucracy. After all these years, after the astonishing progress in so many fields of human endeavour, there remained one constant. The bureaucracy did not change. Well... it did. It took a turn for the worse. It grew. Although eighty percent of the administration was conducted by fully autonomous computers, the residual twenty percent made up for it—with vengeance.

"Only what is available on the 'hypnotapes'. And the media, of course."

John referred to data that could be absorbed by direct subliminal transfer. Colloquially called 'hytapes', as against 'vitapes' or 'Videotapes'. In essence they were neither discs nor tapes, as all the memory was stored on holographic units, wherein the data were stored volumetrically, increasing the capacity exponentially. However, the ancient terminology persisted. It might have resulted from the fact that originally the various terminals had been taped to various parts of your body. The 'hypnotapes' had been introduced centuries ago, but perfected only in the mid 80's. A psychotherapist, claiming to be a direct descendant of Carl Jung, produced the first commercially available helmets in 2184. Since that time the 'hytapes' have been used extensively. Even in schools. Children were given one hour a day of hypnotape conditioning. Then they spent the rest of the day discussing the acquired knowledge, its application to everyday life, and its ethical value. To catch up with the intervening years, John had used hytapes during the planet-falls, and after each of his last three treks. While in space, an induced state of hibernation slowed down John's subjective time to a snail's pace. But the earth-time ticked on. Decades at a time. Time lags resulting in a mass of unpredictable changes.

"I thought as much." The Admiral nodded. He had instructed Psylab on Moon Base to brief Commander Galt fully, but, for now, they may have placed a block on his recall. "You'd better listen to this."

John took the proffered helmet and fitted it over his bald pate. Leaning back, he closed his eyes. Within ten seconds John's consciousness was completely supplanted by hypnotic impulses. Ten minutes later, John took off the headset and handed it back to his friend. As John's eyes once more focused on immediate surroundings, he whistled softly.

"As bad as that?" he asked.

"Those are conservative figures."

The Admiral looked grave. The joyful reunion of a few minutes ago seemed to belong to another era. The data contained on the hytape were classified. TOP SECRET. The matter was serious. It was deadly.

"So we have another eighty years...?" John played for time. The info was still seeping down into his full consciousness. He felt as though he was entering into and recovering from shock. Simultaneously.

"As good as we can project. We have been wrong before. Though not by a large margin." The Admiral waited for all the new data to register fully in John's awareness.

"And there is nothing we can do about it?" The younger man, if one could call John younger, sounded incredulous. "Eighty years... For me, it could mean... a point, a place, of no return. Ever."

Admiral Grant said nothing. The data and the projections on the hytape had been gathered and recorded by his own staff. The info could not be released to the general public. Not even to the Council. To tell the Council would be equivalent to advertising the data on the air. There could be no secrets in an organization where sixty thousand Members attended a session and a further three hundred thousand enjoyed direct access to all info through vi-interface. Confidence and privacy were at a very high premium.

John looked as if the mass of concentrated facts and figures left him a little dazed.

"I had better recap for you." The Admiral understood John's state of mind. "You will recall, back in 2180, that's one hundred and twenty years ago, the Earth ecosystem had been practically destroyed. Prior to the collapse, our forefathers, your brothers, I suppose, had broadcast the dangers of pollution, *urbi et orbi*, with little real results. I say real, because, in as much as the developed countries of the world had made a concerted effort to reduce the emissions of corrosive chemicals, the developing countries had only just began contributing to the global problem. The, so-called, acid rains, resulting in acid lakes and rivers, finally acid oceans, had gradually, over great many years, destroyed most of the biological life in the waters of Earth."

"That's right! Man had been fishing..." John remembered through a dense mist of his own longevity.

"Yes, John. Once." The Admiral's smile carried no humor. "The ultimate death of the oceans stimulated new industries to produce alternative nutrients for the ever growing world population. New industries with the attendant, unavoidable, additional pollutants."

"A vicious circle?"

"Virtually. Later came the massive religious revivals. Thanks to the efforts and generosity of thousands of charitable organizations, hunger and most diseases had been eliminated. The per capita pollution had been cut in half."

"Utopia...?

"Hardly! By 2150, the population had grown to fifteen billion. The gross tonnage of pollutants had thus enormously increased. The worse offenders had been those affecting the ozone layer. In vast areas, particularly over the heavily populated northern hemisphere, it actually collapsed. Disappeared." The Admiral stopped and took a tiny sip of his Venusian brandy.

Throughout his recitation, his voice was calm, almost indifferent. The Admiral could not affect the past. He lived, intensely, in the present. In spite of the gravity of the subject matter, he regarded the Mercurian, opalescent crystal glass with delight. This was the first time he indulged himself with a drink in over a year. John, too, regarded the crystal as though evoking it to reveal the secrets of the past.

"At that time I had been on my way to Van Maanen's system. I read about the riots on my return. But the facts, as I recall them, had been presented in a slightly different way. It was a question of the Big Five: Asia, EuroFed, Indostralia, Africa and the Americas jointly and severally suing each other, in order to attach the blame for the mounting cataclysms."

"That was the way the, so-called, facts had been presented at the time. The economic mega-power blocks were so busy suing each other that few had time, or inclination, to initiate effective action against the real guilty parties." The Admiral affirmed.

"You mean, one could actually identify them?"

"Of course! It may sound absurd, but the only guilty parties were the 'do-gooders'. They sated their myopic, perverted concept of 'charity'. They defied the established, ancient laws of nature. They had saved lives of thousands, then millions, then billions, before anyone thought of the consequences of their magnanimous deeds. Until fifty years ago, I absolved my own conscience by making regular donations to their, seemingly, worthy causes. I assume my share of responsibility."

Hermes D. Grant stared at John Galt, as though defying him to question his integrity. John remained silent. The Admiral sighed heavily, raised his arms in silent supplication and let them fall on the armrests. He looked dejected.

"You see John, nature developed a means of controlling all species; it can control their growth and their numbers. If only we could leave things be. Do you know, that even earlier, when the very first signs of danger had been already lurking on the horizon, there had been some moronic governments who had actually paid people to have children? They had done it, of course, to increase their tax base. Those greedy morons were the first real genocidal criminals, the first offenders against the human race. Later the churches and other, so-called, charitable organizations, took over. When some of the Big Five began to suspect the truth, it had been already too late. Much too late." The Admiral emptied his glass.

"And then came the riots?" John prompted.

"And then came the riots. Large groups of people began to drop dead at a moment's notice. Mostly of skin, and other new strains, of cancer. Mobs formed, ravenous to vent their anger. They attacked factories, manufacturing plants of all types, without any discrimination. Power stations had been demolished, regardless of the degree of pollutants they generated. Every compound which had been deemed, by the ignorant masses, (and in those days as... now, they seem to constitute the overwhelming majority) to be creating *any* pollution, had been razed to the ground. Two billion people

died, directly or indirectly, during those riots. And that's in
addition to the deaths caused by cancer and other freshly
manufactured diseases, and to the four billion who, we are
told, became sterile." The Admiral recited all this in a flat
voice, devoid of emotion. Emotion had done enough harm
over the years. Even in his own lifetime.

"And what is the Earth population now?" John asked.

"The Federated Republics hover around eleven billion."
The Admiral said.

"So, since, we managed to keep pollution down?" John
looked pleased.

"Down, but not down enough."

The Admiral added a few drops of brandy to John's and
his own glass. Then he sat back and seemed to study John's
features. Commander Galt was used to prolonged silence.
The silence of space. He remained relaxed. Finally, Admiral
Grant, evidently, arrived at a decision. He leaned towards
John, a touch of conspiratorial tone affirming his inherent
trust of his friend of many years.

"You must realize, John, that today, the standard of
living is comparative the world over. There are no such
factors as undeveloped countries that do not contribute
substantially to the pollution problem. In spite of our best
efforts, we cannot reduce the overall emission levels any
further—short of drastically reducing our population, or
limiting our life span. Neither alternative is sociologically
acceptable. We must manufacture and distribute our produce
to sustain our present standard of living. If we don't, we are
damned. If we do... we have eighty years."

The Admiral sounded grim. The fact that he would no
longer be alive when the next catastrophe took place did not
seem to matter to him at all. He was a lot more than the Chief
of the Galactic Navy, the Presiding Member of the Federated
Republics Council and, until recently, a loving husband. He
was the concerned father of mankind. His almost limitless
power seemed matched by his equally unlimited compassion.

"Why did you call me in today?" The word 'Sir' seemed missing at the end of the question. John's intuition told him that Harry Grant, friendship notwithstanding, did not call him to his presence just for old time's sake.

"I hate doing it, John, but I have to ask you for absolute confidence." The Admiral did not wait for any affirmations or assurances. Having studied John's features, he assumed them as automatic. The Admiral leaned over to his desk and switched on a scrambler. Should anyone, by some inordinate electronic means, manage to listen in on their conversation, from now on they would hear only gibberish. "There is one, perhaps the last, chance we may have. As a species, that is."

The Admiral paused again. He had to tell a friend, a man who had been away from Earth for the last forty years, that he wants him to leave again. Soon. Perhaps, at a grave risk to his life.

"For the last two years, we have been monitoring signals from the Lyra sector. We have every reason to believe that they originate with... with an intelligent species."

The Admiral took a deep breath. He had recited similar stories to other astronauts before. Nothing had ever come of them. No dreams realized, no hopes fulfilled.

"Yes, Sir?" This time John was more formal.

The Admiral sighed shaking his head. "The problem is that the Council has forbidden any flights for purely research purposes. I have no idea if I can convince them that the purpose is more than just research. We are now grasping at straws." Suddenly the full eighty-four years of Hermes Grant's life seemed reflected in his steely, gray eyes. His gray hair looked whiter, his face paler. "Eighty years, that's all the children have..."

"Isn't the Lyra sector within eight parsecs? The return trip would take a little over seventy years. Seventy earth-time years." John had those figures in his fingertips. He calculated the time by assuming a constant acceleration of one gravity, or one gee, equivalent to ten, rather than the more precise, 9.7536 meters of acceleration per second. He rounded off a parsec to 3.25 light-years, skipping one hundredth of a light-year. 200,000 astronomical units he converted as 30 trillion kilometers. He enjoyed playing with figures.

"Sixty-three-point-one-seven, at one gee acceleration, constant. We can shave off about seven years. Depending how the new drive works. Plus, assuming we're successful, the on site research, of course." The Admiral added.

"A new drive, Sir?" Unwittingly John sat up.

"Still top secret. We managed to isolate a field in which the matter/antimatter is held in balance. The near absolute zero temperature of Outer Space gave us the permanent condition of superconductivity we needed to do the trick. The experiments never worked on Earth. They couldn't. The whole business is, I am sorry to say, a bit experimental. We need another ten years..."

"I wouldn't worry about that, Harry," John returned to the previous informal form of address. His face beamed with a big smile. "If that is all that worries you, don't forget that I am, by your, er... standards, about one hundred and ninety years old. I already had my fling. I could now take a little risk!"

The Admiral looked at John with wide, incredulous eyes. Then, first slowly, then with growing volume, he began to laugh. He knew of John's earth-time age, of course. It wasn't that. It was that this man, who had spent practically all of his life in Outer Space, constantly being at risk of losing that singular life at a split second's notice, considered himself about ready to take, finally, a 'little' risk!

"You know, John..." The older man continued haltingly, his voice still interrupted by laughter, "you know, they don't make them like you any more. Not for some two hundred years!"

"I only meant that a risk was never something I avoided. I think I'd find life rather dull, if it were devoid of a risk." John tried to explain himself.

"My dear boy, surely you do not need excuses!"

The Admiral was beside himself. It took a while before he returned to his normal, well-contained self. He regarded John with fatherly love, forever forgetting that John had been born over a hundred years before him.

"I gather, from your reaction, that you would be willing to assume the risk, if called upon to do so." The Admiral finally found his normal voice.

"I would like to have a look at those engines, Sir." John's eyes were eager.

Since he'd left the moon base, some three and a half weeks ago, John couldn't really settle in on this wondrous mother planet. He had grown used to space. Used to days, months of total, near-absolute silence. Used to gazing into infinity through the ports and visors, to hearing the unsung melodies which seemed born in his own mind when suspended in the middle of nowhere, in the bleak yet drawing, magnetic silence of the expanding universe. A lot has happened on Earth since his first solo flight to Proxima Centauri; a star just a little over four light-years away. Those were the old days. Every time John had come back to Earth, the technology had jumped by some forty years. But even the later more distant treks, encapsulated, in a sense, within a fragile box of fleeting puny metal had imprinted on his mind, his heart, perhaps his very soul, a need for being out there. There, in the great, limitless Beyond. John had developed a yearning for the smell of the distant stars, as much as for the strange intoxication of true solitude. He developed a yearning for the dreamy state of half-life. For the flamboyant dreams of suspended animation. Whatever John Galt had once been, he was no more. He could not be compared to any human being alive today. Or ever.

Yet, even that was not all.

On this occasion, there was something strange in the air of Earth. John detected certain lethargy, a milling mass of people who did not seem to care what happened to them. The radio and the video channels, thousands of them, were filled with countless, self-appointed prophets announcing a fast

approaching end for the human race. They did not base their
prognostications on any rational arguments. Rather, they
seemed to draw on some secret messages seemingly received
by reputedly gifted individuals, who claimed to maintain
constant contact with the dearly departed, the dead precursors
of their own esoteric talents.

John had witnessed such quasi-religious trends in the
past, but never on such a preposterous scale. Now, fully 75%
of all the mass media were preoccupied with such nonsense.
This mass hysteria fuelled an unspoken consensus, within the
already lackadaisical humanity, to reject any idea of
partaking in any effort; of partaking in any constructive work;
of advancing the cause of the human species. On the contrary.
From a number of chance meetings he had during his last
three and a half weeks on Earth, John concluded that just
about everyone devoted more time to sleeping than to any
other 'pastime'. The human race was rapidly falling into a
lazy, lethargic, uncaring slumber.

The corps of the Galactic Navy were the few, the very
few, whose lives pulsated with the old vitality; with a desire
to conquer, to breach the unknown. But they were the
exceptions. The odd men and women among the semi-
comatose billions.

The Admiral stood up. The interview was over. The old
man shook John's hand, then took him in his arms and
hugged him in a spontaneous embrace. For a moment they
both felt embarrassed. They broke away in an awkward
hurry. They both tried to hide the longing for that elusive
something which was no longer theirs to possess. Perhaps it
was a longing for a true, lasting, tangible friendship. Perhaps
their physical closeness brought to the surface the sense of
loneliness. A feeling long held in check, a luxury denied,
through no choice of theirs. Each, in his own way, was
travelling through time in an endless search of his own,
private, imponderable heaven.

"I know where to find you. I'll be in touch. Soon." The Admiral smiled and waved his hand even as John saluted. "You can bet on that."

The door slid silently open and Commander John Galt found himself standing in the sterile corridor of the Federated Republics Galactic Navy Headquarters. His mind pictured the mulling masses of vacuous, equally sterile faces outside. He shivered. By the time a young ensign approached him to guide him to whatever destination, a whimsical smile began to lift the corners of John's mouth. He was thinking of the new spaceship engines. New! The progress must have been fantastic! New engines always spelled Adventure. Of that he was quite certain. He wondered what his old friend Harry had in store for him. John's fertile mind was busy playing exciting guessing games. For the first time since returning from his last trek, his veins pulsated with restrained vigour. He felt alive again. The future, his future, seemed to hold a new challenge. His nostrils flared as though smelling fresh blood. Then, a young man interrupted his thoughts.

"I have orders to act as your guide if you need me, Sir!" the ensign recited in one breath, his right arm raised in a full, precise salute. Then the young man's mouth fell wide open. "Ah, aaah, aren't you *the* Commander John Ga-a-a-alt, Sir?" His eyes were in great danger of popping out.

"Actually I'm his twin brother," John assured. "Take me to the canteen, Ensign. I am rather hungry."

"Yes SIR!"

There was enough enthusiasm in the young man's voice to conquer the entire universe. Single-handed, of course. Isn't that what the legendary Commander Galt would do?

***

Chapter two

The Council

"All shall rise!"

Some Honorable Members were standing already. Some appeared to snore in total disregard for the oncoming proceedings. Still others, their overstuffed carcasses sprawled nonchalantly, lackadaisically babbling at large. Not one them however, not a single Representative of the Federated Republics made the slightest effort to reduce the pandemonium generated by sixty thousand overworked mouths. Their gaping orifices remained open exuding endless voluminous bombast. A forest of arms continued waving, feet stumping ferociously, to underline some persuasive Point of Order.

The Honorable Members of the Council were busy exercising their electoral privilege. Their right to pressure, threaten, hoodwink or otherwise bulldoze the more timid Members to his or her own opinion, his or her own will. Sixty thousand people will not be hushed suddenly. Particularly people who came here to be heard—not to listen. Not even sixty thousand individual viphone speakers could silence this mass of festering nobility. Not even when announcing the arrival of the Presiding Triumvirate. Sixty thousand Honorable Members ignored the first announcement.

"All shall rise!"

This time the honorable promulgating hordes abated somewhat their inherent ferocity. The roar lessened, the decibels ebbed slowly, rather as diminishing breakers of an outgoing tide. Soon the waves rolled back but with a lesser force, carrying the echo of their incessant bickering. All present carried proxies of many millions of people. In addition, up to three hundred thousand Out-Members, Members in absentia, could and often did take part in this ravenous struggle for votes. A vicious contest for the opportunity to leave his or her personal stamp on the affairs of man; to affect, nudge, or to impress one's self, one's ego, on the future of mankind. To buy, steal, or wrench by any means possible, a tiny niche in the annals of immortality. Those physically excluded from the Council Chamber participated through reciprocal instant-replay viphones. With the replay lag reduced to a fraction of one second, the Out-Members were convinced they were partaking in live proceedings. This minor deception had been necessary, sometimes even useful, for those in control. For years the Earth's ether had been saturated with the incessant cacophony of broadcast entertainment. As a result all government communications had to be piped by superconducting fiberoptic cables. Eleven billion people talked; about half of them—simultaneously. The other half slept.

"All shall rise!" The individual speakers whispered for the third and last time.

From the cavernous innards of the underground Federal Complex, at the centre of the Council Chamber, a transparent plexion bubble emerged, exposing the top of its polished, bald head. The dome rose majestically, ponderously, elevating the Elevated, the three presiding Members of the Federated Republic's highest governing body.

The Triumvirate. The Presidium. The temporal gods.

The plexion bulletproof dome had been introduced some seventy-five years ago, shortly after all three Presiding Members had been murdered by a paid assassin. Poison arrows, together with synthetic skin piping, had been grafted, like veins, into his homicidal left arm. The modern adaptation of the prehistoric weapon had remained undetected by the security scanners. The man had pointed his arm at the three presiding Members as though driving home a point of argument, while simultaneously blowing into the tubes that started at the raised collar of his tunic and terminated at the tip of his accusing finger. The assassin would have remained undetected if it had not been for the fact that he, himself, had been murdered the moment he left the Council Chamber. Poetic justice? Perhaps, but the killer's killer had never been traced.

As the plexion dome rose to its full height, a tentative, grudging silence displaced the fomenting jangle of the vast Chamber. The Speaker's monotonous voice began reciting the agenda for the day's proceedings, followed by a detailed report and then the minutes of the previous session. Progressively, a steady murmur from the bored audience grew then overwhelmed the Speaker's droning voice.

The Council's jurisdiction was limited to five principle areas:

* To the updating (rarely) and the enforcement (daily) of the basic Charter of Individual Rights (police activities);
* To the Exploitation of the Solar System mineral and manufacturing enterprises and administration of the Extraterrestrial Colonies;
* To the Galactic and the Global Communication Network (mass media);
* To the administration of the Credit Bank (global fiscal policy determining the credit rating of component Member Republics of the Federation;
* To the activities, (including financing), of the Galactic Navy (defense, overall security and exploration).

All other areas of administration remained within the jurisdiction of the individual republics. Should any participating nation became dissatisfied with the way the Council conducted its business, it could, on requisite notice, cancel its Membership and declare independence. The longest time however, that any Republic had lasted without the obvious benefits of the Federation had been less then a decade. Invariably all separatists became financially, morally and culturally—bankrupt, and after a trial period of ten years the errant Republics were once again allowed to rejoin the Federation. This single experience of unnatural insularity seemed to be a great deterrent for the errant Republics. Nobody learns as slowly as politicians, but even they do learn.

Although the Speaker of the Council concluded his reports by declaring lunch recess, few Members left the Chamber. Soon a persistent murmur rose to the previous impassioned roar of arguments. Again the Honorable Members stretched their backs, their legs, their mouth, and dialed for a wide array of nutrients. All this, simultaneously, while conducting their last minute lobbying.

During the afternoon, the first part of the session consisted of voting on all the outstanding Propositions. The votes on each motion were taken three times. If carried, the Proposition would be enacted by the Executive Council. The period from motion to enactment could last from six months to ten years. The Council did not believe in rushing things unduly.

By the time John returned to Earth the Council employed a half billion public servants. A rise of 17% since John's last visit. An equal number of citizens were gainfully employed in numerous colonies. This latter group included the Galactic Navy and the few remaining professions that could not, as yet, be replaced by automatic labour-saving devices, such as robots. Another six to seven hundred million people were deeply involved in the entertainment industry. This group had to keep the remaining nine billion people happy. Nine billion people with time on their hands, and little or nothing to do.

Nothing useful, that is. Nine billion relegated to sating their minds with vicarious pleasures, with pathological escapism into the worlds of holographic projection. A vast faceless mass committed to satiating their sensual needs with gluttonous overindulgence, invariably resulting in long, vastly excessive, sleeping habits. In fact, among this idle rabble, an inordinate amount of sleep became fashionable. Little wonder! The cause? Inordinate boredom perhaps?

As boring as the voting procedures taking place in the Council Chamber?

Voting on first, second or third readings of over three hundred motions, ninety-two propositions, seventy-nine amendments, forty-two points of order, fifty-seven... On sixty thousand screens inside the Council Chamber, and five times as many outside, little red and green lights blinked, computer memories hummed, and statistical data was updated.

Finally, the voting was over.

For a brief unaccustomed moment a ponderous silence hovered over the Assembly, while Members weighed the pros and cons of the latest results. Finally, new matters, as per agenda, could be tabled and added to the previous, voluminous procedures. The three Presiding Members stirred. They seemed to be emerging from a deep sleep. Until now the Triumvirate had been absorbing the hytapes designed to bring them up to date with the thousands of bits and pieces of information needed to conduct the business of government. Their presence during the morning session had been little more than symbolic. They had lent an air of official dignity to the procedures.

There were seven new items on the agenda. Most dealt with the fiscal reports and with the current data from the Colony J/27 located at Ganymede. The discovery of almost pure titanium on three of the outer, lesser moons, of Jupiter generated a lot of interest. The extensive use of this element in the Galactic Navy was the direct motive behind a number of speeches; each proposing increased efforts to enhance terra-forming on the already established colonies. The overt object was to make the outer colonies more attractive; to make them sufficiently inviting to instigate a dent in the population of the mother planet.

When the applause following the speeches subsided, the Munificent Right Honorable Archdeacon, Moses VI, raised his impressive bulk as a sign of willingness to impart his wisdom to the Assembly. A series of flashing lights further reaffirmed his intent, thus instantly switching off the two-way system of viphones to the receiving mode only. Without this precaution, the few who may have been interested in what his Holiness had to say would be unable to do so. The general decorum in the Assembly called for listening, during the first five minutes, once a week to any Member of the Council. This privilege had not been extended to the Presiding Members. The moment any of them rose to their feet instant raucous hurrahs and boos precluded any possibility of hearing what they may have had to say. Only by shutting off the outgoing speakers on the sixty thousand individual viphones could the message be delivered.

Each Member of the Triumvirate had been assigned up to fifteen minutes, per day, to make his or her point of view known to the world. A time allocation long-contested by the General Assembly. Since, however, each Presiding Member carried around 60,000 proxy votes, the three of them together, providing they did cooperate, could not be outvoted during their term in office. Although the General Assembly's theoretical voting power boasted 360,000 proxies, only a show of unanimity could upset the power of the Presidium. And unanimity among such numbers had long proven quite impossible—on any subject.

For his full fifteen minutes the overflowing Archdeacon spoke against the proposal. Whatever it was. He invariably spoke against any innovation. He represented the status quo. The conservative, passive, sleepy legions.

"No change is a good change. Let us protect that for which we have fought so long and so hard to accomplish. Let not the labours of our noble fathers and our caring mothers be in vain. We owe it to our forefathers!"

"...to do nothing," the Admiral snorted. Although, he mused, in a way it did reduce the pollution...

With this last call for temperance, His Holiness collapsed, exhausted, into his rotating, soothing, vibrating, massaging armchair. He immediately closed his eyes in a courageous effort to recover from the taxing exigencies of his office. The labours he referred to remained, alas, a mystery shrouded, presumably, by his predecessors. Or by the layers of his lard.

Throughout this charade Admiral Grant continued running his affairs from the Assembly. Microchips, implanted subcutaneously, afforded him instant and continuous communication with the outside. The real world. He had the Galactic Navy to run. Colonial explorations to control. The vibrant live world to worry about. He hardly ever listened to His Holiness. Moses VI had never made any sense before—there was no reason to expect any today. The Archdeacon represented the very, very idle masses.

Following some acrimonious debating on the pros and cons of the new propositions, the Speaker called for another break in the proceedings. The Admiral rose quietly and disappeared into a small elevator. Six levels below, a hand scanner-operated door let him out into a dimly lit corridor. He stepped directly onto a moving walkway. Instantly, a speed synchronized handrail and a protective seat slid out of the wall on his left. Sensors, detecting his weight, accelerated the walkway to seventy kilometers per hour. He activated a small keyboard in the right armrest. The Admiral programmed his desired destination. The walkway doubled its velocity.

Four minutes later the Admiral arrived at his secure underground quarters. A wall-panel slid silently open giving access directly into his private office. For a moment the Admiral stood undetected. He watched John Galt nervously pacing the length of the large room. The 'young man' seemed restless. Twenty minutes ago John had been instructed to report immediately to the Admiral's office. A herculean ensign examined his hand scan. Another, almost as large, let him in.

John came in, sat down, then got nervous. He started pacing.

Three days had passed since their last meeting. John had spent the time flying here and there, wondering, trying to find his place on this, his mother planet. Not that much had changed since his last visit. It was he who had changed. Each trip into the spangled darkness of space made him a different man. A man more aware of Infinity—the outer and the inner. The two seemed to expand together. John felt part of the silent darkness, of the eternal Void, with himself as the center of life within it.

John Galt had no idea why the Admiral had summoned him. Yet the moment the helio he was flying picked up the communication, John broke all speed records to the roof heliport of the Federal Complex. His flyer had been equipped with the latest antigrav capability. None such had existed the last time he had visited earth. Just one he thought, of so many, often hardly discernible changes...

"John, I am glad you could make it!" With the panel sliding silently shut behind him, the Admiral appeared to have emerged from the wall. "Come, I have some news for you."

The Admiral's face forewarned that no news was good news, although his stern features looked more determined then worried. He sat at his desk, back ramrod straight. He seemed to be gathering his thoughts. Then his unflinching, steel grey eyes found John's searching stare.

Three days ago John had not experienced the full power smouldering in the Admiral's gaze. Now, John pressed his shoulders deeper into the contoured back of his armchair. Whatever was coming was serious. Of that he was certain. John's adaptable brain shifted into instant overdrive.

"I am at your service, Sir." Unwittingly, even in a sitting position, John assumed the stance of rigid attention. Unwittingly, the Admiral smiled.

Hermes Grant recalled his own words of three days ago: "they don't make them like you any more..." Then the fleeting smile gave way to an expression of deep concern.

"Do you know how we conduct our business of government nowadays?" The question was rhetorical. "Sixty thousand people prattle and promulgate at great length. Periodically the Presiding Members join in. It's all an elaborate sham. A traditional carefully observed pantomime. A studiously maintained nonsense. In fact, all the real dealing is done outside the Chambers. It is conducted without any fanfare, in fact very quietly, by clever amoral lobbyists. By men and women who are not always on the right side of the tracks. But always extremely professional." The Admiral studied John's face. "Do you follow me?"

John nodded.

"Basically it is a question of votes. More precisely, of power." The Admiral continued. "With sixty thousand voting Members inside the Chamber, and three hundred thousand outside, we must concentrate on the Outmembers to get any of our policies adopted." He paused again to check John's expression.

"We?" John asked.

Admiral Grant's smile returned to his tired features. "Yes, my boy. In time you will find your own answer to this question."

The Admiral dialed for a glass of water.

"This evening I shall make a speech, the usual fifteen minutes. I shall table a motion that a consolidated effort, and the attendant fiscal commitment, should be made, immediately, to launch new expeditions in search of intelligent life. At the very least we must renew our search for planets capable of supporting human life within all neighboring star systems. With our present day terraforming capabilities, we must reexamine all the star systems that had been previously discarded. In essence, this will be my motion. For the last ten hours my staff has been equipped with the pertinent data." A sad smile twisted the Admiral's firm mouth. "My men are in constant touch with our pollsters distributed throughout the body of deputies. They tell me that I shall fail to sway the majority of voters. We must therefore take surreptitious, subversive if you like, action." The Admiral took another sip before continuing. "Past analyses indicate that whatever decision is made by the Council today, will be reversed in six to seven years. For reasons already known to you, we cannot afford the delay."

The Admiral closed his eyes. He sat back evidently waiting for John's reaction. Only seconds had passed since the Admiral finished talking, but the silence seemed almost painful. Then John stood up.

"What do you want me to do?" John was blunt and direct.

"Go to the Moon Base and await orders." The Admiral spoke slowly, precisely, enunciating every word.

John remained standing to attention. Though he considered the interview finished, he found it difficult to make his way to the door. Something remained unsaid.

"Shall I see you again?" John Galt asked very quietly.

The Admiral also rose. Suddenly he looked older. He turned away from John, perhaps needing time to steady his voice. They had met once in the last forty years. This had been their second meeting. As Harry Grant turned to face John, his eyes said it all: Why was this man, this intrepid starman, the closest human being on Earth, in the Solar System, in the whole world, to my old, lonely heart?

"Even if it's the last thing I do," he said through clenched teeth.

Commander Galt saluted and left the office. Seven minutes later Admiral Grant's head appeared from below in the glass bubble of the presidential platform. The venerable Donna D. Dobbs had just risen to talk. She, the third Member of the Triumvirate, represented the active part of the human race: the Federated Union of Public Employees. A one-half billion people. It was not really a union at all. They were just people who worked, as against people who did not. Donna Dobbs was one hundred and twelve years old. No one ever dared to challenge her right or her ability to represent her people. She served them well. She and the people both knew it.

Donna Dobbs was preparing the ground for Admiral Grant's speech. The Admiral knew he could count on her. Who knows? Perhaps the pollsters had been wrong—for once. The Archdeacon insisted that miracles could always happen. The Admiral knew, that regardless of what took place in the Council, whatever had to be done—would be done. This sentiment might have negated some primitive concepts of democracy. But the Admiral also knew, and it was the worst kept public secret of all time, that of the eleven billion people populating this poor over-exploited planet, about 99% of the citizenry did not give a damn what happened in the Council. Now or ever.

Perhaps, just perhaps, the people were right?

The diminutive venerable lady, Donna Dobbs, wielded her personal power from a stature of no more than 162 centimeters. If one were to regard her from some distance, she would strike one as an energetic woman of, perhaps, forty or fifty. Her actual age, her longevity, was not that uncommon. An awful lot of people—if they hadn't died of boredom—sustained good heath well into their twelfth decade. What was unusual, very unusual, was her tremendous youthful perspicacity, the cheerful brightness of her disposition, the deliberate sharpness of her judgment invariably based on solid facts and not on some wishy-washy assumptions.

Donna Dobbs was a very rare woman.

Admiral Grant sat back in his console armchair and activated his subcutaneous communication system. He asked for, and received, the latest poll report. No news was good news. For a few seconds he entertained the idea of telling the assembly about the eighty-year ozone layer projection. Then he merely smiled at his own desire to escape the burden of responsibility. The last time a much lesser danger had been announced, the ensuing panic resulted in mass destruction on a global scale. And that concerned only the danger of overloading the airways with excessive communication channels. People seemed pathologically afraid of being, in any way, separated from anyone else. They needed to be part of this global village. Not being active themselves, they evidently needed the news media to partake, vicariously, in the global events. This desire in no way extended to having any interest in the proceedings in the Council. They needed to feel the pulsations of Mother Earth. The news media gave them the illusion of security—of being part of, and within the global protective womb.

Donna Dobbs stopped speaking.

She sat down, lightly, seemingly unconcerned about the success or failure of her discourse. If she worried about the reaction of some sixty thousand people, she would be in no position to look after the interests of the remaining half-billion. She did her job, as well as her ability and experience allowed. That was all.

After the usual time allowance of two hours for general discussion and Members' commentary speeches, the Admiral rose to do his duty. During the last few seconds, he checked once again with his staff. The figures remained discouraging. His army of negotiators, hand picked lobbyists, would continue their work until tomorrow's Council session. Only then would the vote on today's proceedings take place. Since the Council represented the whole planet, one third of the Outmembers were, at present, asleep. They would only learn about the proceedings from the hytapes and assign their proxies to other representatives. The Council met at different times during different seasons, to allow for full participation of all the Outmembers, at one time or another. The system wasn't perfect but it was as fair as they could make it.

As the Admiral stood up a veritable hurricane of applause filled the Chamber. It lasted for fully five minutes—time that permitted the Admiral to reflect that the apparent admiration of sixty thousand Members had little to do with the acceptance of his forthcoming motion. As the Presiding member of the Triumvirate, he simply represented the hero concept, the Galactic Navy, the knight in shining armor elevated on a white stallion. He personified, even if wrongly, unjustly, the romance absent from peoples' lives.

The Admiral knew the truth but did nothing to dissuade the Members from their impression or perception. He did not shrink from assuming the embodiment of their unfulfilled dreams. After all he had crisscrossed the Solar System many a time. He had been instrumental in establishing a dozen colonies in the still-romantic, enigmatic segments of the relatively unknown, to most still-frightening, space. He also worked harder, longer and with greater dedication than any human being alive. Yet all this could do little, if anything at all, to gain approval for the intended expedition to the Lyra system. In fact he no longer had any intention of telling the Members about his plans. At this stage he merely wanted to reduce the danger of pursuit by the Galactic police who, although under his direct orders, did answer to the Council for their actions. In the long run he could not act against the Council with impunity. In the immediate future, he could try.

He did.

Admiral Grant spoke briefly, not even taking the advantage of his full fifteen-minute time allocation. At the end he received a standing ovation. Tomorrow they would have his hide. By secret ballot of course.

As Hermes Grant sat down, he activated his communication system. His adjutant reported immediately. The Admiral's question was terse, as was the answer he received:

Commander Galt?

Left at seventeen hundred hours.

The Admiral felt a delicious chill run up his spine. A surreptitious smile broadened his face as Harry Grant felt, once more, blood cruise faster in his overtaxed body. He totally ignored the applause. He sat back, closed his eyes and sank deep in thought. His mind reached out into the vastness of Outer Space. He would give the rest of his life, his whole life, to be in John Galt's shoes. Some minutes later he shrugged his broad shoulders.

The game was afoot. And he liked it. Hermes D. Grant liked it a lot.

***

Chapter three

Moon Base

The stationary black disk seemed filled with dark, menacing secrets. From five thousand kilometers, the dark side of the moon looked like a black hole: a round, black void torn out of a somber canvas speckled with hard dots of glittering ice.

The canvas of endless space.

The Executive shuttle, enveloped in utter silence, also appeared motionless, lifeless. Only the steadily growing diameter of the forbidding hole betrayed the otherwise imperceptible movement. A void growing, threatening to swallow the shuttle whole in its impenetrable darkness.

"Give me Outer Space, any time," Commander Galt muttered under his breath. "At least the Void is alive."

Had anyone overheard him, his logic would have sounded questionable.

During the last hundred years the Moon Base became the hub, the central station, the busiest spaceport of the Solar System. The landing pads, strategically distributed throughout the cold, still inhospitable surface, formed part of the main permanent distribution grid. Most Galactic Navy moon-falls had been directed to the dark side. The hemisphere having its share of sunlight, but hidden away from the evocative disk of the Mother Planet. Hidden from the comforting sight of Home. The Earthside, awash either with the hard glare of the sun or at least with the gentler reflected glow of earthlight, had been reserved for commercial traffic.

And what an immense traffic it was!

If Earth, as some said, had become humanity's garbage dump, then the moon was the gargantuan storage depot from which an awful lot of potential and eventual garbage would be disseminated.

The produce of all the colonies had been transported to the Moon Base. There the interlocking grid of under and over ground tunnels united hundreds of, once independent, units into a single massive network of storage processing and manufacturing facilities. This beehive was regarded, by most, as the saving grace of the human race. Had it not been for the removal of most processing functions from Earth, the race would have, by now, surely drowned or suffocated in its own industrial excrement. On the moon the redundant solids had been elevated by reusable antigravs to a certain altitude, and there with only a nominal loss of energy, the slag and suchlike were nudged towards the sun. There, in time, the refuse added fuel to our life-giving furnace.

John Galt had approached the moon from the dark side more times that he could remember. Each time the thrill had been compounded by new technology. Never more so then now. As the shuttle closed in on its destination, the dense surface darkness seemed interrupted by shimmering, oscillating cobwebs of glowworms. The hundreds of geodesic domes, some up to two miles in diameter, became visible against the still impenetrable darkness of their background. As the shuttle grew near, the lesser smaller domes with their interconnecting tunnels emerged from the shadows creating a filigree of incredible beauty and complexity. The structural members of the domes and barrel vaults had all been coated with luminous moss, which accumulated and stored light, then returned it, while simultaneously exuding oxygen from its genetically altered DNA molecules. The mesmerizing beauty of the effect caught John off guard. He stared... gaping, enchanted.

The shuttle touched down as silently as it took off. The antigravs not only eliminated the deafening roar of the engines but also the unnerving vibrations, which John had learned to associate with all the gravity touchdowns. His own spaceships had been just that: space ships. They never touched the solid ground. They remained in Earth orbit, circling at a leisurely distance. From Earth they looked like fireflies... trapped, or lost in the impenetrable vastness of the dark blue starry firmament.

The landing lights snapped John back to reality. He had to wait five minutes for the pressure lock adjustments and the usual landing formalities. Since returning from his last exploratory trek to Altair in the Aquila sector, 4.82 parsecs into the northern hemisphere, John had spent two months at debriefing before being sent Earthside. Invariably, or at least for the fourth time in succession, John found Earth, his ancient intermittent base, his roots, an intense disappointment. He had been away about forty years at a time. On each trek he had spent months, years... idealizing his home and the people he'd left behind; his imagination had built social systems based on an assumed progress in the evolution of man's consciousness. He visualized colossal improvements. His bountiful mind eliminated individual and social friction. It improved the means and the ability to respond to one another's needs. And finally, following millennia of practice, he assumed humanity had learned to truly apply the golden rule to everyday living. After a mere few weeks, seeing the snail's progress of his own species, John was ready to depart into the limitless reaches of Outer Space.

From the corner of his eye, John perceived movement. The young man facing him was the same one who had expedited Commander Galt on his Earth-fall, three and a half weeks ago.

"At your service, Commander"

The ensign saluted snapping John out of his somber deliberations. The ensign boarded the shuttle and stood to attention, waiting for John to rise from his seat. John Galt still couldn't accept the idea that he had become a living legend— among the young and old alike. He did not realize that his reputation had preceded him from the moment his spaceship had entered the Earth orbit some three months ago. Incidentally that had been the principle reason why Admiral Grant has expedited Commander Galt to the Moon Base. Before the vote was taken in the Council. Before any precocious Member of the Council came up with a distorted yet potentially dangerous answer to the impending puzzle.

John looked up at the young man. The ensign could not have been more than twenty. His height, well over two meters, suggested that he had been born and reared on the moon. The lesser gravity added extra height to its progeny. Some effort had been made, recently, to stunt the growth of children born in the colonies—if for no other reason than to facilitate the standardization of living quarters and equipment. The ensign's lanky frame, however, in no way detracted from his sure-footed behaviour. He evidently felt at home here. He probably wouldn't—Earthside.

"At ease, Ensign." John smiled up at the rigid beanstalk. Even after John got up, he was forced to look up at his guide. "Forgive me, I seem to have forgotten. What is your name?"

"Beta Mulligan, Sir!" The ensign, evidently, could not hide his pleasure at being assigned once again to serve this living paragon of virtue. "I have orders to escort you directly to your quarters. For the moment, Sir!" reported the ensign looking straight ahead over John's head.

"Relax, Beta. At ease." As the young man remained in a most rigid attention, John added with a grin: "Now, that's an order!"

At that, the young man actually smiled. Not only had the Commander's exploits been legendary, but so, apparently, was his sense of humor. The moment that any of the reports, which John had been sending back from his expeditions, were taken off the security listing, they became instant classics. As for John, after having met the universe face to face he was no longer capable of regarding himself with any degree of seriousness. He knew himself to be too puny, too insignificant in the vastness of space, to take almost anything very seriously. Let alone himself. Outer space is a great, exacting, teacher of humility.

"Yes, Sir! Thank you, Sir!"

Everyone of the young man's sentences had been accentuated with a verbal exclamation mark.

"John," John corrected.

"Yes, Sir John!" the young man attested.

"Never mind..." John vaguely remembered the awe in which he once held some of the early astronauts. So many years ago... He allowed the ensign to keep his idol. Why was it that people always needed icons? Why did they search for inspiration outside their own self, rather than within? That's another thing John could not have done in outer space. Because out there—there was no one else.

On stepping out of the shuttle, Beta placed his palm on the scanner. The outer lock doors opened with a slight hiss of residual pressure differential. The two men entered the airlock. The doors hissed shut behind them. They repeated this procedure twice before arriving in the Reception. About twenty people waited to be processed through the arrival procedures; or, perhaps, to take care of some customs or other business. The colonies were "Common Good", but the individual Republics, providing they were active members of the Federation, could conduct profitable business with any and all of the colonies directly. Or with any number of the holding areas on the Moon Base. History had provided a great deal of individuality, even competition, between the member Republics. Some of them even retained the original language of the geographical areas that had once defined their autonomy. The majority however used the official language, retaining old dialects only for cultural and, or, sentimental occasions.

Beta Mulligan led Commander Galt directly to a door marked "NO ENTRY". They bypassed all the officials who controlled the access to the circulation tunnels network. Beta again placed his hand on the scanner. The door sign went out, momentarily, to reappear immediately on their clearing the archway. Inside, another tall individual wearing the insignia of the Galactic Navy on a short smart looking tunic, greeted them with a salute and a friendly smile. John had been given a bracelet that gave him practically unrestricted access to all the Galactic Navy Moon Base installations. The young lady, almost as tall as Beta, introduced herself as second lieutenant Omega Brent. She had been delegated to act as the Commander's liaison in all matters of security. Personal or otherwise.

"I mean, should any such problems arise, Sir," she added. The girl had been obviously impressed by John's presence. She almost stammered.

All John had to do was to squeeze, in a particular sequence, the beads on his bracelet, and Omega's face would appear on a tiny viphone dangling from the bracelet. Before coming Earthside, John had been wearing such a bracelet also. He never had any occasion to use it. He made a mental note not to disappoint the young lady again.

The red tape done, John and Beta resumed their progress to Commander Galt's assigned quarters.

The moving sidewalk got them to their destination in under fifteen minutes. John recognized the suite he occupied some three weeks ago. There was a ludicrous sign over the entrance door that read "Home Sweet Home". Some previous occupier must have left it there. Someone, who missed his or her family that had remained Earthside. John had no such nostalgic attachments. He smiled every time he became aware of the sentimental sign. He was glad to be free. Outer Space was his country. A spaceship his home. He needed little more than a berth to sleep in.

Ensign Mulligan stood at the door maintaining a semi-rigid posture, something halfway between 'attention' and a 'stand-at-ease'. John decided to humor the young man.

"What do you want to do when you..." John suddenly realized that he couldn't possibly say 'when you grow up' to a man over two meters in height, "...when you finish the Academy."

Every ensign was automatically a member of the Naval Academy. He had to serve at the Moon Base, then put in time on every single colony in the System. By the time an ensign became a fully-fledged lieutenant of the Galactic Navy, he could make competent decisions anywhere in the Solar System. And then some!

"To follow in your footsteps, Sir," Beta answered.

Almost immediately his young face turned crimson. "I mean, Sir... I mean, ah, Sir, I wish to volunteer for interstellar missions, Sir!"

No one could ever follow in Commander Galt's footsteps. Such things as the Commander did, one could only read about. One could not possibly repeat them. There were people who claimed that the Commander was over three hundred years old. Some said he lived a lot longer. He looked about thirty. Maybe a little more. But three hundred? The ensign knew about the dilation of time at interstellar velocities, but... three hundred?

"Why?" John asked.

"Why what, Sir?" The young man seemed lost and flustered.

"Why do you want to go into space?" John prompted.

There was a momentary silence. Beta looked a little ill at ease. How does one discuss space with a space legend? He was searching franticly to find words to express his dreams, his desires, his aspirations... practically since the time he was born. His mouth opened and shut a few times.

"Because it is there, Sir!" he said at last, the exclamation mark at the end of the sentence a bit weaker.

John regarded the youngster with new respect. "That is the best answer anyone ever gave me, Beta. Would you like to sit down?" he asked gently.

"If you say so, Sir!" Beta immediately resumed his previous rigid posture.

"Here." John gestured to an armchair. "A drink?"

Beta marched to the proffered chair and sat down. At attention. John dialed two light refreshments tasting and exuding the aroma of freshly squeezed oranges. He gave one drink to Beta. The ensign took the container and held it as if not quite knowing what to do with it.

"How old are you?" John asked.

"Sixteen, Sir?"

"What?" John asked in such disbelief, that it brought the ensign to his feet in near panic. "I mean I didn't expect you to be quite so young..." He tried to placate the young man. Or was it a boy?

"I am sorry, Sir. Would you like me to ask for a replacement?" Beta's voice strained with self-imposed discipline.

"Good Lord, no! And do sit down, Beta. You look untidy." While earlier Beta suffered from a stiff dose of rigid attention, now his long arms dangled awkwardly in a state of perplexed indecision.

"Untidy, Sir?" His face paled a little.

"Forget it. It's just a figure of speech from a few centuries ago."

Beta Mulligan's mouth fell wide open. Then it must be true. The Commander must be a few centuries old. Three hundred? Maybe even more. Leaping Lunites! This is just fantastic!

When the boy finally sat down, John asked him another question. He tried to learn something about the youth of today. About mankind's future. The hytapes dealt principally with the official version of Federated Republic Council news releases and with the considerable, ever growing update on technological innovations. The subliminal hytapes allowed John, for instance, to operate a helio equipped with an antigrav, but it took personal instructions to learn how to dial for a drink or a meal. The latter had been taken for granted.

"When did you join the Academy?" John asked.

"Two years ago. When I turned fourteen, Sir." Beta sounded more sure of his ground.

"Isn't that rather early?"

"Early, Sir? It is the normal decision time. We all have to do it." Beta sounded surprised.

"Explain."

There was a barrier between them: a rift of forty years of John's absence, a chasm of some centuries in attitudes. In John's time one had not been allowed to use child labour. After a moment or two, Beta's young features showed a glimmer of sudden realization. It grew into understanding that Commander Galt might really not know what took place on Earth, or the Moon, or within the System, to children. To youth. To such as he was.

"Where would you like me to start, Sir?" He wanted to be sure.

"The day you were born?" John said.

The young man smiled. "I don't think I can remember exactly that far back, Sir, but we are given hytapes at the age of two. That way by the time we are thirty months, we can read and write. The acquisition of theoretical knowledge is complete by the time we reach twelve. We are taught with hytapes, discussions, exercises, and labs. We also learn speed reading, especially those of us who are interested in history."

"Why is that?"

Beta smiled as if given a distinguished service medal. This was the legendary Commander Galt actually asking him, Beta Mulligan, to explain things to him. The squadron will never believe it. "The hytapes were initially limited to the technical, sociological and legal data. And later, because there was so much new stuff, nobody ever got around to getting the old stuff on them."

"I understand," John thanked him. He regarded the lanky young man. A boy of sixteen sounding like a mature man. John smiled a little sadly. "And what do you do for fun?"

"For fun, Sir?" For a moment Beta looked lost again. To him nothing he did could be excluded from fun. "Ah, you mean free time?"

"I suppose so...?"

"Well, my favourite exercise is leaping. I mean leaping in the Lunar Caves." When Beta noticed John's blank expression, he continued. "In the Condorset... just south of the sea of Crises, the Mare Crisium, they discovered, I think about twenty years ago, some very large caves. The caverns are all of six hundred meters in clear height. Some chimneys go up another hundred meters or so. After plugging most of the natural openings with standard lavoid and sealing with pladenium the smaller ones, they pressurized them. For the next five years nobody had any idea what to do with them. The caverns were too far off the beaten track for any immediate practical use. By the time the Moon Base expanded to be within reach of the caverns, the, ah, younger... ah, cadets claimed squatter's rights to them. The cadets and ensigns have been using them for leaping ever since. That's a sport, Sir, in which, due to our gravity, we can be fitted with wings and leap from a high platform into re-circulating air currents. We, sort of, fly, Sir." Beta's eyes were shining now. For the moment he forgot he was in such a distinguished presence. "It's quite marvelous, Sir. You'd love it! If you're really good at it, you can wear a badge of the Leaping Lunites." And then Beta remembered. "I mean, I am sure it is nothing special for you, Sir. I mean..." his voice trailed off.

John was not at all sure it would have been 'nothing special'. He made a mental note to check it out, time permitting. For now, he directed his attention to their previous discussion.

"You said something before about a time of decision. What did you mean by that?"

"You mean Decision Time?" John nodded. "Well, Sir, we all do it. Whoever turns fourteen reports to the Psy Center for the test. He is placed under hyphones and, for a specified time, I believe it is twenty minutes, he is questioned about his preferences. The test determines whether the boy or girl will be a doer or not. Also, which functions he or she is best suited for."

Beta reported this as though it was the most natural thing in the world. A natural thing to decide one's fate at the age of fourteen.

"What if you want to be something else?" John asked.

"Something else than what, Sir?" Beta looked puzzled.

"Something other than what the test indicates, you should be."

"I do not understand, Sir. The test does not tell you what to do. It finds out, from your subconscious mind, what it is that you want to do." Beta tried to explain.

"There is never a conflict?"

"Oh, yes. People sometimes claim that they want to be doers, or lay claims to all sorts of aspirations. But, as far as I know, very soon they find out that the test had been correct. Sometimes they think they want to be or do something, but they are not willing to make the effort."

The young man smiled again. By now he seemed quite relaxed.

"Pay the price?"

"I suppose you could put it that way, Sir. Except that when you are doing what you rally want, you do not actually pay anything. It is like having everything free. You are always having fun. That is why, before, I didn't quite understand... "

"...when I asked you, what do you do for fun?" John nodded his understanding. He knew exactly what the mature ensign meant. Perhaps he had been wrong about the people on Earth. Perhaps there has been progress. Or perhaps he should have stayed on the Moon Base and visited the Lunar Caves. Of one thing John was sure. He should have shared his time with the young generation. One can learn from them the true pulse of the race. The pulse of the planet. The hopes for the future of mankind.

"Do you like going Earhside?" John asked.

"No, Sir," Beta answered at once. He gained in confidence minute by minute.

"Why not?" John prodded.

"They are all so... old," the boy answered, and immediately bit his tongue. "I m-m-mean, Sir, ah..." Beta was in well over his head.

"Not half as old as I am?" John had no mercy.

"Oh, no, Sir! Oh, no, never. You are really so young... I mean..."

This time John couldn't help laughing. He knew what the young man meant. The people Earhside did not look into the future. They did not really live in the present, either. They seemed concerned about keeping what they had, rather then in risking all to conquer new horizons.

"And the people on Moon Base are... young?" John asked, after the young man's cheeks returned to their normal colour.

"Not just the Moon Base. All the colonies. We are not afraid to... die, Sir. In fact, that is what makes living exiting!" Beta's bold eyes were shining with the essence of life.

The young man lacked words to explain his sentiments any better. Yet, once more John felt a strange bond with the lad assigned to him as his guide. They had something in common. Perhaps it was their love of life. Or, perhaps, they were both talking about a different kind of life altogether.

***

Chapter four

FRS Blake

A series of sharp regular stabs of three little needles on the inside face of the wrist bracelet brought John Galt to full consciousness within seconds. He activated the bracelet to two-way communication. A youthful face appeared on the tiny viphone. John propped himself up on one elbow. Were all people on the Moon Base so young?

"Galt here," he said. It looked as though he spoke into his sleeve,

"Good morning, Sir!" A smiling face said. "My name is lieutenant Gamma Princeton. I am speaking for the C.O.. Could you please be at gate 49 dash 11A at 0800 hours?"

John glanced at his watch. That gave him one hour. He found it amusing that they were using earth-time on the Moon Base. It seemed to him that universal time would be more practical. Then he reconsidered. After all, there was a sunrise and a sunset up here. Even on the dark side.

"How far is it from my quarters?" he asked.

"Ensign Beta Mulligan will pick you up in forty minutes, Sir."

"Thank you!" he said.

"Thank you, Commander Galt," the face said, and the tiny screen went blank.

What was it with these people. They seemed to enjoy reciting the ancient Greek alphabet to him. What happened to good old Christian names? In fact, what ever happened to organized religion? Apart of the Archdeacon he saw little evidence of it.

John shrugged, stepped out of his night garb, and walked into the shower. A powerful atomizer sprayed him from some thirty or forty jets with an invigorating yet, strangely enough, simultaneously soothing massage. After sixty seconds the same nozzles pushed streams of alternating hot and cold air at his body. Another minute later he felt like a new man. Clean, massaged, his skin pink with a slightly scented fresh glow.

John put on his tunic and punched for breakfast. The only problem with these gadgets was the variety they offered. To learn how to make an informed selection from the menu would take a good hour. He dialed a protein/carbohydrate drink with a fresh orange flavour. The two months he'd spent on the Moon Base, before going Earhside, he drank more oranges than he could count. Most of the items on the computerized menu were unknown to him. He had spent too much time in space to become a gourmet. Perhaps one day...

Next, John put on the helmet and listened to the latest hytapes. There was still no news from the Council. Too early. Nothing much else interested him. Not there and then. He removed the helmet and dialed for Mozart. He smiled. Every forty years his spaceships had returned him to Earth. Every forty years he listened to Mozart. Some things never change. Minutes later there was a gentle buzz at the door. John pressed a button on the armrest. Beta Mulligan walked in. He looked even younger than yesterday.

"Good morning, Beta. Have you any idea where is Gate 49 dash 11A?"

"Good morning, Sir! Yes, I just come from there." Beta looked wide-awake.

"Don't you guys ever sleep?" John saw no evidence of any tiredness in the young man's features. Yesterday, after completing his official duties, Beta had returned to John's quarters. He'd asked if he could be of any help, on his own time. John appreciated the gesture. John Galt had no idea that had he asked the ensign to walk out onto the moon's surface without a space suit, the young man would have done it without hesitation.

They had shared a light dinner and then talked well into the night. John wanted to know everything about the younger generation. Perhaps, John wondered, it is my latent, unrequited paternal instinct.

"Usually four times a day, about ninety minutes at a time, Sir," Beta answered with a straight face. He no longer questioned when Commander Galt asked the seemingly obvious.

Of course! There was no real day and night on the moon. One could jog along, or take a buggy, and remain in the sun all the time. The sun did not affect Beta's biological clock. 'I should have known better,' he realized. John, himself, did not have any regular sleeping habits. He only slept when duty permitted. Sometimes, for a few months at a time. Even years. John grinned at the young man. He liked his unspoiled, straight shooting approach to life. Perhaps we were all like that once. At sixteen.

"Let's go," he commanded

"Yes, Sir!" The exclamation marks came back with renewed force this morning.

"Lead on, Mulligan."

John stepped onto the moving sidewalk immediately behind Beta. In less than two seconds they were moving at a good pace. The breeze felt good against John's face. It was almost like being outdoors. For obvious reasons, all the sidewalks were designed for one-way traffic. On the Moon however, the sidewalks had three fixed speeds, on three individual adjacent strips. A good walking pace, a brisk jog, and a 'running for your life' strip, against the wall. One stepped from one strip to another if and when desired. The handles hanging from above assured one's stability at greater speeds. One could also increase one's pace by actually walking on the moving surface.

Beta discouraged John from attempting this exercise. Especially on the faster side strips. He did demonstrate the trick himself though. With his extra long legs and one-sixth Earth's gravity, the young man disappeared far ahead in seconds. The technique was to convert one's kick or push into forward momentum rather than forward and upward. If Beta were to have run the way one runs on Earth, his head would have punctured holes in the ceiling. Alternately, he would have knocked himself out with the first uncontrolled leap. John decided to continue walking. He was fond of living. Five minutes later he caught up with Beta at the first direction transfer. Beta was leaning against the left wall, his breath quite normal, as if he'd done no running at all.

"Sweet sixteen," John muttered. "Where now?"

"Just follow me, Sir!" And Beta stepped on a new sidewalk veering off to the right. The sign read: F.R.G.N. ONLY.

"As if I have any choice... " John sighed. Until he met Beta, he regarded himself as a reasonably young man. Subjective time-wise, of course. Now he wasn't so sure.

In another ten minutes they reached their destination. Beta transferred his lanky body from one moving sidewalk to another, slowing down his pace, with the ease of a chimpanzee out for a Sunday stroll. Did they still have chimpanzees here, John wondered? Maybe the Moonites used them as instructors.

They stood in front of a gray door with the blue, gilt-edged emblem of the Galactic Navy. Beta put his hand on the scanner. The door slid open. They passed through a corridor of flushing lights and humming instrumentation. Then through another door. John remembered this was the security check for Naval Personnel only. No firearms, chemicals, stunners, lasers, or even compressed air or gas, had been allowed below the rank of full lieutenant. In circumstances where the pressurization was a matter of life and death, even the apprehension of an individual criminal, if such were to be found, had to be offset by the risk of endangering the lives of many. At any rate, for Navy personnel, only electronic stunners had been issued, permanently set to a one-minute cardiac paralysis. People with congenital heart problems shouldn't take up crime as a career. Especially on the Moon.

Finally, John and Beta arrived at the Central Reception of the Academy. Beta saluted the officer on duty and made for another single-speed moving sidewalk. In two minutes they stood at gate 49—11A. Beta saluted again.

"Reporting with Commander Galt as ordered, Sir." He was almost as rigid as when John first saw him yesterday.

The middle aged officer—finally someone out of the kindergarten John thought—not nearly as tall as Beta, returned the salute.

"That will be all, Ensign," he told Beta, while keeping his eyes on John. "You may return to your duties."

It was evident from Beta's face that he would give his right hand to be able to stay, to tag along. Just to watch what was going to happen. Whatever it was. Alas, duty called. Beta saluted again and, with only a sidelong glance at Commander Galt, spun on his heal. John felt sorry for the punctilious ensign. Beta Mulligan was a good kid. From what John had learned since yesterday, they all were.

"I've been asked to be here at 0800 hours," John said glancing at his watch. He had less than a minute to spare.

"Yes, Sir. Thank you for coming so promptly. I am sorry we were unable to give you a longer notice. Allow me to introduce myself. I am Commander Drake. Brad Drake. I have been following your exploits with considerable interest. Perhaps, sometime, we might compare notes."

Commander Drake pressed a button on the side of the desk and directed John to the room to the right of the lobby. As they left the desk, a wall panel slid open, allowing three men to enter and take charge of the area. To John they looked very much like a security squad.

"Where are we off to?" John couldn't help asking.

"You expressed a desire to have a look at the new... ah, engines?" Commander Drake smiled. "You seem to have some good connections, if I may say so."

It was then that John's memory caught up with him. Commander Drake, the first and, to John's knowledge, the only man to have survived seven gee's compression over a half hour period, when coming out of free fall over Jupiter. Later Commander Drake had led an expedition to Sirius in the Canis Major sector, some 2.67 parsecs out. They had not found any signs of intelligence on any of the planets, but the Commander had picked up a remnant of a space object orbiting one of the smaller planets. The object, apparently very old—it was hard to be precise since things in space tend to last a very long time—but it was definitely a technologically advanced, 'man' made object. Whatever 'man' had once been somewhere in that sector of space. The rest was history. Drake's discovery had spurted a renaissance for the Galactic Navy. Great fiscal appropriations had followed. An injection of credits and an awful lot of hope.

"Forgive me, for a moment I didn't recognize you, Brad. I am delighted to meet you at last." They shook hands.

"You must drop in more often, John!" Commander Drake encouraged. "You spend all your time having fun, leaving us to do all the work."

John was about to reply in kind but they reached the first pressurization lock. The ensign at the door saluted and placed his hand on the scanner. The two astronauts walked inside. The door hissed shut and another lock later they were in a shuttle. The silent perfectly smooth liftoff again gave John a sense of great pleasure. Here's to progress, he muttered.

"I am told that you have not as yet been briefed. May I suggest that you put on your helmet and the hytape will give you all the basics you need," Commander Drake suggested.

John did as he was told. About forty minutes later, the shuttle stopped with a tiny clinking sound. The magnets touched, pulled, and the first air lock hissed with incoming air. The sign above the air lock door read: FRS BLAKE. Underneath were the words 'Galactic Navy', a serial number, and the round FRGN logo.

Federated Republics Starship BLAKE. John knew from the hytapes that the ship had been so named after a historic character called Adam Blake. A man who had once taken a one way trip into the heart of a Black Hole. Some said that

Blake had reappeared later on the, then, tiny Moon base—a single small colony of scientists—to help decipher his own messages. Some people were apt to believe anything, John mused, a whimsical smile playing on his lips.

The air lock hissed. Commanders Drake and Galt stepped in.

The inner lock opened onto a compartment the size of about three spaceships put together—three spaceships that John had ever flown. John had the data from hytapes, but there was a world of difference between theory and practice. This ship was enormous. One could live on board in comfort for years... if one didn't have to hibernate to conserve one's supplies and ageing process.

My God, this ship is big! John stood riveted to the floor, as if his own feet were locked in with some kind of magnetic device. Directly in front of him was a large holographic projection of the whole starship. It indicated their exact, present location. John noticed himself and Commander Drake actually within the scale model. A nice trick, he whistled softly.

The gravity felt about the same as on the moon. There was no sense of transition from one to the other. In the shuttle they were strapped in and travelled at one gee. That is a very civilized way to travel, although reputedly, not for the Moonites. For them, if it weren't for their genetic predisposition, such gravity would be equivalent to six times normal!

"She had the same effect on me, when I first saw her..."

Brad Drake understood John well. No one respected the designers of spaceships more than the men or women who spent their lives within their innards. As the two Commanders stepped forward, a woman wearing insignia of a starship pilot walked in from an elevator at the back of the docking area. She saluted.

"Lieutenant Delta One Blake!" She snapped to attention. "At your service."

Women look great when they snap to attention. Beautiful women—look fantastic!

John examined the face, the figure, and again the facial features of the woman. If there had been a flaw, he could not see it. Her beauty was almost distracting. Almost. Were it really distracting, it would no longer be perfect. She was.

Delta One's stance accentuated her trim, lithe and definitely very feminine figure. Her height was above average, a bit over one hundred-eighty centimeters, but quite normal for women raised and bred on the Moon Base. Her body implied rather than flaunted a springy serpent like quality. It suggested a coiled restrained strength, well in control, but ready to be released at a moment's notice. Her face, perhaps a little too pale even for a classical beauty— many people on the Moon Base exhibited the same parlor— was dominated by larger than average steely blue eyes. Those steady unblinking metallic irises seemed to welcome and scrutinize him, both at the same time. In fact, those eyes were just a little unnerving. John felt stripped, dissected, examined in minute detail and reassembled in the time it took him to return her salute. Those piercing eyes were protected by dark lashes, framed by dark eyebrows, in full contrast to her short, apparently natural, curly blond hair dancing over a high, smooth forehead. A small straight nose, a narrow, full mouth and a strong yet softy rounded chin completed the well-disposed features. If it weren't for her poise and those steady eyes, she might be called very attractive. With them, she laid claim to unquestionable beauty.

"I'll leave you two alone. I have some things to do. Delta will tell you whatever you want to know, John. I defy you to find a lapse in her memory!" Commander Drake slapped John on the back and disappeared inside an elevator.

"I am glad to meet you, Commander John Galt."

John offered his hand. The handshake was firm and friendly. John felt that they were going to get on well together. "If this crib can sleep forty-seven people, I would like to see the engines that make this possible. Unless this is a space hotel, of course!"

"Right this way, Commander." Delta turned gracefully and walked to the elevator to the right of the one taken by Brad Drake. When the doors shut behind them, she spoke into the air: "Engine room oh-three."

John hardly felt the elevator move. It seemed to descend on a cushion of air. The next instant the doors behind them slid open. Silently. This place was smooth. Lieutenant Delta led the way along a gallery into a room about six stories high. The cylindrical room surrounded the magnetic coils, which were, in effect, suspended outside along the ship's vertical axis. Imagine a yo-yo with a circular hole in the middle. The circular hole, the axis, was the atomic pile. It had the biggest cooling system possible. The universe. All of it. The chamber surrounding it was the engine room. The slot of the yo-yo, instead of coiled string, housed sixteen directional acceleration funnels distributed symmetrically around the whole perimeter. The spaces between the funnels took care of four shuttle landing docks, four emergency holding areas, and four quadruple laser guns augmented with four photon-torpedo outlets.

Some arsenal!

They now stood on the lowest floor of the engine room, three levels below the slot of the yo-yo. Level 03. Through the narrow plexor slot, John could see the atomic pile. Suspended in a magnetic embrace, it hovered, pulsating, half-dormant, idling effortlessly. It was only 2% operational. John stood in awe. The flexible design, which distributed the funnels in sixteen different directions, made navigation within any stellar system easy. The reverse thrust provided automatic deceleration. A child's play compared to all the ships John had ever flown. Until now, he could get to the stars, but entering an orbit of a specific planet was a time consuming, difficult, often dangerous operation. This lady permitted—nay demanded—precision navigating.

John stood in front of the vertical port, his eyes misty, his head trying to translate the information from hytapes into its practical equivalents. As he looked on, it all became real. The hytapes had saved him two years of intensive study. Still, he would not like to navigate this lady alone. FRS BLAKE. The ship may have been named after Adam Blake, but she was one hell of a lady. A Lady demanding an awful lot of respect.

Above the middle, or zero floor, there were three levels, as there were three levels below. The bridge was at the third level above the main deck, or the funnel/docking/defense level. Got it? John Galt did. But, of course, he listened to the hytapes.

John got it, absorbed it, was rapidly falling in love with it. So that was the secret of the new engines. They not only seemed to have practically unlimited supply of fuel, the 100% efficiency of the pile assured that, but they allowed for superb navigational adjustments. John was well aware that the solar system is moving gingerly along, around the Galactic centre, at some 250 kilometers per second, 900,000 kilometers per hour. Under such conditions, he wanted all the precision he could get. John could translate it into additional propelling stimulus. He could also make use of the centrifugal sling effect of the whole Solar System. If he dared, of larger planets... He could really fly this Lady.

Could I ever! John mused silently.

"Where did she go through her paces?" he asked Delta, without taking his eyes off the impressive engines.

"She hasn't. Or at lest, not in her present form," she replied.

"What the devil do you mean by that?" John looked at his guide and practically blushed. The last time he swore in the company of a woman must have been some time in the last century. Of course, he hadn't met many ladies lately. None during the last forty years. Delta didn't seem to have noticed.

"The engines had been flown before the decks were constructed. We took them..."

"We? You were there?" John couldn't imagine a woman doing a man's job. He was about one hundred and fifty years out of date.

"Yes, Commander. I and two other engineers..."

"You're an engineer?" John was again caught off guard.

"Why, yes, Sir. Do you mind?" Delta smiled a most disarming smile.

"I am sorry." John felt embarrassed. "It's just that I have flown for some years now, and I've never, I mean, I have never...."

"...you have never flown in the company of a woman?" She sounded very innocent.

"You could put it that way." John sounded contrite.

"The Galactic Navy is maintaining a full time personnel of one hundred million of which ten million are qualified pilots. Of which five million are women. These are round figures, of curse. If you want me to be more precise, there are four million nine hundred seventy four thousand eight hundred...."

"I believe you, Lieutenant Delta One Blake. And I apologize. Please don't feel offended."

"I do not get offended, Commander Galt. I am here only to advise you." Her voice really was perfectly relaxed, not in the least bit offended.

John regarded Delta with new admiration. This had nothing to do with her looks. She was beautiful, she was obviously extremely knowledgeable, and she had superb self-control. Frankly, too good to be true. In his thoughts he almost added: 'for a woman', and immediately bit his tongue. Come out of the jungle, John, he admonished himself.

"By the way, what does the 'One' stand for?" He asked.

"If you are referring to my name Commander, I have been the first lieutenant assigned to the FRS BLAKE. Hence, Delta One," she answered.

"That's quite an honor, isn't it?" John tried to study his companion. She had all the right answers but didn't give anything away. Did that make any sense?

By now they had walked around the circular pile and examined the instrumentation on three decks surrounding it. Galt could have stayed here forever, if not longer, but there was the rest of the starship to examine. The hytapes gave him the theory. He wanted to 'practicalize' the knowledge. To translate the theoretical hytape info into tangible components. He decided to test himself and directed his steps toward an elevator. He found it where he expected it to be. The doors opened only, however, when Lieutenant Blake approached.

"They have not been sensitized to your presence, Sir. Where to?" Delta One asked.

"The bridge," he said.

"The bridge," she repeated. "Or to your voice. You can use the manual override, of course."

He wondered if she was trying to comfort him, or was she simply reciting the information?

The bridge was three more levels above them. As before, the elevator was completely silent. The doors opened and John walked into a room washed with gentle, diffused light. The walls were covered with screens. They concealed ports, Galactic star vi-charts and a large, about twenty foot wide, high resolution vi-projector. In front of the projector stood a broad shouldered man. He seemed to be studying some figures popping up on the screen. Finally the man seemed to give up. His shrug suggested he was disappointed but not dejected. He said two words:

"Vi out." The screen went blank.

John knew that voice. He recognized it before the man turned around to face him.

"Ah, there you are my boy. I see you met Delta. A hell of a girl, isn't she?"

John was facing Admiral Hermes D. Grant. The Admiral looked tired but otherwise none the worse for wear. For crying out loud, Harry is eighty-four years old, John thought.

Didn't the man ever sleep, either?

**

Chapter five

Test Flight

The Admiral should have been on the stage. He would have made a fortune. Here, on the bridge, he stood in a balanced relaxed posture in a room large enough to hold a drinking party for thirty or forty men, and he completely dominated the entire space. Admiral Grant did so effortlessly, without sticking out his chest or looking down his nose. Wherever or whenever he was, the Admiral was in charge. Always. John wondered if Hermes Grant had been born with this truly dramatic presence or whether he acquired this unique trait over a lifetime. Probably both, he concluded.

John and Delta stood to attention. The Admiral dismissed their posture with a wave of his hand. He certainly was not a stickler on protocol. He was the most relaxed man John ever met.

"And just how do you like the new jewel of our Galactic Navy?" The Admiral asked, his piercing eyes studying John's face.

"The jewel and I had hardly met, Sir. I only got here..." John glanced at his watch. "...Leaping Lunites! I got here over fours hour ago!"

"I see you spent sometime with Beta Mulligan." The Admiral smiled easily as if the problems, which the vi-projector revealed a minute ago, were of no importance.

"Why, yes, Sir. I..." John was surprised, very surprised, how much the Admiral knew about his movements.

"Harry," the Admiral corrected.

"... ah, yes, Harry. Are you keeping tabs on me?"

"You'd better believe it," Admiral Grant assured. John had no idea whether the Admiral was joking or not.

Hermes Grant asked Lieutenant Blake to join them at the helm. The command center consisted of three identical consoles, each with moulded body-contour adjustable armchairs. Each position echoed the same navigational equipment as the other. Pressing one of an array of keys in the wide armrests, the consoles slid out and about to allow the three chairs to face each other. The chairs, together with their consoles, could rotate horizontally and vertically with equal ease, relative to the direction of acceleration. The bridge had obviously been designed for a triumvirate of command. Probably a Commander, a navigator, and the pilot. On smaller, much smaller ships, which John commanded over the last hundred and sixty odd years, the three functions had been invariably carried out by one man. If two men were present on board, the other was simply an insurance against unknown or unpredictable factors. There had been no other duplication apparently, until now.

"How would you two like to take her out for a spin?" The Admiral asked when all three were comfortably seated.

"When?" John couldn't help hiding excitement in his voice. Lieutenant Blake remained silent.

"When do you think you'll be ready?" The Admiral asked, still smiling.

"Give me a couple of hours!" John kidded with a wide grin.

"All right. In two hours I shall leave the bridge in your hands, John. Good luck." The Admiral's voice was perfectly serious. So was his face.

"That's not very funny, Harry." John really wasn't amused.

"No. It wasn't meant to be. I would like you two to give her a test flight. You have all the theoretical knowledge you need. Delta knows more than anybody about this ship. She also has the practical advantage of having already put in a half a billion kilometers with the engines intact, and her own condition unimpaired. Come on John. A spin will do you good!" The Admiral could be quite persuasive.

John knew from hytapes that there was nothing aboard this ship that was not automatic. He only needed to program his instructions, and the rest would just about take care of itself. He hoped. In addition, every single item on board that had any bearing on the safety of the crew, or the ship, had been, to say the least, duplicated. Even the engines could, for the most part, be replaced in outer space with the use of robots, without the engineers ever leaving the engine room. The main computer itself had an 80% backup, and the other 20% one could, quite frankly, do without. And then, as the Admiral said, there was lieutenant Blake. Delta. John was damned if he was going to continue addressing her as Delta One Blake. Or lieutenant Blake, for that matter. Delta, as Harry called her, sounded just fine.

"What do you think, Delta?" John tested his theory immediately.

"You are the commander, Commander," she replied with a straight face.

"Commander, Captain, Skipper and an oddball, to boot. What do you think, Delta?" he insisted again. She wouldn't get away with it that easily.

"The ship is ship-shape, Sir. Fully loaded, so as to accurately simulate expeditionary conditions. Except for the crew. We do not take the crew with us on test flights." She smiled as if embarrassed at having said the obvious.

"I gather that to be a yes. Are you going to be my Number One?" John asked.

"I am Number One, Sir," she asserted.

"Ah yes, so you are." John turned to the Admiral. "Harry, whatever happened to the months of training on flight simulators, medical tests, briefing and God knows what other red tape, which would extend the programming to at least six months?"

"The two months you have spent, or should I say the two months you thought you had spent, on Moon Base in the, so-

called, debriefing period, you have been simultaneously
tested in every imaginable way possible. We do it all a bit
differently, ah, these days. The testing—debriefing and all
that, has been done, principally, by hyphones. Didn't you
realize you had spent most of your debriefing time in the Psy
Center?" The Admiral looked genuinely surprised.

"You mean I have been brainwashed?" John's eyebrows
rose questioningly.

"My goodness, you have been away along time! A man
can be brainwashed, as you call it, for a very limited period of
time. If the artificial programming were to be introduced, that
is, programming which is done against his free will, his own
definition of his own best interests, neurosis sets in. A
neurosis that can seldom be completely eradicated. As such,
one can never brainwash a person who is to be of any long-
term use to society. The residual subconscious memory we all
carry rebels against any deleterious imposition..."

The Admiral went of for a little while. Evidently, he was
determined to make sure John understood fully his debriefing
period.

"You made your point, Harry. I must have read too many
historical novels on my last trek," John admitted. "So you are
telling me, that whatever they did in the Psy Center had been
for my own good? Rather like in 'Decision Time'?"

"So you know about that? Good man." The Admiral was
impressed. "Yes, in addition to many other tests, they probed
your subconscious to find out, as accurately as they could, not
only what your capabilities are, but what you think they are.
If the two are incompatible, the testing and programming
takes a lot longer. I don't mean to be patronizing, but you are
one of the sanest men on earth."

"One of...?" John teased.

"I scored higher." There was no bragging in Admiral's
voice. He made a statement of fact.

"You were tested?"

"Once a year, regularly as clockwork. Why does that
surprise you?"

"I suppose it shouldn't. Again, it is simply at odds with my latent memory fragments. You must realize, I still carry some baggage from nearly two centuries ago." John sounded almost victimized by his subjective, or was it objective longevity. He could never quite figure that one out. It was forever relative.

"Well?" the Admiral asked.

There were a few minutes of silence. The silence of space. Total and absolute.

"This is probably the most idiotic, irresponsible answer I have ever given in my life. But if Delta is willing, so am I, Sir." John further qualified his answer with a long, protracted sigh.

Hermes Grant knew all along that John Galt would not be capable of saying 'no' to such an opportunity. A space hound, as the Admiral had known John to be, could never resist trying out new engines. Especially engines as impressive as the ones FRS BLAKE offered. The Admiral's question was, practically, rhetorical. The answer, a foregone conclusion. The Admiral knew his officers, and what is more, he trusted his instincts. His intuition. But more than any of the above, the Admiral knew John Galt. He also knew, that he was losing him. Life wasn't always easy.

"That's settled then."

The Admiral dismissed the matter, as though nothing of any particular consequence took place. He turned to Delta.

"Could you look after the launching procedures, Lieutenant? I shall need ten minutes notice."

Delta saluted and left. John was well aware that even punching all the right keys on the computer in the engine room was a job that would take a good hour. The engines were kept idling at all times; if for no other reason than to supply the ship with electricity, heating and air. The Maridian crystals, however, were insinuated into the atomic pile 1.46 hours before the engines were to develop their full power. To do so earlier, would be rather like using a stellar laser projector to kill a mosquito. Assuming they still had mosquitoes, nowadays.

John suddenly realized that he'd been on earth only three and a half weeks. Adding that to the two months on Moon Base, it still didn't offer much time to catch up with the forty years of absence. He absorbed all the hytapes, of course, but that was purely mental. The emotions were not involved. And he could not really learn about anything until he also felt it with his emotions. Or, to put it differently, he could learn a whole musical score by heart, know it forewords and backwards, but still not *feel* it until he heard the composition with his own ears. The senses, the feelings, were strange traits of a human being. Perhaps it was better to be a robot after all. You cannot break a robot's heart. Or can you?

"Harry?" John broke the silence. He was attempting to translate hytape info into a practical application on the disposition of the bridge. Satisfied, he turned to the Admiral, who in the meantime, had again switched on the vi-projector.

"Yes John, what is it?" Half of the Admiral's attention remained on the screen.

"The hytapes do not specify the purpose of the third consol on the bridge. Can you enlighten me?"

"No." The Admiral shook his head, without much conviction. "When you carry forty seven people aboard, it is reasonable to assume that you might want to have at least three people on the bridge. Don't you think?"

John accepted this as a reasonable hypothesis. The Admiral switched off the screen with command 'vi-out', and turned to face John.

"You know that the construction, or at least the design, of this vessel, and another one exactly like it, had began sixty-two years ago. It had started the day after Drake got back from Sirius with his artifact. I had known, then, what effect his discovery would have on the Council. I took it upon myself to authorize the new design, there and then. It had coincided with the discovery of a sustained ultra-magnetic field generator, which could, for apparently indefinite periods of time, contain the matter-antimatter reactor, as well as channel the resultant energy. All I had was specs. At that time, the field had been tested only on Oberon, that's the furthest satellite of Uranus. We did not want to play around with antimatter, contained or not, anywhere near any of our colonies." Admiral Grant gave John a knowing wink.

John nodded. There seemed so much more to history than just hytapes.

"Anyway," the Admiral resumed," we could not find a practical application for it for another eleven years. After all, one can hardly use such sustained power for little 'hops' within our own Solar System. Even Pluto is less than five and a half light hours away, and our fusion engines are more than adequate for such distances. In fact, our limitation had been, and to a great degree remains, imposed by the maximum gee's which both the crew and even the vessel itself can take. There was little point in spending billions of credits on a new engine, for which there was little practical application. And you know how the Council feels about pure research. If you can't wear it, eat it or feel better because of it, it is of little interest to most Honorable Members."

"So what had changed the situation?" John was fascinated by the account.

"In 2253, that is eleven years after we managed to gain control of the ultra-magnetic pile, Dan B. Kadynski came up with the graviton deflector. It worked in theory. A year later, it worked in practice. It is still limited to a maximum of three gee's, but it is ample for our purposes. We were now upping our interstellar speed by nearly 20%, plus the benefit derived from the antigravs, which did not work on the mass of the ship proper, but it did on the crew and cargo. We were now, or really then, talking about placing another forty or more stellar systems within a practical accessible time frame."

Harry Grant sounded as exited as if all this happened only yesterday. In fact, as if it was still happening. In a way it was, or was about to.

"The antigrav doesn't work on the ship itself?" John heard the hytape, but it didn't click.

"To deflect a graviton you need a mass to absorb it. It is a derivative of inertia. Or partially so. All you need to know is, that if you can take three of four gee's under normal conditions, then here, in this lady," the Admiral patted the console, "you can go up to six or seven. It gives you quite a margin of safety."

"Brad Drake will be happy to hear that," John smiled.

"He was. He'll be taking out the FRS ADAM, on a test flight, the moment you report positive results," The Admiral said.

The two men sat for a while, each with his thoughts. John imagined that he should be running about this colossal starship checking things. Closing all the hatches, so to speak. The info John had absorbed from hytapes, kept him in his seat. He felt almost redundant. Every damn thing was automatic. There was no noise, no engine vibration, no people scurrying about looking busy. The chronometer continued on its silent journey. It had been preset to Galactic time, counting from two hundred down, towards zero. John stared at it with a jealous eye. Even the clock did its work, while he, the Commander of this vessel, did nothing. The dial had just indicated minus 120. The Admiral's time on board was ticking away.

"Why is it Harry that I have a strange feeling, that there is something you're not telling me?" John mused, not looking at his old friend.

"Perhaps, there is. Do you want to change your mind?" the Admiral asked very quietly.

For a moment John felt that he detected hope in Harry's voice. That the stalwart gentleman was actually hoping that John would change his mind and remain on earth. The moment passed. John shivered, as if a cold gust of wind touched his naked back. There was no wind. And John wasn't naked. He shrugged.

"How did you take to Beta?" the Admiral asked out of the blue.

"Mulligan?"

The old man nodded.

With seconds ticking away, John felt an absurd need to talk about something other than scientific advances. Seizing the opportunity, he went into a long discourse about the hours he'd spent with the bright, delightful young man. He told the Admiral how he had found him precocious, very mature for his age. How he admired Beta's friendliness as well as his personal discipline. John also said, that as long as the rest of the youth of Earth was of such a caliber, than there must be hope for the future. A lot of hope.

"Would you believe, Harry, the lad was actually teaching me, with the patience of a professional educator. He's almost wasted in the Navy. He can explain things better than any young man I ever met." Then John's eyes drifted to some distant star left behind on his lonesome journeys. "You know, Harry, if it had been meant for me to have a boy, that's the sort of son I would have wished for."

The Admiral turned his head to check something on the armrest consol. He blinked hard and tried even harder to swallow. He cleared his throat noisily. Then he faced John again. "Do you mind if I tell him that?"

"Mind? Of course I don't mind. Why should I?"

The chronometer dial registered minus 100.

Both men noticed it and got up simultaneously.

"John... " The Admiral started and then seemed to have changed his mind about something. "...I just wondered, you do not have to go through with this. There..."

Why did this sound like a good-bye? John was taking out a spaceship on her maiden voyage. It was hardly the end of the world. There was something more to it. If John had any suspicions, he kept them to himself.

"Will you make a tour of the ship with me, Harry?"

"Be glad to!" Harry Grant seemed eager to leave the bridge, to go somewhere, anywhere, to do something. They

turned toward the elevator. John suddenly remembered
something and went back to the Commander's console. He
dialed a code, pressed his hand into a panel, then recited his
name rank and function to a speaker in front of him. One
word appeared on a small console screen: *Confirmed.*

John rejoined the Admiral at the elevator and as he
approached it, the doors slid open. "Down one" he said, and
the silent machine obeyed instantly. They came out on the
floor below. Here were all the laboratories, medical center,
canteen, hologram deck and recreation rooms. They walked
quite briskly, John touching a button, here and there, taking a
quick, cool drink at the self-service bar. Suddenly time
seemed in short supply.

There were a thousand things each man wanted to say to
each other. Neither said any of them. There are things that
remained too difficult to be said. Difficult, man to man.
Especially for men who—one in the vastness of space, the
other on Earth—had both been, for many years, equally
alone. Alone in the whole, wide, wondrous, overpopulated
world.

The next floor down, more of the same, particularly more
laboratories, hibernation cubicles, medical back-up and the
officers' living quarters. They didn't spend more than a few
minutes there. They both sensed an undefined air of haste.
Wherever they looked, their eyes unwittingly found a dial of
a chronometer on its relentless journey. It seemed alive: 87,
86, 85, 84...

At zero level they walked out onto a gallery just to be,
even for a minute or two, in the engine room. Two levels
below them, they both noticed Delta moving about, from one
computer outlet to another. For some reason the input panels
did not appear centralized. Later John remembered that they
were, but Delta took the precaution of checking all the
sixteen funnels individually. Funny, John thought. I wouldn't
have thought of that. Well, not all at once. After all, they
were unlikely to use more than one funnel a long way down
the road. Not for quite a while, yet.

As John glanced at the Admiral he saw signs of quiet distress on his worn face. For a while, he couldn't identify the reason. And then John realized. The Admiral would have given the rest of his life for the privilege of being the first to fly his spaceship. FRS BLAKE was his beloved son, his daughter, his love, his passion. Now he was handing over the bridge to the man he trusted most in the whole world. It was the best he could do. For reasons known only to himself, Harry Grant could not or would not fly with them. Whatever the reasons were, they seem very serious and painful. Painful to him, personally. John thought it best not to ask. We all have to bear our burden. Almost invariably—alone.

The dial over the bulkhead registered minus 27. About fifteen more minutes. The Admiral, still looking down into the lower level of the engine room, said quietly, a tone halfway between an order and a supplication:

"You will look after her for me, won't you John."

It wasn't immediately apparent whether the Admiral had been referring to the ship or to Delta. It did not matter. John did not have to answer. As of the moment he boarded this ship, he became wedded to her. He and the ship had been bonded with ties stronger than any marriage ceremony could ever assure.

The two men didn't bother with the lower decks. In another short while, still standing on the gallery overlooking the engine room, the enormous, six-storey chamber, Admiral Grant turned, and for the last time faced Commander John Galt. The Admiral put his arms around his transcendent, unique friend. For a brief moment, the two men held each other. Nothing had been said. Then the Admiral shook John's hand, the way one would, when seeing one's friend off to a weekend in the country.

"Thanks for what you said about Beta." The old man smiled a strangely fatherly smile. "When he was born, we decided to raise him under his mother's name. We thought it would be easier for him."

"You... you're...?" John was aghast.

"You never guessed, did you? He was born on the Moon. Spend half his time there. He can take three earth gee's and smile. Yet on the Moon he moves like a ballet dancer." There was an unabashed pride in the voice of Beta's father.

"He never told me."

John still hasn't fully recovered.

"When you get back, you might look in on him. He will need..."

"You can bet your life on it, Harry!"

"I do," The Admiral said and turned lightly on his heel.

The next moment the inner lock door closed silently behind him. John walked to a wall outlet and punched: 'dock 4 vi-external'. Two minutes later, a slim silhouette of the Admiral's shuttle separated itself from the Starship. For a short while it picked up glancing rays of the setting sun. Then it was swallowed in the voracious darkness of heaven.

John glanced at the chrono. The dial registered -10. He made his way to the bridge. At -05 Delta joined him. She sat down and awaited his orders. He gave her the coordinates. She repeated them and punched the numbers into the computer.

"Take her away, Number One," John said.

And she did.

***

Chapter six

Delta One

So long Harry, so long Beta. So long...

John glanced at Delta One. In spite of being more than used to spending long years in abject solitude, John derived distinct pleasure from having Delta at his side. Not because she was an extremely attractive woman—although that didn't hurt. John had learned not to develop any permanent ties with anyone, particularly not with women. When he got back from any of his treks, they, the women, were either dead and buried or, what had proven a lot worse, about to be.

Likewise, a test flight is not a test flight unless one takes the spaceship to the limit of its capability. One can even venture beyond that limit to find out about the margin of safety. One can also stop short of it, but only if experiencing trouble which cannot be handled in space. In Outer Space, that is.

There were many tests to be performed. The accuracy of projection, suppleness of navigability—particularly as pertaining to changes in direction, braking power, and, more than any of these, the ultimate practical velocity. The word practical was very important. When a spaceship exceeds 85% of the speed of light, its mass swells to almost double the original. Double its mass 'at rest'. At velocities approaching that of light, the mass increases at a rapid rate. While accelerating up to 85% of the velocity of light the ship's mass reaches 1.8983 of its original mass, during the remaining 15%, the hurling mass balloons to... infinity. If only it were possible. It doesn't sound like a fair deal, John mused. Then his thoughts wondered to XM742. A Singularity. A Black

Hole. Falling into one did not present a major problem. It's the coming out of it in one piece, preferably larger than a neutrino—did. John smiled at a latent memory of Adam Blake, some 160 years ago, earth-time. Infinite energy attracting infinite mass. A stunning concept. Moving towards infinite time...

So what's all this hurry with getting there?

Within the solar system the BLAKE was advancing at a snail's pace. Their present acceleration increased their velocity at a mere one gee per second. At one gee constant, John had plenty of time, to put on his thinking cap: he was used to quick, rounded-off calculations:

"At this acceleration, we can reach 85% of the speed of light in... just over 300 days. It doesn't sound like a long time, but then we would have to slow down, and start again in the direction we came from. Then slow down again, well outside the limit... from sol."

John scratched his head.

"Unless, on the way out, we could swing around some sort of celestial body, which, without tearing the hull with centrifugal forces into space debris, could whip us around to face the other way. Only the ship's computer could figure that one out. We could consider Jupiter. Or Saturn..."

John glanced at the chrono. They were now 45 minutes out off orbit. Their present velocity had climbed to 26 kilometers per second. "Chicken feed as space goes, but I would hate to park my helio at this speed."

"Now, if we were to trust the antigravs and put on four gee's, that is to accelerate at one gee plus the three neutralized by the antigravs, we might pick up a day or two. At 4 gee's constant acceleration, 85% of the velocity of light would be ours in..." John' fingers played with his armrest keyboard, "oh my goodness, 1815.5688 hours or in... just over 75 days! Of course, I might have divided 300 by four. On the other hand, what's the hurry?"

He smiled to himself.

"Assuming that the whiz engines can give us enough kick to move this crate along when it's mass will have doubled. This crate? You are talking about the woman I love!" he admonished himself.

"Commander Galt?" Delta's soft voice invaded John's mental meandering.

There is no astronaut alive who doesn't talk to himself at great length. A life's habit is hard to break. A single untoward blip on the consol screen would send John's adrenaline soaring. Yet Delta had to repeat his name twice before he became aware of her presence. That was the price John paid for spending most of his life in space. Alone. He smiled his apology.

"Yes Delta?"

"It has been six hours since you ate anything, Sir. Can I dial anything for you?"

My God! Can the woman also cook? She's not going to mother me, is she? John scrutinized Delta with critical eye.

"Delta, you are spoiling me. Can we leave the bridge alone?"

"I am sure we could, Sir, but it is inadvisable within the Inner System. The colonies have more than tripled their traffic in the last five years."

Delta had the perfunctory politeness of an officer knowing his, sorry, her duty.

"The hytapes didn't say anything about traffic jams," John muttered.

As a matter of fact, he wouldn't have left the bridge for all the goblets of Ganymede Ginwine. Not that he actually had ever tasted any, but it was reputed to be our Solar System's delicacy. Why is it that for the first few hours in space it is almost impossible to leave the bridge? It is not as if he was doing anything constructive here. Yet... I suppose it might be a little like letting your wife drive your brand new helio. You know she can do it, you know she might well do it even better than you, yet... purely emotional, John mused.

"You go ahead and eat. I will follow you when you get back."

"I am not due for leave for another four hours, Sir." Delta replied.

"Are you another one of those rare Lunar creatures who never sleeps or eats?" John remembered the Moonites.

"I can go on for quite a while without any recharging," she assured him in a confident voice.

Her eyes continued darting among all the dials. She scanned not only her individual console, but also the large, wall chart projector, which monitored their exact location within the Inner Solar System. Whenever another vessel, or any space object, came within 0.5 astronomical units of their location, a coloured beacon began tracing its trajectory on the screen. The computer would interpolate their velocity with that of the other object and, if necessary, adjust their own course to assure a healthy safety margin.

"I bet you can. So can all your friends on Moon Base," John said. "Very well. I shall dial for a protein-rich concoction I had for breakfast. It seems to suit my metabolism."

John was ready to rise from his console armchair when Delta's raised hand held him back.

"You don't have to go yourself, Sir. There are a number of latest editions on board, which were not yet fully covered on the hytapes. Once we clear the System, I shall be happy to show them to you."

As Delta talked, her fingers played with the keyboard of her console. Within ten seconds a stiff looking 'ensign' walked in carrying a drink John had ordered. To say John had been surprised would be an understatement.

"Why in Holy Space had I not been told about it?"

"Well, in a way, you were, Sir. You knew, from the hytapes, that the exterior pile could be repaired in outer space with the help of robots. You can well imagine, that a robot capable of working on the intricacies of an antimatter pile, can also serve you a drink. In his spare time, so to speak."

There was no cynicism, preaching, or the slightest suggestion of a patronizing attitude in Delta's voice. She simply stated the facts, as she knew them. Pure and simple.

"How do I address him, it... whatever?"

John appreciated her help. It had never been his ambition to be the smartest. Only to be the best that he could be.

"There are thirty-four robots. They respond to vocal orders, when preceded by R1 to R34. As per the number on their breast-plate and the back of the trunk.

"Why robots?" John asked.

"The residual radiation within the engine area could delay repairs done by EV astronaut by, up to, six months. And that only if he, or she, wore an extra protective suit, which would severely inhibit his or her movements. Robots are an obvious solution," she recited, as though she was reading from a ships manual.

"That's it?" John asked, half-mockingly.

"They can also lift about three tons of dead matter with one hand. Not that that is much needed in weightless conditions, but there is still the inertia. Also, we had no idea under what conditions trouble might arise," Delta added, as though it was the most natural thing in the world.

"Why thirty-four?" John asked.

"There was no room, for more. The units are all interchangeable. If any were to be, inadvertently, put out of commission, the remaining Rs could repair them from spare, or their own parts."

"Sounds like cannibalism."

"Or using the spare parts from another helio," she corrected.

Why was it, John wondered, that we never assign human characteristics to anything which does not have a head, a torso, a pair of arms and legs. Some of the automotive devices, this ship itself was the ultimate example of them, exceeded the capacity of a human brain by countless billions, perhaps trillions, of neurons. Yet we don't think of them as human, as alive. But make something, no mater how dumb, unto an image and likeness of man, on the outside, and it becomes harder to consider it disposable. Emotions? Or is it just pride, that anything resembling us must, per force, be superior to whatever is different.

John drank his energizing mixture.

The ship's chrono registered one hour twenty-six minutes. They would continue to accelerate at one gee for a long while yet. System regulations, excepting emergencies. At least out to ten astronomical units from the sun. After that, theoretically, light was the limit. Their velocity was now a slightly more respectable 50 km/sec. Not much considering it amounted to 0.017% of the velocity of light. BLAKE had a long way to go. At their present velocity it would take them just about a year to clear the ten astronomical units.

John sighed: 'thank God for constant acceleration.'

John felt little consolation that even at only one gee, within another six and a half days they would leave Saturn behind them. Only then they would be free to try out the antigravs. This time he smiled at the thought. That should by something! John tried to visualize a 4 gee constant acceleration. First time in the history of human race.

In the meantime, they could not cheat. John would be willing to bet his bottom credit that the Galactic Navy had been, still was, following their every move. For the moment, space travel was not all it had been trumped up to be. John grinned, again, at his thoughts. He loved it.

Suddenly, for no apparent reason, John felt tired. It could not have been lack of sleep. Must have had something to do with his emotions. If regular exercise kept his body in a good condition, then his emotional body was lagging well behind.

In space, John had ample opportunity to exercise his brain, but there was very little to get exited about. In spite of enormous velocities, whatever happened, it did so, in a manner of speaking, in very slow motion. With the possible exception of a planet-fall, John had learned to take all events calmly. But planet-fall could only happen once every few decades, and he had months, if not years, to prepare for it.

The rest of the time, there were no emotional upheavals. The fabled warps, the instant jumps through space at velocities, which defied the laws of relativity, were the domain of science fiction, not of real life in the physical universe.

Until a few weeks ago, John had no emotional attachments. He was free. Perhaps too free? Now he missed Harry. He missed Beta. He missed not having them around. John wanted to pick up a viphone and see one of their faces smiling, friendly, perhaps caring. Yes, perhaps just caring. A magnificent machine, such as this incredible starship, might well have the mental capacity of a million men put together. But could it care? Is caring what makes us human?

John glanced at Delta.

In a way, she was like this beautiful ship. Superbly proportioned, beautiful finishing materials, eminently efficient. Apparently very knowledgeable. Yet, John did not, could not as yet, develop any feelings for her. Or about her. Maybe it was her very beauty, her apparent error-free demeanor that had created a barrier.

She cared. She thought of reminding him about his missed meal. Or had that been no more than a manifestation of her efficiency. A fulfillment of her duties as the Number One officer on a Starship. John might have acted similarly, in similar circumstances, whether he cared for the captain or not. Perhaps, for human beings, caring was so natural that it became automatic. Like having an emotional body, so to speak. If you have it, you are prone to use it. Or else, as the saying goes... lose it?

"We still have a couple of hours to go until we hit ten parsecs. Since you insist on being glued to your console, I'll take your advice and grab a bite. I'm a bit tired of the same old concoction. You will stay at the helm. Call me if anything unusual or interesting happens," John admonished Delta quite unnecessarily. He suspected that she knew very well how to act on her own cognizance.

"Yes, Sir," she replied, with her usual radiant smile.

How come she had always been so radiant? Then John remembered that that was very much the way Beta behaved. The Colonials were evidently a slightly different species.

John took the elevator to the canteen and dialed for a balanced meal. He ate slowly, making it last. You do not rush things in space. You learn to extract every single bit of interest out of any activity you perform. There were not that many things you could do out here. Even on the BLAKE, which offered a bigger choice of activities than all the ships ever built put together. John decided to examine some of the amenities while still practically coasting at the controlled, Inner System, velocity.

His next stop was the recreation room.

There were three: the music/reading room, the physical exercise/massage and physio-therapeutic room, and the holo deck. The music room was stocked with a full range of musical expression. From ancient classics to the most modern Music-of-the-Spheres compositions. John made a mental note of some of them for future examination.

Although John wasn't quite ready for any physical exercise, he sat down on a lounge chair fitted with about twenty buttons on each armrest. Rather than read the instructions, he pressed some of them at random. He woke up fifteen minutes later. The program, which he had unwittingly dialed, was based on alignment of the chair's vibrations with those of his heartbeat. In addition, the electromagnetic impulses stimulating various parts of his body were synchronized with his brain-wave pattern. The result was an instant state of an incredible sense of balance, and the attendant relaxation. His immediate subliminal response was to fall asleep. Presumably, in order to prolong this delightful massage. When John did wake up, he felt sorely tempted to dial for a repeat. He struggled to free himself from the hypnotic attraction. When he regained his self-control, he felt as though he just had a full night's sleep. He wondered if the Moonites employed such gimmicks to maintain their inexhaustible energies.

Next, John took a peek at the officers' quarters. He placed his hand on a number of scanners. Nothing happened. Closing his eyes, he reached back into his memory programmed by the hytapes. There was nothing there. Obviously hytapes dealt with all the command functions. They had nothing to do with finding one's sleeping quarters. Particularly on a ship, where, in theory, there would be forty-six personnel, each capable of directing him, the Captain, to his private accommodations.

John decided to use his common sense. He located the nearest elevator and dialed for holographic sectoplan. A pulsating red light identified his exact present location. John then spoke into the mike requesting the Captain's quarters. Instantly, an area on the plan, to the immediate right of his present location, became flooded with pale blue colour. John walked the ten paces. At the door he put his hand at the panel. The door opened silently.

John entered a chamber of about eight by five meters on plan. The ceiling was a good two and a half meters high, awash with a seemingly natural, slightly diffused daylight. As John took four steps into the room, the far wall seemed to dissolve.

John caught his breath, thinking that it had been his last.

However, no swishing sound of de-pressurization followed the apparent disappearance of the far wall. The next instant, John realized that the view of the black sharply speckled sky had not been provided by an outside porthole. It must have been created by a hidden vi-projector. Once the view lost its initial terrifying impact, the effect became truly mesmerizing.

Fighting disbelief, John realized that the suite had been designed for a single occupant. The furniture, while inviting up to eight people to relax in comfort, had been evidently conceived for a man of high rank and quite patrician tastes. John, still stunned by the room's grandeur, sat down on a deep, reclining armchair. Instantly the chair adjusted itself to his body contours.

John looked around.

Gradually he became accustomed to the sheer size of his private quarters. His memory retreated to his first interstellar trek. For almost forty years he had been, more or less, confined to the Commander's navigational console. In it he had lived, ate, hibernated. In it he had been massaged by electrical synapses every four hours, to assure muscular resilience. There had been no question of having more than one space, no matter how small, into which he could have retired for a change of scenery. Those had been the pioneering days. If it had not been for induced hibernation he would have gone mad as a hatter on a Psy Sunday picnic.

Now, John could do with a unihelio or one of those ancient engine-cycles to move around. Already he had spent practically a whole day on this ship and he still had not seen a half of it. Still, there was time. Just about a whole week, before they would even consider hibernation. If then. John got up, shrugged, and left his palatial quarters. He walked to the elevator. "Bridge" he commanded. The intelligent machine delivered him to his destination.

"How do you like your quarters, Sir?" Delta asked.

"How did you know I was there?" John Galt was not used to being spied on.

Delta pointed to a mini screen below her consol. "With only two of us on board, I think it best to keep in touch, don't you, commander?" She smiled sweetly.

At this moment John did not feel at all like a Commander, or a Captain. In fact, for the second time since breaking orbit, John felt redundant. He said so.

"Since you are evidently competent to run this ship alone, I wonder why did they put me in command?"

This question was as much addressed to himself as to Delta. Not surprisingly though, she felt obliged to answer.

"I am sure the reasons will become manifest to you, Sir, in due course," she said.

"What the devil do you mean by that?"

The emotional strain John had been under, these last few days, was beginning to surface. Delta did not seem to notice.

"You are man of unparalleled experience in handling the unexpected. I can cope with everything that is predictable. I have no idea how I would react to..."

"I am sorry," John interrupted. "I didn't mean to imply... I didn't mean to offend you in any way."

"Offend, Sir?" Delta looked and sounded genuinely surprised.

My God! These people don't sleep, hardly ever eat, and don't get offended. This trek will give me an inferiority complex to last a dozen light years.

Delta was right, of course. On every single trek, John has had to face exigencies that could not have been foreseen. Invariably he had improvised and had survived, to tell the story. Space was as relentless, perhaps more so, than the turbulent oceans of John's great, great forefathers. It had not been just knowledge that had saved their lives. It had been the inherent instinct for survival. In stellar terms, not one, not a single one, among the eleven billion members of John's intrepid species had lived longer than he. This fact alone had to amount to something. He hoped!

"Thank you Delta!"

Once again she made him feel good. There seemed to be a lot more to Delta than met the eye. Maybe she had been trained at the Psy Center. Who knows?

***

Chapter seven

Pursuit

Every sixty seconds a stream of coded photons reported the coordinates of FRS BLAKE to the Moon Base. Confirmation of the reports was conspicuous by its absence. It had been judged vital to maintain maximum security for the test flight. The reasons for such measures, had been hinted at, but never clearly postulated. John was happy to maintain communication silence. The automatic dispatches from BLAKE were all scrambled. Deciphering codes were necessary to understand them. Hopefully.

John had learned, from hytapes, that the Galactic Navy had conducted vast majority of colonial operations. There had been, however, as in every free society, a vanguard of private enterprise. Such organizations maintained a vigilant eye on any opportunities of raising additional credits. Their activities included attempts at usurping mineral rights, or acquiring technical data on new manufacturing processes. In a way, such people were the pioneers in search of new horizons. Put differently, they conducted a well-organized network of industrial and mining espionage. Both terms applied to them, depending on one's point of view.

These entrepreneurs, more bluntly space pirates, had been the culprits responsible for the stringent security arrangements. Any advantage, any edge, which the freelancers might gain over their competitors, would be grasped immediately, tenaciously, with absolutely no regard for possible consequences. Competition, in a world where eighty percent of people lived permanently on subsidized credits, was stiff. Very stiff. Ironically, or perhaps logically, the greater the overpopulation the cheaper became human life. The Council could only allot a miniscule portion of the Federated Republics' budget to the protection of human rights, namely, to police activities. Periodic motions to increase spending on internal security had been voted down with persistent regularity.

Live and let die.

The BLAKE continued to steadily accelerate its velocity at one gee constant. After twenty-four hours, the dial registered a 850 kilometers per second. John had just returned from his 'midday' meal, and asked Delta for an update. She was about to report when Moon Base communicator showed first signs of life. It's blinking was accompanied by a repetitive series of short buzzes.

"The Moon Base, Sir. Do you wish to take it yourself?"

"Put them on vi-screen."

"It is audio only, Sir."

John put on his phones indicating to Delta to do likewise. As they pressed the receiving buttons, their ears were filled with a babbling staccato noise. They both punched the decipherer simultaneously. The noise now changed to an artificial, mechanical voice.

XY4 immediate 4 gee or max.

The message was repeated three more times and the earphones went dead. John knew that XY4 was the incoming code for BLAKE.

"You heard the man!" John ordered. "Make it so."

Delta's long, slim fingers performed a little dance on the keyboard, and... nothing, well, *almost* nothing happened. It felt like nothing. Only the dial registering the velocity began to spell out numbers faster. Much faster. Within ninety seconds it was spitting figures four times as fast as before. John felt absolutely no acceleration. The extra gee's were completely absorbed by the antigravs. He grinned his satisfaction.

"This is more like it," he mused wistfully, remembering his previous treks. Then he frowned. "I wonder what made them give us the OK to add gee's earlier. The Base never does anything without..."

John didn't finish. Two little pulsating lights, rather like glowworms, appeared in the top left corner of the main wall screen. Both dots seemed to advance on a convergence point with their own future trajectory. At least, it would have been so, if BLAKE hadn't accelerated. According to the screen readout, the points of light were accelerating, at about ten gee's.

"What the..." John leaned forward in his armchair.

"Freelancers." Delta advised. Her voice was perfectly poised and relaxed.

"What the devil do they want?" John wondered aloud. He vaguely remembered some things Brad Drake said to him, but he did not immediately put two and two together.

"If they ever did catch us, I suspect they would first want to board our ship and then, later, negotiate with Moon Base for immunity from prosecution, in exchange for our lives. Or something like that. They would probably attempt to park the BLAKE somewhere hard to find and, some time later, trade the coordinates of its location for credits or other goods," Delta said lightly, in a dismissive tone of voice. Then she smiled as if she were actually enjoying herself.

John had spent his life in space. His fate had been threatened by many formidable, dangerous situations. But never, never had he been threatened by another human being. By man. It was evident, that he had not spent enough time on Earth to learn about some present conditions. There were items obviously missing from standard hytape releases.

"You're serious, aren't you Delta." John had slight problems believing her.

"I suggest we prepare for evasive maneuvers, Commander," Delta said very quietly. She appeared to have no nerves at all.

"You seem to be enjoying this," John remarked. A hint of a smile raised the corners of his mouth. "Well? Aren't you?"

"Well, Sir, according to the screen, they have been travelling at ten gee's for about three hours. Assuming constant acceleration, that would give them an approximate velocity of a 1000 kilometers per second. With their technology, I suspect it will take them about half an hour earth-time, 28.843 minutes precisely, to affect any significant change in the direction of their trajectory. With our capability of sixteen acceleration funnels..."

"...you find it quite amusing!" John was drawn into the spirit of the game. He resented, just a little, her lighthearted attitude. He regarded their predicament a lot more seriously.

"Does this sort of thing happen often?"

"In the outer colonies only, Sir. The Navy estimates that there are probably up to two hundred settlements on the outer moons which are in private hands. About one third of them may, on occasion, take a chance at a little bit of piracy. The Navy escorts all the main colonial shipments with battle cruisers."

"But how in Holy Space can those guys accelerate at a constant ten gee's?" John wanted to know.

"There are a number of possible explanations. One—their vessels may be operated by robots pre-programmed to perform a sequential operation. Two—the crew, probably a maximum of three men or women, may have immersion tanks, in which they are totally submerged and communicate with the ship's sensors through psytronics. That, in combination with antigravs, might keep them alive for up to six hours under such acceleration. Three—they may have a technology we know nothing about."

While John listened to Delta, his eyes were peeled to the main screen. Delta was right. The two glowworms continued to move towards a projected convergence point, which no longer applied, due to BLAKE's sudden acceleration. John smiled at the pirates' apparent inadequacy. However, even as

John enjoyed these disparaging thoughts, the two bleeps showed first signs of adjusting their trajectory to the BLAKE's new velocity. Although the change in their trajectory was hardly noticeable, John stopped smiling.

"They must have been watching us for quite a while and assumed that we are limited to a one gee constant capability. Most heavy transporters are, I understand. Our antigravs must have come as a surprise to them." John reasoned. He glanced at his consol. On the right top segment, the communication screen displayed a programming keyboard for navigational changes.

"Did you ever practice using all the sixteen funnels?" John asked.

"Well, yes and no. I did fire all the engine funnels, but I did not do so in space under four gee's constant."

This apparent lack of experience did not seem to bother Delta in any way whatever. Her face, her voice, her demeanor remained completely at ease. "Would you like to try them out now, Sir?"

"No, Number One. We shall let them develop a little more velocity before we give them a slip." I would love to see the expression on their faces when we do that, John mused; a latent, atavistic memory of a prey becoming a hunter stirring in his veins.

"If worse comes to worst, Sir, we could use our artillery."

This was neither a statement nor a question. It was a supposition that sounded strange to John's ears. He did not recall ever having killed a fly. There are no flies in space.

John and Delta's eyes followed the progress. which the two blips traced on the screen. The trajectories, exactly as Delta had predicted, were very slowly adjusting to a presumed new point of convergence. The pursuers must have been quite ignorant about BLAKE's capability. Hardly surprising. In shear, physical size, the BLAKE must have registered, on their scanners, as a very fat, juicy carrier, for reasons of economy, without a Navy escort. A loot not to be ignored when offered practically on a silver platter.

Within a half-hour the pursuers were directly behind the BLAKE, and closing. By now, BLAKE's velocity had climbed to over 900 kilometers per second. The blips continued to accelerate at ten gee's. Delta was calculating their probable point of convergence.

"Are these modern day pirates armed?" John asked almost as an afterthought.

"Oh yes, Sir. Always." Delta smiled her usual smile.

"Aren't they likely to use their lasers on us?"

Commander Galt didn't have much... actually, he didn't have any, experience with lasers, photon torpedoes, or with being shot at.

"That's very unlikely, Sir. They would be destroying the very goods they spent time and money to acquire," she argued persuasively. "They might fire a round of torpedoes to persuade us not to run quite so fast. But even that does not seem very likely. If they disabled our engines, they would have to haul us to a desirable hiding spot. The nearest Navy detachment is on Titian, and I am sure they are hoping to board us well before we get there and then make a run for it by releasing a lot of space debris behind them."

"You speak as if you went through this sort of thing before."

John listened, in disbelief, to Delta's reasoned approach to their problem.

"Oh yes, Sir! I have been escorting commercial carriers for eleven years as part of my training." That carefree smile refused to leave her mouth. "We all have to go through all aspects of Solar System navigation. Inner and Outer. What all Naval officers are hungry to experience, Sir, are the interstellar treks."

It was John's turn to grin.

"You can be very sure that those coveted treks are extremely dull as compared to the experiences which you have, apparently, already acquired."

John's opinion of his Number One officer was growing in hops and leaps. He wondered how many of such expert lieutenants the Navy could boast. Once again he felt a certain sense of redundancy.

beep-beep-beep-beep...

John punched the incoming communication button, bridge speaker and the Galactic Navy decipherer, all in quick succession. The message was terse as before:

Scramble repeat scramble repeat scramble

"I think they want us to scramble!" John repeated, his voice almost flippant. His disorientation lasted no more than one or two seconds. All at once, John's adrenaline caught up with his cardiovascular system. He felt very alive.

"I think we are about to get into trouble, Sir," Delta advised in a sweet voice.

The same instant one of the glowworms following BLAKE's symbol on the main projector blinked repeatedly and went out. Immediately after that, three more *new* tiny lights appeared on the screen, apparently coming at them from the direction of one of the Jupiter moons. They were approaching fast. Possibly, they made use of the sling effect of Jupiter to gain such a velocity in a relatively short time. The disappearance of one of the glowworms did not look very friendly!

"Arm torpedoes!" John ordered, while scanning the trajectories of the three converging vessels. Strangely enough, only now was he becoming calmer.

"Photon torpedoes armed, Sir" Delta reported.

"Compute convergence point of the three bandits with BLAKE."

A short performance on the computer keyboard and Delta reported the coordinates. John scanned the System chart for the least amount of traffic. The next instant a vibrating glowworm detached itself from the remaining vessel still in their pursuit. It described a fast arc towards the three new spaceships. A few moments later some kind of explosion took place, with no apparent effect on the three new bandits. John had no idea what method the new arrivals have employed to destroy one of BLAKE's initial pursuers. Neither laser nor photon torpedoes registered on the screen. He was sure that the ship's array of instruments had ample capability of providing the answer, but it could wait. For the moment, the remaining original pursuer was still accelerating at ten gee's. It was evident that his intention was no longer to board the BLAKE but to run for his life. His trajectory was now overshooting their projected convergence by a good margin.

According to hytapes, the photon torpedoes had an effective spread of five kilometers. The BLAKE could arm, simultaneously, eight projectiles. Each could be recharged and fired within five seconds. The procedure could be repeated at equal intervals.

The purpose of a photon torpedo was not to disable the pursuing vessel permanently—laser guns did that—but to scramble their electronic systems by the creation of a temporary but quite powerful electromagnetic field. The disturbance in space dissipated in ten to twenty minutes. However, a vessel traversing such a field for not less than 0.015 of a second became encumbered with considerable difficulties. Even the briefest exposure to the powerful electromagnetic field scrambled most electronic devices, including the main navigational computer. Reputedly, it could take up to three weeks to unscramble the effects of a single torpedo.

John's mind, semi-dormant for the last two and a half months, finally found circumstances that justified his presence. He felt dynamic, confident, sharp. John's strategy was relatively simple. He instructed Delta, to commence firing, on his command, all eight photon torpedoes. She was to continue saturation firing forward, until a sector of space covering the convergence area with the three new pursuers, would be charged with electromagnetic disturbance. This point, of course, was also directly in their own projected flight path.

John intended to draw the enemy, for surely such they must be, into this quadrant of space. Then, immediately before reaching it, BLAKE would veer in any one direction, thus himself avoiding the affected space. John preferred this idea to a laser shootout with the pursuers. Even if the BLAKE had superior firepower, being shot at from three different directions, did not appeal to John at all. He preferred using his brain to his muscle.

Delta listened to his instructions without any comment. Even as John talked, her fingers were playing the keyboard. John's orders were carried out immediately, without question. If ever a Captain needed such a response from his Number One, this was the time.

"Pursuers' velocities 647 kilometers per second and mounting. At eight gee's, in thirty-two minutes they will achieve 796.81 kilometers per second. Assuming standard fusion engines, at that velocity they will be unable to veer away, in time to avoid the quadrant of 960 square kilometers," Delta reported.

"That's... two minutes of firing, at eight torpedoes every five seconds. Looks like a good spread."

John was satisfied.

There would have been no way John could have avoided the quadrant with any ship he had ever flown in the past. He counted on the BLAKE to stand up to her specifications.

"Now you, Number One, have taken our engines through their paces. Tell me, what margin of safety do we need to avoid our own electromagnetic pollution?"

Delta's deft fingers again danced on her keyboard. "Five point oh seven nine minutes, Sir. From the first firing." Delta replied. "That would be at six gee's lateral, Sir. I could cut it closer if you wish..."

"I don't think we have to, do you Number One?"

John was quite happy not to subject the ship to still greater stresses. They were already accelerating at four gee's, and even though, as far as their bodies were concerned, three gee's were dissipated, or absorbed into the mass of the hull,

the actual stress on the vessel would then rise to ten gee's. He
did not doubt that the structure could take it, but he had not
been commissioned to test flight to destruction. John's policy
had always been to get the maximum result with a minimum
of effort. Conservation of energy had become an unwritten
law for all who ever ventured into Outer Space. This law
applied to all the vessels he had ever commanded. John knew
very well, that the hull had been designed for stresses up to
forty gee's. Unfortunately, he was not.

"Number One. Set a program for three additional gee's
after the evasive action, for..." his fingers did a keyboard
dance of their own, "...for one hundred sixteen minutes."

Delta repeated the instructions.

The next thirty minutes were the longest John
experienced in a very long time. At any moment the pursuers,
the pirates, the bandits, could have fired on them with their
lasers and or other weaponry. John was not afraid of dying,
but he despised the idea of dying for an unworthy cause. A
man who lived for one hundred and ninety years, who
sacrificed all his attachments, comforts, rewards of every day
living, for the privilege of serving humanity, such a man had
an aversion towards dying unnecessarily. Or, for that matter,
for dying to make some pirates richer. That dubious privilege
John left to other pirates.

"Let the greedy feed upon the greedy," he muttered
under his breath.

Now the chronometer seemed to move at a snail's pace.
The dial took on a different significance. If Delta's
calculations had been out even by a few seconds, they would
be in danger of losing any advantage over the pirates. If the
BLAKE veered too early, the pursuers would increase their
opportunity to avoid the electromagnetic quadrangle.

"Firing minus ten minutes." Delta reported, her voice as
calm as ever.

Once again, John found her self-control annoying. He
expected her to get a little nervous or, at the very least,
exited. She seemed neither. Perfect officer, doing her job

perfectly. An incongruous thought crossed John's mind: 'It's not feminine to have such iron control over her emotions.'

He glanced at Delta. The trouble was, she looked more feminine than just about any woman he'd ever seen.

"Firing minus nine minutes." Now she sounded mechanical.

Was it he who was nervous? Was there anything to get nervous about? Or am I just growing too old for this game? John shrugged. Maybe in another nine minutes I will not have to worry about my age any more!

"Firing minus eight."

He had to say something; if only to hear his own voice.

"Evasive action in firing plus two-point-five minutes," he ordered.

"Evasive action in firing plus two-point-five minutes," Delta repeated.

Would she have acted on her own cognizance? Would she have taken an extra margin of half a minute? Or would she had gone by the book, and veered at firing plus 3.079 minutes? Just how perfect and cool was she?

"Firing minus seven."

At firing minus five the speaker would take over and count out the seconds. The firing had been preset, automatic. So would be the evasive action. They could both leave the bridge and cuddle up in their respective bunks, in their private quarters. Tomorrow they would find out if the evasive action had been successful. They could do it, but they didn't. One seldom crawls into ones bed to die. They didn't expect to die. But one of the original pursuers did disappear from the screen. It stopped existing. It was now part of the ever growing, unwanted, sometime dangerous space debris. They had no intention of polluting the Inner Space. Time enough to die later. In the Void. At three quarters of the velocity of light, even a small fragment, could punch a hole you could climb through. All the way to nowhere.

Photon torpedoes firing in minus 300 seconds, 299, 298, 297...

The audio took over from Delta. Now that John heard the machine, he realized Delta's voice had not been mechanical after all. There seemed to have been a subtle tone of amusement in her voice. As if she was really enjoying it all. Who knows? Maybe she was.

All this time John had not taken his eyes from the main screen. The three glowworms drew progressively nearer to the BLAKE. Since the screen now represented the whole Solar System, the pirates seemed very close indeed. About an inch in real scale.

187, 186, 185...

John glanced at Delta. She too kept her eyes on the main screen. She seemed neither tense nor exited. Or had he noticed all that before? John ran a final, quite unnecessary, check on his console layout. Delta's figures were all perfect. No more than he'd expected. This was the third time he had checked her calculations. He wondered if she did—even once.

60, 59, 58...

Won't be long now. John's first ever armed conflict with other human beings. Perhaps not ever, but in a very, very long time. Not many people in Outer Space. None that he had met!

Firing in minus 5, 4, 3, 2, starting firing sequence

The audio restarted immediately.

Evasive action in minus 115 seconds and counting

The moment the pursuers recognized the trap they have fallen into they might well take a few potshots at them. With their laser guns. John had gambled that by the time they did that, the evasive action would have taken BLAKE out of harm's way.

An ear piercing buzzing had overridden the audio.

Secure all quarters for six gee maneuver

The system had been designed for a full crew. The personnel, throughout the ship, would have been directed to their secure positions.

60, 59, 58...

At sixty seconds, clamps emerged from behind John and
Delta's shoulders and secured them both to their respective
armchairs. Helmets descended on their heads. At minus 10
seconds, the clamps tightened. For the next twenty seconds
they would be unable to move, regardless of circumstances.
John took a deep breath.

And then six gee's hit him with an all-wrenching power.

***

Chapter eight

The Message

His throat dry, burning, John barked new coordinates. It would take him a while to recover from the tearing effects of six gee's. The prolonged effect of the three gravities that followed contributed further to his soreness. The BLAKE was still within the Inner System as defined by 3.5 astronomical units. Well inside Jupiter's orbit. Their velocity has climbed to 1900 kilometers per second.

"Your coordinates place us too close to Jovian atmosphere, Sir. May I program a sling effect?"

Delta did not seem to suffer from the after effects of the additional gravities. Her voice sounded quite normal.

"Make it so," John growled.

John wondered what made him give Delta the new coordinates to start with. He had given them quite instinctively. Did his subconscious mind realize they had an opportunity of putting the BLAKE through the sling effect? Or had it been an intuitive reaction to buy extra security. The greater the velocity, the more difficult target they would present to the pirates. Was he to expect any more enterprising pursuers?

As an afterthought, John plotted the coordinates he just gave Delta on his own console. The small screen indicated a trajectory pointing in a direction quite foreign to him. He reduced the scale of the chart in order to enlarge the space shown on the screen—rather like looking through the wrong end of binoculars. The screen now displayed a segment of space spanning ten light-years. Void. Nothing but void. John shrugged and increased the segment to thirty light years. This time John gasped. He sat up, blinking. The coordinates he had given Delta were pointing towards Lyra sector. Albeit, that's hardly an accurate description, considering the size of the Lyra quadrant. Still, the coordinates seemed unmistakable.

John wondered again what prompted him to give Delta those coordinates? After all, they could have carried out the tests in just about any quadrant of space. So why towards Lyra? Was he responding to some previous programming? Perhaps they brainwash people, these days, after all. Had he trusted his old friend, Harry, just a little too much? In fact, had he become a pawn in some political game the Admiral has been playing for reasons of his own?

"Six gee's max, progressive, for twenty-seven-point-eleven minutes in three hundred seconds from..." Delta's report had been interrupted, intentionally, by the audio.

minus 300 seconds to 6 gee maximum lateral progressive, 296, 295, 294...

The mechanical countdown again took over.

"...I programmed six maximum gee's, Sir, but only for eleven seconds. I thought that perhaps after only a few minutes break since the previous extra gravities, we might..."

"Quite right, Number One. Thank you."

John was grateful that Delta did not attempt to maximize the sling effect so quickly after the BLAKE emerged from the three gee's they suffered for nearly two hours. His lungs demanded some breathing space. With Jupiter's mass 318 times that of Earth, Delta could have made it much harder on his already aching bones. She meant, of course, six gee's plus the three absorbed by the antigravs. Nine gravities in all. Strangely enough, John had a distinct impression that Delta went easy on the extra gee's for his sake, not her own. The girl must have a constitution of a horse. A mare. A powerful mare.

They might as well use the sling effect Jupiter had to offer. As the largest planet in the System, with a diameter one tenth that of the sun, Jupiter seemed by far the best opportunity to test this technique. By countering the centrifugal force sweeping them away with the gravitational pull of the gaseous monster, they could increase their velocity, quite considerably, in hardly any time at all. The trick had been near impossible in his previous commands. The structure of the older ships simply would not stand such colossal stresses.

260, 259, 258...

The drone continued the countdown. This time, to his pleasant surprise, John did not feel nervous. Pained, tortured, abused—but not nervous. He had two reasons to feel confident. One—he now had a reason to trust Delta, and two—he had reason to trust the designers of this ship. So far, so good, he grinned his satisfaction.

In time, John's eye sockets cleared sufficiently to study the main screen. BLAKE was completely alone within their present quadrant. A space quadrant was represented by a modified astronomical unit; a square of one hundred and fifty million kilometers. The grid gave the basic scale to the chart. Next John glanced at the velocity. Almost 1950 km/sec.

That's over seven million kilometers per hour, and climbing.

The three pursers must have encountered some very unpredictable problems. Two hours had passed since BLAKE entered the six gee swerving maneuver. There had not been sufficient time to remove the pirates from their quadrant. Or vice versa. The photon torpedoes must have given the pursuers more trouble then they bargained for. An engine burnout? If they were merely floating chunks of metal, the screen scanners would not readily pick them up. The computer scanners would, of course. The computer scanners would pick up even the smallest space debris floating, or approaching, BLAKE's path. An adjustment in BLAKE's trajectory would be quite automatic. Their lasers would also vaporize the smaller items. For the moment they were safe. Assuming the sling test did not tear them apart at the seams.

200, 199, 198...

The armchairs began to swivel to provide maximum support to the occupants' bodies. If the six gee's had been negative rather than positive, John would now be ready for a very long vacation. Probably a permanent one!

160, 159, 158...

"Couldn't we switch off this drone?" John muttered. He did not expect an answer.

"Against Navy regulations, Commander."

He got one anyway. Apparently excellent hearing was another of Delta's countless attributes.

Delta may be perfect, but I can't say too much for her sense of humor... John kept this thought to himself. He wondered what had she been told about him. He wondered how little they, the Navy, anyone, can really know about him. It was a matter of record where he had been, what he had accomplished. About the things he did, but not about himself. What was there to know? What can be said about a man who had spent virtually his whole life in Outer Space? And most of this time in a sound, deep, comatose sleep?

His life certainly had moments of great interest. Back in 2140, John had helped to decipher Adam Blake's often cryptic, frequently amusing messages, incoming from his historical one-way trip into the XM742 anomaly. There had also been great, exhilarating moments every time he made a planet-fall. Especially towards his old, old, home planet. Each time the changes John encountered had been staggering. But these were items of interest to himself, to John Galt, not to the faceless 'others'. True, no one had as much time to develop a unique perspective on all things human. But if he, himself, had been of so much interest to his fellow men, how come they did not try to hold him back longer? Earthside? To keep him home longer between his interstellar treks? Or was it, that men were more interested in people who listened to them, rather than listening to what he may have had to say. By now, John has become a walking, breathing encyclopedia. He has read more books, listened to more tapes, absorbed more hytapes, than any man alive. Ever. Even on Moon Base, during his last debriefing, John had spent practically all his time with a helmet over his head. Hours and hours on end. Weeks. They'd never even told him why.

60, 59, 58...

The protective clamps again grabbed and held John in their powerful embrace. The helmet held his head in a fixed position. John was held rigid, trapped, imprisoned with his thoughts.

What did Delta One know about him? Probably things he didn't know himself. On the other hand, he knew next to nothing about her. Perfect or not, the moment we pull out of this sling, I'll start finding out, he promised himself.

minus 10, 9, 8, 7...

John braced himself for another battle with his pulmonary and cardiovascular system. On all his treks he avoided the extra gee's as best he could. He would rather spend another year in space, than spend one hour subjected to extra three gee's. One did not get used to it. It was like a toothache: the longer it lasted the worse it got. One hundred and sixty years ago he had all his teeth removed and a permanent implant installed.

John hated toothaches.

Jupiter was awesome. To avoid an army of moons high-tailing around the whirling ball of gas and liquid, the BLAKE had to maintain a respectful distance. At least seven million kilometers. Although Jupiter moons reached out to almost three times as far, Delta found a safe trajectory for BLAKE to sneak through a lot closer. They would pick up a lot of velocity from the sling effect.

John was grateful that this time the six gee's did not hit him like a thousand suction cups from the rear and another thousand implanted under his skin. The gravities increased gradually and, in the same, progressive manner, they would diminish in twenty-seven minutes from now. Thank heaven for little mercies!

As BLAKE neared the giant planet, John placed its swirling image on the main screen. He increased the magnification until the convoluting gaseous mass filled the whole wall. Every time John encountered this Olympian monster, he felt hypnotized anew. The gargantuan, churning gasses. The permanent, vicious hurricane. Velocities of wind created when a giant, eleven times the diameter of earth, rotates in under ten hours around its huge axis. Stunning. Humbling.

Delta's smile waned. It was replaced by an expression of intense concentration.

Then came the additional gravities. Once more John felt all blood draining from his face, his hands, his exhausted body. His heart was pounding somewhere in the middle of his back. Every breath became a painful gasp. Gradually the pressure began to relax, release, stabilize, until they pulled away from the harrowing grasp of the giant planet.

John felt totally spent. He had no desire to repeat this performance for the rest of his life. The purpose of his vast, interstellar experience had been, still was, to avoid the necessity of such stresses—not to willingly subject himself to them. Still, this was supposed to be a test flight.

Or... was it?

John glanced at the velocity dial. The operation proved worthwhile. Just before the sling effect experiment, the dial registered close to 2000 kilometers per hour. Under four gee's constant acceleration, they would have increased their velocity by about sixty kilometers per second. The sling effect had exceeded nearly twenty two times their normal acceleration.

The dial registered over 3300 km/sec.

With continued acceleration at four gee's they would cross the remaining 5,130,000,000 kilometers between their present coordinates and Pluto in under nine days. By then, their velocity would be in excess of 13,300 km/sec. So far, so good. One thing was certain. Other than a laser beam, nothing that had not been accelerating already for quite a long while was likely to catch them. That was the direct advantage of using the sling effect. That may have been the reason why he had given Delta the new coordinates—subconscious act of self-preservation. A reflex.

John began to breathe easier. The electrical pulsations emitted by the backrest of the command chair massaged his still aching body. Through his tunic John felt the searching, prodding mechanical fingers. They helped a lot but did little for the internal abrasions. Only time would take care of those. John had gone through such stresses before, over the years, but never twice in such quick succession.

He looked at Delta.

Throughout the ordeal she hasn't said a single word. John could hardly blame her. Even now, speech was not something he relished. His lungs were filled with fire, his throat unnaturally dry, his bronchial tube felt as if some sadistic son of a mongrel had shoved a red-hot poker through his gullet. It was not pleasant. John thought that, for a member of the, so-called, weaker sex, Delta held up very well. The next instant she must have sensed his eyes upon her. She smiled encouragement.

"Is there anything I can do for you, Commander?"

Her voice sounded normal. Uncanny. In fact, incredible. John moved his head minutely from side to side. He felt very tired and completely useless. He closed his eyes.

When he opened them again, the main screen displayed the Outer System. Jupiter was a good twenty million kilometers behind them. John had slept for over three hours. The BLAKE had cleared most orbits of Jupiter's outer, comparatively, tiny moons. John wanted to switch the screen to take a look at Saturn. He was still too stiff, too exhausted. Prolonged exposure to high gee's had a paralyzing effect on him.

"I must be getting old," he muttered.

John glanced at Delta. She seemed in total control. What was the matter with this woman? Was she made of steel? She looked relaxed, her fingers resting gently next to the keyboard, ready to take any emergency action as might be necessary. Surely she knew that the computer guidance system had been programmed to act automatically. She seemed part of the ship, in total harmony with the perfect, intelligent machine, which carried them, at millions of kilometers per hour, through the relatively crowded Solar System. John wasn't sure whether to admire the girl or envy her.

"Are you feeling better, Sir?" she asked, with her usual relaxed, encouraging smile.

John wished Delta would stop smiling. Under the circumstances such a facial grimace looked almost indecent.

"Yes, thank you. Yourself?"

John's vocal chords were in better shape than he'd expected. He sounded almost normal. Then he remembered that on previous occasions he flew alone. He had no opportunity to find out how soon his vocal chords recovered, when there was no one to try them on. He frowned. It did make a difference to have someone on board. Someone who cared.

"Our trajectory is giving us a wide margin from both Saturn and Uranus. We shall be within 1.621 AU's off Pluto," Delta reported.

Over one-point-six astronomical units. That's close to quarter of a billion kilometers. With computer enhancement, pretty close for a good look. Throughout his life John measured distances in light years, or even in parsecs. Yet, whenever he entered the home System, he amused himself in translating everything into kilometers. Whenever possible. It seemed to extend his stay on Earth, the feeling of being close to home, that much longer. And why not? He certainly had time enough, and it kept his mind busy. There is not that much one can do in space.

The same wordplay applied to the misnomer: 'tapes'. Many, many years ago tapes had been used for information storage. Now laser disks served this purpose. Yet John had never met anyone who used an expression such as 'scanning the disks', or even 'hydisks'. It just sounded all-wrong. It would be like calling from space 'up' to Earth, instead of 'down' to Earth. The actual, true direction may well have been sideways.

John's breathing was becoming easier. A soothing drink, seeped in individual drops from a tube dispenser over his left shoulder, did its job. He felt better all over. The drops carried a gentle anesthetic.

For the next few hours John had little if anything to do on the bridge. He asked Delta if she wished to be relieved.

"No, thank you, Sir," she said. "I'm good for another five or six hours."

John left the bridge and, for the first time since breaking orbit, decided to take a rest in his own cabin. After all, that's what it had been designed for. That, and a number of other more formal functions which, in the absence of a crew, were hardly applicable.

The door opened at the touch of his palm. This time, John experienced no shock from the sudden disappearance of the outside wall. He sat down and looked at the breathtaking view. Someone had tossed extravagant handfuls of diamonds into boundless expanse of black velvet.

As so many times in the past, John wondered whatever made him venture out. What compelled him to give up all creature comforts for the solitude of Outer Space. Perhaps it was a form of escape. A need of freedom? Perhaps curiosity? No answer, he had ever found, satisfied him. He did what he had to do. As always, he finished his inner probing with a shrug of indifference. Or perhaps, acceptance?

He leaned back on the deeply cushioned lounge chair, stretched his legs and loosened his tunic at the neck. The long hours of additional gravities claimed their toll. He dreamed as he always dreamed, in rich colour. His dreams were therapeutic. They did for his emotions and imagination what mathematics did for his mind, what the exercise room and the electronic massage did for his physical body. All his components, his bodies, needed rest. All needed exercise. All claimed their share of the totality of John Galt.

He woke up some hours later. Certain tiredness still lingered on. He expected it to do so. In time it would go away—and he had plenty of time. It would take seventy more days for BLAKE to reach eighty-five percent of the velocity of light. Time enough to rest. Time enough to recover from the taxing acceleration. Time enough to dream.

He dialed bridge and asked Delta for a report. She gave him their velocity, lapsed time, percentage of engines' efficiency—the usual technical data.

"Anything out of the ordinary?" John asked unnecessarily. She would have told him if there has been.

"No Sir. Everything is GO."

"Thank you, Delta." John cut off. He hoped she had taken enough time off to sleep.

He looked around his cabin. There was room enough to dine six to eight people in great comfort. Probably useful, with forty-seven people on board. The bathroom had all the fittings one could hope for in a five-star hotel. These were no Spartan quarters he'd spent three quarters of his life in. This was true comfort. By John's standards—luxury.

He dialed for entertainment. A panel emerged from a wall offering audio, video, viphones, hytapes and holographic projection. He selected holo and sat back. The panel lit up with an extensive menu arranged in alphabetical order. Plays, operas, comedy routines. Ancient and modern. One holo selection seemed out of place, out of alphabetical order. The first. It was marked, "FOR CAPTAIN'S EYES ONLY."

John sat up. No name, just 'Captain'. Impersonal. He pressed the key. Nothing happened. In a second or two, a tiny red light flashed on and off, and a recording asked for voice identification. John gave his name, rank and function. Then he sat back.

Admiral Hermes D. Grant's face shimmered, hovered and solidified in the middle of the room. The Admiral was sitting in his office, behind his large desk. He sat in silence, as though gathering his thoughts. Then the sound track came on.

"I am speaking to both of you: John Galt and Brad Drake, without whose dedication and courage, we would not have the Sirius artifact, and I would not be taping this communication. You might not like everything you hear, but these are difficult times, and we all have to do things, on occasion, which we do not particularly like doing.

Enough of this.

At the time of making this holo, I had not yet decided, which of you will be the first to leave orbit. Conditions change every minute. Literarily. There had been threats on my life if either of you were to break orbit without the Council's permission. I am telling you this now, after the fact, to protect your innocence, should you, by some means, which I cannot foresee, be apprehended by my own Galactic Navy. Sounds absurd, but I cannot stop the Navy from performing their duty to the Federated Republics. A duty they had sworn to uphold.

The first man out, commanding FRS BLAKE or ADAM, will be attacked by two robot ships. The attack will be carried out at the earliest opportunity, which will not endanger the lives on any of the Colonies. The robot ships will accelerate at ten gee's, thus forcing you to invoke the emergency clause and accelerate at four gee's or more, within the Inner Solar System. Once you reach a desirable velocity, you will be safe from intruders and, all things being equal, you will achieve your final destination.

Should the first ship fail to leave the Inner System safely, the second ship will be deployed under comparative conditions. Robots will also be expedited to simulate the necessity of accelerating within 3.5 parsecs of the sun. If necessary, you may both shoot down one or both of the pursuers. They are obsolete models but have been modified to suit the purpose they are going to serve.

I needn't tell you that I hope the second option, the backup ship, will not be necessary. Whatever happens, I shall not see either one of you again. The chain of command stops at my door. I shall accept full responsibility, for one or both of your actions. Such deceit of the Council, on my part, cannot go unpunished. You both know the law.

I must impress upon you, however, that your mission must succeed. The human race has sixty to eighty years of life left. We are a dying species. Of the eleven billion people, nine billion are now sleeping an average of thirteen hours per day. During the last twelve years, the number of hours of REM sleep has been increasing at the rate of two percent per year. The condition appears to be a syndrome of causes unknown. Growing millions of people have problems identifying let alone defining conscious reality. Those few who refuse to be part of the stagnating corpse of humanity, are forced to choose the hardships of the colonies.

Back to your mission. I am sure you do not need my help. You're both—the best.

If you come across this message in time, beware of freelancers. You are armed. You must regard your mission to be of greater import than the lives of the few enterprising bandits; even though, a century or two ago, those same bandits would have been regarded as pioneers.

Your mission—Get help! Humanity is losing its awareness. We are falling asleep. Dying. Within sixty years, the effects of radiation shall accelerate the death of our species. No one knows better than you that we have been searching for benevolent intelligence outside our System for the last one hundred and sixty years. So far we have failed. We cannot fail this time...

We need help!

My thoughts and my heart are with you. Somewhere out there, there must be a species more advanced then we are. Bring us salvation. Bring us a solution. Bring us hope. If that is not possible, tell them about our planet... I can do no more.

May God be with you both."

The image shimmered, and the Admiral's features dissolved into thin air.

"And with you Harry," John whispered. "And with you, my old friend."

John sat for a long time in total silence. The silence of Outer Space.

He felt very alone.

***

Chapter nine

So Long Pluto

It was with a heavy heart that John returned to the bridge. It was not just the substance of the Admiral's message. It was also Harry's tone—an undercurrent of an old fighter's apparent resignation. If such words had come from any other person, they would have been, somehow, more acceptable. A holographic projection had a most unnerving ability to bring its subject to life, to instill a living presence. John had heard, seen and experienced, Admiral Hermes D. Grant's presence in his quarters. No viscreen has ever had such an effect. Perhaps that was why Harry Grant had chosen this particular mode of communication.

John had seen and heard the final goodbye from his oldest friend. His only friend. He knew now—no more speculation—that his mission had been, all along, to find the source of the signals, which the Galactic Navy has been studying for the last two years. John also knew that the Admiral would not have sent him out so soon after the return from his last trek, if the Navy had better options. There was the second line of defense: Brad Drake. But he, John Galt, had been the first choice, all along. Commander Galt was the first choice because Commander Galt knew more about the great Unknown than anyone.

It sounded like an oxymoron—to know about the unknown.

Yet... it was the Unknown to which one had to react with intuition, but intuition based on experience. In space you only had one chance. You did it right, or you were dead.

John has played the Admiral's holo three times. He did not learn anything new from the replays. But he did spend a little more time with Harry. Just a little.

On the bridge, John found Delta sitting, apparently in the same position he had left her. He gave up wondering how she managed to withstand the high stresses, which the prolonged exposure to the additional gravities had imposed on her body. Maybe she was a robot with a human face. Right now, John didn't care. His mind, his heart, his attention had been focused on Harry. On Harry and the Mission. John sat down at his console, listened to Delta's report, and dismissed her from the bridge.

"Go and do whatever you should be doing. Take a rest, check the engine room, eat, sleep. Listen to some music."

John forced himself to return her smile. It wasn't her fault. She probably had not known Harry. Did he? Even now, from the short holo, John had learned new things about Harry Grant. He had learned that the Admiral had been prepared to upset the Council, to upset eleven billion people, in an attempt to save them. The stalwart gentleman had also been prepared to accept full consequences of his decisions and his actions. *Whatever the consequences.* John clenched his teeth.

"Yes, Sir!"

Delta left the bridge without further comment. She obeyed orders.

Yes, Sir, and a smile. She hadn't left the bridge since they broke orbit. John knew that one could sleep in a command chair about as comfortably as in any bunk. He had spent years in less comfortable positions. He had been younger then. But Delta looked fresh and rested. It wasn't fair.

The moment Delta left, John dialed for hytapes on the Lyra sector. He donned the hyphones and submerged himself in the data. After only ten minutes, he felt satisfied that the coordinates he had given Delta have been for Vega, a star of first magnitude, twenty-six light years distant. John also absorbed many other pieces of information. He had a distinct impression, that all the data he had just heard, was no more than a recap of data he'd learned before. He thought of the Moon Base; of the endless hours he'd spent under a helmet in the Psy Center. Even then, someone had been preparing him for the trek to Vega. Good old Harry. He had to have things his own way.

There was no detailed information about the Vega system. A lot of general data such as the star's luminosity, estimated mass, the spectrum; bits and pieces of disjointed facts, which man could gather from twenty-six light years away. Not much to help once they got there. No guesses regarding any planets, their size, mass, diameter or distance from the Vegan sun. All that John and Delta would find if and when they ever got there. No man had ever ventured on such a distant trek. No man thought it possible to go there and return. To bring back knowledge which might be of help to the human race. No man had ever traveled twenty-six light years at eighty-five percent of the velocity of light... or better.

In many ways this was incredibly exciting. John knew, however, that he had to sustain this excitement for some sixty-odd years. A time further extended by periods of acceleration and deceleration on the way out and, again, on the way back.

Back to Terra. To Earth.

Back to the place where, so many years ago, on a cool, crisp, wintery night, he once stood, alone, his head thrown back, wondering. Marveling about the countless, mysterious dots of light, shimmering, beguiling, promising within his youthful heart that there, on the brink of nowhere someone else stood, also looking up, wondering...

...also alone.

Stood so very alone among the churning masses of an over-populated planet... on a world polluted by greed, by want, by desire for possession. Among people who chose to cultivate that which made us different, which set us apart, rather than that which we all shared, which made us all One—in this endless, ever expanding universe.

Had it been worth it? Will it have been worth it? Did it really matter?

Is not the essence of each and every life the quality of the journey one makes, rather than the destination one reaches? Be it among the stars, be it on a forgotten Colony—shivering on an outer moon of Saturn; be it climbing the highest mountain, or the ceremonial steps leading to the Council Chamber of the Federated Republics.

The long trek, the journey, the eternal becoming.

John shook his head. The next point of interest was Pluto, still some days away. Then, seventy-one more days of acceleration before they could experiment with speeds beyond the projected 85% of the velocity of light. FRS BLAKE would take them there completely on its own. Completely.

John wondered what Delta was doing.

He left the bridge to finish his tour of the starship. Halfway down, on the intermediate engine room level, John looked again through the vertical, plexion visors. He pondered, again, on the design of the monstrous coils within the central axis. The tremendous source of power suspended within an eternal stasis of near absolute zero, protected from any untoward infrared radiation by the bulk of the ships hull. So simple, so logically obvious, yet it took many generations of scientists to put it into practice. It seemed that nothing could happen before its time; that all knowledge is available, but we cannot grasp it until we reach a certain, particular stage in our evolution.

Our awakening?

When the time is ripe, someone, somewhere, will put two and two together, and trip over an answer that will *then* seem obvious. Yet, an answer untenable for centuries.

John thought that we, as individuals, never make history. On occasion, we are chosen by the current of life, by a flood of circumstances, to fulfill a mission, which might change the course of history.

Future history.

But it shall not be our will, the elusive free will of some metaphysical demagogues, which will precipitate such profound effects. We are no more than pawns on the endless journey, a trek through the great Void. The most we can hope for is to become willing, rather than unwilling, subjects to that Power, that Life-Force within us. To become willing students, channels, of the Energy that guides us with infinite patience, from grain to grain of sand along the endless ocean...

Later, from star to shimmering star which, until approached and witnessed with our own eyes, seemed destined to remain no more than a concept, an idea, suspended within the expanding matrix of space and time. A figment of our ephemeral existence.

Rather than take an elevator, John walked down the spiral staircase to the lower levels. He was determined to remain sufficiently interested in the immediate surroundings to avoid becoming lost in a torrent of thoughts, which invariably invaded his mind the last few days before hibernation. It was is if John's brain was determined to exploit the last few available moments; to practice its equations, not of mathematical progressions, but to add up the sum total of its acquired knowledge. In a way, during those last few days, John was no more than a passive spectator of his own mind's wonderings; a bystander tacitly involved, yet essentially indifferent—contributing little, expecting even less. Observing.

John's feet led him on, forward.

And then he stood at a gallery. From this vantage point he could look up and down at the cathedral like engine chamber. This was the hub, the core, the heart of the starship. To John, the engine room *was* the ship. All other areas were no more than appurtenances to this nerve center. The main computer continually scanned the ship's innards. It also scanned the outside, the Outer Space. Through hundreds of minute lenses, direct, telescopic, many capable of microscopic adjustments, zooming in and out, examining, recording, transferring the information to the internal memory microchips capable of painstaking analyses, coordination, deductions, and final integration through an incredibly complex synthesis into action which kept them alive, breathing, fed, and on course.

Man had changed little during the last few millennia of his existence.

What had, and continued to change, was the produce of his creative, imaginative genius. Strange, John thought, how strange that man continues to change his environment rather than learning to adapt himself to new conditions. Perhaps, one day, perhaps...

Perhaps one day man will change?

John's eyes wondered down, to the lower engine room level. There he saw Delta. She was sitting up, straight, motionless. Her attention seemed totally absorbed by something, apparently at the expense of her immediate surroundings. Rather than disturb her, John took the spiral staircase to her level. There he looked again and caught his breath. In his travels, Commander John Galt had been very seldom surprised. Less seldom dumbfounded.

He was, then! Stunned!

Delta sat very erect on a throne-like contrivance. The front of her tunic was open. Two mechanical arms were making some sort of adjustments in the complex, exposed hair-like wiring protruding from her chest. The whole heterogeneous matrix was partially embedded in a gelatinous substance. A moment later, one of the mechanical arms reached into this resilient compound of her body, pulled out a tiny microchip, and disappeared within the console. A third mechanical arm, looking like a device the medical doctors used to perform painstaking micro-surgery on people's retinas, emerged from the left armrest, hovered over the seemingly dormant patient, and purposefully inserted itself into her open abdomen. All this time Delta's eyes remained closed, her long eyelashes resting gently on her pale, alabastrine cheeks. Her full lips seemed frozen, very slightly ajar, as though blowing a kiss to some invisible lover standing in front of her.

Otherwise, she seemed dead.

The single sign of life came from the fingers of her left hand, which periodically came to life, performing, at an incredible speed, some strange, dervish, whirling dance on the keyboard. Those beautiful, long, delicate, feminine fingers moved so fast that John was quite unable to follow the individual instructions they conveyed to the computer. Whatever Lieutenant Delta One Blake was, she was not human. Not like any human being whom John Galt had ever met.

For, perhaps, half an hour, John stood, unable to move, unable to speak, to take his eyes off the strange sight before him. In time, Delta's right hand came to life, if life it was, and, her eyes still closed, it reached up and out. Then, with deftness of a task performed many a time, the hand replaced a pliable plate in her abdomen. An automotive finger pressed around the edge where the plate connected to the rest of her skin, sealing the opening. In seconds, the seam became invisible. Finally, in a most human way, it, the live hand, closed the tunic to cover her pinkish-white, surely warm, living, breathing flesh.

At that moment John felt the need to lean against the handrail of the spiral stair behind him. Not satisfied with the support it offered, John, in an agonizingly slow motion, sat on the first step. There he remained until blood returned to his head. He closed his eyes, did his best to breathe deeply, regularly, to pump oxygen to his starved brain. He did not faint, but came as close to it as any man can without actually loosing all sensory contact with the world around him. Gradually the unpleasant coldness he felt at the top of his head eased. He became acutely aware of an army of minute ants chasing each other along his whole body. He waited, for a considerable time, for the numbness to pass.

"Is there anything I can do for you?" A feminine voice asked gently.

John opened his eyes. Looking up, he saw Delta's beautiful face, her perfect features arranged into an expression of concern, caring, almost worry. No nurse on earth could produce a better, more appropriate facial expression when looking down at a patient needing help.

"Delta One...?" John managed, after some more heavy breathing.

"Yes, Sir. Is there anything I can do?"

Her expression had not changed except for a gentle smile of encouragement slightly parting her lips.

For a brief moment John allowed himself to think that everything he had seen during the preceding half hour was the result of excessive tension, tiredness and overactive imagination. No woman could look more feminine, more human, than Delta did at this particular moment. Even her eyes seemed to radiate a deep concern for his welfare. John decided to let time arrange his thoughts into some kind of comprehensive, coherent order.

The decision to delay the acceptance of reality helped. It stabilized John's breathing, removed the vise from his nerves. It even enabled him to get up and walk. It refused, however, to erase the clear, vivid image of Delta, or someone exactly like her, sitting in the contraption of an armchair, with surgical spiders diving into her abdominal cavity as though performing some futuristic, science-fiction surgery. That image refused to go away even after John looked again at the high backed chair, which now appeared quite normal, perhaps a little different from other chairs or armchairs in front of several control panels throughout the multistory machine room, but normal nevertheless.

John managed to calm and control another wave of vertigo, this time less powerful, less vivid, even as the image his mind refused to accept gained protection of time.

He glanced at Delta.

He did not dare, as yet, to scrutinize her breast or stomach, where the offensive operation took place. He had to wait and see what would happen.

"I think I am a little bit tired, Number One," John offered a lame, understated excuse for his behaviour. He needed time, particularly time to study. "I shall be in my quarters."

John walked quite steadily to the elevator. He felt the need to be alone. On entering his private quarters, he did not even glance at the wall display. He sat at the computer terminal, and punched the code for information access. When the ready light appeared, he dialed: "Lieutenant Delta One Blake, comprehensive." Immediately the screen filled with a statement of available data. Each line was cross-referenced for additional information. John scanned the screen, punched a few keys, then read again, this time more slowly:

> Lieutenant DELTA G.N. basic prog. Hd. Pns. FO.
> Andr. Class ONE, assigned FRSS BLAKE prot.
> dev. stage init. ALFA 03052287, reprog. BETA
> 11042293, GAMMA 09122295 autogen/auton
> 01032297...

The information went on. Cross-references gave details of Delta's development over the preceding seventy years. John had spent the next fifteen minutes looking up references, translating the initial cryptic, concise message into intelligible English. It read: Lieutenant Delta, Galactic Navy, basic programming Humanoid, Positronic nervous system, female orientation Android, Class One, assigned to Federated Republic Spaceship BLAKE prototype, development stages initially as Alfa in 2287, reprogrammed as Beta in '93, as

Gamma in '95 and finally as autogenic autonomous entity in
'97. Exact dates had been given.

It appeared that Delta had gone through her own
development process. Even as every one of us, she too went
through her childhood, her teenage stage, her studies. Then,
she had reached her autonomous adulthood.

John understood all the words, he absorbed the facts, but
he had little if any idea what they really meant. He
remembered wondering, a few days ago, whether anyone
really knew him, as against knowing about him. He had now
placed himself in a position to learn anything he wanted to
about Delta. To learn about the incredible storehouse of
knowledge that she carried within her 'body'; a storehouse, to
which she could add, or subtract, at will. Her will. She could
add or subtract billions of bits or bytes of information, by a
simple process of inserting or a removing a few microchips
into or from her homogenous body.

John knew all this about her, but was there not more to
it? More to Delta? Did he or anyone know her—
individuality? If she was autogenous, self-generated since her
Gamma stage of evolution, her 'student days', did she not
become that which she herself wanted to be? What, if
anything controlled her own programming? Did she have a
conscience? What in Holy Space was a conscience, anyway.
Was it anything more than the instinctive reaction to
conditioning of thousands of years of evolution? And was the
conditioning anything more than programming?

John had spent the next few 'days' brooding in his
quarters. He absorbed hundreds of hytapes on the subject of
genetic engineering, on positronic brain development, on the
early work going back some three hundred years. He studied
the gradual development of individual parts or organs. Over
time, painstaking time, the pioneers overcame many, many
blunders, some tragedies. Their dedication resulted in final
rewards.

Ultimately in Delta.

Delta One, the First Officer of the Galactic Navy's latest, most brilliant, most complex, most advanced starship ever conceived by the human race. And why not?

After all, during the last three years FRS BLAKE had been the product not so much of human brains, as of deliberations of a positronic brain of one Android named Delta One. A thinking machine? Whatever Delta had become, without her the incredible complexity of BLAKE's innards, would never have happened. Without her, the incredibly powerful computers would have never been programmed. Computers so powerful, that only the perfectly superconductive elements protected them from an instant burn out. Computers whose job it was to tune, control and sustain the matter-antimatter pile within an ultra-magnetic containment field... None of this would have ever happened without Delta.

John ate little, slept even less, read, scanned vi-screens. He immersed himself in heretofore-foreign sciences, ever new, ever advancing. He refused to leave his quarters. Somehow, he could not face Delta until he established, in his own mind, a form of relationship with her. It already became to 'her', not to 'it'. He had crossed that bridge. For hours John wondered how he would think of Delta if she had not been contained, enclosed, within a beautiful, female form— or, for that matter, in any human form. Would he still be able to think of the entity as a he or a she?

Was the form so very important? Was it still the question of judging the book by its cover, now, in the year 2300 of the new area?

When John finished studying the technical aspect of genetic and positronic engineering, he dove, head first, into another ocean: into the latest, and the oldest, and all the in-between philosophies, which attempted to define the nature of man. Of a human being. He tried hard to be dispassionate in his research. Even when he came across postulates that sounded like total nonsense, he gave them equal time.

John left no philosopher's stone unturned, no page unread in his search. Today's technology enabled him to cover enormous width and depth of human thought. He included in his study a vast array of religious and quasi-religious reflection and speculation. He slept with the hytape helmet on, loaded with data. By then, John's study had transformed itself into a passionate search for himself. He already knew what he was.

He searched for who is he, whom men call, John Galt.

The communication bracelet buzzed incessantly.

All these days Delta had left him alone. She respected his need for privacy. John knew that she kept tabs on his wellbeing. The medical computer monitored his pulse, automatically. A substantial deviation from norm would have sounded an alarm.

John appreciated Delta's thoughtfulness. Would a human being afford me as much privacy under similar circumstances? He wondered.

"Yes Delta, what is it?"

"I hope you don't mind my interrupting, Sir. We are approaching our nearest point of convergence with Pluto. I thought you might want to see it?"

"I'm on my way."

In less than a minute John joined Delta. He looked at the main screen. The small, almost forgotten planet on its strange, eccentric orbit was just edging onto the screen. It performed its slow, ancient dance with Charon, its lone, frigid moon. Just like mother Earth. Only much, much more lonely. John turned to Delta. Her smiling face seemed pleased to see him. How human, he thought...

"Thank you, Number One. It was good of you to call me," John said. He meant it.

And then they sat in silence, together, each saying his and her own, private goodbyes to the lone planet. John sighed as he had done, always, when passing Pluto's orbit. His impassive face, this time, showed a touch of sadness. He waved his hand.

"So long, Pluto," John said.

Delta remained silent.

And then the Solar System was behind them. At over thirteen thousand kilometers per second, close to fifty million kilometers per hour, he and Delta and BLAKE had just entered the great Void of Outer Space.

***

Chapter ten

A different Perspective

One can delay the inevitable, though only for a limited period of time.

As so often in the past, John felt engulfed by the immense, intangible cobweb of Outer Space. The days and nights became marked with sameness, filled with an undefined melancholy. Time passed unresisting, swallowed inexorably by the voracious jaws of the great, silent Void.

Yet, there was a difference.

On his past treks in search of life, intelligent or primitive, biochemical or any other, in search of any life form characterized by autogenic reproduction, John had set his coordinates with little discrimination. His sole controlling factor had been the distance his spaceship could travel. John's lax, indifferent, hibernating body, trapped in the entombing, flying coffin, had been preset to reawaken at the appropriate time. Once there, the flying Lazarus would be raised from his deathly coma. Once there, John Galt, restored to a breathing, thinking entity, would direct the persistent search.

A search for Contact.

So many times, while maintaining his ship in a tight orbit, John had bombarded the prospective planets with exploratory messages—on all available wavelength. The ship's tele-cameras had scanned the alien surfaces below, recording, analyzing, computing. Hoping, always hoping, for a sign, perhaps a smidgen of proof, that Human Species was not an accident of nature, was not the sole, lone owner of the countless star systems, countless galaxies of empty deserted universes.

A search for a Contact.

A Contact, a connection—with anyone. Anywhere. To sate the gnawing hunger of hollow loneliness. To share the vast universes. To share...

But this present trek was different.

On this occasion hope preceded even the braking of the orbit. The signals originating in the Lyra Quadrant predetermined the coordinates of this, by far, the longest voyage. The signals had been carrying that very smidgen of hope. Not necessarily of any form of life as man knew it; but an orderly progression of symbols, repetitive yet inventive cycles, that contained a number of variants suggesting an attempt by someone to communicate with another. Someone, perhaps, equally as lonely in the vastness of space.

For millennia man had been well satisfied with the exploration of his own planet, his lands and his oceans. Then, within a few short centuries, the whole Solar System no longer sufficed. Man felt confined, restricted, trapped on a carousel of an insignificant star. A small star set apart on the periphery of the galaxy, away from the hub, the core of the Galactic centre.

Suddenly man felt provincial, puny.

In his pride, man resented being ignored by Others. For surely there were, there must have been, Others. Even in man's exorbitant complacency which, on occasion, compelled him to lay claim to divinity, creating gods in his own image, seldom compelled him to imagine that the whole universe had been created for his sole exclusive benefit.

It had been a while since man claimed that Earth was the centre of the world. That he was the sole, divinely inspired creation, at the world's inarguable center. Such pathological stupidity was now the domain of only a few, quasi-religious sects, which even now argued their exclusive claim to a divine origin. The rest of humanity grew up.

What then of all those Other, more advanced species?

John watched man learn to be somewhat more humble, to admit to himself his frail limitations. Too many aspects of man's life seemed to be coming to a dead end: the long-sleeping billions, the loss of ambition on a global scale, the apparent indifference with regard to the threat of racial extinction.

This threat had been leaked out, in a controlled manner, to test random reactions. Rather than creating panic, the news did no more than raise a sleepy eyebrow, a compassionate shrug of a shoulder, an acceptance of the inevitable with stoic indifference. Had the human race guessed, instinctively, that the end was coming? Had it reconciled itself to the countless apocalyptic oracles which history had spawned in such exuberant profusion?

These were questions that John Galt now studied.

The sum total of man's knowledge had been placed at his disposal. John had to know everything that could affect his journey. And even then, by the time he'd return from this last desperate trek—assuming he survived it—Earth would be in her death throes. The final warrant had been issued. It was up to John to find the eleventh hour reprieve from some other than human sources.

Up to me?

It was at that moment, as the full impact of this portentous realization reached the fullness of John's awareness, that his thoughts, as though guided by a single sweep of a magic wand, returned to Delta.

"I am not alone," he whispered. *I am not alone.*

Surely, he thought, surely, if such a task had been placed squarely on my human shoulders, then Delta, a product and the crowning glory of human ingenuity, must shed light on the human dilemma. Perhaps she could advance a totally different perspective on the human equation. Man had searched stars expecting that his problems must also, per force, exist elsewhere. The centuries-old enigma of the human neurosis, of the need for an echo of man's own problems, man's own aspirations.

But had it been so, really?

Perhaps we, the Navy, are the select few. Perhaps we are only the odd members of the racial compendium who suffer from this recurring state of nagging dissatisfaction. We, the offspring of the ancient free spirits—the offspring of the Marco Polo's, Columbus's, Gagarin's, Adam Blake's bloodline.

Perhaps even... John Galt's?

Though that last seed will never be passed on to future generations.

FRS BLAKE continued augmenting its velocity at the rate of four gees. The outer reaches of Solar System, though officially regarded as Outer Space, did harbor some forgotten remnants of doomed worlds' collisions. Dark, frozen boulders trapped by far-reaching, constraining arms of our jealous sun. Some rocks were as large as minor planetoids. Lonely, with a quick glint, a frozen tear in their otherwise blind faces, they stole furtive glances at wandering, vagabond comets. These celestial maidens proscribed to their far-reaching elliptical orbits grateful for any, even transient, signs of admiration, extended their long glittering hair—beguiling. Such diverse fragments, though many in absolute numbers, did not present any challenge to BLAKE's navigational system. And at their present velocity, some 17,000 km/sec., they no longer expected any challenge from the enterprising pirates.

To alleviate monotony, John invited Delta to his suite. He wanted to talk to her in different, less formal surroundings than the bridge. Until then, for some strange reason, he was reticent. He did not know how to begin.

They sat in deep relaxing armchairs, chatting like old friends about this and that. John's idle fingers nervously caressed a goblet of fragrant Venusian brandy. A background of Yng's innovative variations on Mozart themes provided an atmosphere conducive to carefree wellbeing. At least John thought so. He wondered about Delta.

The perimeter wall maintained an illusion of Space. The Void. Its call seemed to penetrate the darkened chamber, its mesmeric arms alluring with a powerful seductive embrace. The Sirens of endless oceans sang their silent compelling airs. Peace, they lied. No more demands, no duties, constrains, obligations. Just peace. Cold, undemanding, all forgiving Eternal. Persuasive, distracting lies.

An astronaut not well-seasoned, well-hardened to their seductive call, would soon succumb to the relentless vertigo. Like a man drawn into a blinding black snowstorm.

John was indeed a well-seasoned sailor. He and Delta sat back regarding dispassionately the distant, nameless stars. At BLAKE's present velocity the tiny sparks moved slowly aft. Soon, the stars would appear like streaks of light, splashed with a deft hand across black canvas. Appearing ephemeral, only to perish into boundless oblivion.

"Is there anything I can get for you, to add to your enjoyment?" John turned his attention to Delta's relaxed features.

"I am very content, Sir," she assured him.

John knew that Delta was waiting to hear the real reason for his invitation. Androids do not get bored or lonesome. Do they? She probably found it difficult to understand John's hesitation. Or was it just that John's emotions still refused to accept everything he'd learned about her. Delta continued to look, move, and talk, even breathe, like a perfectly normal woman. Her beauty made it even harder to think of her as anything but human. John decided to treat her the way his senses commanded.

"Were you fully briefed on the purpose of our mission?" he asked.

"You mean the Test Flight?" Delta raised a delicate eyebrow.

"Is that all that they told you?"

John wondered why she had not been briefed in advance. Surely Delta couldn't possibly be a security risk.

"I am to serve you, Commander, with total commitment," Delta looked surprised. She seemed to be searching his face.

John put down his glass and switched on the holographic projector. After identification, Admiral Grant, his desk, and office once again solidified in the space in front of them. John let Delta listen and watch the whole recording. Neither of them spoke while the message was in progress. When the image disappeared, John turned towards Delta.

"Is all this new to you?"

"Only the part about 'final destination'," Delta's face was devoid of any expression.

"Would you warrant a guess what the Admiral meant by it?"

John was still trying to find out not so much what, but rather how Delta was thinking. How she arrived at conclusions. What motivated her judgment.

"The rest of the message, coupled with the coordinates you gave me, lead me to a single conclusion, Sir. That is why I have added additional data to my RAM storage. It was then that you saw me..."

"You can add or remove Rapid Access Memory at will?"

"Of course, Sir." Delta looked genuinely surprised. She evidently expected John Galt to know that.

"You knew that I had watched you?"

"Not at the time, Sir. I deduced it later, from the info you requested from the library."

"And you said absolutely nothing?" John sat up.

"I could only tell you, Sir, what you already knew. It seemed redundant."

Her logic certainly wasn't human. It did not suffer from an emotional quagmire. It was pure—simple—objective. John wondered if he would ever be capable of such detached reasoning. Would any human being? Who wouldn't be hurt by being 'found out'? John wondered if there could have been more to it.

"And there is nothing you wish to add to the data I have studied?" John's voice couldn't hide a dash of hope. He wanted to hear about some kind of a weakness, perhaps some limitation. Something a little more human.

"The data was factually correct, Sir," Delta replied. Then for the first time, she hesitated. "Since the first of March, ninety-seven, it would be impossible to define exactly the specific progression..."

"...progression?" John didn't understand the context.

"The specific direction of my evolution. The autogenic capability offers autonomy, which in turn offers virtually unlimited variants. In theory I could review all the data and retrace the steps in my self-programming. Perhaps it would supply you with the missing data?"

She looked directly at John, her face registering concern. He remembered that look. Again, it was perfect.

John didn't answer. He felt at sea. What he wanted to tell her, he would find hard to define even to another human being. He took the bull by the horns.

"No. Delta. That is not what I am after. I no longer need to learn much more about you. What I want, if you allow me, is to get to know you!" John spoke quietly, yet articulating each word.

"You seem to delineate a difference."

Delta also spoke more slowly. Perhaps she imitated John, but her thinking could not be faster than human. Her positronic brain functioned at the speed of light, as did human, but she had infinitely more data to reach back into, and from which to draw conclusions.

"Are you sure that there isn't?" John asked.

"There is in the case of humans. The reason, as I see it, lies in the fact that human reaction to external stimuli is motivated by facts not readily available from their subconscious. I do not have such a problem. If you know all

about me, you can predict my reaction." Once again her logic
was flawless.

"Are you not affected by your previous experience?"

"Only to the extent that it stands up, or doesn't, in the
light of my present knowledge," she answered, again quite
slowly.

John had an impression that she had not been reciting,
but evaluating each question, placing it against all the data in
her possession and reaching a conclusion. After all, isn't that
what she just said she was doing?

"Then you exclude the possibility of an error?"

"Oh, no, Sir! The data available to us is invariably
limited. We can only aspire to do the very best we can with
the available data."

John had to smile. Can we ever expect anything more
from any man, woman or child? To do the very best we can
with the available data. That is all anyone can ever do. It was
not the result that mattered. It was doing the very best one
could.

"Always?" John prodded.

"Why would anyone do otherwise, Sir?" Delta asked.
Her lips slightly open, her eyebrows knit together and gently
raised, her head turned a little to one side. A detailed study of
an expression of surprise. Once again, it was perfect.

This time John could not help grinning. Even as he
laughed, he felt a sense of release. His built-up tension was
finally dissipating. Why would anyone do otherwise? A
question Delta could not answer. Her innocence was
endearing. She already possessed what humans were still
trying to master. She did not accept the reality of evil. Of
anyone doing something that was less than their best, in given
circumstances. Could such thinking process be the result of
mere programming? Or was it only because the apple of Eden
had not soiled her.

John got up and started pacing his room.

He realized that he had come to know her. Even as he
had come to know Harry, after only a few hours, he began to

know young Beta, so now he had a window into Delta's character. Character, personality or individuality. In a human being John would call it soul.

John had discovered what motivated Delta's actions, what motivated her thinking, the purity of her deductions. Was there room for compassion in such a paragon of virtue? Would she risk her own 'life' to save her companion, an associate, a co-traveler? Somehow John thought that he knew the answer. At least, he was prepared to act and behave as though he knew it. They both would do their best, under any circumstances. This philosophy had served him well. Throughout his life.

"Delta," John changed the subject. "I gather you are familiar with the Galactic Navy projections regarding the chances of survival of the human species. Can you comment on that for me?"

For the first time since John met her Delta had not answered at once. She must have been weighing countless options. She seemed to be digging to the very last microchip buried in her gelatinous innards. John could only call it thinking. After all, what does a man do when faced with an impossible problem? Think, think, then think some more, and then... and then do the very best he can.

"I am not sure, Sir, that I understand the problem." She looked directly at John. "There are a number of options. Surely there must be countless people who would gladly give up their lives, terminate their existence, in order to save their offspring. I calculated that if twenty-four-point-seven-two-seven percent of the population were to terminate their biological existence within the next three months, the resultant reduction in the production and the attendant emission of pollutants having a derogatory effect on the ozone layer, would assure the survival of the human race for another two hundred years. During this time, it would be logical to assume, alternative *modus vivendi* could be established which, in turn, would prolong the survival still further."

How very logical. A suicide of one in four and the rest can live happily ever after. Or pretty close to it. In the meantime we abolish having children, perhaps limit the number of years one is allowed to continue living...

"You said a number of options?" John asked instead.

"As I said, Sir, there are a number of options. One can substantially reduce the present standard of living. One can offer an option of limiting the life span, while also limiting the number of offspring to, say, one per one thousand. One can introduce an option of mass hibernation, thus limiting the need for food, housing and transport. One can combine any of the above to give people a maximum of free choice."

John smiled sadly. What could he tell her?

"You have a very fertile mind. But you know Delta, you were right as usual. You cannot predict peoples' reactions. Well you can, but not always—or not all peoples'. Would you believe that any of your options would be likely to spark global riots? That people do not accept restrictions imposed on them by anyone? Ever? Oh, humans are quite capable of great sacrifices, but only when the beneficiary of their sacrifice is connected with them by strong emotional bonds. Never by the processes of logical thinking. We are emotional animals. We always were, and we always shall be..."

"I know, Sir. That is why I said, at the very beginning, that I am not sure that I understand the problem. It is... ah, well, Sir, the problem is illogical."

Delta came as close to stammering as her perfect vocal chords allowed. John was quite sure that her statement had been enunciated in this fashion for his benefit only.

So there were limitations to a walking computer, even one nanotechnologically enhanced. The problem remained in spite of Delta's undivided loyalty, in spite of her deductive, analytical and synthesizing powers, or her practical options of sociological improvements. She could expand her abilities to cover an even wider ground, to further apply her knowledge. But Delta could not understand the limitations of illogic. At that particular moment of her peculiar existence, Delta was perfect. Always, without any exceptions, doing what she ought to. She was a child of Eden. Could the human race ever reach such empyrean levels? Or were we humans destined to fall inferior to our own creation.

"Do you think we'll find an answer at the end of this trek, Delta?"

"It would be illogical to speculate before we have the data," she answered promptly. This time there was no hesitation.

"Yes, of course you're right Delta. It would be illogical. But is it impossible?"

Delta looked at John, her head coyly turned to one side as though deciding if he had been joking. Her smile displayed two rows of perfect ivory-white teeth. A perfect smile parting full, sensuous, perfect lips.

"I do not believe many things are impossible."

"Good for you, Delta."

"Unless they defy the laws of logic, Sir."

The laws of our logic. Logic with which man had contaminated this perfect, innocent being which, or who, refused to leave Eden. John tried his best to return her perfect, ever-present smile.

***

Chapter eleven

The Void

FRS BLAKE passed the velocity test showing no signs of wear and tear. When the ship reached 85% of the Velocity of Light, nothing at all happened. The BLAKE continued accelerating although the velocity no longer increased at the previous rate. John and Delta remained on the bridge.

At 265,000 km/sec John examined the available data. The engines gave growing indications of inefficacy. It was a question of balance. At 85% VL the system had worked smoothly—100% efficiently. The BLAKE had been coasting. Now the engines laboured. Hard! For no appreciable gains in velocity.

Also there were telltale signs of a quite different nature: John noticed first indications of visual and audio distortions; the enigmatic, incomprehensible, though theoretically predicted distortions in the space-time continuum.

BLAKE's engines had been designed to be magnetically suspended outside the ship's body. It should be, and heretofore it had been, impossible to hear them. Empty space, cannot convey sound. There is no medium to carry the vibrations. Whatever the noise, it would be dissipated, completely devoured, by the eternal silence of the Void. In theory.

John Galt heard the hum of the engines. He sensed the vibrations.

Something had distorted, modified, the very fabric of space. The immediate environment chose to ignore the laws defining its properties. At 265,000 km/sec space no longer played the game according to the rules of the physical universe.

For a moment John wondered if it was he who had undergone some kind of change. Perhaps, he thought, at such enormous velocities man's senses became sharpened— augmented? Then John remembered: a hazy dim impression from a far distant past. He tried to reach deeper into those latent nagging images.

He came up with nothing. Nothing precise. John sensed, no more than a vague notion, that velocity affects the vibrations of physical objects.

Then, suddenly, his thoughts jumped centuries to vague memories of Adam Blake, the ancient astronaut. It was as though John was eavesdropping on someone else's memories:

...a dark grey emptiness... featureless—a Void... solidifying into a devouring blackness... a voracious anomaly. A Black Hole? Then, a flash of light—blinding, all consuming Light. Then... nothing... The scattered fragments dissipated in an outer nothingness; lost somewhere in another place, another time.

Another life?

But something remained. Images of altered vibrations, of frequencies affecting the density of matter, persisted. Vague recurrent images.

Troublesome.

John considered asking Delta for her impressions. An undefined whim held him back. Whatever velocity did to the space around him, it seemed—well, it seemed subjective. Individual. It didn't make sense. It was as if Delta did not share his private space. She could not share the input from his senses. His impressions seemed his and his alone.

Intuitively, John decided to scrap any further attempts to achieve higher velocity. He could not rationalize it but he was now convinced that there was a connection between velocity and frequencies of vibration. Or perhaps between velocity vibration and mass. BLAKE had ventured into no-man's land. Whatever happened, it affected John's perceptions. BLAKE was on a mission of prime importance. He could not jeopardize it to study side effects. No matter how interesting.

All this happened since the BLAKE crossed the theoretical barrier of 85% of the Velocity of Light. A barrier to what? From what? That was what John was so desperately trying to discover. In addition now there was waste. An overflow, a spillage of energy. A poor return on investment. Old Newtonian law had been vindicated again. Acceleration is inversely proportional to mass. And since 255 km/sec, BLAKE's mass had been growing along an exponential curve. Again vague memories stirred in John's pulsating head: a point of no return... A point of no...

"Cut acceleration, Number One!" John snapped.

"All acceleration, Commander?"

"Cut the Main Pile. Now!"

"Cutting Main Pile now, Sir. Reducing to 2% idling."

So that was that.

John breathed deeply. He felt a strange sense of relief. He wondered why. He knew that at the Velocity of Light their mass would have become infinite. Infinite as in omnipresent. Such velocity could not be achieved of course. It would require Infinite Power. But as the BLAKE approached this enigmatic paradox... Again those vague memories. Blake... Adam Blake...?

The engines were about to receive their first, well deserved, rest. John watched as Delta's fingers deftly phased out the Main Engines. Within seconds the energy trail disappeared. If there were an outside observer to such, FRS BLAKE would have disappeared. The ship now cut an invisible line through the fabric of Galactic Void. A strangely indifferent state of being. The state of free fall.

Towards Vega.

For John and Delta's convenience, the antigravs had been programmed to maintain one sixth gravity. Up remained up, down, down. They did not walk on the ceiling. This nominal gee had no effect on their velocity. It was fully absorbed by the hull. By the mass of the ship. And the mass had increased considerably.

It was time to retire.

Time to visit once more the strange dark land of delta rhythms; a domain of brain activity so insignificant, of cycles so slow, as to be comparable to prenatal fetal condition. The suspension of Delta One's functions would not be so complete, and the decision to restore herself to full operational status would remain in her hands. Not so for John. His metabolic rate would be reduced by 95%. John's life would hover on the brink of death.

On the brink of eternity?

Some two hundred years ago, attempts had been made to reduce the astronaut's metabolic rate even further. The scientists had even attempted to suspend all the vital signs of the biological process called life. Such experiments had been long abandoned. While the bodies of the test subjects had been restored to full physical vitality, the hapless volunteers had often suffered considerable psychological disorders. There had been cases of total amnesia. A loss of basic skills such as reading and writing. In all cases subjects' speech had been significantly affected. Not only had their physical and mental dexterity been inadvertently, often irreversibly, impaired, but emotionally the subjects had become less than juvenile. Some of the volunteers had regressed to the level of a newborn baby. Babies imprisoned in bodies of men and women. They had to be taught how to eat. Often, from a bottle.

In John's case the support system would maintain his body in a condition of near stasis. If his body were to be left alone, it would die. Precise body temperature, regular electrical stimulation of muscular tissue, and the plasma which temporarily replaced blood in his circulatory system, had to be maintained. In a real stasis, there would be total suspension fluids flowing within the body. In the induced condition, the flow of plasma was maintained mechanically. It was the plasma that brought about, and maintained, the lowered temperature of the body through the circulatory system.

Before prolonged hibernation, John had to undergo extensive cleansing procedures. These included rather unpleasant flushing of intestines and other internal organs. This was followed by selective sterilization, to inhibit any attacks of microorganisms while body defenses were at their lowest. The latest, more complex technical aspects of the procedures were available on ship's hytapes, but John's couldn't be bothered to learn them. As with the BLAKE navigational system John trusted the designers.

In Delta's case the process was considerably simpler. Rather than reducing her whole body's metabolism to a lethargic condition, she would switch off the majority of her functions completely, while still maintaining sufficient awareness at the sensual inductive level, to be able to restore herself to full operational status in under two minutes. A considerable advantage over her own creators.

John retired to the medical centre with his usual bravado. The prospect of being nearly dead no longer bothered him. After all, he had spent an overwhelming share of his life-span being 95% dead. To him it was neither a laughing nor a somber matter. It was just a fact of.... life. An astronaut's life.

There was one thing, though.

John wondered why people capable of designing starships, which traversed space at near-light velocity, could not design a medical room which did not look, smell and feel like a hospital. The insipid green walls with touches of phlegmatic pink, the inherent smell of anesthetic in areas where no microbes could possibly exist, the indirect, oh so inoffensive, nauseatingly soothing lighting... John wanted to get it over with before he became sick. Sick enough to fit into his surroundings.

John went through the cleansing procedures with his usual diligence.

Then he checked, personally, all the installations: the cubicle, the sterilization, and stasis maintenance equipment. Satisfied, he quite unemotionally bid Delta so long, and subjected himself to the inevitable. He would be restored to full life in good time to take active part in the planet-fall.

Assuming Vega had planets!

The timer has been set for the maximum length of subjective time. There would be no reason for John to leave stasis until BLAKE shed its velocity to a planetary mode.

As for any maintenance that BLAKE required, the robots had been programmed to take care of everything. From highly technical tasks of engineering maintenance to the mundane jobs of keeping the ship clean and tidy. John had no idea who was supposed to create a mess or raise dust on the antistatic floors. Still. This was a test flight. Wasn't it?

Once John entered the deep sleep, even the life support system was required to work at only 5% efficiency. The whole ship became 95% dead. Asleep.

An empty shell cutting a silent trail through the great Void.

For John the last moments of full-consciousness had always been very important. He firmly believed that the state of mind he maintained and held during those last minutes, had a profound influence on the whole period of hibernation. The Void was not really a void. Or to put it differently—the Void was not... empty.

There were traces of hydrogen atoms spread thinly over vast interstellar spaces. But there was more, much more to it. There were dreams out there. Dreams of the Void. Dreams very different from those John experienced under normal conditions.

Here, the dreams were no longer therapeutic. There was no need to repair the damage done to his psyche by the stresses and strains of an awakened existence. He was in a stasis, a state of suspension. Yet, whenever John had been brought back resuscitated after prolonged deep sleep, his mind had been bursting with memories. His dreams would have been easier to recall if there had not been so many of them. It was almost as though he had conducted a normal, rich, possibly ebullient life during his sleep. Life much richer in diversity of events than any astronaut could hope for. It was as though some part of him, at a very different level of perception, refused to be passive, to do nothing, to sleep, and continue instead in a flamboyant mode of living. This inner life compensated for the lack of sensory inputs in a manner as generous as his imagination allowed.

Subliminal uncontrolled imagination.

John's body might well have been practically dead. His mind, or whatever defined the intangible unit of consciousness named John Galt, was and always had been very much alive. Alive and happy.

Within John's dreams time seemed to obey a different metronome—to create its own rules. Events unfolded in an orderly fashion but at a different pace. John could accelerate their progress or slow them down, particularly when his chimerical activities generated particular interest or pleasure. In most episodes John played the role of a spectator. In others he took part, became involved. When his interest waned, he would transfer his attention to other realms, other events or vistas, which instantly became impregnated with new potent reality, and engaged his interest for another segment of, apparently, flexible time.

John recalled that soon after resuscitation, the memories generated by his dreams began losing their potency. They became shrouded with new fragments generated by conscious living. The more intense the problems immediately after awakening, the more demands on his faculties, the sooner his dreams dissipated into oblivion. It seemed that each state of awareness, as far as mental processes were concerned, had its own priorities, perhaps its own rules of behaviour, or even of intuitive responses.

There was a time when John attempted to make an in-depth study of such matters. Early in his career. Later, unable to share his conclusions with anyone, he let the memories of his findings dissolve into the greedy envious devouring Present. John developed a deep conviction that everything had its time, its place. He held a firm belief that when time was ripe, he would gain conscious access to those enticing, abundant, inner worlds.

With that thought wavering on the very edge of his consciousness, in joyful expectation of what was to come— John slept.

Delta double-checked John's life support monitoring system. She made a grand tour of the engine room. She again checked the star-charts, meticulously reviewed calculations of their trajectory, taking into account the dilation of time, velocity, and the deceleration procedures. Then, once again, she checked John's life support system. It wasn't that she didn't trust her own ability to do the job right the first time. Of herself she was certain. She did it because this was still a Test Flight, whatever destination or additional purposes had been added. Most of the equipment had been used under field conditions for the very first time.

John's life depended on it.

Even the efficacy of the laser and photon torpedoes systems came under her scrutiny. Just in case. She remembered that it had not been checked after their first application—still within the Inner System. Delta checked, and double-checked, everything. She was compelled to do her best. Compelled by her own auto-programming.

Finally, with what sounded like a very human sigh, she positioned herself on her throne-like chair in the engine room. Once more her slim elegant fingers performed their inimitable dance on the computer keyboard. Then she placed her left hand within the cover of the armrest and leaned back. Her eyes lost their, so very human, sparkle; her body seemed to stiffen. Her magnificent positronic brain ceased to monitor her complex metabolism.

Delta had put her vitality in abeyance.

FRS BLAKE hurled through the Void at close to one billion kilometers per hour.

In a world where some life forms create conditions of extreme overpopulation, the great Void denied the necessity for such aberrations. Space seemed to invite all to spread their cosmic wings. To fly in abundant freedom—anywhere. Anytime.

No man who had not experienced the infinity of the unchartered cosmos could possibly imagine the sense of freedom that the Void imposed. The boundless vastness, pensive, sometime brooding vacuum, waiting to be filled, sated. Often repelling, forbidding until breached—only to embrace and invite any daring intelligent presence. Then, and only then, the Void exploded with countless fragments of infusive thought. Fragments of those who once had been, who were no more, yet lingered on within its sable matrix of existence; drawing, enticing, onto consecutive steps of inner awakening.

This great Void of the Cosmos can be breached by the genius of human engineering, coupled with an inordinate number of credits and self-denying toil. On occasion it can also be breached within a deep, induced state of hibernation.

John did both. He had no idea what Delta was doing.

***

PART TWO

Zircon

Chapter twelve

STAR FALL

The digital dial on the left indicated standard earth-time.
The one on the right recorded subjective, spaceship time.
Essentially, the latter recorded the biological time that took
into account the effects of John Galt's vastly reduced
metabolic activity. It also calculated and recorded the effect,
which the velocity of the ship had on the dilation of time. The
dial on the left indicated that just over thirty-four years had
passed since BLAKE had left the Earth orbit. The one on the
right registered a period of a little under two years.

Both chronometers were right.

The temperature of plasma pumped through John Galt's
cardiovascular system has gone up to 35^0 Centigrade. The
composition of the fluid has been gradually changing in
consistency. It was becoming thicker, darker, until it looked
like real blood. Nutrients had been added to the reddening
mixture. Nutrients which offered support to the recumbent
body asleep for more than thirty-four years. Yet when the
time finally arrived for John to leave the transparent,
hermetically sealed coffin, his body would be neither weak
nor stiff. Well, perhaps just a little. But not so as to inhibit his
immediate return to captain's duties. The magic of micro-
voltaic nerve stimulation has maintained John's body in a fit,
almost agile condition. John had often felt more stiff after an
uncomfortable night's sleep, than after spending some ten or
twenty years in a controlled stasis.

As his body temperature rose, so the deep hold of the
Void, the chimerical creations of his fertile imagination,
began to recede.

John's eyelids trembled as his chest heaved, slowly, haltingly, drawing air into his lungs. The first breath under his own volition in many years. With that, the support system began phasing itself out. John remained motionless for a good fifteen minutes before attempting to open his eyes. His throat was parched, stiff—normal condition even after only a few months of hibernation. It would remain sore for some days. It couldn't be helped. No reason for despair, though. Three days from now he would be as good as new.

John's pupils and optical nerve had been adjusting to the light through closed eyelids. Neither his throat nor eyes could be stimulated with an electric current. All that the medics could do was to motivate his glands, artificially, to produce more secretion during the last ten days. It had been enough. Almost. His eyes opened with relatively little pain. The light seemed still too bright. Irritating, but no longer painful.

Then John saw Delta.

Her beautiful face was displaying that marvelous mixture of concern and smiling encouragement. John wondered how long she had been standing by his side. She was a mother hen extraordinaire, a nurse Nightingale, a preoccupied obstetrician watching over a newly delivered baby.

John tried to smile. This small jerky grimace seemed to work without undue stiffness. 'Perhaps the medics managed to advance the art of human resuscitation since my last trek,' John thought, with considerable satisfaction. He recalled having had portions of his physiognomy stiff for days after awakening. 'Good for them, even better for me.' All the same, John didn't dare to speak. Not yet.

"Welcome to the land of the living!" Delta spoke softly, as though unwilling to invade John's silent world too quickly. She could not have had any experience of someone in his condition. The degree of tact she displayed was truly amazing.

John blinked, repeated his weak attempt at a smile, and raised an eyebrow. She took it to be an inquiry into BLAKE's condition. There followed a brief yet precise review of the ship's status. She touched all the bases that would be of interest to a man who just awakened in the middle of nowhere.

Nowhere.

A miniscule grain in the vastness of the universe.

"...and so Commander," Delta concluded, "at the present rate of deceleration, we have five days before entering the orbits of outer planets of the Vega system."

Commander John Galt was more than satisfied. On his previous treks, it had taken him up to two weeks to gather all the information, which he just received on a silver platter. Delta's efficiency, her ability to, in a way, scale down her report to two or three decimal places, her superbly organized mind remained a source of wonder. John could no more regard her as a convenient admirable creation of genetic engineering, then to think of himself as merely a biological construct. He was acutely aware of his growing affection—of an unavoidable bond of friendship.

It was not Delta's efficiency that was the most staggering. After all, the BLAKE was eminently efficient. Perhaps more so. Neither was it the physical beauty with which her creators had endowed her. Nor was it even her mindboggling knowledge. It was none of those formidable traits.

As time went on John was becoming increasingly conscious of Delta's commitment to his welfare: physical and mental. Perhaps, if it were possible, even emotional. John smiled at the thought that if she had the physiological capability she would also offer him her body. A strange thought. John decided to look up pertinent information on the hytapes. When his eye caught the chronometer, he could not resist a mental equivalent of a disparate shrug. Commander John Galt was now two hundred and twenty-four years old. Earth-time. Not bad, he mused.

On the other hand—not very sexy.

An overhead mirror, running the length of the capsule, reflected his reclining body. John looked at a man in his late thirties. At worst, young forties. What would have made the stirring memories of latent desires more difficult to fulfill, had been the many extensive sterilization processes. To say the least, they dampened John's sex drive. Just as well. Otherwise, on his previous treks he would have climbed on the tail of his rocket. Any tail. He smiled. Paradoxically, these thoughts in no way diminished John's interest in Delta's anatomy. Nor did they wipe a supercilious smile from his curiously virile features.

Too bad, John mused. Ain't that just too bad... He swallowed hard. The stiffness of his throat brought him back to the present.

"Signals...?" A muted whisper left his parched lips. The effects of dehydration.

"I monitored the signals periodically, Commander. They continued to repeat or rotate the same, extended cycle. So far, we have had no success with deciphering their meaning."

"Messages...?" John had been referring to possible laser messages which, at the speed of light, might have caught up with them during his long hibernation. Whatever news any messages carried would be unlikely to affect them directly, in the here and now, but they might be of academic, if not sentimental interest.

"I think you should see those yourself, when you'll be up and about," she said.

So there had been messages.

John detected a smidgen of reticence in Delta's voice. 'Or am I assigning her too many human qualities?' he wondered. Still, right now John had to accept her judgment and wait. Whatever messages were waiting for him, must have been sent and received a good many years ago. Later, the BLAKE had become too small a needle in the cosmic haystack for the messages to find them. Laser beams had to be extremely narrow and accurate in order not to dissipate their potency over interstellar distances.

That was an additional reason why the signals from Vega
had been of such interest to man. The source of the signals, at
the point of emission, must be incredibly powerful. Well
beyond any power that man could control. Or, the signals had
been directed at them, specifically. At the Earth. At humans.
But if it had been the latter, why and when, or for that matter
how, did the Vegans learn that Earth's Solar System had
spawned and harbored intelligent life? These were some of
the questions Hermes Grant hoped they would answer. Even
if nothing else came of man's aspirations. Harry, John,
humanity, all hoped to find a Rosetta stone. To decipher the
signals.

Three hours had passed since John's temperature
returned to 36.6^0 Centigrade. His pulse was normal, his
breathing a bit shallow but sufficient to adequately oxygenate
his blood. His brain seemed in a good working order. John
felt ready to attempt getting up. Officially he was supposed to
remain recumbent for the first ten hours. If possible. John did
not spend his life in Outer Space because he liked obeying
orders of some long-dead theoretician; especially now, when
Delta was at hand to give him a hand. Should he need one.
John suddenly realized that there had never been any physical
contact between himself and Delta. He wanted to touch her.
Was her skin as soft and as smooth to the touch as it looked?
Was it warm and silky? Not like plastic but...

John whispered his intent to Delta.

No. Not to touch her—to get up.

He was almost surprised that she voiced no objections.
He expected her to do so. To object. Why? Was he not the
Captain? Commander John Galt being nursed on his own
spaceship by a beautiful woman. What will they think of
next?

At that moment, for the first time since regaining full
consciousness, John remembered why he was there. The
human race was dying. He had been sent here to save the
Earth. To find a panacea. To help Admiral Hermes D. Grant
in his task, in his endeavors. To help Harry...

Harry was dead.

Harry was dead, cremated, scattered in Outer Space. Only senior officers of Galactic Navy held that privilege. Everyone else was recycled.

Delta stood by as John attempted to rise. She was watchful, attentive, but did not interfere. She had already completed the necessary disconnections from the support system before John had regained full consciousness. She had been at his side for the last five days. Like a mother. A loving mother. She could have left John all to himself—the stasis unit was fully automated. But she didn't want to. She enjoyed helping. Being useful. She scanned her memory banks for a facsimile of what it would be like to be in abeyance for such a long time. Would all her synapses work as efficiently? What about the lubrication of her positronic brain. It was a very delicate matter to be left in the hands of robots, machines. 34.8749 years is a long time to lie still. Admittedly the Commander's cardiovascular and respiratory systems had been mechanically maintained. Partially. The same had been true of his main muscle groups. But all this was not the same as walking and talking. Or thinking.

Commander John Galt was up.

A wave of vertigo forced John to lean against the cubicle behind him. He waited five minutes. Then he stood straight and let go of the support. He stood, unmoving, remembering how to walk. Not consciously, but at some lower level of the medulla oblongata. It came back. Quicker than he'd expected. He smiled confidently. He took two steps towards Delta and collapsed into her arms. The last thing John remembered was that her body was as soft as it looked. And her skin... her skin was as soft as that of a newborn babe. A baby girl. Soft, very soft, smooth...

John awoke in his Command armchair on the bridge. His console was switched on—as if he'd been working. John had no idea how he got there. He remembered his head spinning in anti-clockwise direction, just before everything went blank. Or was it black? The blackness then dissolved into a most beautiful landscape. The green had been greener than he remembered on Earth. The sky was bluer. There had been no people there, but he did not feel any need for them. He was in Eden. Perhaps he was Adam before God even had a chance to mould Eve around his rib. He had lain down on tender grass, by the still waters....

"How long have I been out?" John sat up. His voice was near normal.

Delta did not need to look at the chrono. Such simple devices had been all built into her matrix. Her face no longer indicated concern. She obviously knew that John was all right.

"Six-point-eight-nine hours, Sir."

Delta had switched to Galactic time. Ten hours per day, hundred minutes per hour. With no days or nights, it was a lot easier. John had slept almost seven hours.

To his considerable chagrin, John realized how much he'd learned to rely on Delta's support. Not that she really doted over him. She was much too smart for that, yet... When he'd been alone and a trillion miles from home, from anywhere, making decisions had been easy. He had to make them. It had been easy to make decisions when he had no choice. Now he had a choice. It was harder.

"Why?" John asked.

"You had been only minutes away from a powerful stimulant injected intravenously just before you were disconnected from the support system. When you stood up, too early, your heart compensated by feeding extra blood to your brain with the resultant massive overdose. Your brain rejected the drug by contracting the blood vessels," Delta explained. There had been no criticism, stated or implied, in her answer. It was a statement of facts.

"Are you a medic?" John asked.

"Yes, Sir," she smiled sweetly.

"Am I all right now?" He intended to be facetious.

"Yes, Sir."

"How, in Holy Space, do you know?" John stared at Delta, thinking he caught her at last.

"I have been monitoring your metabolism for the last week, Sir. You are all right now," she answered, with the innocence of a nurse proficient in her duty. How could he have imagined otherwise? Could she do less?

"Even now?" John sounded aghast.

Delta's fingers played an atonal tune on the keyboard. "Your screen number six, Sir," she said, pointing to her own and his left hand armrest console.

John looked down. A tiny display indicated his pulse, blood pressure, latest electro-cardiogram, electroencephalogram, body temperature, his skin fluids secretions, his blood analysis... Blood analysis? Only now John actually looked at himself. He had been connected to a number of tubes and wires dispersed from his toes, all the way up to his apparently still poorly functioning synapses. He hasn't felt the connections and was not been aware of them. Only now John did fully realize that he had gotten up from his stasis too early.

"When you got up, Sir, all your subcutaneous connections were still functionally operational and accessible. I simply reconnected them to your chair, in order to save you the necessity of getting up, after you'd awakened." Delta sounded as though she had done the obvious. Perhaps she had.

"Thank you, Number One."

John felt a little like a small boy who'd not only done something wrong, but had been caught at it. For a man of his not inconsiderable age, it was a very strange feeling. Very strange indeed!

For quite a while they sat in silence. John scanned the endless data recorded over the last thirty years. The computer had already reduced the info to a manageable volume. A preliminary review could be covered in two or three days. All repetitive data had been eliminated, the plates only indicating the number and duration of repetitions. In outer space, that's quite a reduction. The computer compensated for BLAKE's motion to assess the relative changes in the phenomena or objects recorded.

John spent the longest time studying the recordings of nine novae and five supernovae. People who assumed that the universe was a neat, orderly place, should look at some of these plates. The explosions had been, in the truest sense, of cosmic proportion. Two of the supernovae had been so huge as to 'ignite', or accelerate the evolution of, other stars, light-years away, creating, in a way, an astral chain reaction. Whoever or whatever was in charge of this world had its hands full to keep it together. It seemed to John that life was the sole manifestation of order. Life, the power that wrenched order out of chaos; wrenched and maintained harmony within an endless, seemingly eternal, ocean of systemic, cosmic anarchy. John was glad that he was, once again, alive.

"You should get up and do some walking, Sir."

Delta's voice reached him from a great distance. John left the supernovae, the churning, hurling, gargantuan expanses of fire, and turned to Delta.

"Thank you, nurse," he smiled. "Will you also disconnect me from this mass of wiring?"

He was perfectly capable of doing it himself, but... when you sleep for a third of a century you feel like playing around a little. Or it could have been his dreams, which invariably left him in an impish mood for many days after restoration.

"Certainly, Sir."

Within seconds Delta's hands were moving over his body, prodding here and there, removing subcutaneous connections, her face, once or twice, within inches of his own. She, an android woman, smelled better than many a woman John had ever met during his stays on Earth. Or the Moon. Or any of the colonies. She smelled like a springtime breeze. Like his last dream. Like a breath of sunshine.

She was a robot. An android. She was beautiful.

He was a man. Healthy. He was two hundred and twenty-four years old.

And then the moment passed. The wires had been removed, the tubes disconnected, the implants, temporarily sealed. Delta stood a few feet away, ready to help, if he needed help getting up. For crying out loud, I don't need a bloody nurse! John fumed inside. He said nothing. He got up. For a brief moment he toyed with the idea of collapsing, again, into her arms. Except this time he knew that she knew that he was all right. Why in all the Blasting Novae had she told him? Did she suspect? That could not be possible. That would have been devious, surreptitious, human behaviour. Emotional.

Or would it?

John's steps were firm but lacked confidence. Thirty-four years is a long time. He paced the bridge, slowly, rather stiffly. That reputed instant agility had been vastly overrated. John refused to show his weakness. In the past, on resuscitation, he always remained in his command chair. The ships had been small. The quarters cramped. Exiguous. All he needed, on waking, had been his arms. Now he walked.

John glanced at Delta.

She stood, unmoving, her face indicating pleasure. How did she do it? How do you program pleasure? Can one? John looked at her sharply, his forehead furrowed. The last few years, even in Earth orbit, she had been autogenic and autonomous. One could study her memory tapes. Possibly. Rather like deep hypnosis in humans. But no one could swear what went on inside that positronic brain of hers at this moment.

"Is anything wrong, Commander?" Delta's look of concern had returned.

"Wrong? Ah, no. It's nothing. I just remembered something," he lied to an android. He also just remembered, again, to look up her physiological capabilities. I must be crazy. For crying out loud! Those dreams must have sent me over the edge.

Twenty minutes later John sat down. It felt a lot longer. Enough for the first time. John wanted to sit down before

Delta suggested that he do so. He had to rebuild his ego. The darn woman was much too perfect. He dialed for a robot to bring him his first meal. It was a container with a plastic, self-sealing straw. His diet would remain liquid for a week. For no reason at all John felt annoyed. He wondered why. He couldn't think of a reason.

Sipping his nutrients, John continued to scan the tapes, then hytapes. After three hours, he asked Delta for a review of the Vega system. It was a vastly more detailed account than anything they had on Earth. Although still a good few million kilometers away, even from the outer planetary system, the scanners had been accumulating masses of information. The new charts included the number and mass of Vegan planetary bodies, their equatorial diameters, surface temperatures, possible chemical compositions of their atmospheres—if any, and even principle mineral structures. The scanners also accumulated a veritable library of the lunar satellites of the various planets.

It was a rich, diverse solar system.

The star Vega claimed eleven major planets, four minor ones, and two asteroid belts—probable results of collisions between ancient members of the bright sun's family. The single most interesting phenomenon of the system were the seventh and eighth planets, which played hide and seek with each other, pretending to be each other's moons.

"Rather than any rings adorning their planetary systems, they appear to share a sort of funneling chain, rather like a mobile link, or bridge, between themselves," John thought aloud.

Delta nodded.

Indeed, each time one of these two Mercury sized planets reached an orbit further away from Vega, a mass of particles, shimmering with a mass of iridescent sparkles flowed from it towards the planet closer to the sun. After their relative positions reversed, the flow followed suit and shimmered towards the planet it had come from. By some strange balancing act, in spite of enormous torsions, which such action must have created on the surfaces of the twin planets, there had been, so far, no evidence of any volcanic activity on either of them. In all his light-years of travel, John had never witnessed such a fantastic display. So far John only saw it in miniature, though under great magnification. A computer enhanced simulation. In real life it would have to be a most fantastic spectacle.

To John, and Delta, this binary system was of even more particular interest. Although it was much too early to be certain, there were indications that the signals, the long monitored signals, had been originating from somewhere within their orbit.

Patience.

Thirty-four years of waiting seemed to vanish into oblivion. Patience was needed from now on. Badly. John knew from sad, frustrating, past experience, that jumping to any conclusions prematurely, invariably led to scientifically unfounded and later disproved conclusions. Mind and emotions seemed always at odds with each other. Patience. John had long learned to avoid repeating his early mistakes. Patience. It should by now be easy, even natural to him. After the long stasis, it was now only a question of days. Days! Then why did he have to repeat the word to himself? Over and over?

Patience.

He glanced at Delta. She seemed perfectly relaxed. He envied her.

Patience.

***

Chapter thirteen

View from Above

During the next few cycles, John's dreams were more expansive than those that had recently emerged, so to speak, out of the Void. John awoke from each rest period with lingering images of flamboyantly verdant, immense panoramas of idyllic surroundings.

Day after day, upon rising, John had problems reconciling the intensity of his chimerical reality with the ship's hard, sterile interiors. He suspected that the deep recesses of his mind, starved of simple, natural surroundings, had been digging out from his memories such pastoral fragments, and putting them together in order to balance his subconscious needs. An exasperating aspect of the dreams was that there had been no man or beast present in them. At the same time, John had awakened repeatedly with a feeling of being watched. As though some living, breathing entities had been present within those idyllic environs, but chose to hide their presence from his eyes and ears.

By the third rest period, John's feeling of disorientation upon waking still lasted over ten minutes—a condition quite rare when affecting a Commander of a Federated Republic Spaceship. Very rare for a man who, for many years, took pride in having an ability to finish a sentence on waking, which he'd started the previous night. Such quick reflexes, such instant ability to invoke full awareness of his whereabouts, had been useful. On occasion life saving. Particularly as John had to snatch moments of sleep, cat naps, only when duties permitted.

Now, of course, there was Delta. If need be, she could carry out the whole mission single handed, and the final result would be none the worse for it. John recalled his sentiments of this very nature, when he first met and set out with his Number One officer. Her answer then had satisfied him. Now he was in need of reassurance, of a reassessment of his personal worth, a confirmation of his own identity. Even of his personality. It had become evident that Delta had maintained a consistent watch on the ship's automatic, yet complex, operations. She kept tabs on the multitude of details, many of which he could not even imagine. The ship was simply too big, too intricate, for one man, a mere mortal, to operate. John tried to rationalize that the ship had been designed for a crew of near-fifty trained personnel. Under such, 'normal' conditions, the Captain would not be expected to carry a greater burden. To do so would be inhuman.

This thought brought him again to Delta. Inhuman. In this starship John was apt to keep turning and turning and inscribing ever-diminishing circles. And they all lead to Delta.

Since the day of awakening, John spent one hour in ten, exercising his body. The gym, designed for so many, was uncomfortably empty. John wanted to get physically tired. He wanted to sleep due to physical exhaustion. He needed a deeper sleep, with dreams less vivid. On the fourth day, John increased his exercise period to one and a half hours. If he continued in this fashion, he would soon qualify for Naval Olympics.

The physical activity reminded John of Beta. The young man—now around fifty—may still be finding release in Lunar Caverns at Mare Crisium. Leaping and soaring in air currents of freedom.

A young man of fifty!

The lanky, smiling, punctilious Beta. John wondered if he would ever see him again. Right now, BLAKE was thirty-four years away from home. If John turned the ship around, this very minute, he could shake hands with a man thirty-two years his senior. Beta would be a lanky, punctilious eighty-four-year-young Leaping Lunite.

John's preoccupation with the past had been, at least partially, due to Delta's presence. In the past, on lone treks, he had so much more to do—so much more to remember. Or... pay the consequences. And the consequences, on occasion, had been serious. John's very survival attested to his ability. Or had it been merely his powerful inherent instinct.

John shook his head. It was time for a jet shower. John Galt was beginning to act like a neurotic. It wasn't like him. Not like him at all.

In his quarters John examined, again, the last messages, which had been recorded 29 years ago. There was no need for a more precise time record. Time, here and now, was of no consequence. The messages were obsolete. Five years after BLAKE broke orbit, the Council approved the expedition. The name of Admiral Hermes D. Grant had been reinstated to hero status. Two years after the Admiral's death.

There was also a personal note for John. It read: "Love and respects from all the Leaping Lunites."

John discovered a strange thing about himself. For many years he did not need company. He had no need of a personal friendship. Nor did he expect anyone to think about him. Now, that his last friend was dead John felt a great vacuum. An emotional emptiness not unlike the Void he just emerged from. John felt as though he had been totally alone; in the whole world; the whole vast infinite universe. There were the stars and he. No one else.

Except for Delta.

'Tomorrow' they would cross the orbits of Vega's outer planets. For more that two months, BLAKE's velocity had been shrinking to a manageable magnitude. For the last ten days, the star-fall had been conducted along a spiral trajectory. By tomorrow they would have circled, or rather super-scribed an ellipse, around most of the Vegan solar system. The scanners were busy recording data. All of John's previous commands put together had not had BLAKE's number nor scope of scanners. By the time BLAKE entered the system, the preliminary analyses of all the planets was completed. John felt hard pressed to examine the voluminous conclusions. To do them justice would take John two years. Theoretically he had time.

"After all, what are two years in the history of mankind?" he said, then realized that no one was listening.

"How come my heart isn't in it?" he said out loud. He often did that when he was alone. It filled the Void. Somewhat.

But if time was of no essence, why did John feel a strange, inexplicable agitation? Was he, himself, in a hurry? Was he keen to return to Earth? To die on the dust which had spawned him?

Patience. I am here to do a job. That is what I'm paid for.

And for the first time since awakening, John laughed. He had used an ancient expression: *That is what I'm paid for.* John had been around for 224 years. The last time he received a salary had been when he was thirty. Or thereabouts. I must have been crazy! Then, as well as—now.

John wondered what Delta had been doing.

"Sir? Could you come to the bridge, please?" There was no panic in her voice.

Why had she called him just now? In addition to all her incredible talents, was she also a telepath? Both he and Delta left their communication bracelets open at all times. The incoming option only. There was no point switching it off with only two people on board. People? Only one of them was ever likely to swear under his breath. Or mutter something to himself.

John was up on the bridge in minutes.

"What is it Delta?"

"I think you should look at these."

She played on her keyboard and the main screen filled with a mass of figures. The end product of the scanner recordings, organized by the main computer, reduced to conclusions and arranged by Delta.

"My God! You have been busy!" John was flabbergasted.

"It was really a question of selective programming, Sir. The Main did the actual work."

Talk of modesty!

Of course, John could do the programming himself. He always did in the past. But then, he'd left stasis a month earlier, he'd worked eight out of every ten hours, and the data he'd had to choose from had been about one ten thousandth of the present avalanche of info. Whatever Delta said, whatever the capabilities of her positronic brain, she still was, well, incredible!

John studied the figures for a good six hours. Occasionally he made cryptic notes on his own console. His fingers could never match Delta's digital speed, but he held his own in confidence and purposeful determination

At first sight, the conclusions were both, encouraging and depressing. The depressing part was that all the scanning carried out so far, failed to reveal any sign of intelligent life on any of the planets. Primarily, the computer scanners listened for any 'noise' indicating the presence of any communication systems within the electro magnetic wave spectrum. Neither radio, nor laser, nor any other organized emissions of waves has been attributed to any of the planets. Other than the 'signals', of course.

Heretofore, there also was no evidence of any discharges of energy, either on or between the planets, which would indicate the presence of large, energy-intensive projects, or interplanetary travel. What was worse, the preliminary atmospheric analyses did not indicate the presence of any conditions conducive to supporting any live forms based on hydrocarbons. None of the above was conclusive, but the results did not inspire excessive hope for an interstellar, fraternal reunion.

The single encouraging aspect remained the signals.

The very same signals that had initiated this expedition were definitely originating from, or within, a very short distance of the binary planets. From the Waltzing Duo which after closer examination strongly suggested an unnatural relationship.

An artificial configuration?

Too many factors would have had to have happened in too short a time, for the two planets to have arrived, in their symbiotic relationship, by accident. Nature was very good at creating chaos. Not good at all at introducing order and harmony. That potential belonged to some higher influences, an altogether different axiom scribed in the secret annals of evolution. Ever assuming that the evolution did, in fact, take place. There was a body of evidence that we lived in a world, at least on Earth, which had been grinding to a faltering halt. Such evidence would suggest a condition of devolution. It all depended on your point of view.

"All right Delta, let's have your inferences."

John having drawn his own conclusions was not about to miss out on the benefits of a positronic brain.

"There is so much data, with new factors coming in all the time, that it is really much too early to draw any conclusions, Sir. I merely thought that we had enough info to be of interest to you. Particularly regarding the binary system. Had I been correct?" Delta sounded on the defensive. For her it was an unusual condition.

"You have been, Delta. Nevertheless I would like you to speculate. Extemporize."

"I can do little more than repeat what you have already witnessed, Sir."

She pointed to the screen. After six hours of study, John forgot, that the screen represented Delta's enormous scope of 'conclusions'.

Was there a reticence in her voice, though? If so, why?

John decided to let go of the subject, particularly since his rest period was coming up. He wanted to read some works of old literary giants. The Classics. For reasons he could not explain, John felt a great need of poetry, of great fantasy wrapped in a poetic, engrossing fashion. He needed to soar with the human spirit into realms where only imagination could take him. This need felt like a hunger, which John discovered within his psyche. It was one he could attempt to fill.

He glanced at Delta. I wonder what are her needs, her desires. John asked Delta if she had been taking her own regular rest periods. Periods of reflection?

Delta, sounding as though the answers were available on the hytapes, replied that she liked to do her own realignment once every two years.

"...and as you know, Sir, my energy source would last me for approximately two centuries. The Commander's questions were, therefore, a little incomprehensible to me, Sir," she said.

"I had been referring to your, ah, shall we say, psychic overload. If you continue to absorb, at the present rate, new data, new information, does this not result in a..., well, a sort of overload? I rather imagined that you might need time, a sort of passive time, in order to consolidate your knowledge..."

As time went on, John's interest in Delta grew in areas that they had in common.

"If I had not eliminated a number of redundant factors from my memory, it might well happen, Sir. But, again, as you had noticed, a few years, a few earth-time years, ago I did some realignments which afforded me a good margin of safety." She looked at him with a renewed interest. "If I may ask, Sir, why are you asking?"

"I am interested in what we might have in common." John decided to be quite blunt.

"If you mean in terms of interest..." she began.

"No, I do not mean in terms of interest" he cut her short.

"Then I do not understand, Sir."

Delta appeared to be studying her Commander with those big steely blue eyes. John felt as though he had been dissected, cut into little pieces, and reassembled together once again. It was the second time he had this particular impression. The first time John experienced this feeling was when they first met onboard the BLAKE. At the time he'd dismissed it as imagination. Now he wasn't so sure. What other powers may she have acquired since she became autogenic and autonomous?

"Never mind for now," John shrugged, and left the bridge.

Perhaps his sudden feeling of loneliness led him to look for traits in Delta which she could not possess. But if that was so, then why was she so infernally human? Why had they made her so womanly? Surely her designers, of all people, could not have suffered from a lack of imagination. Yet they seemed to have completely ignored the effect she might have on a man, on her fellow crewman. Particularly on long treks. Or could it have been intentional?

In his quarters John ignored his need for literature. Instead, he dialed, yet again, for information on Delta. He hoped she had been too busy doing her job to monitor the hytapes he had selected. Why should I feel embarrassed about what an android might think of me? John felt a little ridiculous!

The pulsating light announced that the hytapes were ready. John put on his helmet and swiveled the video attachment in front of his eyes. Almost immediately his body relaxed under the influence of hypnotic induction. He reviewed the hytapes for additional info. Most of it he had absorbed previously. His left hand played with the keyboard. Part of his brain, which retained a degree of normal awareness, dialed for video tapes of Delta's construction. He reviewed them from the inception to the present. A half hour later, he dialed 'reset', scanned the videos again, and dialed 'stop'.

Slowly, John removed the helmet. He sat for an hour without moving. He was totally absorbed by the new data. Until studying the visual tapes, the hytapes did not convey the whole picture. Now he knew. He knew, but had no idea what to do with his knowledge. A few times John shrugged then seemed to slump into deep thought.

The protracted brainwork did not lead John to any specific conclusions. It failed to provide the reason why the Navy had offered Delta autonomic programming. Also it did not really explain whose decision it was to make Delta autogenic. The woman, the android, had full capability of reproducing herself. Not through a sexual method of course. But the whole creative process, and therefore reproductive technique, had been made available to her. She could clone a new 'Delta' from her own brain cells. Why?

These were questions to which John could, theoretically, find the answers on his return to Earth. But there was one other enigma. Why had Delta, within seven months of achieving her autonomy, completely redesigned her external appearance? She used to look like a glorified robot with a covering surface reminiscent of skin. Within seven months of her 'coming of age', she had reconstructed herself to look, move, feel, act and even smell like an attractive and beautiful woman. Did this 'improvement' have anything at all to do with her functionality? With her ability to serve mankind better? Was her intention to be kind to... man? Or was it for control.

Control meant Power.

During the next rest period, John's dreams did nothing to resolve these questions either. For the first time, however, his dreams were not completely devoid of a human element. At least, quasi human. Humanoid. He strolled the luscious gardens with Delta. They walked arm in arm. Like two good friends. Or had it been more than friends?

John woke up with a headache. A jet shower, a thirty-second electronic massage, and the headache was gone. The memory remained. He drank his usual liquid breakfast and went to the bridge.

Delta seemed absorbed in computer data analyses. She smiled her greeting. John nodded and went to his console.

The BLAKE was about to enter the Outer Planetary System. For reasons of efficiency, the Main has divided the System into Outer and Inner Systems. With so many planets the subdivision was useful. Almost necessary.

The first planet was magnified on the main screen: a rounded flattish ball of methane ice and dust. Surface temperature an uninviting minus 246^0 C. 27^0 Kelvin. That's pretty cold. Damn cold. Diameter 3,900 kilometers. A large snowball. It could not possibly support life. Any life. It could preserve it in a deep freeze. John wagered it didn't. It reminded him a little of Pluto but Charon was missing. It had no moon. A lonely planet.

John studied the left hand side half-screen on which Delta has projected a computer facsimile of the whole Vegan System. The orbits of all planets were indicated in different colors. BLAKE's trajectory was shown in red. It spiraled through the system gradually approaching the binary planets. Had John calculated the trajectory himself, it would have been exactly the same. Exactly. Perhaps his Number One was a mind reader.

"There, Sir. I think I have it now."

Delta leaned back from her keyboard. She'd been typing with two hands simultaneously, each hand on a different keyboard. John had not seen her do that before. Theoretically—why shouldn't she? Pianists had done it for ages. Had she concealed her abilities on purpose?

"You have what, Delta?"

"I have a report for your inspection, Sir." She sounded pleased but did not look it.

John thought he might be imagining things, but didn't Delta look, sort of 'flat'? A deadpan, noncommittal expression? Or was it... sad?

There again, she always sounded happy and he didn't always check on her appearance. He might not yet have learned the full range of her facial expressions. She must have worked nonstop since he had left her 2.74 hours ago. Patience. There had been no hurry. The orbit of the outer planet, which Delta named V17, averaged almost seven billion kilometers from Vega. There was plenty of time.

Delta transferred her findings to the main screen. It was a mass of figures, calculations. Enough to keep his own reputedly experienced brain busy for a week.

The numbers proved more complex than he first assumed. John spent the next five hours going over them. More than once. That is what one did, mostly, on star treks. Not in science-fiction, of course. In real life. Figures, calculations, projections, brain twisters... The life of an astronaut; a lot of sleep... a lot of loneliness... sometimes boredom... and figures, figures and more figures.

The numbers looked right. Did he expect otherwise? He couldn't find any loose ends. The calculations and assumptions, both looked very convincing. Only the incredible BLAKE scanners could have supplied data necessary to put these numbers together. Only Delta's positronic brain could organize them into a coherent whole, suitable for translating into actual equations. Delta could have been wrong. There may have been missing factors. Factors they hadn't thought of, as yet; some hidden ingredients.

The unknown—the unexpected.

But until they found them and translated them into a different theory, it would appear that the Waltzing Duo, the enigmatic binary planets were no longer as enigmatic. Or, perhaps, more so. The calculations indicated that the two planets were, have been, in their present configuration for the last 150,000 years. One hundred-and-fifty millennia. Give or take a thousand or two.

It also appeared that the binaries did not converge on each other. Nor had they come into their symbiotic relationship by an accident of nature. They had been placed or nudged into their present balanced positions by an intelligent will.

They had to be.

If not, they would have crushed into each other about hundred millennia ago. Given their mass and distance to each other, they had no right to be where they were.

John leaned back and withdrew into deep thought. Again. It was habit forming. Delta seemed to be the cause of most of his cerebral trances. He spent the next hour just trying to imagine conditions which might have precipitated, resulted in, the relative orbits of the planets which was studying. He needed more data. Much more data. Or a miracle.

Or perhaps... Delta?

"What made you think of taking this direction in your calculations?" John asked.

"The fact that the binary system appears to be the source of the signals." Her answer was logical, but not satisfying.

"That was all?"

She seemed a little reticent. She looked at the wall screen covered with her calculations. The deductive assumptions, the synthesizing computations, as well as the actual mathematical calculations, even when aided by the ship's main computer, would have taken John, or any reasonably intelligent experienced human astrophysicist, a week to figure out. A good week.

Not 2.74 hours.

"I suspected that the binary system, if it had been artificial, could not have been put together by... by..."

"Come on Delta. I can take it!" John encouraged. This was most unlike her.

"...by an intelligence such as the human race, Sir," Delta answered quietly.

John sat back, his eyes widening, his mouth falling wide open. He caught himself holding his breath. The substance of what Delta said was beginning to sink slowly, ever so slowly, into his cluttered mind. A mind so clogged, hampered, fettered with his puny egotistical problems and his emotional tantrums—the juvenile prerequisites of the human race. For a moment John thought that Delta has been stammering because she has been graciously attempting to protect his infantile feelings. Then the real meaning reached his recumbent cerebral cortex.

Could *not* have been... she has said.

Delta was lonely.

She had left the human race as far behind as we had left the hairy apes fighting over a banana. Delta saw, in the creative process, which had been manifest in the binary system, a kindred mind. A kindred ability. Someone with whom she might have had something in common. For a while John was stunned. Speechless. Then, recovering sufficiently to take his mind off himself, even if only for a moment, John looked at Delta with true compassion. He tried to imagine how she felt. At last, someone of her own stature almost within her grasp, and the scanners indicated no life forms on any of the planets.

"I am sorry, Delta."

She looked at him with her usual serene smile. Perhaps a warmer smile than ever before. She said nothing. What was there to say?

***

Chapter fourteen

Contact

Two weeks have passed. BLAKE continued shedding its mind-boggling interstellar velocity. Every hour their speed decreased by more than 140,000 kilometers. Well over three million kilometers in a single earth day.

Delta continued her vigil on the bridge.

During the first week after his resuscitation, for six hours out of every ten, John kept her company. The rest of the time he spent reading, learning, exercising, resting, eating and indulging in as wide a range of activities as the ship's facilities offered. He searched for ways to convert the theoretical hytape knowledge into some practical use. The volume of information John had to catch up on was astounding. His treks had left extensive gaps in his education. As John's knowledge grew, his hunger for more became obsessive.

By the end of the first week John left Delta in complete charge of all operations. Trusting her implicitly, he plunged into the ship's extensive library. He studied alphabetically, all subjects, absorbing knowledge at an ever-increasing rate. He could never have done it without the aid of hytapes. His brain, progressively augmenting its capacity, soaked up the data at the rate of ten to twelve hytapes per hour. This was equivalent to reading as many books in the same period of time.

John couldn't explain his hunger. It grew, as if fueled by influences outside his own will.

Within two weeks, John not only decreased his bridge presence to a perfunctory minimum, but skimped on physical exercises, reduced eating habits, and even cut down on sleep. All to sate his new craving. It would take BLAKE another three weeks to reduce its velocity sufficiently to enter into any selected planetary orbit. John felt there was no need of him on the bridge. Whatever he could do, Delta could do better—of that he was now convinced.

Many a time John searched his unconscious mind to explain this churning desire to raise his scope of knowledge, to increase his mental capacity, to improve on the power of his acumen.

To move closer to Delta?

Could knowledge forge a bridge between his own perceived limitations and Delta's awesome potential?

As John absorbed more—more became clear to him. When he finished the alphabetical scanning and an in-depth review of advances in all pure sciences, he turned to history. He studied the history of human race. The slow pilgrim's progress of his species. From man's straggling descent from trees to his incredibly rapid rise to the stars.

It has been a stumbling yet magnificent journey.

Rather than pity his forefathers, John grew in awe of their titanic struggle. Man had been lumbered with every possible difficulty, every encumbrance, along his audacious path. It became evident that it had not been man's eventual ability to reach for the stars that was his ultimate objective. It was the journey itself that mattered. The greatest moments in man's history were not synonymous with great discoveries or some awe-inspiring conquests. The greatest moments, so often unnoticed at the time, had been manifested in and by man's innate ability to rise above his own inherent limitations. The elusive, ephemeral, immortal moments when One had given all for the good of Many.

The efforts of the few had been so exhaustive, so demanding on the Life Force which stirred within them, that many died before seeing the results of their magnanimous labours. The mist-shrouded history still preserved records of the giants, of the 'immortal mortals', the altruistic saviours.

They were the youthful fearless conquerors that showed mankind ever widening horizons. They were the inspired prolific creators who molded the Life Force, Itself, into works of eternal enlightenment. Men showing man his ultimate potential.

Those few who claimed that men forgot how to be gods.

The philosophers, the lovers of truth, of wisdom, the composers, poets, sculptors, painters, writers, musicians... all man, women, asking naught in return for their total commitment. Their one desire in life was: to be a pure channel for Creative Spirit. For that intangible Energy which inspires all who know how to listen to Its vibrant, ostensibly silent Voice. They had been Saviors of the human species. They had been the few amongst the many, amongst so very, very many, who raised mankind towards a higher level of consciousness. Towards an awareness affording a more intense participation in the art of living. In the fullness of Life Itself.

It had not been only their deeds, per se, which John found so inspiring.

John was fascinated by the individual yet diverse journeys which each of these ancient giants had travelled. It seemed as though these few humble beings, these magnificent channels, seldom, if ever, attempted to extract any reward for their efforts. The creative act itself had been, for them, the essence of their life. These youthful, young-dying immortals, never allowed their feet to leave the dust from which they raised themselves to such esoteric heights. They soared by being the best that man can be. Their spirit had reached the most distant stars, galaxies, worlds endless, eternal. They brought heavens down to the dirt of Earth, always humbly, to the floundering masses. To the two-legged ape ever trying, often vainly, to become, one day... Human.

What am I doing here?

John, stretched himself on his favorite lounge chair. He took off the helmet. Almost as an afterthought, he switched on the wall screen. Beguiling space invaded the large, darkened room. John felt tired. His eyelids heavy, he let his mind drift far, yonder...

...he sensed his body floating, aimlessly, among the stars.

A strange, sparkling, opalescent body. A body, a union, of a million stars. Each spark an independent cell, hovering, spinning, working, ever working. Busy at its prescribed, specialized assignment. Carrying out its duty without interference, jealousy, in perfect consonance with every other cell. With every tiny universe. Each tiny cell knowing its function, precisely, its particular place, responsibility. Each fostering the greatest benefit to the Whole.

Such was the accord in his own, private universe. A Universe of universes.

A perfect scheme of things.

John's mind and body succumbed to this overwhelming concordance. A serene harmony. A peace beyond words. Satisfaction. Fulfillment.

Slowly, awed with celestial marvels, John opened his eyes.

The wall screen shimmered with tiny pinpoints of light, suspended, each in their appointed place, travelling. A ocean of spaceships on their silent journeys. Now, in full, sharp awareness, John reached out, once again. Boldly traversing the Void, his mind embraced the stars—even as moments ago he espoused the cells of his own body. Now the stars were as cells. First within a Galactic, then a Universal body. Each performing its function. A function unknown, yet strangely, intuitively, each manifesting its purpose, united in a cosmic, infinite Gestält.

John closed his eyes again. And then...

...and then heard the sublime harmony of creative effort. The awesome, majestic, Music of the Spheres...

The next time John opened his eyes, three irregular cylinders shimmered against the background of black, starry velvet. Before John had time to analyze what happened, the sparkling cylinders coalesced, solidified into human contours. Into three men. They stood, together, halfway between John's lounge chair and the wall screen. For a moment the three bodies appeared almost transparent. Then the illusion passed. The men's shoulders seemed to lower slightly, as though relaxing after a taxing experience.

John blinked, expecting that his tired eyes were playing tricks on him. A dose of over-study? Lately, not quite enough sleep? Before John had time to decide if he had suddenly gone crazy, one of the figures spoke. At first it sounded like gibberish, an incomprehensible *mélange* of sounds. Within seconds the words cleared, becoming fluent, Standard English.

"We believe you are looking for us," said the man in the center.

The other two men continued to study John with undisguised interest. All three strangers, or apparitions, were clad very similarly to John: a just-over-the-knee length tunic, long, semi-loose leg covering; easy, comfortable looking footwear. Their heads were uncovered. A good head of hair... John thought incongruously. Indeed, all three wore their hair nearly down to their shoulders, loosely tied with a narrow ribbon. The man in the middle wore maroon, the other two pale-blue, almost white apparel.

"What... who are you...?" John sat up on one elbow. "You're not real... surely?"

Then John smiled. Of course. I am dreaming. He leaned back. Or else my mind created this mirage image.

The images remained.

"In a way, we are real. In a way, you aren't," the man in the center answered. "My name is Gamman. This is Zooron and Kdoba." The man nodded to his left and right, pointing to his companions.

Frankly, John found it difficult to distinguish between them. Apart from the color they wore identical clothes, their faces had a very slight sheen to them, the color of golden suntan. Their hair was in shades of chestnut, cut to the same length. To make things worse they all looked about forty years old. His own actual age. With an indulging smile John decided to play their game. It wasn't often he had a chance to indulge in conscious dreaming. Although it did happen, a few times, lately.

"And my name is Commander John Galt, Captain of this vessel. The Federated Republics Starship BLAKE."

This time John did get up and offered a cursory Navy salute. He found it difficult to be very serious. Dreams have a habit of suddenly disappearing. In spite of that, John remembered his manners. "Do sit down, won't you?" he gestured to the chairs.

"Thank you, Commander." Gamman, evidently the spokesman for the trio, accepted the invitation. The other two followed. They all sat at the conference table with an air one would ascribe to experienced diplomats.

"What can I do for you?" John asked.

John played his part of the dream to the hilt. The three men looked knowingly at each other. The middle one smiled.

"We find you have difficulty accepting the evidence of your senses. For the purpose of this meeting, may I suggest, that we shall continue to, ah, pretend, that the testimony of your eyes and ears can be relied on as valid."

As Gamman spoke, his serene yet strangely penetrating eyes never left John's face. He seemed to study intensely John's features.

"That's fine with me." John wasn't about to argue with a mirage. A phantom.

The only problem was that John developed an overwhelming desire to pinch himself. He needed confirmation that he was dreaming. Then John remembered his bracelet. His hands dropped to his lap and there, under the table, he switched the bracelet to two-way communication. For the last few weeks, unless otherwise required, the communication device remained in receiving mode only. Now he relaxed. He knew that should any of this charade not be the result of his over active imagination, Delta would hear all that was said at his conference table. After all, according to Delta, this Vegan civilization had been more advanced one hundred and fifty millennia ago than man was now. In spite of all this John could not help smiling at his own rationalization.

"I am sorry, Commander, but it's not going to work." It was Zooron who spoke. The others only smiled.

"Not going to work?" John asked.

"The bracelet," Zooron added.

This time John did not feel embarrassed at all. He grabbed the skin of his cheek between his finger and thumb and squeezed hard. Viciously. He looked down at the surface of the highly polished table. It was like a mirror. The skin turned red and hurt like hell. A few seconds later the area of pinched skin was the only red spot of John's face. The rest turned deathly pale.

"There is no need for alarm, Commander. After all, you did invite us here?" Gamman spoke very softly.

The last sentence had been phrased like a question. All three visitors maintained a relaxed friendly demeanor. Even their smiles were reassuring. John remained sitting. His initial tension began to lose its vise-like grip. My God! John thought. Isn't this what I've spent the last two hundred years striving for? So why the hell am I nervous? He felt annoyed with himself. The annoyance gave way to embarrassment.

"You must forgive me gentlemen. I am not used to hosting such distinguished visitors in my humble quarters." Even as he spoke he knew that every word sounded pompous, if not utterly ridiculous. My God! Two hundred years!

"It was meant to be?" offered Kdoba.

There was a long silence. John needed time to get his blood flowing in both directions. As it began finding its way to his brain again, he felt better—just a little.

"You did say I called you?" John asked.

"Yes. We three listen for Contact. I am the translator, Zooron the telepath, and Kdoba works a lot, ah... in an advanced time dimension."

John had an impression that Gamman was looking for a different word but couldn't find it.

"Forgive me, Mr. Gamman..."

"...just Gamman. The name includes the title."

"Very well, Gamman, forgive me if I do not understand your answer. I asked you to explain how is it that I called you." John was beginning to stand his ground.

"In a million and one ways my friend." It was the telepath who answered. "These last few days you have been calling out with considerable fortitude. Finally, when you tuned yourself to the music of the spheres..."

"....we decided that you were ready," Gamman finished for Zooron.

"I am afraid that is not very clear to me..." John confessed lamely.

It was then John realized that when Zooron was talking, his lips were moving. And how in Holy Space did these guys get here anyway.

"By means which in your world would be called a transporter. It is now beginning to be used on the Moon Base to transport fairly complex molecular structures. Our mode is similar but it works on the principle of differential vibrations."

Unwittingly John sat up. "How do you know what is happening on the Moon?"

He looked at the three faces. All three remained silent. This time only Zooron was smiling. Telepath of course. John wondered if he could hide any of his thoughts from him. John shook his head trying to clear the cobwebs. All this was very different from anything and everything he'd ever imagined. Assuming it was really happening.

"You mentioned earlier that the bracelet is not going to work. Can you explain?" John remembered Zooron's admonition.

"We have rendered it inoperable to save you embarrassment. Your Number One officer would only be able to hear your voice. By the same token your ship's instrumentation will not register our presence," Zooron answered.

This time his lips were moving. John had a distinct impression that using his mouth to talk was a concession for his benefit only.

"I can't say that you made it much clearer...?"

In fact John didn't even begin to understand what was going on. He wanted to ask about ten million questions and instead he was talking about a stupid bracelet.

"We are communicating with you at a different frequency of vibrations. You might say that we feel your thoughts rather than hear them. Conversely, we emit certain vibrations when we address you. You receive them at the emotional level, then your mind translates our concepts into symbols which you can then comprehend visually and audibly," Zooron continued, while studying John's face as though to assure himself that he had been getting through. "Delta, whose mental capacity exceeds our expectations, does not possess an endocrinal system which would enable her to communicate at this particular level of vibrations."

"If you cannot communicate with her than how do you know about her mental capacity?" John was still confused.

"Why, from you, Commander. All that we know about you, your species, or about the history of human race, or about Delta, is only from you. You are our only source of information," Gammon assured.

"You mean that you read my mind?" John thought it had been presumptuous of them.

"We have kept pace with you since you emerged from the stasis. With the exception of your dreams, we did not approach you. In your sleep, your Alpha brain waves, or rhythms, indicated to us the first aspects of your psyche, which we studied only as concerned spectators. After all, Commander, if your planet had been approached by an interstellar spaceship wouldn't you attempt to learn as much as you could about the newcomers?" Gamman's logic was convincing. "And by the way. We did not read your thoughts, we only listened to your strongest emotions."

"There is a big difference?" John asked.

"In a practical sense only. Thoughts can be masked, distorted, influenced by many external factors. Emotions on the other hand, particularly in one's dreams, cannot lie." His quiet, calm 'voice', indicated that Gamman, as well as the others, held large reserves of tolerant patience.

"Are you the people who put up the binary planets in their orbit?" John jumped the subject like a little boy who finally realized that daddy knows all the answers.

"Not exactly us. You might call them our forefathers." It was Kdoba who answered.

"So it is an artifact... " Delta's been right. Again.

There was a moment's silence. Suddenly, without any warning, Gamman rose and bowed to John. The other two followed in quick succession.

"We must leave you now Commander Galt. If you allow us, we shall be glad to show you our planet. We hope you will find it as beautiful as the gardens we have seen in your dreams."

At this, all three smiled as though sharing some private joke. John had not seen anything funny in Gamman's invitation.

"You mean you are going now?" John jumped to his feet, suddenly realizing what Gamman just said. "I mean... must you?"

The three men were already in the middle of the room in the place where he first saw them.

"We shall be in touch..." John heard, or rather felt, the words, even as three shimmering cylinders of light enclosed his visitors.

John stood rigid for some minutes, his breathing a little irregular. Then he walked to the spot where the three men just disappeared. There was no sign on the resilient flooring, or ceiling, or anywhere, of their residual presence. No telltale energy burns on the ornamental rug. No sign that the trio had ever existed. John wondered how long it would take his mind to reject the meeting and reclassify it as an imaginary experience. He looked at the table. There too he found no signs of anyone uninvited ever visiting his quarters. No one had left behind an item, a memento, a bracelet or any tiny, elusive, priceless artifact.

And then the full impact of what had just transpired expanded, virtually exploded, in John's head. His iron willed self-control had left him. John staggered. His feet refused to support him. He leaned against the table to keep himself from falling.

He'd made contact. The first ever Contact.

CONTACT.

They were not alone. The human species had not been alone. John reeled towards his lounge chair and collapsed, exhausted. The magnitude of the event was only now reaching his full awareness. With superhuman effort he rose to his feet only to collapse once again. John wanted to run to the bridge—to share his news with Delta. But... he had been warned. He had to think this out. My God! The human race makes its first contact with another species and there is no one he can share his news with.

No one.

Suddenly John felt even more alone than he did before he had met his three visitors. From which planet were they? Can I be sure I did not imagine all this? I've been reading too much. Much too much. Did I not imagine all the stars in a cosmic Gestält? Is that not a sign of mental aberration? My God, I am tired.

I am so very tired...

It was not John's physical body that was drained of its strength. It was the whirlwind that assaulted his inelastic emotions. John would learn later, much later, that the first conversation of this nature, conducted at such length, can exact a much more severe toll than he was now paying. That is why, he also learned later, the three men had left in such a hurry. One of them, the Kdoba, had sensed that John was at the end of his 'emotional' rope. Had he been subjected to any more of this Contact, at the very first session, the results may well have been much more traumatic.

There was so much to learn.

Normally it takes three days before the first conscious Contact is attempted. Three days during which the subject is divorced from any sensory inputs. During this time the subject is allowed to relax in, a sort of, no man's land. In a state where the old and the new are witnessed but only as a spectator. Not many men can face the completely alien and retain their sanity. There lurked, in every man, the desire for the unknown. This desire was delicately balanced with a redeeming influence of xenophobia. True, the cure had often proven worse than the disease. But, as John also learned later, there was a reason for everything.

Yes... everything!

The lounge chair embraced John like a forlorn lover. It gave way to his contours, it vibrated with the gentlest massage. John slept for over three hours. He needed every second. He did not dream at all. He woke up with a single thought on his mind. The thought repeated the name: Delta.

Delta, Delta, Delta...

He had to be able to tell Delta of his contact. Not just for his sake, but for hers.

Without rising from his perennial lounge chair, John dialed for all data on the endocrinal system. He learned an awful lot about glands and glandular secretions. In his mind he dissected the thyroid, the adrenal and the pituitary, the glands that secreted directly into the blood stream, and those which dealt with expulsions of substances from the organism. He searched for a single mention of any emotional linkages. Other than finding that some secretions had a direct bearing on human behaviour, little was said about direct emotional tie-ups.

John refused to give up. There had to be a way. And then he had it.

If those beings contacted him again, he would ask them for assistance. He would ask them to find a way, in which he could share the good news with his only partner. His only friend, Delta. After all, in so many ways, she had proven herself a lot more than human. It was she who truly needed Contact. Oh, surely, the human race was dying. John would gladly, without the least hesitation, offer his life to help his distant cousins. But John knew, that when the last curtain had fallen, and the echoes of final applause dissipated in the empty theater, the human race would have brought its demise upon itself. But Delta? What had she done to deserve such a quick ending? The linage of her race had only just started.

John needed help. For her. He was going to get it.

***

Chapter fifteen

Ziircon

"When you have time, Delta, would you extract for me from the ship's library, or from your own records, anything you can find concerning the relationship, if any, between human glandular system and human emotions?" John asked as he entered the bridge.

"Anything, Sir? Endocrinology is a broad subject."

"I have reasons to believe that our endocrinal system, if I can call it that, may have a bearing on the intuitive range of our emotional response," John said, in an attempt to explain.

Not being at all sure of what he was talking about did not make it any easier. John was groping in the dark, but anything was better than doing nothing. The alternative would be to tell Delta about his "Contact" and wait until she stopped laughing. John did not relish the prospect. "Very interesting, Sir," she'd say, politely, adorning the answer with her usual smile. Then the smile would be replaced by a superb expression of concern. "Have you been sleeping well lately, Sir?" she would ask.

No. It was definitely a safer course to prepare for all contingencies before coming clean, as the saying goes. The fact that John found nothing conclusive in the prodigious annals of the ship's library did not mean that Delta would meet with equal disappointment.

"Perhaps, Sir, if you might narrow the field a little. Are you principally concerned with limiting, or with acquiring a greater control over the range of your emotional response? Or with improving on mine?" Delta asked innocently.

John took a sharp breath. Could she be that intelligent? Or did she really possess and hide some germinal telepathic abilities. John studied her beautiful features but found no answer. No clues whatever.

"Why do you ask?"

"To limit the range of research," Delta repeated.

"No other reason?"

"Should there have been any, Sir?"

Delta's face looked as far from devious as any face can. Correction. As any human face can look. Were all her facial reactions premeditated? Were there any built in, automatic grimaces? Would she be able to hide her feelings, if she had any? Questions that needed answers. At least John needed them. Badly.

"What do you think about human emotional response?" John answered with a question.

"It seems to interfere with logical analyses and the subsequent synthesis. That is why I had been given, by my creators, the automotive capability. At a certain stage of my development, my creators realized, if I surmise correctly, that their emotions had been interfering with my, if I may use the word, natural development?" Delta explained.

"Elaborate, please."

"My Creator, I use the term generically as there had been a considerable team involved with my coming into existence, realized that their emotional reactions would have led them to build into me not only the rationality of a human brain, but also their own, personal, weaknesses."

"Then they regarded emotions as weakness?"

"Not as such, Commander. Only in the absence of controlling factors. At the time of my autonomic freedom, humans had not, as yet, discovered any mechanical means of controlling their emotional responses." Delta appeared to have a perfect recall of her past.

"Drugs?" John offered.

"Drugs subdue or exacerbate the emotions, not control them. In order to control ones emotions at will, it would be necessary to be able to increase or decrease the range of the response to a much greater and reliable degree." Delta glanced at her Captain. "Even as a positronic brain can be controlled and therefore used beyond the limitations of a biochemical brain, although both are grown, or cloned, from human neuronic tissue."

So that was what all this was about. Control. John began to understand. Delta's positronic brain wielded, like it or not, an enormous power. If she suffered from uncontrolled emotions, she could abuse that power, to the full limit of her mental capacity. She could easily become a fully-fledged dictator of the human race. By the power of her brain alone. What could the answer be, then? Was there an answer?

"Would you like to have the capability of an emotional response?" John asked.

"Only if it could be proven that there is an advantage, a pluralistic benefit, to having such a dangerous... weapon," Delta replied gravely.

Why is it that people are not capable of such an unselfish comment? John was as sure as one can be, that when Delta said 'advantage', she did not mean—to herself. "One has to be the very best one can be," she'd once told him. "Isn't this true of every one?" she'd added. Could any thinking entity, human or android, be that innocent?

"What if it could be proven?" John asked after a protracted silence.

"I keep my mind open."

"And how would you go about it?"

"How would I go about proving that the possession of a fully controlled emotional response would be advantageous to furthering ones development?" Evidently Delta needed to be precise.

"Yes."

"It doesn't need proving, Sir. The answer is: of course. It would be advantageous." The answer, to her, sounded obvious. The question—elementary.

John sat up, his brow knitting together. This was a completely new tack. A different, fresh wind was filling John's sails.

"The problem remains, Sir, that the human race did not, as yet, think of a way of controlling it."

Delta put a damper on the new tack. John had been right back where he came from. He tried one more stab.

"And why do you think it would be advantageous to have such capability, assuming one could fully control it?"

"There are two basic reasons, Sir. One, evolution has proven that any additional capability, when exercised properly, can open new horizons. New capabilities are needed to assure survival. The second reason is, in a way, connected with the first. You see, Sir," her voice sounded sadly persuasive, "I can only induce, adduce, analyze and synthesize. That limits my thinking processes to those we can define as deductive. I am not capable of, what I can only call, creative thought. There appears to be an intangible link between creativity, I use the word in its strictest sense, and the emotional response. I do not mean manufacturing, making, producing, or any method or manner of transforming one into another. I mean creating in the sense of thinking about something which had never been thought of before."

Delta's voice was well 'controlled', but John thought, perhaps imagined, that there was a sad note there, somewhere. But isn't sadness a feeling, an emotion? If it were possible for an android to have misty eyes, then Delta, at that moment, had misty eyes.

Some time later John returned to his private quarters.

Delta's, or rather BLAKE's, probes, sensors and scanners had not revealed any intelligent life on any of the planets. Not even a smidgen of hope. John knew that if he had not dreamt about the meeting in his room, then they, the trio, and God knows how many others like them, would reveal themselves when they were good and ready. Not before.

Certainly not before.

John's enigmatic visitors had an edge of 150,000 years over human technology. According to Delta, probably a lot more. That's quite an edge. John wondered if the Vegans, as he thought of them, had their own 'Deltas'. Their own creations which jumped ahead of their own creators, yet continued along; coming for the ride, perhaps, for reasons of their own.

John once again felt tired, preoccupied, a little nervous. He had no idea what to do with the knowledge he carried in his head about the Contact. He began pacing his room. After a while John walked over to the spot where the three men had appeared out of nowhere. He stood there thinking about their sudden arrival. He tried to imagine, to feel their presence. Nothing happened. He shrugged and sat down on the carpet as though to meditate about his unenviable situation. John enjoyed sitting cross-legged. After spending most of his life on his back, half-lying or sitting position sitting cross-legged was fun. Closing his eyes, he breathed deeply, endeavoring to relax his wrought nerves.

The room was spacious, airy, off white. Diffused light was emanating from the walls, the ceiling, all around him. John felt 'light', physically and mentally. He felt no fatigue, no tension. He had no desire to move, to do anything. It was nice being here. Just being. Relaxing.

"Welcome to Ziircon, Commander." The voice came from behind him.

Slowly, almost against his will, John turned his head. He was still sitting cross-legged on a white floor. The surface was soft and tepid to the touch. As John turned, he saw Gamman sitting on a simple bench, possibly carved out of a single slab of white marble. Only, it looked soft. For reasons John could not understand he did not feel nervous.

Zzzeeerc'n? Planet Zzzeeerc'n? It sounded like a long zzz followed by a long eee. John's inner eye saw it as a long

iii. A little like a buzzing of a bee cut short by the last syllable.

"Gamman?" John made to rise, but his host's hand restrained him.

"Relax for a minute longer. There is no hurry," Gamman assured. "We do not rush things here. There is no need to. Time is a little slower, so we have plenty of it." There was a soft, reassuring smile radiating from Gamman's eyes.

"I am on your planet Ziircon?" John pronounced the name as best he could.

"You did want to visit us, did you not, Commander?" The question, although academic, sounded genuine.

John's emotions took the better of him. He began shaking in a silent, deep felt laughter. It had not been a case of puerile merriment. It was a release of tension. A tension built up over some two hundred years of his wondering life. The emotions swirling within John's heart were powerful, having never been acted upon. Just felt intently.

Gamman was as good as his word. He neither pushed nor interfered with John's need for a slow acceptance of the elusive becoming real. He may have reached back in his own ancient memory, or perhaps he remembered other intelligent species going through the same stages of acclimatization. Although lately, the last thousand years or so, these had been fewer and fewer.

Gamman's smile carried a trace of melancholy. Yes, he did remember what the various races had gone through. He knew that sooner or later he would have to tell John the Truth. Not all at once, though. The shock might send him over that precarious edge dividing the sane from those who relinquished their conscious sanity to protect their subconscious stability. The reality was seldom as easy as one would have liked. It was also seldom as beautiful. Although that, too, depended on ones point of view. If only people realized that sooner...

"How did I get here?" John asked, his voice almost normal.

"The same way we visited you."

Gamman very presence exuded serenity. The sage knew that the beginning, for new comers, had always been very difficult. "In time you will understand this mode of transportation better. For now you must trust me that no harm will come to you, neither here nor in transit."

"I wasn't worrying about that. I am simply trying to learn," John countered, a little hurt at having his courage questioned. By now he fully recovered from his initial nervous reaction. "Gamman, I must learn as much as is physically possible. You know that. If you can read my mind, you also know that my race is facing extinction. Therefore you know why I am here."

"Is that all?" Gamman asked.

"Are you testing me?"

"I am not testing you, Commander. And I cannot read your thoughts. Zooron can but he is busy elsewhere right now. Remember I read your emotions not your mind. Your emotions tell me that you left something unsaid. If I am wrong, I apologize," Gamman continued in a very calm, soothing voice. It was as if he'd said: I am dealing with emotions, not mental concepts.

John smiled in spite of himself. "It is I who must apologize, Gamman. You are right of course. There is another reason, but it is... more personal."

"All things are personal, Commander. You are the center of your universe. It cannot be otherwise."

Gamman looked pleased. He felt, in John, a recognition of what he just said. He also remembered the images John had invoked immediately prior to their first meeting. "But you already know that," he affirmed, a deep satisfaction in his eyes.

"It is about Delta. My Number One officer," John sighed. "My only officer."

"The officer without the capacity to feel emotions," Gamman offered. "At least not in the human sense?"

"Must that remain a permanent condition?" John couldn't hold back a tone of hope in his voice. He probably needed a positive reassurance on this subject more than on any other subject under the sun. Including the Vegan sun.

"Few things in life are permanent, my friend. Those few which are—must be accepted. But the impossible, as your saying goes, usually takes just a little longer."

Gamman continued to regard John with paternal concern. It was a little strange since the two man looked about the same age. Perhaps here, on Ziircon, age was counted in a different way.

"How old are you?" John changed the subject for no reason he could fathom.

"One thousand one hundred and twelve of our years. About seven thousand Earth years. Why, does this matter?" Gamman looked surprised.

"It explains your patience with me. It also says a lot about your disinclination to hurry things. I do not share the same advantage."

On Earth John felt like an ancient. Here he qualified as a juvenile—in more ways than one.

Suddenly John felt a pang of panic. The reason for his expedition flooded his mind.

There was a lengthy silence. For a while Gamman sat motionless. Then he rose slowly and walked up to one of the vertical slots seemingly carved in the tall walls. He appeared to study something outside. He looked pensive.

John felt he might have gone too far. He came to ask for help. To beg, if necessary. Not to admonish or instruct on ethical duties of human pilots who, together with a few billion people, got themselves into a terminal condition. The condition was hardly Gamman's fault.

"First, I must ask you to trust me. Even if the way we do things here may seem slow or strange by comparison to your ways. You must trust me, my dear friend. If you do not, there is very little I shall be able to do for you. Or for your people."

All this Gamman said in a voice that, while still calm and kind, did not encourage discussion. The tone implied that he did not state an opinion, but an immutable fact.

"I am in your hands." John knew it and meant it.

"Could you come here, to the window?" Gamman asked.

John joined his host at the vertical slot. It was wide enough for both of them to enjoy a panoramic view of the... city? It looked more like a park with enormous sculptures. The sculptures seemed to have some utilitarian purpose. John felt that. He had no idea how, but he did. The object straight ahead corresponded, in height, to about twenty stories. But the building, if that's really what it was, looked like a giant fountain, which discharged its waters at a great height. Then, while the water continued to cascade downwards, it froze, creating a semi-transparent, greenish crystal. The crystal looked completely solid, inert. Yet, as John continued looking at it, the greenish translucent material began to shimmer, giving off reddish sparks, rather like a burst of dry snow against a dying sunset.

John stood, flabbergasted, stunned. The beauty was unworldly, in the truest, most precise sense of the word. Impossible. Yet happening in front of his eyes. Time slowed down, hovered, became immaterial. John perceived new waters creating minute rivulets at the top of the building. The tiny streams descended in a grotesquely slow motion, insinuating themselves into the frozen sculpture. They were the shimmering waters of... there really were no words to describe John's vision. One had to feel it...

After an indeterminate time, Gamman waved his hand and the window became opaque. The fountain was gone—a figment of John's imagination? John felt a pang of annoyance at this sudden dismissal. He wanted the view, the creative process, to continue. He wanted... and then John remembered Gamman's admonition about a 'different' time passage on Ziircon. How long has he stood there? A minute, an hour? How did they measure time here?

Once again, John forgot why he was there. It no longer seemed so important. Particularly the problem of the human race. Delta? Delta was different. She deserved to see this. Could she? Could she ever?

"You feel very strongly about Delta," Gamman observed.

John finally accepted that while his host could not read his thoughts, he could construe an awful lot from his emotions.

"How did this happen?" John pointed to the darkened window.

"You do not know?" Gamman raised one eyebrow. His, heretofore, passive features had been rapidly acquiring a broad spectrum of human facial expressions.

John was a little startled by Gamman's question. There had to have been a reason why Gamman asked it. A reason. Hasn't Gamman already said, once, that there was a reason for absolutely everything? Or was it someone else. After thirty years in a stasis, too much was happening, all at once. John had difficulties concentrating. Who said what, when, and wherefore? Did it matter that much? He had no idea what Gamman was talking about. John thought, that at Gamman's age the ancient could be...

"No, Commander, he is not as yet senile. I can testify to that. Upon my honor!" The voice belonged to Zooron, who either walked in silently, or insinuated himself into the large chamber without John's knowledge.

"Ah, Zooron! I didn't..." John started.

"Of course you didn't. And he isn't, and I am not. Hungry, that is," Zooron assured, a twinkle in his eyes.

Zooron's white-blue clad figure seemed to float rather than walk along the white floor. When John walked on it, the floor gave way under his weight like a deep plush pile carpet. There was no such a reaction from the carpet when Zooron approached him.

"I feel rather lighthearted today..." Zooron threw over his shoulder, turning towards Gamman. "Should you not offer

our visitor some refreshments?" he asked, a pretentious
accusation half-hidden in his voice. Somehow John did not
think that Zooron was serious. Why?

Gamman waved his hand to the right, and as John turned
he saw a white marble table displaying some fruit and a
carafe of red liquid. John could have sworn the table had not
been there when he'd walked to the window. Zooron filled a
tall, cut-crystal glass and drank with considerable gusto.
When he finished, he turned to John.

"I firmly recommend it. It quenches thirst, replenishes
lost energies, and stimulates good digestion. Further more, I
must..." Zooron was in a very good mood.

"All right, Zooron. Thank you for the reminder."
Gamman turned to John. "Would you care for some
refreshments?"

John was halfway between being annoyed at Zooron's
interruption and laughing at the telepath's antics. He decided
on the latter. He walked to the table, chose an apple and bit
into it. It was juicy and sweet. Not too sweet. It was perfect.
After a few bites he had to ask: "How come your apples are
so much like our own, on earth? Only, I must say, even
better."

"You have only yourself to thank for that, Commander,"
Gamman assured gravely.

"And me, since it was my idea to start with!" Zooron
would not give in.

"And Zooron's," Gamman admitted.

After finishing the apple, which had an almost
nonexistent core, John tried some of the liquid. It was less
sweet than the apple but a lot more thirst quenching. John,
used to the continuous eating and drinking of synthetic food
on board the BLAKE, could not imagine any better fruit or
drink on Earth. Or on Ziircon.

The thought of Earth brought John back to his mission.
He began to feel guilty at having such a good time. The two
Ziirconians became instantly serious and attentive.

"Ah, yes. Your mission." Zooron said. "Gamman told me." He pointed to his head. Then Gamman took over.

"I can set your heart at rest that the human race is not facing such grave problems as you presently imagine. It may be difficult to do, but... you must trust me completely. I guarantee that you will return to your Earth with a much lighter heart." He looked at John with a strange, almost enigmatic kindness.

It felt as though an ancient grandfather was talking to a small boy sitting on his lap, trying to explain things which the youngster would find easy to understand in time, but which appeared, at present, quite incomprehensible. John was not prepared for such an answer. His first reaction was to quote, verbatim if need be, extracts from the Galactic Navy confidential report which had proof, beyond a reasonable doubt, that the days of intelligent life, indeed any life on Earth, were quite definitely limited. Yet, when John looked at Gamman, then Zooron, he decided to keep his council.

At this moment their faces indicated compassion rather than readiness for a scientific discussion. It would have been easier if the Ziirconians disputed his figures. Or even mentioned the G.N. report. But they didn't. It was as though their confidence was based on completely different points of reference, which appeared to have nothing at all to do with any scientific facts.

It was hard on John.

Hard on a man whose whole life, whose day to day survival, relied exclusively on scientific data. On proven facts. Not figments of his or anyone else's imagination.

"Delta is quite another problem," Gamman said slowly. "You must let us dwell on it for a little while. But remember John, never, never lose faith. More importantly, never loose hope. The residual quality will then take you through. Always."

Now Gamman talked in riddles.

John felt tired. Not physically; a different type of fatigue. He felt a diminished capacity to keep facing, absorbing alien concepts. John felt that what was being said was but a small part of that which registered in his subliminal awareness. He had no idea how long he was already down here. Was it down? Closer to the sun, to Vega? John still had no idea which planet they were on. Where was Ziircon's orbit in relation to Vega? Did the instruments really not show any signs of life in this system? John felt drained. Too many unknowns...

"So there is hope...?" he whispered.

"I think you already know the answer to that, John." Gamman's words were strangely reassuring. More so than a direct affirmation.

Only then did John notice that Gamman had used his first name instead of the formal 'Commander'. A serene, trusting smile slowly replaced John's uncertainty.

And then a shimmering cylinder of light enclosed John's body and deposited him on the rug in his private quarters on the BLAKE.

***

Chapter sixteen

Delta Dobbs

Biting ones tongue is not the most recommended pastime.
Particularly if and when carried out on a regular basis. It can
lead to infection, certainly frustration, and the resultant
dejection. Yet dejection was the last word that could possibly
apply to John Galt under the present circumstances, though
each time John faced Delta, he bit his tongue.

John's emotional body was humming at such exuberant
frequencies, that if it weren't for his previously established
precedent of spending most of his time in the seclusion of his
own quarters, he would have exploded in the form, if not
force, of a minor nova. Figuratively speaking of course.
Although, at times, he wasn't so sure.

John found it extremely trying to spend any time in
Delta's company and maintain a stony silence about Contact.
After the first meeting in his quarters, he had considerable
difficulty reconciling himself to the new reality. Now, John
would no longer be willing to swear that his apparent visit on
Ziircon could be dismissed as a latent effect of his overactive
imagination. An imagination held at bay for some thirty odd
years in the straightjacket of hibernation. After all, John had
never spent such a long time in stasis before. Who could tell
what would be the psychic, psychological, or emotional
aftereffects of such a long withdrawal from physical reality?

That was then. This was now.

John's residual doubts were gradually dissolving, leaving
behind a deep conviction that although he did not understand
too much of what was going on, neither would a monkey if
faced with the latest human technology. There were subtle

details that remained unexplained. These fragments continued to have a dream-like intangible quality.

But I have been down to their planet, John repeated to himself again and again.

Down to Ziircon.

He had walked on their soil, or at least, their floor. He had visited, even if only through a window, their city; eaten their fruit, tasted their strangely satisfying nectar. He spoke with them—at length.

The Ziirconian logic was persuasive even though, on occasion, testing his credulity. John could even testify to Zooron's, sense of humor. But the most vital aspect of Contact had been his total and absolute recall of the encounters. John's recall included the visual, auditory, olfactory, tactile, and even the sense of taste. It further demanded of him to exercise his knowledge, imagination, faith and cordiality. In fact, the experience of Contact was a Total Experience. This all-inclusiveness was not in the domain of dreams. Dreams may have invoked some of these characteristics but there were always a few loopholes. Little missing fragments. Here, John could recount the course of both encounters in minute detail. He could repeat, verbatim, all that had been said. He could accurately describe Ziirconians' facial expressions.

And this was exactly what John did.

He opened a file, protected it with "CAPTAIN'S EYES ONLY" encoding, and proceeded to describe what took place at the two meetings. Even as John dictated his report, his fantastic recall continued to amaze him. If anything, it seemed to be improving. Was that a hidden clue? Or was it merely that Contact was the single most important event in history? Well, in the most recent history of the human race, at least. As such, it may have mobilized his mind and his psyche subconsciously, while mobilizing the potential reserves of his beingness. It was a subliminal effort to record all details, no matter how small, in case any single item might prove of immense value later.

When John completed what he considered his duty, he felt a lot better. He even thought of facing Delta, pretending that nothing has happened. How he wished the Ziircons would release him from an implied obligation to keep silent; to hold back until they could furnish Delta with the capacity to recognize them. To see them. To feel them? Did this make any sense? Capacity to recognize them. For that, according to them, Delta needed an emotional response capability. Isn't that, essentially, what they said?

John took the shuttle to the bridge, said hallo to Delta, and sat at his console. It was hard to accept that the first Contact took place only two days ago. Two days ago, after a two hundred year Galactic search. It seemed that ages had passed since the three enigmatic beings stepped out of their shimmering cylinders of light, their transporters, and met him, face to face, aboard his own ship.

"Anything to report, Delta?" John watched her from the corner of his eye. He was beginning to feel guilty.

"Yes, Sir. I have prepared a brief for you. Here it is."

She dialed with her left hand keyboard and the main screen lit up with charts, diagrams, and a three dimensional trajectory simulation.

John could hardly believe his eyes. The masses of data had been subjected to such orderly screening that he, who had hardly kept in touch with the bridge during the last three weeks, could, within minutes, catch up with the essentials of their Vegan system exploration.

"How do you do it...?" he wondered out loud.

"I surmise your question is rhetorical?" Delta smiled sweetly.

To look at her, one would imagine that Delta was a young lady who had just spent an extended holiday on one of the colonies. Perhaps leaping in the Lunar caverns. She looked relaxed, perhaps a little pale due to spending all her time indoors, but fresh and rested. In truth, Delta, to John's knowledge, had not left the bridge for at least three weeks. She didn't even look bored.

Now that John had the entire ship at his disposal, he seemed to forget that he had spent many decades sitting in very much more cramped quarters than Delta was now occupying. John had sat or reclined in a commander's chair, the only chair, in the only compartment, hooked up to a thousand and one tubes and wires, which, in turn, fed him, vacated his wastes, maintained his muscle-tone, took his temperature, pulse, brain waves... Compared to such conditions, Delta was enjoying palatial comfort. Did she need comfort? Was it part of her programming, self-induced or otherwise, not to need periods of either mental or physical relaxation? He'd asked her that once before. He was not satisfied with her answer.

"Thank you Delta. This is the best report I have ever seen in my life. And since for the last two hundred years all the reports I ever saw had been prepared by myself, I know what I am talking about!" There was humor, somewhere there, in his statement.

"Thank you, Sir. I try to do my best." She took it as a direct complement.

"Delta, what would you do if you ever made a mistake?"

"I would correct it, Sir. Why do you ask? Have you noticed an error in my report?"

She was not on the defensive. She simply wanted to know. Surely the Commander would not have asked such a question without a reason.

"I am creating a hypothetical situation. Would it not worry you, so to speak?"

"Worry is an emotional response that delays implementing corrective measures. I do not believe I would delay such measures in order to 'feel' sorry for myself, Sir." Her explanations sounded logical enough to John. He was not ready, as yet, to give up, though.

"Wouldn't such a condition, this emotional response, also stimulate one to put a greater effort into the execution of the remedial measures?"

"Greater than what, Sir?" Delta's positronic brain, apparently did not foresee putting in a lesser effort.

John realized that he had been walking in circles. He could not punch a single hole in Delta's armor of logic. Not even a chink. Yet he desperately needed to break through, to find a weakness, to find something in common with this beautiful paragon of virtue. Even the Ziircons did not claim perfection or omniscience. Did not Gamman say that in Delta's case they, those immensely advanced beings, needed time to dwell on the problem?

John began contemplating some ridiculous ideas to provoke Delta into an emotional response. He could attempt to confuse her, by accusing her of imaginary errors. He could try to accuse her of deliberate lies. Or he could strike her. Physically. In relation to him, her specs gave her strength factor edge of thirty-four to one. In her favour. Could she kill him accidentally? In self defense? Obviously John had no desire to hurt her. Only to provoke her to an irrational response.

My God! John suddenly realized the implication of his last thought. He equated emotional with irrational. Was that true? Are emotions in direct opposition to rationality? If so, this was the single greatest challenge the human race had to face. Rather than think of ways to add this capability to Delta, he should be thinking of ways to eliminate his own glandular system.

A moment later John remembered Delta's own words: *I am not capable of creative thought.*

So that is the price for emotional response. Delta may well have superseded man's mental potential, but if it hadn't been for man, she would not exist. She referred to the team that had put her together as the 'Creator'. It appeared that, as usual, she was right. John wished that he had other things to occupy his mind. At least for a while. The moment John formulated this thought he felt a powerful desire to go to his quarters. He was becoming impulsive.

"I'll be back, later," he threw over his shoulder.

John felt compelled to go to his room at once. Now. Even as he stepped into the elevator, he began to 'feel' their presence. He was developing new abilities. Something like an emotional telepathy. Whatever that might be.

Impatient with the door scanner, John practically ran into his room. He made a mental note to switch the security scanner off. Permanently. After all, who was likely to enter his quarters without permission? Who from among the ship's crew, that is?

The same trio who had visited him on the first occasion stood in the middle of the decorative rug. John was on the verge of assigning some mystical, or at least magic, properties to this piece of yarn. The Ziirconians bowed their heads, then smiled, rather like meeting an old, respected friend.

Gamman spoke first.

"Forgive this assault on your privacy, but you gave us the impression that the matter of Delta is exigent for you. Am I right?"

Gamman's question seemed a matter of politeness. John was convinced that the Ziircons knew better than himself what went on in his own head.

"That is only because we communicate at your subconscious level," Zooron offered, answering John's unspoken suspicion. When John looked blank, he continued. "The next stage of your evolution will be to treat your subconscious as your conscious and your unconscious as your subconscious."

Now that made things perfectly clear!

Finally John knew that he did not dream of the three men—he merely went nuts. Crazy. Mentally bankrupt. As these dire thoughts invaded his mind, the three men began laughing. The leader of his particular chorus was none other than Zooron, who seemed bent on confusing John as best he could. Finally the three calmed down.

"I often think that we all are a little crazy—at times. Taking life too seriously, for instance, should be regarded as telltale signs of mental ineptitude. To take oneself seriously, is a definitive admission of such a condition," Gamman said this in a circumspect voice, but laughter was still dancing in his eyes.

Somehow, John felt that he had passed some sort of a test. He wasn't clear what was its precise nature, but it had something to do with Gamman's statement. John felt that he was now an accredited delinquent, or the very opposite. He wished he were sure which. This time only Zooron opened his mouth to emit another hilarious roar, but Gamman waved him down. Zooron looked a little hurt.

"What Zooron was attempting to tell you, John, was that different vibrations correspond to different levels of consciousness. When you communicate with us, you do so at your subconscious level. That is why you left the bridge, not knowing fully why. When you entered your quarters, our presence quickened, or raised the frequency of your vibrations still further, and you were instantly able to communicate with us in full consciousness. Does this explanation help at all?"

As usual Gamman's question was perfunctory. The Ziirconian could see-feel, that John was beginning to catch on.

"But haven't you told me that, with the exception of Zooron, you do not read my thoughts only my emotions?" John was clearer but not clear.

"One communicates in many ways and at many levels, my friend. You do so with your eyes, your sense of touch, taste, your ears. All these must be translated, or attuned, to your subconscious, then translated into a matrix of familiar symbols. I purposely did not say subconscious mind. That would place a limitation on that state of being."

Gamman was watching John's face with his usual intensity. Evidently he practiced what he preached. He was looking for significance at different levels of communication.

It was only after this interlude that John had a chance to ask his visitors to sit down. All three seemed quite happy standing where they were. They were equally as happy to sit down. Their legs, evidently, did not get tired. To return Ziirconians' previous hospitality, John thought of offering his visitors some refreshments. All three declined, without uttering a single word, before he had a chance to ask. John wondered how he knew that.

"We are here to ask your permission to conduct an experiment," Gamman began, his face, at least to John, an unreadable mask. All John could gather was that all three regarded the matter as serious.

"I am at your service," John said, with a slight nod.

Whether John would understand the experiment or not, one thing he'd already learned. He could trust them. He also had little or no choice.

"You may change your mind, when you hear what we need you to do."

Again that somber look.

This time, the silent man, Kdoba, turned his attention directly to John. "Please do not be alarmed, but it seems expedient that you return to your planet a little faster than you intended. The experiment, if successful, would assist in expediting your departure" As John sat up, his face unduly alert, Kdoba raised his hand. "I repeat, there is no need for alarm. I speak of expediency, not of dire necessity."

"Why?" John whispered louder than he normally spoke in full voice.

"You may be of great service to your race. However, only if our experiment works. There are no guaranties." Gamman again proved to be the most comprehensive communicator.

"But why this sudden 'expediency'? What are you not telling me?" John wouldn't let go.

There was a long silence. The room seemed filled with alternating waves of serenity, echoes of profound knowledge, compassion, uncertainty. John felt those currents, but could do no more than observe their presence. He had no power to interpret them or to define them with any accuracy. Of one thing John was sure. Emotions run deep. Very deep.

Finally Gamman broke the pensive, ponderous stillness.

"There are times in racial history, which are best described as periods of great transition. Please believe me when I say that I have no wish to sound patronizing, but to say any more, at this stage, would cause your mind to reject the knowledge."

Gamman spoke quietly, with a measured, almost melodious voice. When he assumed this tone, John seemed to accept his words without question. There was a mesmeric quality in the Ziirconian's voice, as within his eyes. And John had no choice but to look into those eyes. They drew him into their depth even as a whirlpool gathers and draws in, irrevocably, adamantly. Yet rather than power, there was an immense peace within them. Gamman did not command attention, he made it irresistible.

"What will you have me do?" John asked.

"As we already mentioned, we cannot communicate with Delta. Conversely, she cannot communicate with us," Gamman continued. "We need you to obtain her permission to partake in an experiment. If it works, we might be in a position to offer great service to mankind. Your mankind."

"What are the risk factors?"

John was concerned about Delta's welfare. He seemed to care for her in ways he was not ready to admit, even to himself. In spite of her obvious superiority over him, in many areas, John continued to feel protective towards her. Could it be, in a sense, a vicarious heritage of her Creator?

"That is the problem. Our race at no time developed artificial intelligence. We seem to have evolved on slightly different lines," Kdoba answered, evidently peeking into John's thoughts. "We do not have a historical precedent for the experiment. She, Delta, would have to submit to it willingly. We have no choice but to regard her as an intelligent entity. She not only had been given autonomous capability. She took it. She accepted it. She now is a being in her own right."

Kdoba was showing signs of tiredness. It was as though he'd spent endless hours studying the problem. Tireless hours weighing the pros and cons had exhausted him.

"Can you not at least speculate?" John asked.

"Speculate?" Kdoba looked surprised. "I have been doing that from the moment we met you. I have been doing nothing else. How do you speculate on something that has no echo in all your primal memories? No similarity, no point of reference, anywhere, at any time, in all of your racial history?" Kdoba spread his hands, as though asking for help. None was offered.

"You mean that Delta can actually loose her... her... " John needed a word.

"We call it life, John," Gamman said. "The cessation of her independent conscious awareness. A loss of autonomy."

"She could become a robot?" John said softly

There was a moment's silence. Then Gamman nodded his head. "We do not know. That is why she must decide."

John suddenly realized that he still had no idea what was the nature of the experiment. As he gathered his thoughts to ask, answers came pouring in. Silent, wordless answers seemed within him. There was no question about it. The problem rested in Delta's inability to communicate at an emotional level. But...

"Delta is afraid not so much of losing her life, as of abusing any new powers which might be placed at her disposal," John whispered.

And at this moment the full impact of the problem reached John's awareness. The Ziircons were saying that if the experiment proved unsuccessful, Delta would have to be... 'terminated.' In human terms one would say killed. Destroyed. The faces of the three men confirmed his own speculations. What else was there? They might create a saint or a monster. The dice would be cast and no one, not even the ancient Ziirconians appeared to have any idea which way they might fall.

And I? All I have to do is to ask Delta if she would be willing to risk her incredible, practically immortal potential for the glory of mankind. John's thoughts seemed to permeate the room. A possible glory? Apparently, there were no guaranties. Were there ever?

John felt drawn, irresistibly, into a dark abyss of his apprehensions. His eyes closed, his mind whirling like a trapped wild animal in a cage. The Ziirconians rose silently and walked to the middle of the room. The oscillating cylinders swept them off to their beautiful planet. John stayed behind. He needed rest. He, too, was becoming tired. At least, if all went wrong, he would be no less lonely than he had been before he met Delta.

But if the experiment worked...?

John slept for an unusually long time—close to four hours. Apparently, a period of 'repair' had been overdue. The repair of his emotional body. That inner part of him that John so seldom exercised. That part, now, was subjected to an extensive effort. He hardly dreamt at all. When he did, he reverted to the verdant gardens, to whispering brooks, to the scent of wild flowers.

Once more John had lain in fields of tender grass. He walked by the still waters. He became restored.

When John woke up, he not only felt superbly rested, but his brain germinated new questions, if not answers. He remembered that someone had once said, that the real problem was to find the right questions. The answers had been always there. John guessed, or deduced, the nature of the experiment. He also saw the risks. He thought he knew the possible repercussions. The sleep had given him strength he didn't know he possessed. The strength that comes from utter disregard for ones ego for the greater good of the whole. Someone else cannot impose this particular commitment on anyone. It is only valid if assumed by an act of ones own, unfettered will.

Within minutes John rode up to the bridge. Delta looked up. Did she sense something different about him? Surely, she couldn't. Not yet!

John sat at his console and reviewed the latest reports. Even as he did, he realized the artificiality of the situation. Delta continued to perform tasks which he had spent his life doing. She was the extension, the logical conclusion, the ultimate of that which he had been or could ever become, on that particular path. He, on the other hand, took a new step forward. He had crossed a new threshold, opened new gates to worlds of a new and much, much wider range of experience. A new experience of life. A life of new experience.

"Thank you Delta," John said, on completing the review.

As always, her syntheses had been perfect. The conclusions remarkable. There were no errors that he could see, or even feel. Not within the world in which Delta's consciousness manifested its state of being.

John sat back arranging his thoughts in order. When he was ready, John started by thinking aloud. He knew that Delta would be listening. John strongly suspected that she had been programmed to listen when he talked.

"I understand that the positronic brain is cloned from human tissue. It would be reasonable to assume, that one would select the neurons which, one would have reasons to believe, were superior to a corresponding tissue from another human being. So far, I have been thinking only of a nerve cell with its dendron and axon, its communication system. That is, after all, the basis of a positronic brain. The communication system. What I have failed to consider was the most vital characteristic of your particular nerve cells: the aspect that gives it, and therefore you, your individuality. Your personality. That missing factor is the DNA. The deoxyribonucleic acid. The essential hereditary factor that carries the characteristics of your donor."

As he talked, John swiveled his chair to face Delta. She stopped working, sat back, and listened. John did not remember seeing her quite so immobile. "Am I right, so far?"

"Yes Sir."

Delta did not waste words.

"Then, we must assume, indeed, we can be quite certain, that whoever had donated his or her brain cells to you, must have been selected as the very best that humanity had to offer. You carry as good a heritage as the Creator could supply. Still on the right track?" John needed her involvement. He had it.

"Yes Sir."

No false modesty. That would be an emotional, illogical reaction.

"Therefore, we can assume, that you would inherit a predisposition to respond to the needs of the human race even as your donor would?" John continued.

"Yes Sir," she said again.

"And who might have been this donor who's innermost characteristics you carry in your positronic brain?" John knew the answer, but he wanted to hear Delta say it.

"Donna D. Dobbs, Sir," Delta obliged.

Donna D. Dobbs. The longstanding member of the Presidium of the Council of the Federated Republics. The illustrious member of the Triumvirate who had carried on her diminutive shoulders the welfare of the residual, active part of the human race. She and Hermes D. Grant. Donna, who had lived exclusively for the benefit of others. About half a billion others. That's a heavy DNA, a heavy heritage, to carry in ones neurons.

"And how would Donna D. Dobbs respond if she had an opportunity to help mankind regardless of the risk involved?" John arrived at the crucial moment.

"She would respond, Sir, that no risk could ever be too great." Delta's voice was quite dogmatic.

"And tell me Delta. Had she been aboard the BLAKE, right now, would she be prepared to trust me sufficiently to place her life in my hands?" John asked, his eyes resting on Delta's steely blue, unwinking sensors.

"Yes, Sir. Delta Dobbs would trust her Captain with her life in the interests of mankind. Regardless of risk," she added redundantly. She had never said anything redundant before. She never spoke as Delta Dobbs before.

"Thank you, Delta," John said turning away. All of a sudden, his eyes were itching with saline emotion. "I would do the same for you, Delta. Did you know that?"

"Yes, Sir. I knew that," she answered quite simply.

***

Chapter seventeen

The Experiment

For reasons known only to the Ziirconians, the experiment could not take place until BLAKE reached a particular orbit. John has been given the coordinates directly. Mind to mind. Without any further physical contact. He felt them. Although John was certain he would not forget the instructions, he entered them into BLAKE's records immediately.

In general terms, John could have guessed them.

In fact, the coordinates merely set out certain limitations. John had been told to decelerate to a velocity that would sustain BLAKE in a specific orbit around the binary system. A 700,000-kilometer apogee has been given. The perigee has been set more accurately. Under no circumstance was BLAKE to approach the binary system closer than 325,000 kilometers. By planetary standards the nominal orbit was defined very precisely.

John sensed that he would have no further contact with Ziirconians until BLAKE reached the stipulated orbit. He joined Delta on the bridge. Together they calculated the new trajectory. A period of deceleration at two gravities would place BLAKE in the desired location in good time. It would also, more or less, sentence John to two days on the bridge. Moving around under twice normal gravity is not a pleasant pastime. It is like carrying your own weight on your back. All the time. John left the bridge only when nature compelled him to do so. Otherwise, he rested. Finally BLAKE reverted to standard 4 gee pattern. Breathing became a pleasure. Thanks to the antigravs, 4 gees translated to earth normal.

John missed Contact. He missed the presence of the three men. If men they were. Especially John missed Gamman. Something obscure was happening to John whenever he met the Ziirconians. Something that he could not translate into words. John missed his newly discovered emotional capability, or whatever it was, which enabled him to see and hear and sense those advanced beings. It was not just a question of the Ziirconians being absent. John missed the state of consciousness that he seemed to partake in, when in their company. That was what John missed most. That new undefined state of being. The condition in which John functioned within his normal physical state of awareness no longer sufficed. Aboard the BLAKE John felt... not quite alive. He functioned in a half-dream state of awareness, when supposedly fully awake. It was a new paradox. A life within a half-life.

I must wake up... John told himself a thousand times.

John stared at the twin planets growing minute by minute on the main bridge display. Under 1000x magnification, the duo filled the entire screen. The computer-enhanced images were awesome.

The two polished metallic-looking spheres were of equal mass. This alone precluded their natural origin. Nature abhors exact duplication. It thrives on diversity. The planets' close proximity to each other, a concentric distance of a mere 175,000 kilometers, was quite another story. Less than half the distance between Earth and the Moon! Within the known laws of physics, the gravitational forces generated by such contiguity would have, surely, torn these planets apart. Or smashed them into each other with a titanic explosion. Yet, the only visible effect was the mobile bridge of tiniest particles. The simmering dust, flowing between the two flirting orbs.

The Waltzing Duo.

Now that BLAKE was a lot closer, another factor entered into consideration. The densities of both planets had proven far beyond those found within the rest of the Vegan solar system. Their mass suggested many times their physical dimensions defined by BLAKE's scanners. The binary was a rapidly growing mystery.

"Commander, the sensors are detecting a subtle electromagnetic field," Delta reported.

"What is our distance from the binary?"

"We are within 254,000 kilometers of our projected apogee, Sir."

"Calculate optimum deceleration necessary to reach apogee, in shortest reasonable time, and to sustain prescribed orbit."

He was thinking of his own physical limitations.

John wanted to keep as far away from any major electromagnetic fields as possible. Assuming that this field must have been generated by the binary system, he wanted to keep his distance. Did the Ziirconians know all about BLAKE's limitations? Computers did not tolerate electromagnetic fields very well. For that matter neither did human brains. BLAKE was equipped with protective shields, of sorts, but who could guess what a really powerful field might do to their propulsions system?

"We would need to use three additional gee's to enter into a self-sustaining orbit, Sir. Three gee's, for 1.876 hours in 2.47 minutes from now. The rest of the distance we can negotiate at 1.75 gees."

Delta was at her best when faced with complex trajectories.

"Make it so," he commanded, a sigh leaving his throat.

He had little choice.

John braced himself for almost two hours of considerable discomfort. He knew that Delta would have found an easier way of getting there if it were, at all, possible. They could support their orbit with their engines, but again, an unspoken voice within John's head, or heart, or whatever, made him reject this option. They would obviously maintain life support systems, but would reduce any other energy output to a minimum.

How do I know those things? John asked himself a dozen times.

John was learning to trust his inner voice.

He did not assign it to any communications from the 'unknown'. He was sure that this new knowledge did have something to do with Ziirconians, but essentially it originated from somewhere within himself. He just did not, as yet, know how. Or exactly why, for that matter.

In Outer Space the line between the known and the unknown is often blurred. There had been times, on his many treks, when John had reacted to a feeling. Intuition? Instinct? Such reactions had saved his life. Now, this extra sense was growing, ripening, with an astonishing intensity. John has actually *sensed* the orbital coordinates. This seemed a lot more than just a 'feeling'. He had to react to it. This 'feeling' would not be ignored. The first indications of a magnetic field had been, somehow, part of the answer. Without the specific coordinates they might well have approached the binary system too close. Much too close. A powerful gravitational field they could well counteract with their mighty engines. An electromagnetic field was quite another matter.

John's and Delta's consoles began swiveling away from the forthcoming gravitational pressures. When the countdown reached sixty seconds, the familiar clamps secured each of them to their respective armchairs. The helmets slid down over their heads. At three gee's and under, the security procedures were optional, but neither of them pressed the release button. There was no need to take any risks. At ten seconds the clamps tightened.

Three additional gravities weren't so bad. Physically John was in fairly good shape. All the exercising he did after coming out of the stasis helped. Following the 1.876 hours, the residual 1.75 gee's were no great hardship. One wouldn't want to spend a week in such conditions, but a few hours did not leave any scars. The extra gravities were no more tiring than say, making love for the same period of time. Only much less fun.

Delta seemed unaffected. What an incredible constitution! John remembered meeting people on Earth who had up to seventy percent of their body, including all the joints and most of muscular tissue, replaced with bionic components. At times it seemed that only their dubious-quality heads remained intact; and even there, the plastic surgery usually changed them beyond recognition. Long or short noses, whichever became fashionable. Fuller or thinner lips, wide or narrow mouths, strong or delicate chins, all could be purchased for a few credits at the Remodeling Center. John himself had some parts replaced. Not out of vanity, but to improve his resistance to various precarious conditions he had to face in his profession. But none of this even began to approach the efficacy of Delta's body. She could jump from a six storey building, turn a few somersaults on the way down, lend on her feet, and walk away as though nothing had happened. If it hadn't been against her nature to do things that did not result in some definite benefit, she had the ability to do such things—just for fun.

Two hours later John's maturing senses detected the presence of his new friends. He left the bridge, rather heavily—still under 1.75 gees, and walked to his quarters. He was right. Almost right. Only one of the trio was waiting for him.

"Gamman!" John bowed his head, in a manner he found customary on Ziircon. "How good to see you."

"Thank you, John. I missed our chats, also."

Gamman grinned in his usual friendly, relaxed manner. It was evident that the man could never be hurried. Even if he did something fast, good planning, or good foresight, would preclude the necessity of any rush decisions. And Gamman always looked as if he knew exactly what he was doing.

"Do sit down," John offered. Although Gamman did not appear to notice the additional gravities, John did.

"I understand we shall reach our destination in a few hours. When we do, you will ask Delta to enter her reduced efficiency state. It is particularly necessary to free her cerebrum from any positronic activity. We are not concerned with her cerebellum or medulla oblongata. She can maintain those systems as she wishes. Do you think you can do that?"

The usual polite question. Gamman must have known that the matter had been settled some time ago.

"Yes, Gamman. You know I can. But... can I tell her why?"

"I can tell you what we shall attempt to do. I doubt though that the knowledge itself would really help to make things easier for her. You would have to prove to her, logistically, that the effects would be beneficial. And we cannot do that."

"Why? Why can't we?" John remained worried.

"Because pure logic is based on empirical premises. And what we are attempting has no precedent," Gamman spoke very softly.

John said nothing. Delta would obey his request. He wished, though, that he could tell her more. John felt torn. He wanted to treat Delta as a human being. He found it painful to admit that he couldn't. Evidently pure logic had its limitations.

"But didn't she inherit something from her donor? Some traits that would..."

"John, we are counting on it. You must trust me."

Gamman looked at John again as a father would, regarding a backward child. Not backward through any particular shortcoming, but rather due to a condition known, among men, as... childhood. Gamman seemed moved by John's dejection.

"All our knowledge," Gamman explained, "all we know about you, or Delta, or humanity, we know from you. We cannot read your machinery. Computers. Only your mind. I do hope your facts are right!"

John sat up, worried. In spite of Gamman's words there was no lack of confidence in his voice. His eyes seemed to cut through the core of John's being.

"As I was saying," Gamman continued, "we know that Delta has inherited her neurons from a human. The fact that they belonged to Donna D. Dobbs, at this stage, does not enter into the picture. The only thing that matters is that the neurons carry the DNA, which in turn carry all the blue prints for the production of the various specialized cells. In our case the matter is made easier, because what we want to build, or stimulate, the creation of is a body, which normally, in the human sense of the word, exists within the human brain."

"It does?" John interrupted, mostly, because he needed time to absorb what Gamman said.

"It does. The body in question is the pineal body, or the pineal gland, or the epiphysis or the conarium. For some reason, you have many names for it. It all describes a pea sized gland, the shape of a cone," Gamman continued.

"The 'third eye'?" The scientists normally regard it as a vestigial sensory organ. Nobody seems to know what its present function is, if any."

"We think we know," Gamman said with a slight smile. "It is you who showed us."

"I did what?"

"Remember, all that we Ziirconians, as you call us, know about the human race is a direct scrutiny of a single representative of your species. We see Earth, the human race and the world through your eyes. Through the eyes of John Galt. And, of course, through your subconscious mind. The two, incidentally, are quite often at odds. When the disparity is serious we resort to a little test," Gamman said.

"I had a feeling I was being tested," John smiled knowingly. "On quite a few occasions," he confessed.

"It had been necessary. For your sake."

Gamman waited for a comment. When none came, he continued. "When we study your, shall we say, knowledge, or the sum total of the entity we know as John Galt, we do so at three levels. I read your emotional input. Zooron has the ability to read your thoughts. Kdoba can dig deeper. Having the ability to reach beyond the limitations imposed by time, he can sense things that happened before you were born. From him, for instance, we know that you were not born at all, in the strictest sense of the word. Kdoba, working outside the confines of time, can also reach into the future. He cannot say 'when' certain events will take place, (although he can speculate, rather well, in that realm also)," Gamman waved his arm as though dismissing the non-essential, "but he can be fairly accurate with the 'what' of the equation. Kdoba can even tell, with considerable accuracy, what will happen 'if'. Do you understand me?"

"He can see alternate futures?" John asked.

"The alternate possible futures. Exactly. He works on the assumption that all things, which we perceive, are states of consciousness. These states, according to Kdoba, already exist. What he can do is see those states without having to actually enter them himself."

There followed a lengthy silence. What Gamman said called for considerable reflection. There was no time for it now. John wanted to find out all he could, while he had a chance. He would spend hours contemplating on the various statements Gamman had made—later.

"But to reach beyond time..." John was used to scientific arguments only.

"Come, come John. You of all people know that time is relative. You people had known that already in your twentieth century. Time is a component of mass space and velocity. In true reality, we are always living in the present. Right?" Gamman smiled at John's adamant objections to accept what he already knew to be the truth.

"Are we...?"

Science was a lot easier when coming out of a computer terminal.

"You know that at the velocity of light, time 'stops'. There is no more reason for it. After all, with your mass, at such velocity, being infinite, you cannot take any 'time' to get anywhere. You are already there. So what's the point, ha, ha, of having time?"

Gamman was actually laughing. He knew that John knew all this, but continued to have emotional, atavistic attachments to old, earthly, immature concepts.

"Put like that..." John said lamely.

"Now think of your physical consciousness as a pinpoint of light. Within that pinpoint time doesn't exits. You are that pinpoint and the pinpoint is light. Within that micro-universe you are omnipresent. You do not go anywhere to see yourself. You are, so to speak, already there."

Gamman spoke slowly, giving John time to absorb the new ideas.

"As I said previously, this state of consciousness corresponds to your physical consciousness. Each pinpoint is individual, self-sufficient, autonomous. The next step is the subconscious. This time the universe of the possessor of such a state is enormously, you could say, exponentially larger. The exponent being the variable between different stages of evolution. Here the spheres of influence begin to overlap. Your subconscious and mine, overlap, rather like large circles drawn on a piece of paper with their centers less distant from each other than their respective diameters. They overlap. In that common area you and I meet. We share the space, and our relative time."

"Is this the condition which we are now experiencing? You and I being conscious within that which previously had been our subconscious?"

John was desperately trying to grasp concepts that were totally alien.

"You tell me."

"I cannot think of any other logical explanation. Although there are still moments when I associate my consciousness with my physical body," John admitted.

"And so you should. In some moments. You find your expression through your body. In every state, whatever it might be, you always need a body through which to find your expression. Without a body you have no individuality. You are one with the whole. You are no longer a 'you'. You are one with 'All'," Gamman said.

Something strange must have been happening to or with time. John did not feel the pressure of the 1.75 gees. In fact he felt almost as light as he did on that one occasion when he visited Ziircon. He asked Gamman, how come?

"Can you answer that yourself?" Gamman again prodded.

"I am in a different state of consciousness and therefore subject to different laws?" John mused aloud, his voice uncharacteristically dreamy. Gamman only smiled. "Do all these states, as you call them, have their own laws?"

"Oh yes! And until we learn them, and learn to obey them, we cannot live with any degree of effectiveness or happiness within them. No more than a baby can enjoy a walk until it learns, subliminally, about the laws of gravity. But do not worry. You are doing very well. In fact, very well indeed," Gamman assured.

For some reason John felt very pleased. He felt as though his father had finally recognized his efforts. He looked at Gamman with great respect. For an instant, the Ziirconian looked like a much older man. Wise and understanding. A kind, fatherly figure. John blinked and his visitor reverted to his previous appearance. This was a bit too much for John. He needed to learn about the laws of this state of consciousness. At the moment it was all a bit beyond him.

"I think it is time," Gamman said without warning.

John sensed immediately that he was talking about Delta. "Already?" John suddenly felt weak. Almost sick. The 1.75 gee's suddenly felt very heavy. He thought his legs would not carry him to the bridge.

They did.

He didn't have the courage to delay the moment any longer than necessary. He explained to Delta, in very broad terms, the principle behind the pineal gland investigation. He did not attempt to say how he intended to carry out this experiment. He said that he had reasons to believe that under certain circumstances the DNA can be stimulated to produce desired effects. He asked Delta not to ask questions. John asked her to trust him.

"I realize that during the last few weeks you have spent considerable time acquiring the necessary data to attempt something of this nature. In case there are difficulties, in Main Computer file R44, R45 and R46, I have prepared programs for a safe return to Earth. That's in case you wish to use them, of course," Delta smiled and left the bridge.

John bit hard on his lips. He was as close to an emotional breakdown as he had ever been in his life. She is an android, dammit! An android! She does not feel things. She has no emotions. She...

Then why do I feel so rotten? So bloody rotten. I wish I could go and lie down in that torture armchair myself...

Then, true to his conditioning, John checked the trajectory coordinates and went downstairs.

The elevator seemed very slow today. My God! John thought. Time is relative. I shall never get there. She will die alone.

She didn't die. At least, not yet. Hopefully never. Not on this little trek, if he could help it. John found Delta half-sitting in the same throne-like chair in which he'd seen her before. From a distance she looked perfectly relaxed. Her eyes were closed. She seemed to be sleeping. Androids don't sleep. At least not very often.

John remained at a distance. Three men were standing around her. They seemed engrossed, in a trance. Then, another body stepped out of a shimmering cylinder of light. A woman's body. She looked young, although who can tell with those people? Seven thousand years? Isn't that what Gamman claimed to be? Earth years!

The woman looked no more than twenty something. Gamman, Zooron and Kdoba moved slightly away to make room for her. She came very close to Delta. She touched her on the forehead. Then she moved her hand over Deltas body, as though caressing it. A gentle, kind, nonsexual caress. Delta remained quite still. She must have switched off all the nonessential sensors.

About an hour later Gamman left the small group and came towards John. For the first time he looked tired. Whatever the Ziirconians have been doing must have been exhausting.

"This will take quite a while, John. Get some rest. Or better still, keep busy on the bridge. We are all in your hands, you know," he said softly.

Was he trying not to disturb the others?

John felt useless standing there. He went to the bridge. It looked more empty than any bridge he'd ever faced in his life. He wondered if the Ziirconians could remove his emotions from within him. Who needs emotions? What good have they ever done for me?

John felt very despondent. He was scared. A man over two hundred years old doesn't need any emotions...

And then John sat down and got busy. He calculated every trajectory needed to examine the rest of the Vegan planetary system. He examined the voluminous data already acquired as pertaining to every planet. He counted the moons, the rings, the small planetoids. He did a hundred things that the computers had already done during the last two months.

He kept busy.

John had no idea how long he remained on the bridge. Alone. Long ago, the gravities had automatically reverted to earth normal. For quite a while, already, BLAKE was inscribing an almost perfect 690,000-kilometer orbit around the strange planetary artifact. The word 'artifact', is supposed to mean something produced by human hands. Well? Didn't those people look human?

John worked, slept, worked, and slept again. Time lost its meaning. On a few occasions he imagined he was in the engine room. He couldn't have been. No one spoke to him. In spite of periods of rest he felt tired. Once more, he felt drained of emotions. For a short while, John felt nothing. Later he pretended he was Delta—or some other indifferent humanoid. Then the emotions he denied returned with vengeance. They washed over him like gigantic waves. An emotional tsunami, leaving behind a wasteland. John didn't think he could last much longer. The human race was dying. Not satisfied, he had given permission to destroy Delta.

John remembered the years he'd spent alone on the bridge. He'd never felt lonely. He tried to recapture that lost state of emotional stasis. A tacit acceptance of his tiny role in the vastness of the universe. Now, it did not seem to matter. The Ziirconians would have their planet and he would return to Earth. Empty handed. A gift for humanity? A burned out incapacitated android. Dead Delta Dobbs. A gift to remember.

John's emotions were at their lowest ebb when he felt an urge to go down to the engine chamber. He recognized that strange compelling pressure. The Ziirconians were calling. For what did they need him? He could not sense the nature of their feelings.

He run to the shuttle.

As he entered the engine room the three Ziirconians stood to one side. Delta was still seated. Her eyes were slightly open, squinting, as if there was too much light in the room. But the light was perfect. Functionally diffused, not glaring. It wasn't that. It was as if she'd been emerging from a very, very long sleep. She did not look at the visitors. She looked straight at John. Then, very slowly she smiled. A smile of recognition.

"John?" she spoke finally. "John Galt, the Commander?"

John took a few steps towards her chair. He must have looked stupid. His mouth was hanging open, his throat, tongue, like an arid desert. Then Delta sat up.

"I am s-sorry, John. I beg your p-pardon, Sir. I mean Commander. Commander Galt, Sir."

She sounded a little confused.

John tried to swallow. Not easy with a parched mouth. He still couldn't utter a word. He didn't have to. Delta was alive. She was no longer an android. She was a live, gorgeous, wonderful, stammering woman. And then John's knees felt soft and he sat down, heavily, on the floor. A part of him, the part that had been dormant for many, many years, started laughing. Soon Delta joined him. They laughed together. Neither of them had the slightest idea why. It didn't seem to matter.

Gradually, their laughter subsided. They both smiled, sheepishly, something between slight embarrassment and uncertainty. Even as John got up from the floor, a shimmering cylinder of light emerged from Delta's body, separated itself from her, moved away a few feet and solidified into... Delta. The new shape smiled at John and reached out towards him. She didn't speak but John felt a breath of warmth, friendliness, something very close to desire for oneness; her emotions enclosing him with a gentle gossamer embrace. Again he caught his breath. He turned his head towards Delta's figure sitting in the special armchair.

"Was the experiment successful, Sir?" The sitting Delta asked, her voice friendly, concerned, and perfectly modulated.

Unwittingly, John's legs trembled. He staggered backwards. He leaned against a handrail of the spiral staircase leading to the upper level. He leaned on it and then his knees refused to support him. Once more John sat down, this time on the first step of the stair behind him. His veins contracting, his head rapidly draining of blood, he looked up at the four visitors. Gamman slowly nodded. The answer was yes. According to Gamman.

John smiled gratefully, but too late. His consciousness sought refuge in the deep Void of blissful, relaxing darkness.

***

Chapter eighteen

Sweet Sorrow

"I find it strange to communicate without talking. Strange and quite wonderful," John whispered, belying his own words.

Delta walked close, her arm interlaced with his.

"Yet, when we do, there is something missing. I miss the sweet sound of your voice," she, too, whispered unnecessarily.

"I think, we shall find, that hearing also comes. In time. It is probably only a matter of practice. And... trust in your imagination," she added. This time her communication was silent.

Three days had passed since Delta, the new composite Delta, had carried Commander John Galt, in her arms, to his private quarters. He, taller and broader than the feminine contours of her bionic structure, seemed as light as a feather. Delta was delighted with her physical body. She has deposited John, gently, onto his long adjustable lounge chair. She already knew, felt, that it was his favorite recliner. She felt his feelings. Later, John found this emotive knowingness to be the most unsettling aspect of his new awareness. He found it disturbing to have access to his interlocutor's subconscious desires.

When John had fainted in the engine room, his consciousness had escaped into his emotional body. From that vantage point he saw his physical body slumped on the staircase. He panicked; he withdrew even further. One could say that he had fainted again, this time receding even deeper. He searched solace within his unconscious. In physical terms one would call it a coma. A deep coma. A state as far removed from full physical consciousness as it can be, without severing the link, the silver cord, permanently. John was soon to learn that this supposedly full state of awareness, defined a very narrow mode of existence.

There, in that reclusive state, Kdoba approached John's cowering awareness. Slowly the sage unfolded some of the Ziirconian knowledge. John would not understand it all, but the seed would have been planted. The soil had proven fertile.

The entity sharing Delta's android body, inherited her host's memory together with a full range of physical sensors. She inherited physical awareness. Through the pineal gland, developed by the psychokinetic efforts of the three Ziirconians, she could, and did, negotiate a mode of existence with her host's positronic consciousness. The new 'Delta' managed to further attune the android's body responses into a full symbiosis. This had been, by far, the most difficult aspect of the experiment. If the android Delta had been left to her own devices, it would take at least fifty years before her emotional body would develop sufficiently to be of use to her very advanced intellect. Emotionally, the android Delta had become a newborn child. While her positronic brain could be programmed at the speed of light, emotionally there was no known way to accelerate the process. No one knew how to program emotions.

It had been at this point that a young Ziirconian woman agreed to help in the process.

Many millennia ago there had been a planet called Ziiron. The ancient planet was the physical predecessor of Ziircon, the present habitat of Ziirconians. When the original planet had ended its usefulness to the race it once spawned, Q'rran, a woman of Ziiron, had not had a chance to develop her full, physical potential. She did not have to, of course. A physical body has very few assets which, at higher frequencies, cannot be matched or bettered. There was, however, a single yet substantial drawback.

As Gamman had told John, quite a while ago, time was relative. It 'traveled' at a very different pace at a higher frequency of vibration. Whatever one did in physical consciousness, one did many times faster. A centurial life on earth, corresponded to about fifteen centuries on Ziircon. At this rate, Q'rran would need to live a very, very long time to accomplish, in a Ziirconian mode of existence, her personal growth.

When approached by Gamman, Q'rran jumped at a chance of sharing a physical body. Assuming, of course, that there would be a willing host. This willingness had been the essence of the experiment. There had never been any question that the pineal gland would enable the transfer. The big unknown has been whether Delta, the android, would agree to share her body. Her physical consciousness. There had to be a profound compatibility. Otherwise, each of the 'women', would continue her own separate evolution.

Delta and Q'rran had merged into a perfect unit.

There remained a single but important difference between an android's body and that of a human being. A human physical body needed its emotional component, its emotional 'body', to maintain a 'waken' state of awareness. There had been rare exceptions to this preponderant rule. For thousands of years the human race had reared, periodically, some very advanced beings. Those early precursors could, seemingly at will, function at different states of consciousness, simultaneously. They could separate their various 'bodies', each vibrating at different frequencies. But those rare people had been the exceptions. The avatars borrowed from a distant future. They were the test cases.

An android's body could not have such limitation. It operated at a single frequency, without any other components. It was as though the evolution has been reversed. In nature, the seed of consciousness grows, evolves into ever more complex forms of mental, emotional and physical manifestations. There comes a time when a human, while still in the physical body, can become aware of his or her total state of being. Such a gifted human can shift his consciousness from one body to another, entering an ever-higher frequency of vibration. From the physical to subconscious, to the unconscious and even beyond. This singular 'beyond' appears paramount to the condition that occurs at the velocity of light. Mass becomes infinite, time is in abeyance, the state of consciousness is infinite. A state beyond time, beyond space, beyond limitations. The quanta of a body, which vibrates at the velocity of light, could never be described as physical. Yet, if one could accelerate the mass of ones body to such a vibratory frequency, one would become omnipresent, omniscient, infinite, eternal.

If one could...

The Ziirconians had reached only the first step on the upward journey. There they remained for unknown millennia, trying, persevering, reentering ever-new bodies to further their existence. Kdoba had reached a more advanced condition. Although he could not as yet sustain it, he had the ability to enter and function at still higher frequencies. This singular quality enabled him, on occasion, to reach out beyond time-space limitations. Kdoba was the instigator of the experiment. He believed that the new Delta, with her advanced knowledge, could be of immense benefit to the human race. It never crossed his mind that Q'rran might not accept such an exile. He thought of it only as an opportunity. Q'rran had proven him right.

The undulating landscape embraced John and Delta with an enchanting beauty, which only an advanced being could create in his or her consciousness. Q'rran, the new wondrous Delta, left her android body on the BLAKE, and proceeded to show John the magic of her homeland. The city-park had existed for thousands of Earth years. The climate seemed bewitched into a perennial condition of exuberant springtime.

The building-sculptures graced, and complemented, the idyllic surroundings. No two structures were alike. None competed for preeminence. Each seemed conceived with the thought of contributing to the surroundings, while partaking of the enhancement.

"But what do people do here?" John asked, his eyes as wide as a wondering child's.

"What people do everywhere. They learn the art of survival," she answered simply.

Q'rran looked exactly like Delta. She became Delta. By assuming a lower body, she assumed its expression. Had the body been imperfect, that imperfection would be manifest in her emotional expression. One cannot lie within the confines of ones emotional consciousness. Whatever you really are, that is how others perceive you. You are an expression of your subconscious—of the sum total of your present knowledge.

"Don't they work for a living?" John asked.

"Do you?" she countered. "We all have to find our own way to our own advancement. Some of your people call it the road to salvation."

"I thought my people, as you call them, refer to salvation as a reward for becoming a good person," John told her.

"This, surely, must be a great misunderstanding. You are not saved because you are good. You are good because you are saved."

"And just what is this state of being 'good'?" John wondered.

"When I feel I am saved, I shall be the first to tell you!" she laughed. "John, all we can do, all that anyone can ever do, is to be the very best we can be. Delta, my host, that superb body endowed with a magnificent positronic brain, had reached this conclusion by a purely logical processes. Even in her own right, she knows that. I doubt the experiment would have worked if she didn't."

"But don't you people strive for some incredible scientific advances?" John asked, still not satisfied with her explanation.

Q'rran smiled, her eyes sparkling with inherent contentment. "There is no greater reward in life—and life is always in the present and therefore eternal—than to be of service."

She pointed to a building looking like a perfect sphere. The globe seemed suspended in air without any visible means of support. It floated.

"There are scientists who continue the work of their ancient forefathers. There was a time, when our physical world was reaching the end of its usefulness. These men worked to find a way to transfer the remaining people to Ziircon before the physical planet became uninhabitable. Working within the realm of both states of consciousness, they created, or brought into existence, the binary system. After years of heartaches, errors and catastrophes, the binary system produced a sufficiently attenuated electromagnetic field. It produced and sustained characteristics of both Ziiron and Ziircon vibrations. They found that within the range of this field, they could transfer the remaining people, in full consciousness, into our new domain. You could compare it to a, sort of, conscious dying. Except, of course, there is no such thing as dying. There is only a change in the frequency of vibrations." s

"There is no dying?" John stood still, looking the hovering sphere.

Q'rran said nothing. There are things that everyone must learn for themselves. In the meantime, the sphere shimmered and became hazy. Then, in John's eyes, it took on the appearance of Earth, as seen from Moon Base. Before John could react to this mirage, the sphere reverted to its original, semi-polished surface.

"Did you see that?" John pointed at the sphere.

"You did it rather nicely!" Q'rran congratulated him.

"I did what?" John gasped.

"You created the image which, at that moment, was foremost in your mind. Didn't you know that?" Q'rran looked up at him, laughter in her eyes.

"I created the image?" He shook his head from side to side.

"Look!" she said.

And as John looked on, the sphere turned again, for a moment, into an image of Earth. Then into an image of Saturn, then Jupiter, and then again to Earth, before reverting to normal. John took a step back.

"Good God! he whispered. "Is this some kind of magic?!"

"It takes a little practice," Q'rran said, now laughing outright. "There, you try something else. Something quite different."

"Such as what?"

She took his hand and looked into his eyes. Suddenly, they were both a hundred feet above the ground, looking at the magnificent garden city. The metropolis seemed to go on forever. It would be hard to decide, though, whether it was a city, a park, or just rolling countryside; with brooks running through glades between thickets and copses, all interspersed with beautiful sculptures which, John knew, were really functional buildings.

"My God! I am flying!"

John grasped Q'rran's hand even harder.

The next instant he found himself standing near the spot from which some force had raised him to such heights. He was breathing hard. What in the world had happened?

"I looked into your eyes and read your real desire. Then, I just let it happen," Q'rran smiled innocently. She stroked John's face to calm him. "Come let us sit here."

They sat by a brook that whispered a song of serene calmness. John leaned against a rock. Q'rran took his hands, protectively, into one of her own. With her other hand she made a wide, sweeping arc.

"It has not always been like that," she said, wistfully, as though thinking of things she would rather forget. "You must realize, John, that your world and mine are not really so very different. What separates us the most is the fluidity of time. In your world, your truest desires, those wedged firmly in your subconscious, do become manifested in the physical reality, even as they do in ours. The essential difference is, that here, we can make things 'appear' just a little faster."

John thought about what she said and then asked: "And what about flying a hundred feet off the ground?"

"Were we flying? Or was your desire to see our city so great that the only way to satisfy this desire was to regard it from above. To sate such a desire on Earth, you would rent a helio. Here, we create our reality... a little faster. In both cases you would emerge from the experience sated," Q'rran tried to explain.

"And that is all you do? Sate your desires?" John asked.

"In a way. Only, that after ten millennia or so, we seem to realize our greatest fulfillment when attempting to sate the desires of others. We find that, more often than not, this tends to improve our own perception of reality."

"And just what is this elusive reality?"

John felt a little guilty about his previous question. Knowing what Q'rran was doing, what she intended to do, the question had been uncalled for.

"That is what we are attempting to find out. We believe, I believe, that the ultimate reality is a state of consciousness in which we retain our individuality while being one with infinity."

"Isn't that a paradox?" John could not imagine such a state.

"Remember John, I am describing a state of consciousness. After all, everything is no more than a state of consciousness. So far, we have failed to set any limits to ours."

"And, I suppose, when you achieve this elusive state, the horizons with recede still further?"

"Precisely! Isn't it wonderful?"

Q'rran could not contain her ebullience. For a brief moment the air shimmered with tiny sparks, an explosion of joy, a kaleidoscope of pure colour. It was beauty discarnate. John closed his eyes. The sparks continued. When he opened his eyes, they were gone. He sighed.

"When you're happy, you're happy..." he wondered aloud.

"Happiness is an integral part of life. The single greatest gift imaginable," she affirmed.

"But you said that life was, or is... you said that there is no death?"

"Did I?" she teased.

And then John began to sense the formidable power supporting the serenity of the people of Ziircon. That power ensued from knowledge. A state of knowingness that comes from within ones own being. Dry facts, computerized data, can be learned, but only you can make them come to life. You must incorporate that knowledge into your own reality. Your own, private, exclusive universe. John had met only a few Ziirconians. Yet, each person was preoccupied with his, not his or her own, welfare.

John looked at a building some six hundred meters away. A trabeated facade of white marble. Simplicity substantive. Dignity inherent in form and in materials. Horizontal cloisters, perhaps three to four meters high, surrounding a sunken, open proscenium. As John looked closer, he saw three to four hundred people sitting on white marble steps, listening intently to a maroon robed man. The man was talking. Perhaps, giving a lecture? A moment later John caught his breath. It was Gamman. His very own mentor. His initial Contact—his benefactor.

"He is one of our greatest teachers," Q'rran said, her eyes filled with admiration.

"What is he teaching?" John lowered his voice, as if afraid he might disturb people even at such a distance.

"He teaches whatever you want to hear. Gamman has access to most of the unconscious. That makes his knowledge confluent with all of Ziircon. And that, in turn, gives him a good few thousand years of knowledge to draw on."

It was at this moment that John realized what Q'rran was willing to give up. The planet she was leaving, by Earth standards, was heaven. Although people here also periodically shed their subconscious, these 'life' periods could last beyond fifteen hundred years. That's almost like being immortal. Yet she was going, leaving, of her own free will. They were very strange people—these ancient, ever youthful Ziirconians.

"I would like you to come with me," Q'rran interrupted his wonderings.

"Wherever you would take me…"

John trusted Q'rran on Ziircon, the way he trusted the physical Delta aboard the BLAKE.

They walked for a while through the luscious gardens, Then Q'rran took his hand and, a moment later, they stood in the middle of a room. It's size comparable to John's living quarters on Moon Base. Somehow John knew that he was in Q'rran's, house. Her home. This was the place where she could be alone. Where the other Ziirconians would not invade her privacy. John felt honored that she chose to invite him to her inner sanctum.

It was a humble, almost austere room. A table, a bench, two chair, a simple sofa, a few colourful pillows. Each piece of furniture was a study of functional beauty. Each was deprived of any decorations. It was a form, a sculpture, in its own right. The furniture enhanced, complemented, rather than decorated the space it displaced.

Three steps lead up to a large, open, arched window. Two more, lesser archways lead to some other compartments. Two of the walls, and the ceiling, seemed luminescent. They generated or gave off, visible, diffused light. On one wall, there was a painting of a woman. She was very different from Delta. Beautiful in a very different way. Humanoid rather than human. Yet, even as John looked at this painting, its contours began changing. The colors wavered as though in a gust of fog. When the mist cleared, Delta's face was regarding him from the picture.

"What was this?"

"This has been my mirror." A bemused, enigmatic smile wavered on her lips.

"But..." John still did not even begin to understand the strange laws of Ziircon.

"It is as I told you. What you see on the wall now, is my present true image. It displays the sum total of my present reality. I really am Delta." She looked up at him as if to prove her point. "This is what I wanted to see. I wanted to make sure that I am ready for leaving."

"Leaving? What leaving? We only just got here," John recoiled.

The very thought of leaving this Eden, this land of magic and beauty, was as painful to John as... there was no comparison. Apparently people who went through a near death experience had that reticence towards returning to their physical reality. Only John was very far from dead! Even if death ever existed. On the journey of new knowledge, John had just reached the stage of very profound confusion. He did not want to leave. He wanted to see, learn, study, perhaps jump once more a hundred feet above the ground and see more of the city. Or garden. Or anything. Anything at all. John felt like a little boy. He wanted to stamp his feet and have a tantrum. He didn't do either. Instead, he felt a great sorrow.

"Ah, parting's sweet sorrow..." Q'rran said softly. "Surely you know, John, that we shall never leave here. Not really." She stood close to him, stroking his arm with gentle caress. "That which we truly are, we always take with us. We are a state of consciousness. The true reality. Remember?"

John lifted her slightly, to her toes, and kissed her full, receptive mouth. Her arms reached up around his neck and they held each other tenderly, closely... a wonderful feeling of completeness enveloping them. Time ceased to exist. Then, John gently lowered her pliant body to the Spartan sofa. They both appeared to be searching for something. Searching and finding something new, something very, very inviting. Something they could both take away with them, wherever BLAKE would take them. Wherever, whenever...

As John opened his eyes he saw Delta. She was bending over him. He was lying in his quarters, on his favorite lounge chair. He felt quite disoriented. Gradually, memories returned.

"Oh, my God!" he thought, disenchanted. "Surely, it hasn't been but a dream?"

"Did you enjoy your dream, Commander?"

"I have no idea what happened," John confessed.

"You escaped into a coma. At least—to start with," she said.

"To start with?"

"Why, yes. Do you not remember, Sir?" Delta spoke with her perfectly modulated voice.

"Remember what, Delta?" *Would she believe me?*

Delta bent down a little more, pressing her soft sinuous body against his, then brushed her warm lips gently across his. Only then, remembering, John pulled Delta tightly to him. A long while later, she raised herself to a standing position. She smiled at John with her perfect smile.

"Why, Commander Galt, Sir. Had you already forgotten?" she asked coyly.

But John remembered it well. He had perfect recall. For the first time in two hundred years Commander Galt blushed. He had no idea why. In time, he recovered. A little.

"I am afraid I have, Number One. Do you think you could possibly remind me once more?" He tried to look very lost. When Delta didn't move he added very softly: " Please?"

***

PART THREE

Earth

Chapter nineteen

A Parting Gift

"**A time will come** when we shall be together again," Gamman assured. "Now, we must go. Soon."

All five of them stood, once more, in the Captain's quarters on FRS BLAKE. Gamman, Zooron and Kdoba, relaxed, confident. John resigned, Delta bridging the mood with empathy. The lone, independent Commander needed her. More then he's ever needed anyone.

John looked at the wall screen. A three dimensional image of the huge Vegan skyscape shimmered, then solidified before them. Since holographs took over memory storage, the projections became enormous. The memory was now stored in volume, not on surface only. A world of difference. In the foreground, two spheres hung suspended in the rich fabric of Inner Space. Between them, a slim, elongated hourglass: a gossamer bridge, shimmering with gold and silver, binding the planets together. Up, in the left top corner of the screen, a bright, almost white sun stared from behind, unblinking, at the Waltzing Duo. One of the planets was surrounded with an eerie halo. The other smiled a broad, happy crescent.

"So soon?" John hardly whispered. Talk was becoming obsolete.

"Your mission, John?" Gamman shared John's sorrow.

During the first three weeks after BLAKE left the planetary binary, John remained in near constant communication with Ziircon. Delta introduced him to a number of her friends. Most were artists striving to become the best possible instruments for their individual and collective unconscious. Even more so, they each sought to become a clear channel for the creative force, which wrought

their individual, unique traits, to find expression in the
Ziircon world.

Under Delta's patient coaching, John stole a glimpse of
the incredible Ziirconian mind. He managed, momentarily, to
withdraw, in full consciousness, from the sensual, physical
awareness to the subconscious, and then, to the realm of the
unconscious. To say that the experience had been
overwhelming would be a belligerent understatement. John,
for an undefined instant of time, made contact with the sum
total of Ziircon Entity. He became one with the immeasurable
reality of Super-consciousness. One with countless billions of
individual Ziirconians. Simultaneously. He became one with
each   individual   atom,   each   independent,   unique,
indispensable component of an indivisible Whole.

For an ephemeral moment, John shared all their
memories. Their aspirations, their past, present, a great deal
of their future. The Ziirconian unconscious seemed indeed
close to the inexplicable, intangible, 'beyond'. Close to that
singular vantage point from which John could discern time
stretching in both directions. Past and Future exemplified two
sides of a single coin. Two sides of the all-important reality
of the Present.

And there was more.

In this sublime state, John's awareness encompassed the
whole planetary system. He reached out and held each and
every spinning globe in the palm of his hand. He smiled a
benevolent smile of the Vegan sun. He cast life-giving rays at
his adopted children...

...his mind, still hungry, demanded the stars; the
powerful, fiery fragments of ultimate reality. His mind, his
MIND, HIS MIND...

For that brief moment John bore witness to the
magnificent future that awaits each unit of boundless
creation. Frightening, euphoric, divine? The Unconscious did
not belong to anyone of its components. Seemingly infinite,
through mental avarice destined to remain finite. Seemingly

eternal, yet borne by a beginning. But only a as night that must follow a day—an infinite succession of now's. Omnipotent? It ruled. It embraced the lowly.

A paradox.

John emerged, from this fleeting experience, with a sense of wonder tempered by profound serenity. The apparent chaos of the physical universe no longer appeared chaotic. Even the monstrous supernovae fitted into an orderly scheme of eternal purpose. But most of all, John brought back a new sense of humility. The magnificent pride of the mind left him untouched, unspoiled. It had not been the stars that he had touched, John realized. He touched the concepts. The ideas of stars.

Another paradox of the greater reality.

The day after breaking orbit, John discovered that while he wandered on Ziircon, in the realm of the subconscious, his physical body strapped to the bridge command chair could be subjected to much greater stress. Rather like during stasis. Throughout their Ziircon visits, BLAKE maintained eight additional gee's of constant acceleration. A total of twelve gravities for most of the first three weeks.

BLAKE's velocity increased at an astounding rate. Soon they would be outside the range of the Ziircon subconscious. Even this exalted state of awareness has its limitations. The twentieth day was the last day of Contact.

"Your mission, John..." Gamman repeated.

John never forgot. But so soon? He only just got here.

Gamman, Zooron and Kdoba came aboard the BLAKE for the last time. They proved to be more human than John could ever imagine. He read in their faces real sorrow at his and Delta's departure. They neither preached, nor made speeches. They seemed content to share the state of conscious communion. Then, the irrepressible Zooron told a story of his early exploits in the Ziircon advanced awareness. He had all of them laughing, dissolving the lingering sadness. John found it glorious that so highly advanced people were still endowed with such a rich sense of humor. Zooron, reading his thoughts, hastened to assure him that his absurd stories were "based, if only loosely, on absolute, unadulterated truth."

"So help me die," he added, finding a phrase within John's own subconscious. "Providing one of you would care to tell me, just how to accomplish this elusive feat. As I recall, I tried to affect it by leaping from the tallest buildings." Zooron spread his arms in a gesture of abject despair. "Every time, just before hitting the ground, I seemed to have changed my mind. I jumped back up again!"

There was a great need of laughter.

A while later, Gamman rose and the others fell silent. The teacher, the translator, seemingly commanded such presence without the slightest effort. Approaching John, he embraced him. Then Gamman held John's head, firmly, in the palms of his hands. He looked deeply, intently, into John's eyes.

Later John claimed he did not remember this particular moment. Gamman bypassed John's subconscious. Zooron, Kdoba, and Delta knew, even then, that at that juncture, the great sage has given John the greatest parting gift imaginable. He imbued John with the ability to find him, to find Gamman, in the great realm of the near limitless unconscious. Gamman would now remain John's teacher, a devoted mentor, for as long as John desired.

It was indeed a rare, later the most cherished, gift. A gift that few people on Ziircon could lay claim to possessing. A gift not easy to merit, even for a Ziirconian.

Then Gamman embraced Delta. She had her own gifts already, beyond anything that John could aspire to at present. Yet, since she now represented the human, rather than Ziircon race, Gamman did not leave her without enriching her consciousness. Again by prolonged eye contact, he passed on to Delta the Knowledge of the Spheres. The secret of the binary system. Should the human race wish to take advantage of this knowledge, they could now do so. On BLAKE's return. A gift equivalent to salvation. To the next, conscious step of human evolution.

Then they all rose, and formed a circle. No further words were necessary. They chose, quite simply, to partake in the final goodbye by sharing each other. All five closed their eyes and, for a wondrous instant of infinity, became one. When John opened his eyes again, his arms were encircling Delta.

They were alone.

The listless Void swallowed BLAKE at over 200,000 kilometers per second. The velocity was still climbing.

FRS BLAKE was going home.

The stasis was still necessary. John tried to argue that he could acquire immense knowledge from Delta, during their return journey. She replied that he also would age to well over seventy, while she would remain her gorgeous self. She teased him. What they now shared had little to do with physical attraction.

John had no choice but to agree, but only on condition that Delta would join him, at least periodically, in his subconscious state. Outside the influence of the binary system, John lost his ability to leave his physical body. His inner threshold was a lot more accessible in the dream state than in a waken condition. In some ways, the subconscious and the dream states were similar. Most people experienced both. Unknowingly. When people slept, on occasion, they not only dreamed, but actually did breach their subconscious. Those who had learned to recall their dreams could easily tell the difference. It was a question of maintaining a state of full awareness. While 'dreaming'. To participate knowingly. To retain control over unfolding events. A lot greater control than in their waken condition. Within the inner realm, there were fewer limitations. A greater scope for emotional fulfillment.

Delta stayed at John's side until the electroencephalogram registered theta rhythms. Deep sleep.

She was fully aware how difficult it was for John to sever conscious links with her. It was yet another goodbye. She, too, would miss his presence. Delta felt that John always regarded her as a being greatly more advanced than himself. She also knew, that the one sure measure of ones own lack of advancement, was to consider oneself superior to another. Pride and humility were the great equalizers. The real worth of an intelligent being did not lie in the duration of his or her conscious existence. Q'rran learned, long ago, that it lay in the ability of total commitment. On the ability to sublimate her ego. By those standards, John was a very advanced entity. An advanced being. Even Gamman has born witness to that.

Later Delta rechecked BLAKE's trajectory.

Satisfied, she set about lowering her own bionic functions. Next came the reduction of her positronic brain activity. Only at this moment did she feel free to withdraw her subconscious from her new host's bionic body. Yet, in a manner that she couldn't explain, she felt that there remained a constant, if intangible, link between herself and her physical 'container'. A silver thread of awareness. Only then did Delta realize that she'd lost part of her freedom. She also knew that she had lost it by an act of her own will.

While John attempted to retain his awareness within the realm of his dreams, Delta elected to recede deeper into her unconscious. She couldn't do it. On Ziircon, the condition she attempted to achieve would correspond to sleeping. The Ziirconian bodies did not require this form of rest. Instead, people employed different forms of contemplation. To recede into ones unconscious in full consciousness, required practice. Delta's attachment to her new, physical body made this transition unexpectedly difficult. She smiled at the prospect of having some thirty years to practice. "They have a funny attitude towards time, those Ziirconians", she remembered John saying. She laughed when she thought of the Ziirconians as 'They'. A physical body held a powerful, magnetic attraction.

The timer had been preset for periodic inspections. As on the outward trek, Delta hooked up her bionic body directly to the main computer. Only now she was ready to leave her physical body.

She projected herself to John's cubicle.

Commander John Galt looked dead. His emotional body was still interwoven with his physical form. Delta sighed at human limitations.

"You'll learn, Commander," she smiled, giving John a mock salute.

Next she pictured the engine room. The next instant she was there. What magnificent design! She, Delta-Q'rran, shared all Delta's positronic brain's memories. The atomic pile looked exactly the same as on the day her host left the Solar System. The Earth System. Some forty years ago.

The beauty of engines with no moving parts, she mused.

Delta was proud. She had played a good part in the design of these engines. She now enjoyed what her host could not previously have experienced. Emotional pride is hardly a creative concept but it carries connotations of great satisfaction. It should be taken in very small doses. It can be deadly, if taken in excess.

Delta returned to her body. It felt good. Congenial. A base of operations.

She managed to withdraw into the unconscious.

Years passed. An influx of energy. Delta was back in her emotional body. Another bridge inspection. She could see, hear, experience, but she couldn't do anything. For that she would need her physical body. She pressed the requisite buttons. In seconds she was fully operational.

"What a magnificent body they gave me!" she actually said it out loud.

Delta checked the coordinates a little less than five years ago. At 255,000 kilometers per second, a millionth of one degree would make a profound difference. She scanned and analyzed data from the leading edge sensors, computed the adjustments and reprogrammed the main computer. The new trajectory, imperceptibly different from previous one, would bring them into orbit around Moon Base in 23 days.

Delta could make it much sooner, but she had promised to awaken John before entering the Outer System. Once he awakened, the rate of deceleration had to be reduced. Unless, of course, John would continue his journey while in the subconscious.

For a brief moment Delta was terrified that John may have lost his ability to do so. A moment later she realized, to her considerable amazement, that the panicky reaction had originated in the emotional body, which was developing, independently, within her 'physical' body. Her positronic cortex had been inactive during most of the trek, but there, obviously, had been some very rudimentary movement. Delta made a mental note to be on her guard.

John, as expected, emerged from stasis unscathed, if temporarily weakened. He had to subject his physical body to the usual discipline of liquid diet, electronic massages and physiotherapeutic exercises.

"The penalties for running a 'biochemical sensory device'," a name Delta coined for John's awakened body. John hadn't laughed. So much for my humor, she thought.

John was used to his body—for a great, great many years. He identified with it. Judging from the ship's records so did most, perhaps all, people.

"What a strange race of beings", Delta pondered. "If only they knew what they were all missing!"

BLAKE was well inside Neptune's orbit before they picked up the first communication from Moon Base. Apparently the Galactic Navy did not expect their return for another five years. They could not understand why BLAKE did not announce their arrival sooner. Surely, Commander Galt could have set up an automatic laser beacon? It was customary to do so. A few hours later, the Moon Base admitted that it had been customary only during the last sixty years. BLAKE, and the crew, was forgiven.

From that moment on, masses of information flooded BLAKE's communication sensors. Moon Base endeavored to furnish them with as much data, of what transpired on earth, as possible. BLAKE's sensors loaded all data directly into hytapes. It could wait. Two days after the information glut began, came the first question.

Anything to report?

Delta and John both knew what the Moon Base was asking. During the last few days the computerized data, which the ship's sensors had gathered in the Vegan System, has been broadcast directly to the Moon Base computers. The scientists must have been poring over the bountiful info, looking for that one telltale sign, foremost on their minds.

The restrained, held back question was asking: Did you make Contact? Any Contact???

John spent the last week worrying how to answer this question. He knew that it would come. It had to. Eventually, after many discussions, Delta convinced John to reply in affirmative. After all, in her positronic brain Delta carried blue prints for the magnetic field. They would need full support from the Galactic Navy to put it into existence. The sooner they prepared Earth for such a contingency, the better. Better for the whole race. They decided, however, to communicate this affirmation under a scrambled code. The code, in itself, would make the communication top secret. Assuming that the system had not changed in the intervening years.

It was time to don the hyphones.

The matter of convincing the Federated Republics Council Appropriations Committee would not be easy. John's claim of Contact could only be backed by two sets of data obtained by BLAKE's sensors. The unusual, unprecedented, magnetic field. That, and the source of this emission were the sole tangible evidence of Contact.

The binary, at best, might be regarded as artifacts. On a planetary scale, but still—artifacts. The rest, the vital part of Contact, could not be proven. Not by the, so-called, scientific methods. The question was whether such evidence would suffice to convince the Council to spend untold billions of credits to build Earth's own 'spheres'. It would probably convince the Moon Base scientists. But the Council?

The binary system could not sustain a state of equilibrium under the laws of physics presently known to science. Or at least, not by science as defined seventy years ago. Only time would tell. According to the communications received from Moon Base, time was now at a premium. Earth had entered her terminal death throes.

Earth was dying.

John and Delta had about two weeks, and a little more three million kilometers, to decide on a plan of action. Under normal circumstances, this would be more than enough. These were not, however, normal circumstances.

The volume of information pouring in from the Moon Base had been extensive. Without the hytapes, there would not be enough time to absorb it all. Delta hooked up directly to the main computer. Then she stopped. There was little point to load her positronic memory cells when she now possessed a magnificent, fully 'accessible' subconscious. No machine, regardless how advanced, could compete with the subconscious. Her scope had been, and now had become even more, beyond human limitations. Compared to the laws of physics, Delta's knowledge was virtually infinite. At least, by any known human standards.

Gradually the picture of the present situation on Earth was emerging.

The population had shrunk to just over nine billion. The reduction had not been due, at least not primarily, to damaging radiation. Surprisingly, the ozone layer had thinned and punctured, but still held up reasonably well. The main reason for the demise of two billion people, during just two generations, had been multiple, rampant plagues. All over the planet. Moon Base speculated that the direct antecedent of the infestations was the present life style. An overwhelming majority of people were concerned with little more than extensive sleeping. Total abnegation of physical exercise, of maintaining even nominal conditions of hygiene, of removing garbage from festering dumps, or streets, or sidewalks—these were, according Moon Base, the primary causes of death.

Earth was dying.

This putrid condition was not yet true of the main civic centers. Five world capitals had been kept as clean as the latest technology in robotics would allow. As for the rest of the globe?

Corpses littered back alleys.

In addition to the plagues, (viral infections of new genetic strains), people were dying from exposure to carbon dioxide and methane. When John last walked the Earth, garbage had been re-circulated. Transposed into useful ingredients. Then came the transition era. The administration of Renewal Functions had been shifted from human to robotics control. In the five world capitals, Council managed to complete this transfer. But by the time implementation of the system reached the secondary centers of population, it had been already too late. There was a last desperate attempt to convert water-purifying systems to robotics control. There had not been enough robots. And people? People did not seem to care.

People preferred to spend their time sleeping. It was a strange malady.

Deadly abnegation.

"We are not too late, are we?" Delta's face indicated deep concern. "Can those people really know what they are doing?"

"You once said, that every thing has its reason," John replied somberly.

"It is obvious why they are sleeping. But why the abnegation?" she asked.

"Obvious? Not to everybody!"

Delta looked at John, closely, reading his emotions. When John was angry, it was difficult to read his feelings. Primitive emotions are too physical. She needed to know if she contributed to his mood.

"People escape into dreamland, not into sleeping. The race has long reached the next stage of their becoming. The problem is, that most of those wielding power appear to value only their physical existence. They also seem to reward power that upholds their own aims. And those in power promote the perpetuation of their own, physical species." Delta spoke as if she too found it difficult to understand.

"And...?"

"And the racial subconscious has rebelled. They opted out, from the rat race."

"And became the sewer rats themselves!" John felt angry. Angry at people. At the race. Angry at the death of a beautiful planet.

There followed a pensive silence. Then Delta had an idea. She asked John to sit down and relax. The computer would take care of navigation, for a little while, she assured him.

"Now close your eyes and follow me," she said softly.

It wasn't easy. John took a full minute to relax sufficiently to be able to do as Delta had asked. His previous ability to enter the subconscious instantly, suffered a few setbacks. On the inner screen of his mind, John saw Delta's hand. Before he could reach out and take it, the hand wavered, dissolved. He knew it wasn't the hand that was dissolving. It was his attention struggling under oppressive weight of negative impressions. Finally, they made the connection. John held on to Delta's hand. Gradually, her face came into focus. Then followed a flood of memories of heaven. Of Ziircon. The emotive wave obliterated, swept away, his anger. Even sadness. It cleansed his awareness. John felt free. Free to conquer. Not to be conquered. No matter what the setbacks.

"It's been a long time," he mused, still holding on to her hand.

"Yes, John. Enjoy it. But this is not why we are here," Delta admonished.

A moment later John stood on a stretch of grassland. There was an intoxicating smell of wild flowers. The sky of purest blue touched a distant forest. John tried to remember where he'd seen such beauty on Ziircon. He couldn't place it.

"Where are we?"

He filled his lungs with glorious, aromatic air.

"Would you venture a guess?" her eyes were smiling.

John remained silent. He sat down and leaned back. He looked up at the sky. As though on command, a few scattered clouds appeared, out of nowhere. John amused himself by changing their contours into shapes of various animals.

"John..."

As much as he loved her voice, John resented her encroachment into his private space. After all, it had been over seventy years since he saw the earth sky. And then John sat up.

"That's right, John. There has been no such pure sky on Earth, for centuries. This is the home of the abnegating masses."

"This is the reward for their abnegation?" John asked in disbelief.

"No, John. Not for their abnegation. But this is a place where they can find rest, before climbing the next step. The only reason they can enter higher consciousness is their state of mind. They do not impose their will on others," Delta answered.

"So you don't have to be good, nowadays, to go to heaven?" John looked around again. This was not yet like Ziircon. But it held promise. An anteroom of heaven.

This time Delta laughed. Soon, though resisting, John joined her.

"This is hardly a heaven. But it seems many times better than what they left behind."

"Are you sure they are here?"

John was a true doubting Thomas.

Once more Delta took his hand. Instantly they hovered a hundred meters above ground. As quickly they moved, at a great speed, towards the dark forest. John felt no pressure of air on his face or body. Was the speed an illusion? It may have been the forest that was speeding towards them. They landed gently. From not far away, John heard people playing. At least it sounded as if they were playing. He peered between tree trunks. A short distance away, directly ahead, was a group of—maybe, twenty people. They were running around a sun-swept, grassy glade, as if playing tag. They seemed like children, only, they looked older. Around mid-twenties.

"They are not lacking exercise, out here," Delta observed.

"How come they are acting like children?" John couldn't believe his eyes.

"Because they are. Not in the physical sense, of course. But there again, they no longer are hampered by physical bodies."

"But will they grow up?"

"We all grow up, John. But even when we do, it would be a grave mistake to forget our childhood. We should always visit the perennial playground. Only there can we appreciate how far we have travelled."

At this moment, Delta, herself, looked like a child. Her face was the face of joy. The face of youth, of springtime.

"Thank you, Delta. I may need a lot of reminding," John said, spellbound.

"And I shall always be with you. To remind you."

As she tilted her head back, John kissed her joyful, radiant eyes, and her cheeks, and her smiling mouth.

"Thank you," he repeated.

The next instant they were both on the bridge. The communication panel was going frantic. They smiled at each other.

Why are these people always in such a hurry?

***

Chapter twenty

Planet Fall

The message was quite specific:

Hold explicit continue implicit data only.
Repeat hold explicit...

The message was coded and repeated continually until BLAKE confirmed the instruction. The code was identical to the one used some seventy years ago. Moon Base might not have expected BLAKE's return for another five years, but whoever was manning the laser transmitter was well up to date on BLAKE's history.

It was further evident that whoever was operating the laser must have been overcome by an acute case of cold feet. Implicit data only... The only possible reason behind such instructions would be the two items of exceptional interest: the binary system and the equally inexplicable electromagnetic field.

But why such secrecy?

What was it that could be in any way dangerous to the recipients of this data? No one had objected to direct computer feed which, in Navy jargon, always meant implicit or 'unedited' data only. Explicit would include the crew's conclusions on the said data. Evidently, the analyses had to be reserved for later.

But why?

The BLAKE was now less than three earth days away from entering Lunar orbit. John already converted ship's operations to Earth-time. He had to allow for his biorhythm to adjust itself to a twenty-four hour cycle. Normally, such synchronization required a minimum of three days.

For the last 10 hours, Delta's attention has been riveted on the main computer. Since BLAKE had been programmed to maintain its present trajectory and to enter Lunar orbit autonomously, John wondered what was behind such a fervent preoccupation. Surely there could be little to add to her positronic brain.

He left Delta alone. He had always respected her decisions. Delta's preoccupation gave him time to study the flood of data that the sensors had accumulated on the return the journey. John also needed to recap the Vegan statistics. Some of the facts were staggering. The mass of each of the two planets was about fifteen times that of Earth. Originally the planets must had been colossal bodies, in their own right. If one were to shrink, say, Neptune to the size of Mercury, one would achieve the density of one of the Ziirconian binaries. Not a mean undertaking.

John realized that he still had no idea where Ziircon was in relation to the Vegan system of planets. The fact that he had visited there, while in orbit around the binaries, did not prove a thing. After all, he had no idea what the Ziirconian transporter's range was. If Ziircon had its existence at or in a different frequency from the physical world, then its location may or may not have a relation to the Vegan planetary system. And, for that matter, what were those enigmatic vibrations? Were they referring to some sub-atomic structures, or to quanta of energy such as photons, still in their massless state?

Commander John Galt was confused.

It suddenly dawned on him, that after a seventy-year trek, John had no clear idea where he'd been, what precisely he'd been doing there, nor, for that matter, from where, exactly, he'd just returned. From Vega? A feebleminded understatement. Rather a droll conclusion after an expedition to the most distant star ever visited by a human being. Thank God for Delta!

"Relax John," Delta leaned back from her console. He felt her words rather then heard them. This was still confusing.

Until this moment, her fingers had been playing an elaborate, *allegretto-vivace* on the programming keyboards. Whatever the influence of Delta's emotional body, it did not reduce the efficacy of her bionic host. Some people have all the luck, John mused with quite undisguised jealousy.

"You have other, unique abilities, John. You must learn to use them," Delta said, this time aloud. John completely forgot that she could read his emotions, if not his thoughts. He felt embarrassed.

"You seem a little too busy to teach me, right now," he said. "Are you sure I cannot help with anything you are doing?"

"As a matter of fact, it is done," she replied.

"What is done?" This was a trifle annoying. Wasn't he the Captain of this spaceship?

Delta regarded him with a steady gaze. John's emotions were taking the better of him. Under the circumstances, it was understandable. What a pity that human beings were still at the stage where they expected to be taught. Time was rapidly approaching when each and every unit of consciousness, on Earth, would gain its emotional independence. A much greater achievement than rearing up, not so long ago, on their hind legs.

"I have been working on my gift." Delta evidently decided to ignore her Captain's tantrums. "If you recall, Gamman had given me the basic equations for the transporter. On Ziircon, you referred to it as the binary? I tried to assess, if the Solar System would support such a disturbance, how long would it take to put it in operation, and how long would it have to last."

Suddenly, something stirred within John. When Delta mentioned Gamman's gift, his mind drifted to an indistinct memory of that moment, just before he'd said goodbye to the three Ziirconians. A gift. He, too, had received a gift. It lay buried somewhere deep in his subconscious. Or even deeper?

John shook his head and turned his attention to Delta. "And...?" he prompted.

"It will not be easy."

A flat statement. No emotions.

John knew, that if it were a difficult problem for Delta, for him it would be impossible. Even after his vain attempt to absorb all the scientific data through the hyphones, his recall was still no match for Delta's positronic abilities. Yet, there may have been an edge he could offer. Didn't one of the Ziirconians say that evolutionary direction that the human race had chosen, the path of technology, had not been the Ziirconian way? It could be that Delta, the new Delta, might not be thinking the way that a human would think. In a materialistic, physical way. Could that help?

"I really don't know John. It might..." Delta sounded hopeful.

Her telepathic abilities were evidently expanding to reading his thoughts with ease. Or was it that John could no longer differentiate between his thoughts and emotions. There formed an overlap. A bridge. Whichever it was, she was reading it. John regarded Delta with admiration.

"Both," she answered. "To start with, your thought-patterns have been rather, well, strange to me. Your reactions to any given stimulus, even to your own sensory inputs, are very different from mine. Now, I am learning to understand you.

"Can you tell me a little more about this problem of yours?" John asked.

"Problem of ours. You and I have to solve it. Together. I doubt if anyone else is going to volunteer any help!"

She did not try to reassure him. She sat straight, her beautiful face a mask of concentration.

"Well," she resumed, "my initial scanning of the human primary, or group, subconscious, indicates a much broader range than we, or they, have or ever had, on Ziircon. Or Ziiron, the preceding mother planet from which the

Ziirconians originate. I really do not quite know how to tackle it..."

For the first time since John had met Delta, she appeared to lack confidence. Strangely enough, this alone, made her much more human.

"Is your primary concern with the subconscious, or with the physical consciousness, of the human race?"

"Good question." Delta seemed surprised at John's insight. "To be quite honest, I am not sure. You see, Gamman had given me the principles to be applied, not the method to be used. The latter we must work out ourselves."

"Can you share any of it?"

Delta appeared to be jumping subjects. John doubted he would understand even if she explained the issues, but he was interested. He needed to know. For a while she remained silent. It struck John that Delta may have been trying to translate alien concepts into human words.

"The problem is, John, that to accomplish any major realization one needs a compound effort. Individual people, regardless how evolved they are, have limitations. You and I, we each have ours. To bring about a magnetic field of a controlled magnitude necessary for the transporter to function, we would have to employ vast numbers of people. Millions. We would need a channeled, unified effort, at the subconscious level but with an echo, a parallel, within the physical component." She sounded as though she was thinking aloud.

"And why is that so difficult?" John wanted to know.

"It must be!" Delta looked startled. Then she realized that John couldn't have known. "You see, my friend. Attempts had already been made. Three times. And they, our predecessors, had failed."

"What attempts?" John sat up.

"Why, to create the field, of course."

"What!?" John gasped. "You mean here, on Earth?"

"Well, not on Earth, obviously. But within the Solar System."

John sat back, closed his eyes, and tried doing some slow, deep breathing. Gradually his rigid muscles relaxed. A magnetic field, a binary system right here on his doorstep? This was too much.

"Are you sure?" he asked weakly.

"As sure as I can be. But they had attempted to create it in different ways. The idea is not to copy any one method, but to apply the principles. The first unsuccessful attempt had resulted in our asteroid belt. Since that attempt had not done much good to the atmosphere of Mars, they had decided to try a different method a bit further away from Earth. The attempt, on a minor scale only, a sort of 'dry run', had been attempted on Neptune. Finally, when that offered some promise, they got down to business on Saturn."

As Delta unfolded her speculations, John's pale face grew paler. A blank, vapid expression replaced his usual bright, intelligent countenance. His chin dropped, his mouth remained open. His eyes stared, unblinking, at Delta. His stare also suggested John's mounting reservations about Delta's sanity.

"John! For crying out loud. Read my subconscious. Your are acting like a baby!" Her beautifully modulated voice lost some of its beauty.

John shook his head. He forgot again. All this seemed so desperately new to him. He now remembered that the subconscious cannot lie. He scanned Delta's emotions. She had been speaking the truth. Of course. He knew that, all along.

In a way, John was buying time. Protecting his own sanity from too rapid an input of startling information. These were completely new concepts. More different, more alien, than anything he had to face in a long life of interstellar travel. John was trying, desperately, to make the connection.

"These are not alien concepts, John. These are concepts of evolving consciousness. There is not a single intelligence in the universe that did not have to take these steps. There is no such thing as a free ride. You, like everyone else, have to pull yourself up by your own bootstraps. Keep pulling. I cannot do it for you."

Delta's voice was very steady. These were things that needed to be said.

"If I understand you correctly... My forefathers, my ancient ancestors, had already attempted to terminate life on Earth as we, as I, know it, by creating conditions in which the whole race could take the next evolutionary step." John recited the words like pieces of a puzzle that he finally managed to assemble.

"In a nutshell. Except, they were not attempting to terminate life, only to enhance it," Delta corrected. A smile returned to her lips.

"But life on Earth would no longer exist as we know it now," John insisted.

"This would be rather lucky, don't you think?"

"But... but..." John felt he had to defend something or someone.

"But it would be a little more like it is on Ziircon?"

But it would be a little more like the heaven on Ziircon.

John fell silent. What could he say? By defending the status quo he would be defending the appalling conditions prevalent on Earth today. Was there another way out? Out to where?

John gave in. "Can you explain those unsuccessful attempts of our ancestor?"

"I cannot describe to you the nature of the explosion which resulted in the asteroid belt. We can be sure, though, it had been a dangerous method—not to be emulated. All the surrounding planets, including the Earth, bear scars of that explosion. Imagine, a planet just outside the orbit of Mars blown to smithereens! It must have been quite a spectacle!"

Delta's mind seemed to be reaching into the distant past, visualizing the cataclysmic event. John managed to sense some of her feelings. He almost saw what her eyes were seeing.

"As for Neptune," Delta continued, "only a few rings had been formed by the time the first attempts at mass transfer had been completed. They still exist today. There had been no point continuing, however. From such a distance, by the time the electromagnetic field reached Earth, it would be too weak. Also, the density of the planet was a little too great. As I said, it was no more, than a trial run."

"Are you trying to tell me that those few rings around the Neptune are man made?" John voice carried admiration mixed with disbelief.

"Oh yes. Very much so. There is no other logical explanation. However, they only got down to serious business with Saturn. With a density of 0.7 that of water, the conditions had been, still are, near ideal. The mass ratio of almost 10 to 1 that of Earth, also fit into the calculations. And the distance from the Earth, only a little over a 1,250,000,000 kilometers, is far enough in case of accidents, while being close enough if the conversion worked." Delta was definitely admiring our ancestors.

Our ancestors!

"Conversion?" John asked aloud.

"Yes. The idea had been to convert a percentage of the giant planet's mass into orbiting rings. They had attempted to do so by increasing the rotation of the planet. They, obviously, had partial success. Imagine. Saturn, with a mass 95 times that of Earth, rotates on its axis, in just over 10.7 hours. It makes my head spin! The surface of the planet is moving along at over 11,270 kilometers per hour. You've got to hold on to your hat! When the desired mass had been transferred into the rings, they, the rings would continue to rotate at their present velocity, while Saturn's rotation would be gradually slowed down. This would initiate the collapse of the planet's mass to a much greater density. A rather clever plan, I would have thought. Particularly the idea of the rings. By distributing the mass fairly evenly around the whole perimeter of the rings, there would be no need for the bi-planetary model that the Ziirconians employed. The two planets had to have a similar mass to sustain equilibrium. With the rings, and utilizing a much larger planet, the same magnetic field would develop without the need for the rings to be much more than..." her fingers danced on the keyboard, "...then about 0.127954 of the planetary mass," she concluded.

"So what happened?"

"Not very much, as you can see..."

"Delta. What in High Heaven are you talking about?"

Now John was lost. Completely.

"Well, as you can see, nothing much happened. The problem is, that in order for the transfer to succeed, there must be a proportional effort from both sides of the equation. There must be about eighty percent of effort from the subconscious, and the rest from the physical side," she answered.

"So???"

"So it would have worked fine if it hadn't been for the incomprehensible desire of the human race to remain in the confines of physical consciousness. They appear to think that when they remove their consciousness from their physical bodies, they will, as you call it: 'die'. That they'll cease to exist. That they will be no more."

Delta smiled spreading her arms. John hardly dared to breathe.

"What made them believe such nonsense is truly flabbergasting," she smiled sadly "Every night they go to sleep, they become unconscious and, lo-and-behold, they wake up alive in the morning! Whatever happened to this death business? They probably think that it doesn't work during the night! I don't know, John. Such an incredible attachment to a physical state of existence is without precedent throughout the universe."

John needed time. A time of silence. He was still in the process of converting his inbred concepts. Through his own experience on Ziircon, he knew them to be wrong. It was one thing to be asked to believe in something untenable—quite another to experience the incredible for oneself, and still have problems accepting it as real. A full quarter of a millennium of consistently wrong conditioning is not easy to eradicate.

To John, the universe always appeared as an expression of poetry. As a beautiful idea, rather than a bunch of rocks spinning around with no apparent rhyme or reason. He knew that there was, there is, an underlying Reason. For all things. All actions. He knew it intuitively. He had always known it. Not by a computer printout but through his inner senses.

"Delta, when we visited the, ah, the subconscious environment right here—what is it called, anyway...?"

It was rather funny. The name Ziircon, some 30 light years away, was indelibly imprinted on John's mind, yet he didn't know the name of his own real planet.

"Those who have their existence within the Solar System subconscious, refer to it as Antlantis, after its original, physical antecedent of Atlantis. A vague, residual memory of the period remains in the man's physical consciousness. The previous attempt appears to have taken place during a period sometimes referred to as Lemurian. Before that, I really cannot reach. There had been a long break between the first and the second civilization." Delta seemed to be apologizing for her inability to reach further back into racial memory patterns.

"And what is this problem with human attachment to their physical consciousness? I mean as affecting the creation of the magnetic field." John went back the previous puzzle.

"The problem is that the number of units of consciousness, in any, shall we say, solar system, is finite. Large, enormous, but definitely finite. Mankind, by developing such an attachment to physical consciousness, maintains too large a percentage of its units on... Earth. This is the main problem. Also, there is man's insatiable desire for animalistic sex. Most humans, at some time or another, appear to be in direct competition with rabbits, rampant in a sexual frenzy. Emotionally, all humans are too overheated. And not just sexually!"

"So...?" John was on the defensive.

"So the laws of the physical and the subconscious universes state, quite unequivocally, that every construct, or manifestation, must support the highest state of consciousness it possibly can. This means, that there may not be a physical body, which does not serve as host to the highest awareness, through which this awareness can find its expression. This is the law of economy."

She felt John had not fully understood. She knew he would. Later.

"So even in the sum total of our subconscious we are finite." John was still preoccupied with Delta's previous answer.

"There are very few things which are not. Offhand, I cannot think of anything, that isn't," Delta smiled wistfully. "The Beyond?" she offered. There really was no other name for It.

"So some of us must 'die', in order to restore the balance which would enable us, as a race, to create the magnetic field, which in turn would enable the more advanced consciousness to attract and transfer the more elementary... Delta, this is not very easy to accept."

John felt drained. His head was pulsating as though an inordinate amount of blood tried to aid him in his mental processes.

"Trust your subconscious. Trust your instincts. Most of all, trust your intuition. The latter is the gateway to your unconscious. And there, within that innermost state, few things are impossible. For any of us. We must trust our own higher selves."

Delta enunciated her last words the way Gamman had done, when he wanted to get through the outer layers of John's consciousness.

And, in spite of his disbelieving, rebelling grey cells, and contrary to thousands of years of atavistic conditioning, John knew. He knew without a slightest doubt, that Delta was speaking the truth. She did not try to persuade him. She insisted, that John persuades himself.

Slowly, laboriously, he did.

***

Chapter twenty-one
Beta Mulligan

His broad smile was quite unmistakable.

Something, however, didn't work. The bridge main-screen displayed a twice-life-size image of Beta's face. The moment John saw it, he felt something was wrong. A full minute later John had it. Beta looked no more than forty years old. He should be over eighty. Could this have been Beta's son? Or, for that matter, grandson?

"Commander Galt! I never dreamt I would see you again. Somehow, it didn't seem likely." Beta's grin still retained a lopsided twist of a young ensign who was happy, serious, and respectful—all at the same time.

"Beta? Beta Mulligan? Surely, this cannot be you?"

John steadfastly refused to accept the evidence of his own eyes.

"There, you see, Sir! I told you I would not see you again. This can't be me!" Beta obediently confirmed John's suspicions.

By then, Delta was trying hard to suppress her laughter. She didn't quite make it. The men ignored her. Delta continued to observe, diligently, John and Beta's expressions. It was also her first opportunity to study the emotions of two humans, towards each other. Judging by her raised eyebrows, she wondered what would happen next.

"But you are over eighty... Aren't you?" John almost shouted.

"Well, Sir, some of me is, most of me ain't," Beta admitted lamely.

"What, by the Leaping Lunites, are you talking about?" John remembered the expression he'd learned from Beta—it seemed, in another lifetime. This time Beta Mulligan laughed also.

"Aha! So you remember, Sir?" Beta looked very pleased. Then his face turned serious. "I mean, Sir, that I met with a little accident on one of my missions. Most of my body is now bionic, and my face had been rebuilt to match the rest of my beautiful body."

Beta Mulligan... Beta. Beta Mulligan... Silently John's lips formed the two words.

John did not expect any of his past acquaintances to be alive. What, with the passage of time, the plagues, radiation, the exigencies of duty in the Galactic Navy... Yet here was Beta. Young, smiling, jolly as ever...

Suddenly life was wonderful. Even more so than before. John turned his face away from the screen. He needed to hide a sudden influx of unbridled emotions. A veritable flood of cherished memories swept over him. The images came in waves. Relentless, mounting, piling up, breaking like white crests over subsequent, more recent events. A minute ago a series of impersonal blips asked for visual, two-way communication. The BLAKE was within range. John agreed, neither speculating nor suspecting whose face would appear on the large screen.

Beta Mulligan. The son of his only friend, the last time round. John buried them both. Long ago. Freeing his heart from painful attachments. Now Beta was here. Live, healthy. The Leaping Lunite. He'd be the only one... The only one John still knew, on the entire Earth.

"Permission to come aboard, Sir?" Beta asked formally.

The BLAKE was still thirty-six hours away from Lunar orbit. What was Beta talking about? Delta, with a dainty, practically girlish giggle, explained:

"When we were discussing the, ah, transporter, Sir, a Galactic Navy cruiser matched our velocity. Since we were busy, I've waited for them to initiate dialogue. They can come to, if you so desire, Commander."

After her innocuous giggle, Delta reverted to being prim and proper. John guessed that she might wish to withhold her 'total' identity until she met and studied the 'young man'.

"Permission granted."

John could hardly contain himself. His mind kept repeating: Beta, Beta, Beta... The link with the past. The link with his physical past. The inexplicable attachment to the physical state of consciousness, Delta had said. How powerful it was.

Delta programmed docking procedures. In twelve minutes, precisely, the shuttle elevator doors slid open. A lanky, very tall man stepped out onto the bridge. He stood to attention and saluted. He wore the uniform of a Fleet Admiral. Like father like son. John Galt, Commander, again had difficulty believing his eyes.

Like father like son!

John got up and saluted.

Then he and Beta embraced each other.

Then Delta cleared her perfectly clear throat.

"Admiral Mulligan, Sir, may I present Lieutenant Delta One Blake," John said, his own throat still constricted with emotion.

"The pleasure is entirely mine, Lieutenant." Beta returned her salute and then took another deliberate look at her. "Yes, definitely entirely mine!"

"Thank you, Sir," Delta was gracious.

Delta knew, already, that she was going to like this youthful eighty-year-old. She could read his emotions. It was immediately evident, that Beta cultivated a happy disposition. He could be very serious, she suspected, but only when necessary. He obviously enjoyed life. By far the best way to live, she mused, relatively easy, if you do not take yourself too seriously. Beta didn't.

Finally Beta managed to tear his eyes away from Delta's conspicuous charms and return his attention to John. "I wonder Sir, if I might address you... well, you see, my father and you were close, and I thought that, perhaps..."

Normally Beta had no problems at all with expressing his sentiments. This was not a normal occasion.

"I shall be glad if you would call me John." John assured him. "Everybody else does!"

And there was more laugher. Never, not in his wildest dreams, did John expect such a magnificent homecoming.

"You will, of course, continue to call me Beta. Ensign, if you like. There, I am so glad that's settled."

The two men continued to stare at each other. Whatever each of them had remembered was some seventy years out of date. This was a new meeting. And yet...?

"Sir, I mean, John. I came aboard because it would give us time to have a chat before you enter Lunar orbit. By then, I would not find it easy to keep the media from you." Beta spoke with an unexpectedly deep voice. The voice of his father. John remembered him as a boy. Albeit a very tall boy. Then, Beta spoke with the enthusiasm of youth. Now John was facing a man who made his own decisions. John did not interrupt him. In outer space you have a lot of time. You learn to wait, sometimes for years.

John gestured Admiral Mulligan to sit down at one of the three bridge consoles. Delta swiveled all armchairs to face each other. The main screen was off. Beta's agile, probably bionic, fingers dialed a Galactic Navy standard security mode. The bridge visual and audio censors went off. There was an almost indiscernible sound of an electronic scrambler. Then, the youthful Admiral leaned back and faced John. This was the first time in BLAKE's history that the intended triumvirate occupied the bridge. There was a satisfying feeling of propriety about it.

"We have received certain implicit data." Beta paused, trying hard to read John's eyes. "Data that do not add up."

He paused again. When there was still no comment from either John or Delta, Beta sighed and continued.

"Evidently, I have forgotten that you people are endowed with abundant patience. Well, I'll come to the point. The data pertaining to the magnetic field and to the binary planetary system do not add up. Our computers refuse to process the information. That can mean only one of two things." Again he scanned John and Delta's faces. "It can mean that BLAKE sensors are in error, or... or that the sensors recorded phenomena which do not occur naturally in our universe."

This time the silence was longer. They had thirty-six hours. John preferred to leave this matter to Delta. Delta, on her part, has been scanning Beta for all he was worth. Her sharp senses again confirmed that she liked what she initially perceived. Finally, she relaxed her vigil. She turned to John.

"Shall I, Commander?"

John was surprised that he knew exactly what she was talking about. He nodded.

"Admiral Mulligan," she addressed Beta with all the decorum. Every reaction she could elicit from the man facing her would add to her knowledge of him.

The Admiral held up his hand.

"I gather that you are to be the spokeswoman. I have no objection at all. But if you are, you must address me as Beta." Admiral Mulligan smiled. "When lieutenants report to Admirals, they tend to present facts in an officious way. I don't want a report for the records. I want to know why you both chose not to add explicit data before I managed to stop you from doing so.

Delta was now sure of her ground. She was going to do what was necessary. She needed someone, Earth-side of the equation, to throw full support behind her, and behind her ultimate proposals. She also needed someone who had considerable clout, if such, in due course, was required. There were no half-measures possible.

"Would you allow me to report to you in my own, particular way?" she asked.

"Since I have no idea what your own particular way is, I can hardly offer you my blessing, can I?"

If Beta was matching his wits with Delta then, so far, he emerged the winner.

"I am sorry if I did not express myself clearly. What I intended to ask you was to trust me, on the strength of your friendship and trust which you feel towards Commander Galt," she explained.

Beta looked at John. Friendship is a strange sentiment, he thought. I first met this man, this famous, practically

immortal astronaut, over seventy years ago, and—she is right.
I do feel I can trust him. I am completely convinced of it.
And I feel warm, candid friendship towards him. More so
than towards most people I have spent half my life with.
But... how did she know this?

"John?" Beta asked, his left eyebrow rose quizzically. "I
presume you know what Lieutenant Delta One is talking
about?"

John nodded.

"That's good enough for me, Delta. Do it your way,
whatever that is supposed to mean!?"

Beta knew that he had to trust her. He did not have much
choice.

Delta got up and approached the Admiral. Her smile
reminded John of Gamman. He found it strange. This was the
second time he had thought of Gamman recently. Was there
still some kind of connection? A latent Contact?

Delta positioned herself directly in front of the Admiral.
Even as John watched, there was a noticeable relaxation in
Beta's features. As the Admiral tilted his lean face backward,
to look up at Delta, John thought he saw an almost childish
trust in his eyes. Slowly, as if unwilling to break some sort of
spell, Delta placed the tips of her fingers on Beta's temples.
She held him so until their eyes locked into a peculiar
immobility. John, himself, felt drawn, if not actually
absorbed, into Delta's subconscious.

John had never seen Delta so resolute in her actions. It
was as though she was acting under an influence greater then
her own. Within seconds, Beta closed his eyes and became
perfectly still. Delta also seemed frozen, petrified. Less than a
minute later, she went back to her console. The Admiral
appeared to be sleeping.

"What have you done to him?" John's hushed voice
carried a trace of worry. He also remembered seeing this sort
of thing before. But from a different perspective.

"He will be alright within minutes. I shared my
subconscious with him."

"You did what?"

For some reason John was horrified.

"Why are you so surprised? Gamman shared more than that with you."

"Then how come he looks... he looks... " he couldn't say it.

"Dead? So did you when you were in a coma. That's the way everyone looks when they withdraw into their unconscious."

"But why...?" John started again.

"John, you are not communicating with me as well as you can. Read my feelings. You knew very well that by the time you were granted Gamman's gift, you had already acquired considerable experience in the subconscious. For Beta this is all new. He must rearrange his subliminal concepts. He must adjust in a few minutes to the same degree to which you have adjusted over a few weeks," Delta spoke softy, smiling her reassurance.

"You sure he can take it?"

Half John's mind was dwelling on what Delta said about Gamman's gift. The Gift. He knew it, he felt it. He couldn't define it.

"It will come when you need it," Delta said, once more reading John's innermost feelings.

Even as she said it, Beta opened his eyes. He blinked a few times, then swiveled his armchair to face Delta. He stared at her for a long time. Neither she nor John interrupted the pensive silence. Still looking at her, Beta addressed John.

"And you can confirm all that?" Beta asked.

John was at a disadvantage. He did not communicate with Beta or Delta at the time of the subliminal briefing. He could not know, precisely, what she told him. Then John remembered. She told him nothing. She shared her subconscious with him. The subconscious cannot lie.

"Yes, Beta. I can confirm everything she shared with you."

"Ah yes. That's right." Beta smiled his broad, forty-year-old, boyish smile. "The subconscious cannot lie!"

"Did I say that?" John asked surprised.

"Didn't you?" came the counter question from Beta. "You know Delta, I like it. I like it very much!"

John was just a trifle annoyed. How come Beta could read his feelings on the first try, while he, John, still continued to stumble. He was glad for Beta. He was also more than a little jealous.

"I think it is his mostly bionic body," Delta replied to John's thoughts. "Since most of his parts are no longer of biological origin, he is less inclined to associate his consciousness with them, to the same degree as you do. Could that be it?"

By now, Admiral Beta Mulligan became Delta's most ardent admirer. His face showed admiration, amazement, practically adoration. He couldn't take his eyes away from her. John remembered this feeling well. He went through it for a long time. Even now, on occasion, John fell under her spell.

"So you are not human," Beta said slowly.

"Of course not. I am bionic, a bit more than you, though."

Delta flashed her best smile.

"You know what I mean." Beta returned her smile. "How do you pronounce it... Zeerc'n?"

"Like a bee someone just stepped on. See the word Ziircon. It is easier. And by the way, in everything that matters, I am human. To the extent that John and I have been sharing our subconscious for quite a time now."

"By that definition, I am part Ziirconian!" Beta sounded delighted.

"You certainly do not share your race's predisposition for xenophobia!" Delta said laughing.

"To be xenophobic towards you!?" Beta spread his arms in a sign of despair. "I would have to be crazy!"

"Some might accuse you of being just that..." Delta said quietly.

This put a damper on frivolity. Beta had his mind loaded with truth, but that was a long way from being able to use that knowledge for any useful purpose. It was rather like having been given a magnificent space cruiser. You now owned it, but it was not much good to you until you learned to fly it. And Delta said earlier, that she would need all the help she could get.

They discussed the options.

Who, when, and how would announce the Ziirconian connection? Should they announce it at all? What would be the reaction of the masses, the population, at large? By the masses they meant particularly the Council. The sixty thousand people who, of late, had to be dragged to perform their duties pertaining to the Federated Republics.

Some of the information that had been dispatched by laser to BLAKE had been incorrect. The 'official channels' had to give an 'official version' of the news releases. For political and sociological reasons, true statistics, e.g.: relating to the Earth's population, had been withheld. The populace was sufficiently demoralized as it was.

Beta furnished John and Delta with true figures. The most vital was the population. The last census, or more correctly a head count carried out by infrared scanners from orbiting satellites, recorded less than six billion people. This was about one half of the population that Earth supported some seventy years ago. According to what John and Beta now knew, the human race was finally doing the right thing: shrinking. Strangely enough, this reasoning was harder for John than for Beta. Yet they both loved the Earth, they both served humanity throughout their lives, and they both shared the same inner convictions. Yet John, after spending a quarter of a millennium in a physical body, developed a much greater attachment to his physical consciousness then Beta. Small wonder?

By way of contrast, Moon Base and the Colonies were humming with life. The challenges, which man faced in space, demanded, and maintained, a certain cavalier attitude. A strange, spontaneous mixture of careless disregard, and enormous respect for life. Simultaneously.

Do your best and to hell with consequences.

The buccaneers of the Solar System no longer committed great crimes. The total population, outside the Earth proper, remained at about one hundred million. That included at least two generations who have already been born in 'space'. Born outside the confines of the Earth's punishing gravity. Tall and lanky, like Beta, but unlike him, unable to ever spend, unaided, more than a few hours on Earth. Their bodies simply could not take the downward pressure. Those born on the Moon, at least had the advantage of one-sixth of Earth gravity. The others, born in outer Colonies, or within the enormous artificial constructs welded into the fabric of the asteroid irregular rock formations, did not even have that. They looked like two legged spiders. Wobbly, seemingly on the verge of collapsing. On Earth they walked around with mini-antigravs strapped to their backs. Like very tall humpbacks on an eternal pilgrimage to the ancient bell tower of *Notre Dame de Paris*.

And then there were the androids.

Contrary to the human counterparts, their bionic bodies could negotiate any gravitation that the System could throw at them. Pull at them? They became the 'physical' emissaries representing the Colonies in the Federated Republics Council. They often remained on Earth to supervise the robots, which in turn supervised each other, but without the all-important autonomy of decision.

Androids inherited the very best that the latest technology could offer. Neurons, which were cloned for their positronic brains, came from the pick of the human crop. The donors were invariably of the highest I.Q. available. Furthermore, the donor's character had been subjected to prolong scrutiny before the Lunar Labs would have requested a sample his or her brain tissue.

This last aspect proved extremely important. Within ten years of BLAKE's departure, 85% of androids developed a rudimentary pineal gland. The marvelous positronic brains had been strapped by a child-like temperament. The most dreaded eventuality that the Creators had feared.

Nevertheless, to every problem there is, somewhere, a solution. This one emerged from the cause of the problem itself. The presence of the pineal gland had also stimulated a condition akin to a subconscious mind which, in turn, could be influenced by hypnotic induction. This latter had proven the saving grace. The genius 'children', had subjected themselves, unanimously, to hypnotherapy, which managed to control their periodic, adolescent, tantrums.

By now, androids were practically running the Colonies. No one objected to their near-total autonomy. They regarded androids as their own progeny. Humans regarded themselves as proud parents. It was merely a case of a pupil surpassing his master—a condition repeated throughout human history. And anyway, the Colonies offered enough interests and challenges in anyone's life without wasting time on envy or jealousy. The Colonies were as healthy, physically and mentally, as Earth was not.

None of this has been conveyed to John and Delta until Beta's arrival. What he told them could not be classified as news. It was the status quo. The *modus vivendi*. A way of life. On Earth—a way of dying.

They talked till the proverbial 'early hours'. Each had questions, for the other. The subconscious was theirs to share, but John and Beta still lacked expertise.

When general catching up, and updating, sated their first hunger, Delta wanted to discuss the prospects of their report to the Council. For a while they even toyed with an idea of limiting their report to the Moon Base and Colonies only. Morally, this course was indefensible. Finally, after considerable discussion, they agreed to delay the official announcement of Contact until after official debriefing. That bought them time. Then, after the official quarantine, they would report to the Council. Delta would do the announcing. John would introduce her. Beta would provide the security, in case of trouble. You could never tell, with some of these people.

For Admiral Mulligan, it was time to leave the bridge. He would be the host at the official welcoming ceremonies, on Moon Base. Decorum still laid claim to some official procedures. Beta hated leaving. He wanted to stay. Forever. He said as much.

"You can't imagine what it's like to hear something completely new, revolutionary, and then, only minutes later, to realize that you had known it all, deep down, throughout your life." Beta sighed and stretched as though waking up from a long, long dream. "I feel strangely awakened..." Then Beta noticed the expression on John's face. "I guess, maybe you do know..."

John said nothing. There was no need.

"By the way, how did the signals reach us from Vega, and what did they mean, precisely?" Beta suddenly remembered. Weeks would pass before much of the shared data from the subconscious would percolate down to his physical awareness.

"They are not signals. They are a byproduct of the binary system. The alternating transfer of subatomic waves and particles through quantum field, from one planet to the other, to maintain equilibrium, produces radiation wavelengths which you picked up," Delta explained.

"So we found you by accident?" Beta asked.

"We do not believe in accidents, even within physical worlds," Delta replied.

Beta continued to regard Delta with the same, childlike admiration. He still found it difficult to take his penetrating gaze away from her face.

"No, I do not believe in accidents either. Not any more," he assured her.

***

Chapter twenty-two

The Vega Report

The silence was deafening.

To achieve such a stunning effect, one must amass 60,000 politicians into a single, acoustically resonant space. One must deny them the use of their favorite toys: their electronic communication equipment. One must still their incessant scratching, shuffling, gyrating, stirring and, on occasion, snoring. Finally, one must compel all Members, by a power never yet wielded on Earth, to hold their collective, rasping breath.

And that's not all.

One would have to control, anesthetize (or otherwise render mute) a further 300,000 Out-members. Each would have to forsake his or her constitutionally guaranteed right of self-expression. To give up the use of their cherished individual viphones. Ah, the joys of electronic knickknacks... Then, and only then, might one perceive the magnitude, the uniqueness of the occasion.

Such was the splendor of the Chamber's silence.

It must be stressed, that no audio-visual equipment has been disconnected. No threats have been issued. No bribes offered, no pressures applied, no demands placed on the 360,000 people representing the Federated Republics. No soporific, hypnotic or any other tranquilizing gases had been pumped, or otherwise insinuated, into the air-conditioning system into the Council Chamber.

When speakers murmured the final "all shall rise", the world held its breath.

Admiral Beta Mulligan, Commander John Galt and Lieutenant Delta One Blake met with the three members of the presidium in Admiral Metis's office. John remembered the room well. Once it had been dominated by the presence of Hermes D. Grant.

Beta performed the introductions. The Right Honorable Councilor Chang Chou Peng, represented the Planetary administrative work-force. The Munificent Archdeacon Moses VII, who incidentally inherited his title, position, and responsibilities, as well as his bulk, from his father, Moses VI. The third member was a stunningly beautiful woman. Taller then Delta but, if it were possible, even more beautiful. The Presiding Member of the triad, Mia Metis, a full Admiral, second only to the Admiral of the Fleet, but overriding him in matters relating to Colonial representation. Admiral Metis was an android.

"Not much has changed," John whispered as he drew Delta to one side. "The shufflers, the sleepers and the stargazers. Just like seventy years ago."

After the introductions the group chatted for twenty minutes. Both human members of the Presidium attempted to pump John Galt for advanced information. John, just beginning to get the hang of reading people's emotions, that is to say their true intentions, had no difficulties in avoiding a direct answer. Previously, still during their debriefing on Moon Base, Admiral Metis had been drawn into their confidence. She had been given the duty of organizing the Council session for the "Vega Report". Admiral Metis issued a statement that an important announcement would be made by two surviving members of a seventy-year mission in search of intelligent life. The word 'surviving', added spice to the soup. Nowadays, such innocent seasoning was necessary, to keep Council Members awake.

The introductions over, Admiral Mia Metis led her guests to the moving walkway. A short ride later, her private lift deposited them directly onto the round, presidential platform. The moment they all sat down, the domed podium began rising to the Council Chamber level.

The silence was uncanny. Had the Members obeyed the command: 'All shall rise', the eerie effect would have been destroyed. The command was a procedural tradition. No one had risen for centuries.

The platform stopped.

Admiral Metis stood up to open the proceedings. She was immediately interrupted by Councilor Chou Peng with a point of order. The Right Honorable Chou Peng tabled a motion to dispense with standard agenda and move directly to the Vega Report. Munificent Moses VII seconded. The motion was carried by unanimous silence of the Chamber. A silence of consent.

It was the first unanimous vote recorded in the Federated Republics history.

"They can smell something, but they are not quite sure what." Delta whispered in John's ear.

She could have talked out loud. No sound would have reached the Chamber while her console light was not on. Finally John discovered something that Delta didn't know.

"Gotcha!" he too whispered, pointing to her tiny console.

The keyboard built into the armrest of her chair seemed tiny only by BLAKE's standards. It was a perfectly good terminal outlet. There was no need for more power here. John felt the warmth of Delta's amusement. He hoped the whole session would prove as nice and easy.

Admiral Metis rose again.

"Honorable members of the Council. I have great pleasure to introduce to you Commander John Galt of the Federated Republics Starship BLAKE."

Silence.

"Commander Galt!"

Still no applause, no reaction. Such absolute stillness among that many people was unnerving. John felt tension creeping at the base of his neck.

"Easy," he felt Delta's emotive message, "they already sense something. Just take it easy...Be natural..."

John took a deep breath. He rose to his feet. It was not necessary to rise, but it seemed appropriate. The right thing to do.

"Admiral Metis, Right Honorable Councilor Chou Peng, Munificent Archdeacon, distinguished Members of the Council. I thank you for your attention. Seventy years have passed since my feet touched the soil of our home planet. Seventy years that have left an indelible imprint on my mind, my memory, the state of my consciousness. We are here to share with you all the culmination of our mission. An experience that will ultimately lead us to a greater understanding of the purpose of our existence. To convey this knowledge, to share this experience, I have the honor to present Lieutenant Delta One Blake. She brings from Vega, new knowledge of new horizons. She will define the next step on the endless journey of human endeavor. Honorable members of the Council, Lieutenant Delta One Blake."

Again, this screaming silence.

Times like this are indeed memorable. They are also extremely unbalancing. John savored doubts about his sanity, about the efficacy of the microphones, about the mental condition of his listeners. He also wanted to hide. At least for a while. Or, until the world gets back to normal.

Delta was on her feet.

Almost immediately John noticed a peculiar phenomenon. The last time he had seen it, many years ago, was when he had flown a helio, on a hot day, just above the ground. Light had been refracted by the sudden change in the density of the air. It had created a strange, mirror-like, shimmering effect. It had given an unreal impression, suggesting plasticity of the tarmac surface.

Now, he saw this effect again. Delta stood, silent, relaxed, and the air shimmered around her. A moment or two later, the plastic bubble enclosing the podium filled with tiny, almost insignificant, minute points of light. Glittering, oscillating, as though innumerable glowworms invaded, and became trapped within, the dome.

The next instant, the glowworms dissipated, outwards, as though swept away be a wave of a magic wand. Air shimmered, momentarily, and returned to normal. John wondered if any of this really happened, or if it had been his eyes that created this peculiar effect.

Delta spoke.

"I wish to thank Commander John Galt for visiting my home planet Ziircon. I also thank those who, more than seventy years ago, placed at Commander Galt's disposal the magnificent Federated Republics Starship BLAKE, which enabled me to visit your planet. But most of all, I thank Lieutenant Delta One Blake, who had agreed to share with me her body; who has placed her magnificent positronic brain at my disposal. She and I, thanks to her superb altruism, have become one. That which we now share, we shall share forever."

John listened completely spellbound. To his utter amazement, Delta did not address the Council as herself. She spoke as Q'rran, as the subconscious residing within Delta's bionic body. Delta has become so natural, so completely human, that John already forgot the long, taxing, unnerving experiment. He forgot that the experiment's results have been, even to the Ziirconians, quite unpredictable.

"I bring you greetings from that which had been my home. Greetings from a state of being, which we call Ziircon. It is a planet not unlike your own, though in some ways, quite beyond the reach of any of your spaceships. I wish you to know, that it is only Commander Galt's unique and exceptional sensibilities, which made his mission a success. If it had not been for his ability to step beyond the normal limitations of human consciousness, I wound not be here, I would not bring you the gift of Gamman."

John never thought of himself as exceptional. The late Harry Grant, Donna Dobbs and particularly Delta, were exceptional. He was an astronaut. One doesn't need any particular talents for that. Merely a lot of patience, and the ability to improvise. When necessary. John thought of himself as very ordinary. Now, for the first time in his entire life, facing such a multitude, John felt embarrassed. He wasn't sure why he'd been asked to be here at all.

"People of Earth. I bring you news that many of you will find sad. There will be countless others, who will find it joyful. You will be saddened to learn, that you are the last civilization within our galaxy, which still holds dear life in a physical form. You will rejoice in the knowledge that the Gift of Gamman will enable you, all of you, to take your rightful place in the Galactic, even Intergalactic culture."

"The Gift of Gamman," John whispered to himself. "Of course. That's what it was all about!"

The Gift of Gamman!

A little later, John heard a collective, halting, intake of air. A communal gasp, when Delta told the Assembly that many of the human species had already joined the vast Galactic brotherhood. Then, the ominous silence returned. John's perceptions seemed honed to new heights. He reached out beyond the Chamber. Earth seemed to hold her breath, as though the whole planet has suspended her journal gyrations. Animals, birds, even insects seemed to stop in their tracks, to quieten down their busy wings. All nature took part in this moment of portentous revelation.

"There comes a time, when all people, the whole race, must take the next step on their wandering journey. A journey towards homeland. For millions of years you have been confined to this Earth. You have not labored in vain. You've earned your freedom. The time is ripe to withdraw from carefree kindergarten. You have come of an age. The next classroom is waiting. Already well disposed to receive its new students."

Again there was a momentary wavering, a hesitation in the currents of light. The same illusion as at the beginning, before Q'rran began speaking. In this brief moment, John sensed open fields. He saw the darkness of a distant forest... a group of people, young, carefree, playing. Then the vision was gone. John wondered if Q'rran made this image available to everybody. To everyone who took part in her message from Vega.

The Members seemed spellbound.

"Even as I speak, I sense that some of you have already shed the myopic veil. That you perceive the knowledge that has always been with you. Many of you have forgotten that Truth is the essence of being. A joyful process of eternal becoming. No one can every grasp It. No one can hold It in the palm of his hand. Truth is Life Itself, the awareness within you. The past is behind you. Dreams—are your future. But only the Present you can manifest your beingness."

For the first time since Q'rran started speaking, John sensed that he was not alone. Not in the physical sense. It was a sensation that John had touched on, vaguely, when still back on Ziircon. Now, the impression was different. It was not a feeling of sharing his subconscious with any particular entity or person. It was more like being plugged into the very source of an electric current. Except it wasn't electric. Magnetic perhaps? John didn't know. But he sensed that he was in the process of becoming an integral part of a greater Oneness. In no way did it impede or lessen his individuality. No more than parents or sisters or brothers detract from the individuality of each other. Even as John thought about it his sensibility of Oneness was growing greater, richer.

A larger, much larger family.

The racial subconscious, composed of an immense number of individual spheres of consciousness, each partially interlocking, like a three dimensional chain, of pure, transparent bubbles. A universe of tiny worlds. Each an individual kingdom. Each inter-meshing, drawing strength from each other, expanding into much greater awareness of an integral Wholeness. Could this be the sense of the Unconscious? John's thoughts seemed like fragments of the thoughts of others. Are we all searching? Are we all on the brink of some strange, enigmatic...?

The Gift of Gamman...

"We are all One. But it is up to each one of us, to find the awareness of this Oneness. To give It home in our individual consciousness. To accept It. You were afraid of losing your cherished, tiny selves, in this joyful process. Be not afraid. Those who have made the Connection no longer fear this fear. Deep within your heart you always recognized your invincibility. Even in the innocence of childhood, you sensed the freedom of your unfettered, true Self. It is fragile—yet indestructible. Omnipotent—yet filled with compassion. It dies a million death, yet ever remains immortal. Dear friends. The step you are now taking is for the bold, the courageous. Those who sit on a seesaw, will suffer loneliness. You need not be, you are no longer alone."

John listened to Q'rran with undivided attention. He hung on every word, absorbed every nuance. Yet, each time she stopped talking, John felt that Q'rran did not say anything new. That he, John Galt, already knew the essence of her knowledge. He felt, almost, as though she was reading his mind.

Is that the shared subconscious?

"I shall be here to help you with your individual Connection. Those who need help, including your non-human brethren, will, in time, be given assistance. We shall create a field of magnetic convergence, a transporter, within which influence the transfer will be made easier. Easier for those who will need such assistance. John Galt will bear witness to the efficacy of this method. The process has already begun. It is lodged in the unconscious. What you will see in the night sky is no more than the result. The cause rests always within you."

"So the Saturn project already begun?" John's little, childish ego was bruised. "Why did she not tell me about it?

Or did she, but I didn't listen? Is there no end to this learning?"

His ego partially mollified, John almost laughed at his own, fatuous bias. He was glad he had not vocalized his thoughts. That he'd remained silent.

"There is little more I can tell you. The Truth is already within you. Continue the process of self-discovery. The discovery of Self. You will never grow tired. Each one of you is unique, indispensable to the integrity of All. You are all ready for this step. The gates of your consciousness are wide open. You must cross them yourself. If you need me, you can always find me—within you. That, above all, is the gift of Gamman."

As unobtrusively as she had risen, Q'rran sat down. No more shimmering air or oscillating glowworms. She was Delta again. Her smile was warm, strangely innocent, and friendly. She was one of us. In no way different, in no way superior. She looked like the last person on Earth who would have made the speech she just delivered.

Even now the eerie silence has hardly been broken. There began a slight murmur, a rustle, rather like a shy inception of an early morning; a tentative, almost surreptitious dawn, when nature awakens from a long winter night's sleep.

Those were the audible signs.

There were other indications. John knew he had to learn, rapidly, a better control over his own, new perceptions. Within, he perceived, almost painfully, a whirlwind of activity. A boisterous, quite undisciplined pursuit. People, who outwardly remained almost motionless, at a different level of awareness became assiduous in their ebullient activity. Far from mourning after the loss of their childhood, they rejoiced in their new powers. The slothful became hyperactive, the sleepy—full of vigor. The bored—bubbling with intense excitement. All without moving a single muscle of their physical body. "You are all ready!" she'd said. The air itself seemed the carrier of this expanding and compounding virus.

The inner, wider awakening has begun. In earnest.

A small number of Members remained ill at ease. Yet, they too remained silent. Suspecting, if not realizing fully, the magnitude of what had just transpired. Every now and then, a pair of dim, distrustful eyes, with a haunting look, in a face blank with tacit incomprehension, would suddenly brighten with a new light. A sure sign of new awareness breaking the barriers of pretentious resistance.

Close to an hour passed since Delta delivered her message.

The Council Chamber was humming with activity. The new learning process, which would extend for countless millennia, was greeted as a new toy. On this, the very first day, people were bravely unfolding their invigorating, if tenuous, wings. Though still burdened with physical awareness, many had taken their first, hesitant steps to a greater, previously unattainable, freedom.

Later, much later, they would learn their first lesson about freedom's twin brother. They would learn that freedom and responsibility are two sides of the very same coin. But enough time for that later. This was a day of joyful celebration. A magnificent farewell to millions of years of the humanity's childhood.

The Illustrious Members of the Federated Republics witnessed the second, long promised, heralded, inevitable, consummation.

The First had been the innocence of the Garden of Eden.

That was followed by the stumbling, enduring stay in Earthly Kindergarten.

Today Man took the first step into a Garden of his own, prodigious making.

***

Chapter twenty-three

Adam Blake

"It is strange, living on Earth."
There was a hint of sadness in John's voice. Since
leaving Moon Base, he felt inexplicably tired. The temporary
euphoria of Vega Report delivered in the Council Chamber,
has worn off. What was left was vacuum. A limbo.
"Should it not be I to say that?" Delta asked.
Perhaps, John thought. Perhaps it should be her. But for
Q'rran, this lingering feeling would be, at least,
understandable. For me, well, I have no other Earth. I have no
Ziircon. For now, I don't even have my own Antlantis. I have
no place I can call my home.
"Not Q'rran. Delta," she corrected.
By then, Delta was quite adept at reading John's
thoughts. Her senses advanced well beyond just reading or
interpreting his emotions. She had found, there was a
tremendous difference between the thoughts, or thinking
processes, of a Ziirconian as against those of a human being.
At least of a human still treading the soil. Physical soil. A soil
of coarse vibrations.
These last few days John has been sulking. Not verbally.
He was much too mature for that. But his heart felt a longing
for what he'd long accepted as his true home: the Outer
Space. A billion kilometers from nowhere. John wondered if
even the Antlantis would satisfy his gnawing yearning. For
now, he felt an undefined emptiness—a quite different void
from that which engulfed him halfway between the silent,
twinkling points of light of interstellar abyss. A deeper, more

hollow void. One having its roots within the dark recesses of his own being.

An end of an era.

There was no longer any reason for John Galt to search for other, superior, intelligent species. The Earth people, were the last ones.

"We are the backward children, only just rising from our extended kindergarten," he mused, his pride falling off in emotional chunks.

Many a time great teachers came and went, admonishing mankind of its erroneous endeavor. Mend your ways, they had said. My Kingdom is not of this world... The past Masters tried, so hard, to set the path straight. To redirect man's efforts toward his inner kingdom. The great Avatars had been invariably ignored. Often despised. Some had been slain, murdered by ignorant masses. By us.

The long trek of the spaceship Earth.

There was no longer a tangible reason for John to remain here. There was no special, unique, way he could contribute. The billions whose hands he'd never shaken, whose eyes never met his own gaze, whose path never crossed his own journey—no longer needed him. Those recalcitrant masses now laid claim to the Gift of Gamman. Did I really have to live for two hundred and sixty years, to accomplish this one act?

"No gift is greater than the gift of oneself," John felt Delta behind him.

"But it had not even been my gift..." John's thoughts were still painful.

"That is true. You have embellished the greatest gift with a crowning glory. You offered your life to deliver the gift of another."

John spun on his heel. He faced Delta. She wasn't even looking at him. He suddenly realized that he'd heard her, although she wasn't speaking.

"Can I now read your thoughts?" he asked, strangely afraid of what she might answer.

"You knew it had to happen. You and I have grown very close, during our return journey. A subconscious union was quite inevitable."

Delta turned her head towards him. She smiled her words with so much more than a perfunctory friendship. There was love in her eyes. Her bionic optical sensors seemed imbued with life of a far different dimension.

"But..." John stumbled.

"But you were asleep, for most of the journey?"

And then John understood. During most of his stasis he dwelled in his subconscious. But even his deepest unconscious had been open to her gentle, benevolent probing. He and Delta must have been together most of the time. Most of the thirty years. Travelling as one, through the Galactic immensity. Through the Void itself. In such unrestricted conditions, their subconscious must have expanded to unparalleled distances. They must have crossed...

"Half our galaxy and then some!" she finished his thought. "To achieve the same freedom on Ziircon, I would have had to have worked for five or ten millennia."

Again John felt himself surrounded by an aura of her intense love. An undemanding, unconditional, unearthly type of love. "You see John, it is I who have a great debt towards you. You have advanced me on my journey. You have shared with me your own Gift of Gamman."

Delta's thoughts were becoming clearer every second. John felt that they were like two individuals submerged in the same water. Sharing a sea. A bay of a much greater ocean. Aware of the same feelings, sensing, experiencing.

My Gift of Gamman...?

Rather than analyze Delta's words, John merely relaxed. He leaned back on the broad lounge-chair, which Mia Metis had installed for him. He and Delta have been assigned a suite on a hundred-eightieth floor of the Federated Republics, Western Hemisphere Headquarters. Robots had been programmed to recreate, for them, an interior half way between a lunar luxury apartment, and the bridge on BLAKE.

The Earth no longer suffered from overpopulation. There was plenty of room.

John closed his eyes. Soon his dark thoughts, images, of these last few days, gave way to a pastoral landscape. John languished, neither thinking nor feeling. He hovered in a realm of sentient, suspended being. He was.

"...I AM," was the first realization he formulated after a little while. "I am and I like it..."

John was experiencing the most primal, eternal state of consciousness: the reality of being. Slowly, at great leisure, he directed his attention at the sky above him. The deep blue. The timeless, infinite beyond. He allowed a thought, a concept, an idea of a star to enter the realm of his inner vision. In that same instant he felt himself floating, suspended in nowhere. Outer blackness receded behind him. Ahead, a gigantic ball of swirling, convoluting fire. He shrunk back, apprehensive, and regarded the star from a more distant perspective. If ever man could imagine an expression of Power, this, surely, was Its greatest manifestation. An inordinate, monstrous atomic furnace, suspended in the middle of utter blackness, commanding space itself. Unequal in Its realm. John, his mind reeling, thought of Its countless counterparts. In that same instant a billion suns exploded in an array of exuberant glory. John was surrounded by them. His vision no longer limited to any one direction.

He smiled.

And that, so very human reaction, brought him back, to the tender grass of the humming, pastoral landscape. A gentle breeze swayed the blades, to and fro, as wide and as far as his eyes could see. John thought of a horizon. Instantly a hazy contour defined the line where the blue of the sky met the blue of the distant mountains. He felt at peace...

"That is the Gift of Gamman..."

It was Delta, once more at his side.

"The ability to travel?" John's mind was still reeling from the wonders he'd just experienced.

"Did you really travel, John?" She conveyed to him her emotive thoughts.

"No. That is true. I was already there. In that very same instant..." Then John looked hard into Delta's eyes. "The Gift of Gamman...?"

"It is the ability to reach out beyond the bounds of time and space. It is what we call, on Ziircon, the Beyond."

"But it is greater than even... the unconscious..."

John attempted to define the infinite. The indefinable. He soon realized that it cannot be done. To define It would mean to limit It. To set limits to It, would be to deny It. John's mind whirled at the enormity of the concept. "Are there any limits to this... this..."

"...to this Beyond? We do not have any name for It. It is the Nameless. The only thing that can set limits to It—is yourself. It, in Itself, has no limits."

The Beyond. The Nameless. God? That which is the sum of all the eternal becoming? She was right. There was no point in attempting to name It. It was, is, forever will be, whatever the consciousness, which reaches out to It, will experience. Whose consciousness? That state of awareness which some of us will aspire to, in countless millions of years of becoming? And then too there will be no limits. Beyond time, beyond space. The ephemeral Instant. The eternal Beyond.

"How did Gamman come to possess it?" John asked after a while.

Images of Antlantis dissolved into the hard, restrictive contours of their suite. He and Delta were again sitting in their aerie, Earth-side quarters. The view from their floor reached out to the distant horizon. Funny, John thought. We talk so much of pollution, yet the air seems quite pure. Yes. The view is breathtaking. The distant, blue-hard, majestic Rockies. Carved with a sure hand of a Master sculptor. Yet how puny they seemed compared to the ranges of his inner vision.

"Gamman does not possess It. It is not a commodity. It is a state of being. Gamman has the power to impart his ability, to share his state of consciousness with those who are ready to receive it. He is the only one on Ziircon who has this skill. That is why we, they, call it the Gift of Gamman," she answered slowly. Even to Delta these concepts were not easy to describe.

"So we could never share this ability with another?" John asked.

"Never is a long time, John." She smiled her old, familiar smile. "There are things which cannot be given. In a way, they must be taken. They have a saying, on Ziircon, that he who is hungry will eat. I suppose it depends on the intensity of hunger."

"But that doesn't seem to be enough," John wondered.

Delta regarded John with open admiration. "Once more your perceptions are penetrating beyond the obvious. You are right. The desire is not enough. In a peculiar way, the desire must be tempered by... by..." she faltered.

"...by a state akin to indifference. It is an enigma. When I wanted to escape, I couldn't. Then I thought of Gamman. And..."

"...and the stars were yours to command." Delta rose and came to sit at the foot of John's lounge chair. "I have been attempting to master this elusive feeling from the moment I had met you, wondering, in the unconscious. That had been almost thirty years ago. You took me into the Beyond. I don't know how you did it. It is the Gift of Gamman."

"Dear Delta. My dear Delta. If I knew how I did it I would be Gamman!" John said very softly. Then he asked without speaking: "Do you know why he chose me?"

"I did not know then. I do now." Again she smiled wistfully. "Your consciousness had previously resided in a man called Adam Blake. He, Adam Blake, had earned his freedom by a single act of ultimate altruism. He gave his life for humanity. In the process, he touched the Infinite. Apparently, once you reach the Beyond, it remains latent within you."

"And for that same reason you have now reached it with me?" he asked.

"I have not given my life," Delta replied.

"Haven't you Q'rran?" John asked.

"I am Delta," she replied.

"Exactly," John said. And they both came a step closer to a new understanding.

For quite a while now, John's mind kept returning to Adam Blake. He knew the story of the early, legendary astronaut, as well as anybody. Perhaps, a little better. In the late twenty-first century, scientists had organized a mission to study an astral singularity. Adam Blake, apparently, had volunteered to be integrated into a spaceship. He had been, literarily, wired, clamped, and otherwise integrated into an early Starship. At the time, it had been considered a marvel of science. The human torpedo had been designed for a one-way trip. It was to drop into an anomaly referred to as a Black Hole. Then, an enigma of science. Adam Blake's trip was a success. The intrepid Starship continued broadcasting data up to the very last moment of its existence. Obviously, Adam Blake was never heard of again.

Many years later, a new mystery developed. A legend, dating back to early twenty-second century, claims that some 250 years ago, a man is said to have appeared on the then, still relatively small Moon Base, and helped the scientists to decipher the masses of data incoming from the Adam Blake's Starship. The man arrived at the crucial moment, when the incoming data had just begun arriving from the intrepid Starship. The man's name had been lost in the annals of history. Some say that, even to this day, a lot of data, which Adam Blake had sent back from his mission, were not fully understood. Others said, his last messages had been a total mystery.

John Galt began remembering only a few weeks ago. Even as his subconscious became more accessible to him, he recalled what he described as 'snapshots' of his life. Snapshots dating a lot further back than his present, albeit extensive, life span. John could not understand his newly acquired memories. So many new experiences crowded his life recently, that he simply took all those mysteries as part of the new, growing order. According to Delta, he would now have, if he wished, a few thousand years to arrange all the new, and old, incoming memories neatly in his head. Or in his mind. Whichever.

"It's all a part of growing," she said. "Growing and learning."

John believed her. Whatever gifts she assigned to him, John still held her in an immense esteem. She was his ultimate reference point in the new realm of consciousness. In time, in fact within only a month since the Vega Report, Delta began drawing him into her inner work. Incomprehensible to start with, John soon became adept at helping others reach out into the subconscious. He helped them without stepping outside his assigned quarters atop the Western Headquarters Building. He did so by projecting his own consciousness, his own awareness, and guiding any who would follow into the new realm. He never imposed. He never attempted to convince anyone. He merely showed the way.

First, John had to learn to control his own awareness. The harder he tried, the more he asserted his ego, his power—the less he succeeded. Once again, he refused to ask Delta for help. One day, almost by accident and certainly in near despair, he put himself at Gamman's disposal.

It happened in an instant.

Emotive calls for help reached him from many, still suffering from his inadequacy of a few minutes ago. John did nothing. Almost nothing. He became a channel. An instrument of destiny. He extended his own subconscious and touched the tentative, faltering, often cringing realms of others. He interposed his awareness. Very, very gently. Then, he moved on.

Towards Antlantis.

John did not bring anyone across the subconscious divide. No one could do that. Every entity had to cross the gates under his or her own power. Will power? Paradoxically, by forfeiting it, but by an act of their own volition. By an act of faith. All John could do was to hold the doors open a little longer. Just a little longer.

By the time John acquired some skills in this endeavor, his dark thoughts of some days and weeks ago, were gone. They became a distant memory of a transient, insignificant era. John affirmed what he had known for, probably, all his life, that he would not find peace, unless he helped others. Until now, he never did so consciously. For him is seemed an inherited trait. Inherent. It was not a case of altruism. Rather, an act of self-preservation.

Many questions remained. Infinity awaited him, in which to find the answers. Glorious Infinity.

John and Delta became inseparable. Not physically. But their aims, their desires, aspirations, their objectives united them beyond even the most profound friendship. They became as one. If before they existed as individual atoms of consciousness, now they became a molecule: a larger organ of a still greater organism. While working in his own right, John continued to learn from her. What before he did intuitively, he soon performed in full consciousness. Then, in turn, he made his knowingness available to more and more people.

On one occasion, John found himself perturbed about the countless life forms that found home on Earth. What would happen to them after man departed?

"It is all a process of learning," Delta assured him. "Theoretically, a unit of consciousness could abide in a piece of rock, if that suited its advancement on the journey of learning. Surely, you can see that if we have grass and trees and flowers on Antlantis, the higher states of consciousness, those enjoying a greater freedom, would also be protected from extinction. Or at least for as long as they serve the purpose of learning."

"It is all part of a greater whole?" John wondered.

"Precisely. We are all individual atoms, endowed with an independent state of consciousness, each in the process of self-discovery. Such entities as we are, such units of consciousness as we are at present, had, in the distant past, gained their experience by finding their expression through a variety of life forms. Each species has a centre of consciousness. The more developed, like some advanced mammals, enjoy the expression of many such centers. On the other hand, in case of some lower species, it may take thousands or millions or even billions of such minute, physical life forms, to provide expression for a single unit of more advanced consciousness. We all progress through such a magic chain, on the way to self-awareness. If there are any shortcuts, none have as yet been discovered."

"So we all go through the process...?"

"You remember, when approaching Ziircon, you had pictured your own body as a galaxy of stars, each performing its own, specialized duty? Well, you would never have been able to do so if at one time, in the very distant past, you had not controlled billions of individual life forms, perhaps such as microbes or bacteria, to find your own expression. Now, the control of your body's cells is perfectly automatic. You now call it natural. But it is only natural to those who have learned it. Do you see that?"

"So we all go through the process..." John repeated, his voice filled with wonder.

"Yes, John. There are no exceptions. But do not ever make a mistake of identifying yourself, now or in the past, with a fly or a worm or any animal. You are always you. An indestructible unit of consciousness. It simply means that, at any particular stage of your evolution, you can only find expression through such forms as your state of consciousness, at the time, will permit you. You are, forever, your own limitation. Nothing is, nor could be, imposed by external conditions."

John listened not only to Delta's words but, even more so, to the meaning behind them. His understanding grew in direct proportion to his self-realization. In a way, the two were interchangeable.

"Or, for that matter, I am not to identify myself with my present body..." John remembered their previous discussions.

Delta did not comment. She sensed that John was reaching a crucial stage in his apprehension.

"So the form through which I find my own expression is a result of my understanding?" he mused aloud.

"Of course. Except that it happens at the subconscious level. Some people once called it, an understanding within your heart. It is an expression implying an understanding at a deeper level. Your deeper level is your subconscious. When you accept the truth at that level, you become its expression." Delta tried to help a little more.

"I am the truth..." John remembered once reading.

"You are. At a physical level you can attempt to mask your inner, as yet uncertain self. You can occasionally manage to mask your ignorance. You can treat the world as a stage, yourself as an actor. But at the subconscious level, you cannot. You are the expression of that which you are at the time. You are the truth."

It was all coming together.

John was becoming aware that he could, soon, perhaps even now, leave his present, physical state of consciousness and transfer his awareness to Antlantis. He could do so by an act of his will. By rejecting the limitations of his physical body.

"Easy to say,' he smiled at his own thoughts, but not impossible.

John sensed, more and more, that he was close to becoming a master of his own condition. Within the physical realm, he had fairly achieved freedom.

John changed the subject.

"When you had spoken in the Council Chamber, I noticed some subtle changes in your immediate physical environment. Was that because you had been communicating at different levels of consciousness?" John's question was rhetorical. He already knew the answer.

"There are certain byproducts that come through from the inner realms. They are harmless, often beneficial. My purpose had been to communicate with the Members at all levels. Particularly at the unconscious. That is the realm within which new ideas are born. Or at least, the realm within, where we first become intuitively aware of them. I could not have done it without the Gift of Gamman."

"But is that beyond the unconscious?" John wondered.

"I lay no claims to the understanding of the Beyond, John. I am grateful whenever I feel that I am an instrument through which this Nameless Source chooses to act," Delta said quietly. And then she added. "I wonder if Gamman is overseeing all this..."

They both smiled and became a little pensive. Gamman. The first being from Ziircon with whom John had established a conscious contact. Or had it been the other way round?

"I cannot really leave you here..." John said after a while.

Delta knew exactly what John's words meant. He was unwilling to leave Earth and take the next step. On Antlantis. Delta has known, long before John realized it himself, that he was ready. Her features assumed her old, familiar, undemanding smile.

"Most people have no choice in such matters. They must go when they are ready. With you it is different. Adam Blake earned, for you, a freedom of action. He had settled your accounts before you became John Galt."

Delta said this as calmly as she could, in order not to influence John's decision in any way. Then she could not resist adding: "You also have earned your freedom, many times over, dearest John."

"Would you miss me?" John's voice sounded serious, but his eyes twinkled with badly concealed humor.

"I should haunt you daily."

"Not nightly? On Earth, ghosts work, mostly, the night shift."

John sounded like a flippant expert. Was that a contradiction in terms? Not with some experts John had met in his long, long lifetime. Then his voice changed again. "Will you come and visit?"

"All states of consciousness are contemporaneous. Our presence is defined by where we place our attention. Part of my attention will always remain with you." Delta's beautiful, bionic fingers caressed John's hand.

"Part only...?"

John was still teasing. He had to hide, even from himself, the storm brewing within his heart. Then his voice became serious. "I know that I can help them. Out there. After all, they are still only children. I shall wait for you."

They lay down on John's favorite, broad, lounge chair, their bodies hugging, melting into oneness. Their arms intertwined like liana of a single vine. Such physical proximity was not necessary, but human bodies remain ever human; doubting, divided. Lonely.

John sealed her smile with a gentle kiss. A very human touch. Physical. But the rest of their joining was so much more than human. John's brief lament at losing his identity was soon overcome by a rising rhapsody of finding himself, his image, within her heart. Stripped of all pretense, unmasked, naked, was like finding the Truth. Yet, ever longing. Ever longing for still greater union, in search of the eternal mirror. Then came a sustained orgasm of unremitting merging. Soaring, enduring, unwaning. Roaring. Eternal.

Oh, so much more than human.

For an ephemeral moment they both experienced the essence of Oneness. And then? Then there was silence. An endless, shimmering Void. Beyond it—Light. The hum of becoming lost in the silence of Being.

An hour later Delta regained her physical awareness. John Galt did not.

He became Adam Blake, again.

***

Chapter twenty-four

Homecoming
3581

"**The seed of every idea** is recorded, indelibly, in the racial memory of every species. Even as an acorn carries the memory of an oak tree, so does your mind, record your own genesis. All you must do is learn when and how to read it."

In Delta's lips it all sounded so simple.

Adam had, many times, attempted to reach back into his unconscious. But it must have been elsewhere that the seed had been planted. He was not yet quite ready to venture into the forbidden country.

"Tell me please, Delta. If you feel I should know it."

"Adam, let me call you John. Please. After all, you do have all John's memories, and as John you came into my life. For such I hold affection."

Delta's stay on Earth made her all the more human. More so than John, or Adam. John felt that he achieved his immortality as Adam, but it did not seem to matter. After all, wasn't Delta also Q'rran? And vice versa? In some ways, aren't we all immortal?

"John will be just fine," he smiled his acceptance.

Delta and John had been meeting regularly on, or around, Phoebe. John had learned to project his consciousness from Antlantis with such ease, that he no longer needed anyone's assistance. Delta had always known the art. 'Always' by Earth standards.

They had chosen Phoebe for its remoteness. John badly needed respite from having to screen the subliminal clatter, which filled the air of both Earth and Antlantis. Most people, on Antlantis, hardly knew how to control their emotions, let alone their emotional bodies. For Delta, this unholy mishmash did not present a problem. For John the screening proved more tiring than he cared to admit. At 13 million kilometers from Saturn, the satellite provided ample margin to eliminate most of the subliminal noise. It also offered an inspiring sight, beneath them.

And what a sight it was.

The rings, doubling their size and density by a factor of about one in every decade, shimmered with an opalescent light. Made up mostly of frozen liquid, quadrillions of crystals oscillated with such iridescent beauty, that neither John nor Delta could keep their eyes away from them. In the early years, Saturn seemed hardly to have changed at all. Only later, when the collapsing process had been initiated, had the proud, celestial giant assumed a polished, reflective texture. In this spherical mirror, the brilliant rings flirted with their own, glittering reflected image.

If beauty alone could invite people to shed their physical bodies, then surely, this sight would suffice. Easily.

"Alas, dear Delta. Whatever name you assign to me, it shall be like music to my emotive ears..."

Instantly Johns' ears were filled with Delta's laughter.

"A poet is a poet. I love you John, but a poet thou art not!"

"John will be fine, Madam. Now tell me about genesis."

She did not tell him. At least, not at once. John strongly suspected that Delta, imbued with Q'rran's emotions enforced with Delta's own fast growing emotional body, tended towards the frivolous. Whenever occasion permitted. As time went on, she seemed to find her being in a permanent state of exuberant joy. Her disposition reminded John of

Zooron, who had never missed a chance to gently ridicule anyone who might regard themselves a trifle too seriously. After some more jesting, almost regretfully, Delta succumbed to John's request.

"I must worn you, it's rather a long story."

"How long is it?" John was infected with her tongue-in-cheek spirits.

"Oh, a few billion years. Give or take a dozen..."

"Hadn't you better began then?"

Delta made a fuss of clearing her emotive throat. Not an easy feat to accomplish. Then her face grew more pensive. Time and motion seemed to slow down. As if even the lesser gods of worldly continuum wanted to listen.

"If scribes were to continue recording human history, the year 3581, of the New Era, would have marked the year in which the last vestiges of higher consciousness left the home of their early childhood. No biological life had been left behind to renew itself. No predator stalked its prey; no birds or bees whirled in a lascivious dance of self-perpetuation. There would be no further need of them. Their purpose had been fulfilled. Diverse states of consciousness they had been created to provide had been learned, recorded, immortalized in the great heritage of human subconscious."

Delta continued by direct thought transfer.

"A thousand years will have passed, since FRS BLAKE brought back to Earth two astronauts, bearing the Gift of Gamman. The millennium of peace that followed had been foretold by sages, seers, and dreamers, of long-past generations. Not quite in the manner presumed by vain prognosticators. Nevertheless, it was a millennium of relative tranquility. For the first time in history, the majority of people directed their vision inward, instead of searching outside their own state of consciousness. As time unwound, absolving mists shrouded Man's preemptive childhood. If a more accurate date were to be assigned to this year of Homecoming, the annals would have reached well back into the grey, forgotten millions of unrecorded ages."

At this point in her story, time appeared to slow down—almost to a standstill. John and Delta joined in the Unconscious.

"First, there had been a Whim. A Concept. An Idea."

A blinding light filled John's awareness. He cringed but could not run. He was now one with Delta.

"An Idea, imbued with beauty. It had blossomed and ripened into self-awareness. A brooding awareness of Its own existence. It had waited. It filled the Great Void in search of impressions. In search of a mirror of Its phenomenal Image. It found none that existed. It had become lonely. It had multiplied Itself by spontaneous fragmentation, instilling the first impulse of self-perpetuation. It needed space and time to manifest Its presence."

Silence, seemingly, stretched for light-years.

"Thus space and time had come into existence."

Eons had passed.

"The Idea splintered Itself into countless components. It burst in Cosmic Effusion. Even as later countless Supernovae divested themselves of singular existence, It then, at the pre-dawn of history, multiplied the seed of Its origin. Advancing, expanding, exploding with unrestrained Creative Impulse. After many eons of progenitive frenzy, the fragmented Idea forgot from whence had come Its being. Now, It consisted of innumerable individual fragments of energy, not yet solidified into atoms. Each fragment not sure of its place within the limitless universe of its own creation. Each longing to rediscover its birth, its singular origin. Beyond time and space."

Each longing, longing, longing...

Many, many more eons followed by more eons...

"Before a single unit of consciousness manifested its presence on planet Earth, millions of years had passed in the planet's history. During those formative eons, formless entities, endowed with consciousness, roamed free among the wastelands. The entities seeded the primordial caldron. The barren wastelands turned into wilderness of promise, which later, in turn, matured into abundant and prolific homeland. The individual atoms of consciousness had taken their first, tenuous step, towards self awareness."

Yet the innocence of childhood had failed to provide the answer.

"Then, each despondent atom asked its own proemial awareness: Who, or what, am I?. This single question had set in motion a spiral of evolution. The spiral of awakening. The atoms of consciousness, each in its own right an individual being, each carrying the germ of the Original Idea, searched far and wide to find forgotten meaning. The meaning it had lost in the explosive eons of its unrestrained creation."

The search had began.

"Scattered as far and as wide as the universe itself, the shuttered Idea searched for Its lost Self Awareness. Each of Its components advanced the cause of learning. Each, sooner or later, added its, seemingly insignificant effort, towards Its understanding. Towards remembrance. No effort had been ever wasted. Each fragment, each unique, irreplaceable component continued its enduring search for its rightful place."

And thus, as the very first step on its return journey, many Earths had come into being.

And thus, Antlantis had come, as the next step towards the beaconing homeland.

And thus, the next step will follow, within sight of final destination.

"Perhaps then, a New Whim, a New Concept, an Idea will come forth out of the Beyond."

Gently, with great care, Delta released John's consciousness. At first he seemed lost, bewildered. Gradually he found the essence of his self-awareness. Of his individuality. He smiled, almost shyly.

"Eternity does not have to hurry," Delta felt his emotive whisper. "It dismisses time as an element of being. Nor does space seem to matter. Continuum had been a much later creation. It came forth merely to serve as a homing beacon."

They both looked at the rings of Saturn. A homing beacon of their own making.

But then, there was a different, a much different story.

To those other beings, the advanced entities, which remained within Solar System after the year of Homecoming, history would mark the first year of a new, racial history. The bionic creation, subsisting directly on energy and thought waves, became independent of the biological environment. The positronic brain originally cloned from human tissue, now had been based on a non-organic substance. The beings free of the need to feed or oxygenate their bodies, could concentrate on their emotional and mental development.

Many centuries had passed since the first pineal gland had been recognized, in androids, as influencing their emotional behaviour. As a self-generating magnetic field replaced the need of a glandular body, a subconscious awareness took on a new meaning. The more emotionally advanced androids, thanks to the new, restructured Saturn, could, on occasion, communicate with the Antlantean people. Both races endured in hope of future union. Time was on their side. No one had ever told anyone to hurry!

As for Antlantis? Well, that, too, is yet another story.

Considerable chaos still rules in the new schoolyard. To discipline boisterous children into a semblance of civilized behaviour had not been at all easy. The result was, and remains, a great stratification. Since while in the state of subconscious one cannot conceal ones true colors, those who manifest similar traits tend to live with each other. Many strata, or levels of consciousness, have come into being. Not directed by any external forces, but born of natural expression of people at very different levels of understanding.

Perhaps even more so, than once, on ancient Earth.

Thankfully, there is enough room, here, for everyone. Room for every possible diversity. Antlantis has dimensions that extend well beyond their Earthly origins. The power of imagination, the strength of conviction, the depth of emotion, the ability to recognize and flow with the current: on Antlantis these serve more as true dimensions than any linear or geometric patterns of Earth. The latter could once have been changed at will. The Antlantean dimensions are more of a creative nature.

On the day of Homecoming, the day of final transfer, the air of Antlantis was filled with vibrations of a festive mood. John, Beta, Harry and Donna met in John's Spartan villa to await Delta's arrival. John had modeled his home on his memory of Q'rran's Ziirconian residence. Simple, adequate, in some ways introverted, yet with a beautiful view from a raised platform. The villa's only departure from the original was a round opening in the centre of the living room's ceiling. John felt the need for a visual contact with the vastness of space, which claimed many of his years as Commander John Galt.

John's guests arrived early. The four friends have maintained contact for many, many years now. John, or John-Adam, looked very much like the physical, 'earthly' John Galt but with a mass of black, unruly hair atop his previously bald pate. That was the only concession John had made to his previous existence. Harry looked, well... like Harry. Like Harry had looked when he had been thirty or forty. A few centuries ago. Beta was a bit shorter, a matter of mere convenience, otherwise all in one piece. No bionic parts here, on Antlantis. But the greatest shock to the eye was Donna. The last time John had seen her on Earth, Donna Dobbs had been a hundred and twelve years old. She had been, and played the part of, a venerable Mother. Now Donna looked to be in her late twenties. She insisted that she was too ignorant to look any older. The foursome joked and chatted remembering the days they had spent, way back when, together.

Then John sensed it was time.

All four held hands, as had been customary, to enrich, and simultaneously contain, the emotions that stirred within them at the expectation of Delta's Homecoming. Delta was the true Captain of the planetary Earthship. She was leaving command reins in the capable hands of Mia Metis.

After a few centuries, which had passed since John left his physical consciousness, Mia had been, by far, Delta's most adept student. Mentally she probably exceeded her mentor. She was beyond any definition that could apply to the word 'genius'. Emotionally, Mia was also advancing. She would remain in the System, even as Delta had remained on Earth, until the fulfillment of her own mission.

And then the moment came.

John, Harry, Beta and Donna closed their eyes. When they opened them again Delta was standing in the circle formed by their arms. She smiled the smile John had missed most dearly. He and Delta had met, on occasion, but each had been working on a practically continual basis. Now Delta would stay with them. Delta-Q'rran. She had forsaken her bionic body. There was no further use for it. Not on Antlantis. John had awaited her coming with an open, unabashed longing. After all, Delta was, and remained, part of the core of his being.

Delta transported facing Donna. She touched her with emotions and embraced her warmly. Then she hugged Harry and Beta, before turning to John. The three guests found a pretext to disappear into the next room. To prepare some refreshments. Delta and John remained standing, riveted to the floor, looking at each other. Finally John whispered with evident difficulty:

"I had moments of doubt that this would ever happen."

Delta did not reply. She continued to stare at John. She fought an inward battle to marshal her emotive turmoil. Her once steely self-control, seems to have deserted her on this one occasion. Then she found a way out.

"I am not convinced about your mop of hair, darling. I think I'd love you as much if you didn't have it."

In that precise moment, John's hair disappeared. One moment it was there, the next moment it wasn't.

"Oh my, you are getting good at it! Just for that I shall have to kiss you," she threatened.

She made good her threat. They lingered for a while.

What they said to each other was of absolutely no consequence. They talked the way people once talked on Earth. Just to pass the time. They had to talk about nothing. Their emotions were too overpowering. They shared an inexplicable joy—a sublime feeling of two states of consciousness, overlapping. It was almost like merging.

Later, Donna, Beta and Harry rejoined them. After some more small talk, they all decided to hold hands, again. This time together with Delta. They stood in a circle, fingers of both hands firmly interlaced with each other. They shared their subconscious.

A fleeting gust of air, a touch, a magnetic current, stirred within the circle. They all felt a Presence. John smiled instant recognition.

"You may come home now, if you wish, Q'rran," John sensed the emotive thought.

There was a prolonged silence.

"On the other hand, you would have to bring John-Adam with you... Would you like to come back, John?" the disembodied thoughts asked him.

"I see. Well, you will probably do more good right here." Another silence. Then: "Look after her well, for me. Anyway, I am always with you."

And the Presence was gone.

Five old friends stood motionless for a little while. Harry was first to recover.

"What in heaven's name was that?" he asked, his eyes wide open.

The question hovered, and hovered—unanswered. Time seemed to stretch, to hang limp. Then, John, too, returned to his senses, even—if not completely.

"Oh, that was another gift I received. Another Gift of Gamman," he said, his voice as wondrous as the communion that just took place.

And for some strange, inexplicable reason, they all knew what he meant.

******

Shall I continue?

Before you forget
PLEASE WRITE A (BRIEF) **REVIEW**
Your thoughts are important to me.

Acknowledgments

I would be remiss were I not to thank Madeleine Witthoeft and a host of friends for their diligent comments and proofreading. As always my gratitude to my wife, Bozena Happach, who put up with being a grass widow for weeks on end, and then offered me her inspired insights.

Sincerely,
Stan I.S. Law

A Word about the Author

Stan I.S. Law (aka **Stanislaw Kapuscinski**), architect, sculptor, and prolific writer, was educated in Poland and England. Since 1965 he has resided in Canada. His special interests cover a broad spectrum of arts, sciences and philosophy. His fiction and non-fiction attest to his particular passion for the scope and the development of Human Potential. He authored more than thirty books, twenty of them novels.

Under his real name he published seven non-fiction books sharing his vision of reality. He also composed two collections of poems in his original native tongue in which he satirizes his view of the world while paying homage to Bozena Happach's sculptures.

INHOUSEPRESS, MONTREAL, CANADA
http://inhousepress.ca

www.ingramcontent.com/pod-product-compliance
Lightning Source LLC
Chambersburg PA
CBHW062027170626
46813CB00001B/321